PRA

every time we say goodbye

"Every once in a while a delicious novel comes along, one that pulls you in and twirls you through its world until you look up and three hours have gone by. Or six. While there are many stories about families, what distinguishes this book is the compassionate wisdom that underpins it, the grace that echoes through it. To read this masterful (and humorous!) novel is to feel what it is to forgive and live bravely: with a tender, laughing, ever-opening heart."

Alison Wearing, author of *Honeymoon in Purdah*

"An astute and effortlessly readable portrait of a family in crisis. . . . Zeppa has fortified this raw material with a rich family history, shifting dynamics and a gentle voice that allows the novel to waft, rather than plod, as it pieces together its characters' disparate narratives. . . . A smart, accessible novel that has put Sault Ste. Marie on the map of the family epic." *National Post*

"Jauntily written and stuffed with period details, *Every Time We Say Goodbye* crackles along. It is a good read."

Literary Review of Canada

"It's not your typical *Bildungsroman*. And though Zeppa does childhood exceedingly well, she does adolescence, adulthood and old age well too. The full spectrum of the human experience is spread out for us in an unpretentious and thoroughly convincing way. . . . Zeppa shows off other literary chops as well. The secret to writing good historical fiction is simple: Make us feel as if the past is the present. Easier said than done, but a skilled author makes it look effortless." *The Globe and Mail*

"There is a quality to Jamie Zeppa's writing that aims directly at the reader. Her characters speak their hearts in a way that makes *Every Time We Say Goodbye* read a little like a memoir. . . . Zeppa's narrative flows, linking her characters and their stories as we are pulled deep into their lives, always pleased to pick up their story once again." *The Chronicle Herald*

"Rife with raw and stifled emotion, broken dreams and broken hearts, [*Every Time We Say Goodbye*] is less a quiet triumph than a thunderous tour de force that keeps you laughing, hoping and turning every page until hours have slipped by." *Sweetspot.ca*

every time we say goodbye

JAMIE ZEPPA

Vintage Canada

VINTAGE CANADA EDITION, 2012

Published in Canada by Vintage Canada, a division of Random House of Canada Limited, Toronto, in 2012. Originally published in hardcover in Canada by Alfred A. Knopf Canada, a division of Random House of Canada Limited, in 2011. Distributed by Random House of Canada Limited.

www.randomhouse.ca

The Care and Feeding of Children by L. Emmett Holt (1855–1924) is quoted from on page 50. A copy can be found at gutenberg.org.

Library and Archives Canada Cataloguing in Publication

Zeppa, Jamie
Every time we say goodbye / Jamie Zeppa.

ISBN 978-0-307-39948-9

I. Title.

PS8649.E66E84 2012 C813'.6 C2010-904944-6

Text design by Terri Nimmo
Cover design by Terri Nimmo

Image credits: Radius Images/Getty Images; Killerspud/Dreamstime.com

Printed and bound in the United States of America

2 4 6 8 9 7 5 3 1

For Susan Terrill,
ideal reader and friend

DAWN

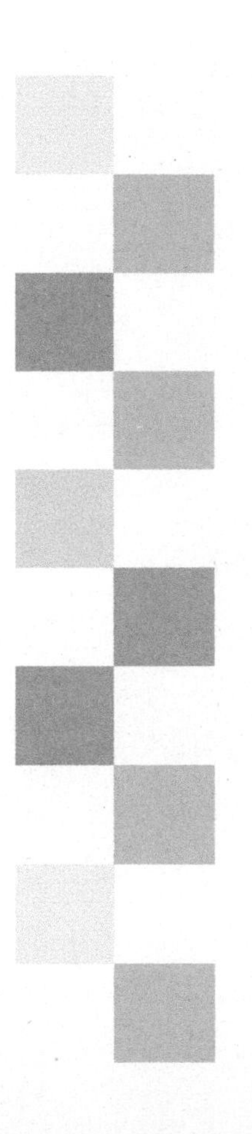

THE BEGINNING OF THE END

Dawn should have known it was over the night the men showed up with the car. The jig was up, the goose was cooked, it was going to get worse before it got better. It was the beginning of the end, her grandparents would have said, only they would have seen it coming from Day One, if not sooner. This was not unusual: in Frank and Vera's stories, things often ended before they began.

But Dawn was too busy on Day One to look for signs of the end. Her father and new mother were coming to take her and Jimmy to live with them, and a lot had to be done to make the beginning work out right. She was up and scrubbed and dressed before the darkness in the dining room began to melt. "For heaven's sake!" Vera exclaimed when she came downstairs in her brown plaid housecoat. She checked the blue-faced clock above the sink. "They aren't coming until lunch, you know."

Vera had short grey hair, which she rolled in curlers and unrolled before going to church or the grocery store, and about five hundred aprons. Frank was tall and thin and wore glasses. He was very good at fixing things other people just threw out, like lamps with frayed cords and toasters that no longer toasted. Vera was good at explaining things. She could tell you the relations of everyone in Sault Ste. Marie, how so-and-so was the second cousin of such-and-such, who married the aunt of the girl you sat beside when you made your First Communion. "And that's who they are to you," she'd say.

"And I'll tell you another thing," Vera called over the running water in the kitchen. "They'll probably be late, knowing your father."

That was something else about Vera: she always wanted to tell you another thing.

Dawn adjusted her ponytails and sat up straight. Very soon, the beginning would begin and none of this would count, especially if she could convince Jimmy to help. But instead of sitting and waiting properly, Jimmy unpacked his cars from the cardboard box at the front door and played in his pyjamas under the table with the claw feet. His blond hair was sticking up all over his head. "You're spoiling it," Dawn hissed at him. He ignored her and whispered to Professor Pollo. Professor Pollo was a brown beanbag monkey smoking a big black pipe. Sitting on the bowl of the pipe was a tiny Professor Pollo, smoking an even tinier pipe. Jimmy claimed there was another, nearly invisible Professor inside the tiny pipe, but Dawn couldn't see it. Jimmy also claimed the Professor could talk, which just showed what babies five-year-olds were. Now Jimmy held the monkey to his ear, listening. "Professor Pollo says, 'Poop to you,'" he said solemnly.

"You won't be ready when they get here," Dawn persisted.

She was three years older and had to explain everything. "Don't you get it?"

Frank said, "They won't be here for a while yet, Tinker. Why don't you see if there's something on the television?" But there was only the morning news, all Nixon, Nixon, Nixon. Vera told Dawn to make herself useful and bring up six Mason jars from the basement; she was going to do down some beets.

Five minutes before noon, Dawn left the kitchen full of vinegar clouds and went to stand on the porch beside their brown suitcases. Then she walked to the driveway and looked up and down Sylvan Avenue. Vera said theirs used to be the only house on the street, when the road was a lane and it was all farmland out here. Now it was a subdivision of beige bungalows with sliding glass doors and patios, and theirs was the only house on the street that looked haunted: three storeys of dark brick with cobwebby attachments like trellises and eaves and storm windows. Even the yard looked spooky: gnarled apple trees on one side, tangled forest hiding the creek on the other. In a few minutes, though, Dawn thought happily, she and Jimmy would also live in a house with a patio.

At one o'clock, she sat down on the steps. Lunch was sometimes at twelve, sometimes at one. It varied with families.

At two, they had pancakes for lunch. Dawn said she wasn't hungry, but Vera told her to stop moping and get to the table or she, Vera, would give her, Dawn, something to mope about. And it wouldn't be pancakes.

At four, Jimmy fell asleep on the couch, Professor Pollo wedged under his arm, while Dawn watched *The Brady Bunch*.

At five, Dawn asked if she could phone them, knowing Vera would say no. Vera said no. She said they would get here when they got here, and god only knew where they were anyway, probably out in some barroom.

It didn't matter, though, because the beginning wouldn't start until they arrived. A beginning couldn't be spoiled if it hadn't begun.

They arrived at dusk, honking noisily all the way down the street and finishing up with *honkety-honk-honk-beep-beep* in the driveway. Dawn followed Vera out to the front porch. Dean had driven Geraldine's blue Beetle right up to the flower bed. He leapt out, crushing a petunia or two, and ran around to the passenger door. Geraldine stepped out. She was wearing a grass green dress with a white sash, an Indian bead necklace and white high-heeled sandals. Her legs were darkly tanned, and her long brown hair rippled to her waist. In one hand, she had a pink carnation. Dean seized her other hand and zigzagged her around in a little dance. Then he bent her back so that her hair swept the ground and one brown leg kicked the sky. She shrieked with laughter. They both straightened up and waved. "Evening, Frank and Vera," Dean called out.

Dean called his parents by their names instead of Mom and Dad. Dawn didn't know anyone else who did this, but asking about it caused silences to prowl and lie in wait like invisible cats with flickering eyes, so it was best to just accept that what people called their parents varied in families.

Now Dean was scratching his head. "Say, didn't I leave a couple of kids around here somewhere?"

They ran down the steps, yelling, "Dad! Dad!" He swung them around and tried to hand them to Geraldine, but she couldn't hold them up, and they ended up in a laughing pile on the grass. Geraldine sprang up the steps, handing the carnation to Vera and giving Frank a kiss. Frank smiled and ducked his head. Vera took the carnation as if she were just holding it for someone else.

Dean had finished loading their things into the trunk.

"We'll bring the kids for a visit soon. Say goodbye to your grandparents, kids."

Jimmy's "bye" turned into a wail, and Dawn would have pinched him if she'd been close enough. Vera stood stout and stern, but Frank's voice stretched thin and tore at the end, and then he turned his head away and wiped his nose on the sleeve of his old plaid shirt. Something dreadful began to bubble up in Dawn, but then they were in the car, and Geraldine was humming "We're Off to See the Wizard," and by the time they reached their new house on the other side of town, the dreadful thing had drained away.

That was the real, true beginning.

Even three months later, puddles frozen and snow falling, it could still be considered the beginning. They were still settling in, which is why there was trouble over who didn't pay the phone bill and who didn't press the shirts and who was supposed to be home hours ago. The beginning was lasting a long time, but there were certain advantages. It was like playing an open hand to learn a new card game: mistakes didn't count.

Some beginnings took longer than others. It varied.

Then the men came with the car. They came after dark, two stick men in jeans and leather jackets, bare-headed and -handed in spite of the snow, pushing a long white car up the driveway. They were friends of Dean's, they said, and they were having a problem with their car. The problem was the starter wouldn't start. They had a friend who could fix it, but he was in Wawa, and in the meantime they had borrowed another car, but they needed a place to keep this one until their friend came back, and Dean, their buddy Dean, they had known Dean since they were grass high to a knee hopper (one started laughing at this and couldn't stop, even when the other kicked him), anyway, luckily Dean said they could use *his* garage for a few days.

Dawn stood behind Geraldine and watched the snow falling in the upside-down V of the porch light. It looked like the light was making snow. It was an illusion, though, just like when the sky caught fire but it was only the steel plant dumping slag. The men lurked at the bottom of the steps, just out of reach of the light. They shuffled in their pointy-toed shoes and mumbled into their jacket collars. Shifty, Vera would have called them if she had seen them. *Go on, get out of here*, Vera would have said to Shifty and his pal Shiftless. She would have put a stop to it, right then and there. She wouldn't have cared what foolishness Dean had told them. *I don't know you*, she'd have told them. *Who are you to me?*

But Geraldine only said, "Well, I guess if Dean said it's okay . . ." So they pushed the long white car into the garage, and the snow fell quickly, filling up the tire tracks and the shoe prints, muffling the sounds of cars whose starters still started. When Dean got home, there was a lot of hissing in the hallway about the car, with Geraldine asking was it something-something because that's sure how it looked, and Dean declaring Jesus, Ger, no it was not. The snow kept falling, and within hours it was the middle of winter, even though it was only November, still the beginning. Dawn drew lemon suns, white houses with orange curtains on lime lawns, but it snowed like that until spring.

That winter Geraldine was sick and tired because of the baby, the new brother (Ryan) or sister (Amy) for Dawn and Jimmy. If Geraldine didn't eat, she got tired. If she got tired, she became nauseated. But when she ate, she threw up. Then she had to go to bed, and they couldn't make any noise; the TV was turned down so low they had to listen with their mouths open.

When she wasn't sick and tired, she wove braids into Dawn's light brown hair and unravelled them in the morning so their hair had the same ripples. She made french fries for Jimmy and sang along with the radio. She knew the words to everything, but her favourite was "(I Never Promised You) a Rose Garden." Dawn sang this at Vera's one Sunday, and Vera asked where on earth she had picked up that nonsense. Dawn said, "Geraldine sings it."

Vera said, "Hmph." And then, "Well, she made her bed. Now she can lie in it."

The truth was—and Dawn would never tell Vera this—Geraldine never made her bed. She didn't care if Dawn or Jimmy made theirs, either. That had been the first shock, at the beginning of the beginning in the new house: all the beds were unmade, even their own beds, even though they hadn't slept in them yet. "Oh, honey," Geraldine said when Dawn went to tell her, "we had some guests last night and they stayed over." Dawn could not remember seeing an unmade bed during the day that didn't have a sick person sleeping in it, and sick meant you had a fever or you were throwing up. Even then, the blankets were arranged neatly, the bedspread folded down at the end of the bed. There was no call to pull the bed apart while you slept, Vera said. Decent people slept neat.

Seeing her slept-in bed, the blankets all twisted up and the sheets pulled off the mattress, Dawn felt the dreadful soup return to her stomach, and for a moment she wanted to cancel all the wishbones and falling stars and coins in a fountain, the exercises she'd made Jimmy practise with her. ("Let Dad marry Geraldine. Come on, say it, Jimmy. Let Dad marry Geraldine and take us to live with them.") Then music floated up the stairs. Dawn opened the door wider to hear. At Vera and Frank's, the radio was not allowed because of Vera's nerves. In the kitchen, Geraldine was singing "You Are the Sunshine of My Life." Dawn made the bed and went downstairs to join her.

The new house did not have sliding glass doors, but it did have a patio and white aluminum siding, and through the park and down the street was Dawn and Jimmy's new school. Geraldine took them to buy school clothes at a place where the sales clerks were teenagers and the music was so loud they all had to shout. Geraldine flew through the store, laying shirts and jeans and belts over counters, asking, "Do you like this? Which do you like better, the blue or the purple? The striped or the plain?" She let them wear their new clothes home from the store, and they didn't have to put them away For Good.

Geraldine had never heard of For Good. She wore her slinky black dress with the fringe of black beads to fry hamburgers and her new shoes to help Jimmy find his GI Joe weapons in the mud at the park. She wore her mauve silk blouse to bed. "Always wear clothes you love," she told Dawn. It was a rule.

This was news to Dawn. At Vera and Frank's, you wore what you were given. Occasionally, most likely by accident, you might be given something you liked, but then someone at school would point out that it was the colour of puke or had seams sewn down the front *and* back legs. You still had to wear it, though, because Vera was not going to throw out perfectly good clothes just to follow the Fads, which were invented to take advantage of people who thought money grew on trees.

There were so many other things Geraldine had never heard of, Dawn sometimes doubted she was a grown-up. "Are you going to do those down?" Dawn asked when Geraldine brought home a basket of fresh peaches. Geraldine looked blank. "You know," Dawn said, "put them into jars."

Geraldine was confused. "Why would we want to do that?"

"So we can eat them in the winter," Dawn said.

Geraldine said, "If we want to eat canned peaches in the winter, we'll buy them. In cans. In the winter." And she grabbed two peaches and tossed one to Dawn. They ate them standing and threw the pits into the sink.

Vera and Frank bought fruit and vegetables on sale and cooked them for hours in enormous metal pots, with Dawn and Jimmy carrying warm jars of dwindled pears and blasted cauliflower down to the cellar. When the next Depression came, and mark Frank's words, it was on its way, they would be prepared. Geraldine shrugged when Dawn told her about the Depression. She said if she wanted to keep herself up at night, she'd do it with something new and interesting, like aliens.

Made of money, Vera and Frank said when Dawn and Jimmy showed up on Sunday in stiff new jeans, fringed leather vests and purple running shoes. But of course Geraldine wasn't made of money. She went to work in her yellow hard hat and big boots, one of the few women working in the plant part of the steel plant. She kept track of parts. She worked hard for her money, Vera grudgingly acknowledged, but then she spent it, hand over fist; she didn't look after her pennies!

Dawn could attest to that. Geraldine hated pennies: she threw them out in fistfuls. Threw them *out* into the garbage can or out the car window into the street. She would end up without a pot to piss in, Vera said. She hadn't been raised right. As far as Vera was concerned, she was no better than You Know Who, and Vera didn't care who heard her say it.

And it was true that Geraldine didn't know how to take their temperature, or which medicine went on impetigo. But she did know the recipe for D&J cocktails (ginger ale, orange segments and a maraschino cherry in a martini glass). She knew how to whip a scarf around a dress to make a belt, call out for pizza and make Dean laugh. He grabbed her around the waist and pulled her down into his lap and growled into her long brown hair. And she knew how to work the Finding Stick when Professor Pollo went missing. She half-closed her eyes and followed the Y-shaped stick upstairs, downstairs, through each room to where Professor

Pollo had fallen behind the bed or was wrapped in a sheet in the laundry basket.

But as the snow rose in dirty hills and bluffs along the roadsides and Geraldine's stomach got rounder, her voice got higher and sometimes she even hit them. She was turning into someone else, and Dawn tried all the magic she knew to turn her back, but nothing made any visible difference. Sometimes, she wished she could vanish her.

Dean didn't need help in that direction. He could vanish all on his own, especially after Uncle Del (who wasn't their uncle, only Dean's friend) convinced him to quit his job at the radio station and work for him, and now he was always going over the river to the American Sault, even on weekends.

"What exactly are you doing for that guy?" Geraldine wanted to know.

"This and that. Keeping an eye on a few projects, scouting for business opportunities," Dean said.

"Business opportunities, my ass," Geraldine muttered.

Dean said, "He's a man who makes things happen."

"Oh yeah?" Geraldine said. "Can he make a paycheque happen?"

"If I just wanted a paycheque," Dean said, "I'd sign on at the plant. You gotta see the big picture, Ger."

Geraldine marched over to the fridge and grabbed a handful of envelopes. "Electricity bill. Phone bill. Returned cheque." She tossed the envelopes one at a time at Dean, who let them fall to the floor. "There's your big picture, mister." Dawn's mouth fell open: Geraldine sounded exactly like Vera.

When Vera and Frank stopped by after school or early on a Saturday morning, they always asked, "Where's your father?" and Dawn and Jimmy were supposed to say, "He's away on business." They weren't supposed to say "for Del Cherniak" because Vera couldn't stand that Del Cherniak and Frank wouldn't trust him as far as he could throw him. Vera and Frank came to bring them the socks or vitamins they had picked up on special. They stood in the doorway in their boots and coats, the bright, cold air swirling in past them. They were always on their way somewhere, the cemetery or the grocery store, so no, they couldn't stay. Finally, Geraldine stopped asking them to come in.

After they left, Dawn stood in the kitchen door to see what they had seen. Dishes in a sink full of cold, greasy water, a cream cake scraped clean of its icing, crushed Mountain Dew cans on the floor. That was Geraldine and Jimmy playing Dew Shot. At least from the kitchen door they couldn't see the unmade beds and the pile of garbage swept behind the TV.

One Sunday afternoon in January, Geraldine invited them in again. She asked three times, hovering and circling, clearing her throat, but still they wouldn't stay.

"Oh god, oh god, what am I going to do?" Geraldine cried when they left. She put her hands to her face and squeezed the sides of her head. Dawn would have laughed if she had been out of arm's reach. Dean had been away on business for two weeks, and Geraldine had taken the phone off the hook because it was always someone looking for him. Vera and Frank had brought old issues of *National Geographic* and Oreos reduced to half-price because the box was a little crushed. "What good are these?" Geraldine cried, knocking the magazines onto the floor. She had only enough money for her bus fare tomorrow, and there was no dinner for the kids. And they weren't even her kids. "Youse aren't even my kids," she wailed. "Oh god, what am I going to do?" She plumbed the sofa lining for change and then sent them to the store with $1.71 for milk and bread. "Close enough," she said. "Just pretend you lost some on the way." But they stopped to play with Vincent down the road, the three of them flying over his backyard snow hill on his saucer sled, and when they got to the store, they didn't have to pretend. Dawn's pockets were empty. They went back and dug frantic holes in the snow until their hands cramped. "We need the Finding Stick," Jimmy said, and it might have worked if Geraldine hadn't caught them in the upstairs hallway.

She said nothing when they told her; instead, she turned and punched the wall so hard her fist went through the plaster. After that, she went to her room and the door closed with the quietest click. Jimmy couldn't find Professor Pollo and went temporarily crazy, shuddering and crying, until Dawn found the Professor behind the kitchen door. She got Jimmy to lean over and sip water from the opposite side of the cup to take away his hiccups. Then they ate a row of Oreos each and put themselves to bed.

When Dean had come last summer to tell them he had good news, Dawn knew immediately that all her wish work had paid off. "Kids," he yelled. "Vera, where are the kids?" They heard his voice and forgot not to pound down the stairs, making enough racket, according to Vera, to be heard all over the Two Soos. "Kids, I have some great news. You know Geraldine, right?" Of course they knew her. Dean had been going out with her for a year. "Well, how would you feel about Geraldine being your new mother?"

Dawn and Jimmy began to jump up and down. "When is the wedding?" Dawn wanted to know. "Can I be the flower girl?" But Dean said he and Geraldine had already got married that morning at the courthouse.

Jimmy asked if they should call her Mom.

Dean scratched his chin. "Why don't you just keep calling her Geraldine for now? That's what you're used to, right?"

As soon as he could find a place, they would all move in together. Dawn immediately began to lobby for the right kind of house, and Dean clicked a make-believe pen to take notes on his hand.

Dawn thought she would float away. At last, at last: father and mother and kids living together in a normal house, instead of father living in a two-room apartment that smelled of cat pee over the Sunset Café on Queen Street and kids living with their grandparents in a weird old house with claw-footed furniture and a cellar full of pickled beets. They would go to Parents' Night with their parents, they would go on vacations during summer vacation, they would go to the movies and then to A&W and it wouldn't be for the birds and a damn foolish waste of money.

"I think I've got it," Dean said, pretending to read his notes. "Million-dollar single-storey mansion with indoor-outdoor pool . . ."

Dawn and Jimmy began to jump up and down again and hoot and holler and Dean jumped and hollered with them until Vera went upstairs with her nerves.

They waited until Dean found the house, then they waited until it was fixed up for them, then they waited for Dean and Geraldine to come and get them before lunch on the last day of August. The beginning began, and it was good at first, or at least there were moments of good, considering it was still the beginning and some things didn't count. But by the time the snow began to melt, Dawn knew it was coming to an end. With beds unmade and clothes unwashed in smelly piles around the broken washing machine, a garbage bag of money squashed flat under the spare room bed and a stolen car in the garage, it couldn't possibly last much longer.

GRACE

THE BLISS

When the sickness woke her early in the morning, just after the birds began to sing, Grace pulled the sheets over her head and thought about her mother. She had to start with the day she didn't want to remember, because, before that, the pieces were too small to make anything out of. That day, her mother dropped her rag and sank into the brown armchair under the lamp while Grace stood beside her, perplexed. The floor was not half-finished. "Grace," her mother said, "come and have a little rest with me." Grace hesitated, then laid her rag down and climbed onto her mother's lap. The room smelled of oranges from the wax.

"Will you tell me a story?" Grace asked.

Her mother said, "First I must sit, Grace."

"I must sit too," Grace said, and laid her head upon her mother's shoulder. Her mother tucked her arms around Grace's middle, and they listened to the drip and fall of rain outside. Her mother said her ears were too tired to listen to the radio. The sheets they had pulled in this morning before the rain started were still in the basket, and they hadn't done a thing about dinner, but they stayed in the chair, not shelling peas or knitting, just sitting, until Frank got back from school. Frank was big. He was twelve. He came clanging in, bringing the smell of wet earth, banging his books down. When he saw them, he went quiet. He shifted from foot to foot, shedding worry. "What's wrong, Ma?"

Grace answered for her. "She is tired. She must sit."

When their father came home from work, their mother got up to make dinner. "I'm feeling better," she told Grace. Grace leaned against her mother and breathed in her smell of white soap.

The next time, her mother stopped in the middle of the washing. "I must sit, just for a moment," her mother said. "Shall I finish the wash, Ma?" Grace asked, but her mother smiled and said no, Grace was too small to work the wringer. In the front room, they sat on the sofa and watched the light grow bright and then dim on the polished floor. "I must get up," her mother said, but she did not move.

When Frank came home, he squeezed the laundry through the wringer and emptied the machine. "Ma is not well," he told Grace. "You have to help with dinner."

Grace said, "I have to sit with Ma."

So Frank peeled the potatoes and fried onions and bacon and set the table, and Grace and her mother sat in the front room under the lamp until it was time to eat. Sometimes Grace opened her mother's button box, a little red tin trunk with yellow trim, and they looked together. Grace's favourite was the bride button, a pink pearl set in a silver curlicue. The large navy button with the gold satin centre was the groom. After buttons, they played hands: Grace's fingers were the animals or the birds, hopping over the hills of her mother's palms, looking for a warm, soft place to sleep. Grace had clever hands, her mother said. They were good at threading needles and lacing boots and fitting the coffee pot back together after her mother had washed all the pieces.

Her mother's hands were not working properly. They broke a teacup, a plate, a jar. Sometimes they could not hold the scrub brush to clean the pots or the wooden spoon to beat eggs. She had to sit earlier and earlier in the day, and her legs ached and twitched. She didn't want to read or listen to the radio or sing "On the Sunny Side of the Street." She just wanted to sit. In the garden, weeds were choking the tomatoes and the berries rotted on their vines.

One Saturday morning, her mother did not get up. In the front room, Grace traced pictures in the dust on the claw-footed table while the doctor talked to her mother upstairs. She drew a mother bird and a baby bird in their nest. The wind lifted the nest from its bough and drifted it down to the cool, green creek, where the water carried it swiftly away. Inside the nest, the mother bird put her wing over the baby bird, and they watched the waves and waved at the fish. When they got hungry, they paddled the nest to shore and ate berries and drank water from leaf cups. Then they got back into their nest and floated downstream again.

The doctor came down and talked to Grace's father in the kitchen with the door closed, and when the doctor left, her father called for Frank. Later, Frank called for Grace. "You know that Ma is sick, Grace. That's why you didn't start school this year. We all have to help. I'll make breakfast in the morning and you wash the dishes. You're six now, you're old enough to do that."

But after Frank had left for school, her mother said, "Leave the dishes for now, Grace. Come and do my hair." They sat in front of the oak dresser that held an oval mirror between its two curved arms, and Grace brushed her mother's hair, lifting the dark waves to her face. Her mother's hair smelled different from her skin—it smelled like lemon tea.

The doctor brought oranges. No one was to have them except her mother. After they woke from their afternoon sleep, Grace peeled an orange and broke it into segments on the plate. Her mother said, "I can't eat it all, Grace. You take half." In the afternoons, they ate orange pieces and rested until Frank came home.

In the mornings, Frank muttered and moped in the doorway of the bedroom. In the evenings, he called out, "Ma? I'm home now," and pushed Grace aside on the bed. "He's mussing the covers," Grace complained, but her mother said, "Shh, Grace, let him sit." She put her arms around them and called them her Two Peas because they looked so much alike, with thick reddish-brown hair springing from broad foreheads and the same sharp little chins. Grace was always glad when the other pea left the pod to do his homework.

On Wednesday afternoons, Mrs. Davies brought loaves of bread and a rhubarb pie. Her mother said, "Grace, go downstairs and play. I want to talk to Mrs. Davies."

Grace pounded down the stairs, then crept silently back up to sit outside the bedroom door. She liked the pie, but why couldn't Mrs. Davies leave it in the kitchen and go home straight away? There was no need to come upstairs and disturb her mother, who needed to rest.

"You see how my legs are now," her mother was saying.

Mrs. Davies said, "Oh, Florence. But you know, they say people can live years with it."

When Mrs. Davies left, Grace said, "Ma, do you want a glass of water? Some bread and butter?"

Her mother shook her head. She only wanted Grace to sit with her. Her mother's arms were heavy now, even though they had grown thin, and she could not lift them to hug Grace, so Grace put her arms around her mother and laid her head on her mother's shoulder and said, "Shall I tell you where the mother bird and the baby bird went in their nest today?" Her mother nodded and closed her eyes.

Frank scolded her. "What do you do all day? Why don't you help?"

Grace said, "I do help."

Frank said, "Pa's at work, I'm at school. I can't do everything around here."

But he did. He made breakfast and supper. He washed the dishes and weeded the garden. He washed the clothes and tried to make Grace hang them to dry. She said she would and then slipped upstairs to sit beside her mother, who was asleep.

Frank said, "Pa, Grace won't listen to me. She's big enough to help a little bit, isn't she?"

In the kitchen, her father answered quietly. Grace could not hear the words, but he must have said, *Frank, let her be*, because after that, Frank let her be.

It was the Creeping Paralysis, Frank told her. Some people could live years with it. Her mother lived two. Violet, a fat young woman with a face like pudding, came during the day to wash Grace's mother and change the sheets and feed her spoonfuls of custard and soft-boiled egg. Violet told Grace to get out from underfoot. She closed the bedroom door when Grace's mother was sleeping so that Grace wouldn't wake her. She cut Grace's mother's hair into an ugly bob, and then she cut the bob into something worse. "It'll be easier this way," Violet said, dumping the dustpan of dark feathers and curls into the compost pile.

In the end, her mother could not lift her head or speak. She had been turned to stone. But her eyes were not stone. They followed Grace everywhere and talked to her. Her eyes said all the things her voice had once said, before her throat had turned to stone: *Grace, how I love you. You are the dearest girl in the world to me. I wanted a daughter so badly after three boys. After Eddie and Joey went up to Heaven, they sent you down to me.*

Her eyes said, *Grace, tell me that story of the mother bird and her baby. Have they got all the way to the sea?* Grace curled up at her mother's side. The mother bird and baby bird were not yet at the sea. They had stopped on the riverbank, and some kindly beavers gave them tea and filled their nest cupboard with chokecherries and nuts.

Violet threw out the chokecherries and little black seeds. "Don't bring a mess in here," she said. She threw out the daisies Grace had picked. "They were dead," Violet said when Grace scowled and sulked. Grace asked her mother, "Does everything die?" and her mother's eyes said, *Yes. All things: birds and bugs and plants and people.* "Why does everything die?" Grace asked. Her mother's eyes said, *I don't know,* and filled with tears.

One morning a terrible sound woke her. Her father was standing outside, in the cucumber bed, choking, she thought, and then she realized: crying.

On Sundays, she went with Frank to the graveyard to see the stone with her mother's name: Florence Alice Turner, 1890–1930. Joey and Eddie's stone was there too: Joseph William Turner, 1911–1918; Edward Albert Turner, 1912–1918. They had died of the flu. Frank told Grace, "Now Eddie and Joey have Ma to look after them. They're all in Heaven together."

"Why don't we all go to Heaven?" Grace asked, but Frank said, "Hush! Don't talk like that, Gracie."

To get to the graveyard, they had to walk up their lane, past the Cherniak farm with its fields of mournful black and white cows, to the wide road and down to the church. Frank said, "If you aren't good, Grace, I won't take you," because Grace had been acting up. Throwing tantrums, refusing to eat and worse: she had taken the scissors and cut the leaves off all the plants in the front room. She had cut off her own hair in jagged strips. And worse than worse: she had taken the photograph down from the wall and cut out her mother's face so she could have it with her all the time. "Leave her," their father said when Frank said she must be punished. Their father went downstairs to the cellar, where he sat in the dark. Frank said, "Grace, I won't take you on Sunday."

Grace cried, and after that she became sick. Her head hurt and she threw up. A rash bloomed along her face and neck. Her teeth chattered, she could not breathe, and her hair was wet with sweat. The doctor said she was hysterical. They were to ignore her. She would snap out of it.

When the doctor left, Grace ran upstairs to her mother's room, with its bed neatly made. She ran downstairs to the front room, where the floor no longer gleamed with polish. Her shoes hammered up the stairs and pounded down the hall, and the horrible noise filled her ears. Frank said, "Stop it, Grace!" but she could not stop. There was a motor and she was caught inside it; the teeth of the gears were chewing through her arms and legs.

Frank grabbed her shoulder and yelled, "STOP!" When he turned his back, she opened the closet and threw a can of floor wax at him. It smashed through the glass door of the china cabinet, and when the shattering was finished, Grace sat in the armchair. "I must sit," she said. The engine inside her was dead.

Frank swept up the glass and brought the dustpan over to her. "Look," he said. "Look what you've done. Ma's best dishes."

Grace closed her eyes. "I am tired," she said. But something about the shards bothered her, and the next day, when Frank was out in the garden, she took the old white and blue creamer down to the creek and broke it into pieces against the big flat rock under the chokecherry tree. With a sharp stone, she pressed the pieces into fragments, the fragments into granules, the granules into dust. She rubbed her fingers together, and the dust disappeared. *So that is what it was made of*, she thought, amazed. *Tiny little pieces of nothing*.

Against the flat rock, she opened a saucer, a candle, a pea, a beetle, an ant, a seed. Inside, everything was the same. Everything broke into smaller and smaller pieces, until it disappeared entirely.

Some things didn't break. She asked Frank, "Frank, what is inside this?" It was a screw she had kept from a clock she'd taken apart. She was able to snap the outside plates back into the rim, but had to throw out the metal innards.

He told her how the screw was made. "They take iron ore, you see, and they—"

"But what is inside iron ore?"

"It's a rock. Like a lump of coal."

Grace was disappointed. She knew what was inside coal. She asked, "What happens to people after they die?"

Frank sighed. "I told you, they go to Heaven."

"I mean, what happens to the body?"

Frank told her how God made the first man and woman out of a handful of dirt in the Garden of Eden. "Ashes to ashes, dust to dust."

Grace went back out to the flat rock by the creek. Dust to dust. Everything, even people. The mystery was not why everything died, but why anything lived in the first place. What made the tiniest particles cling together to form dust and rocks and seeds? Frank said all the pieces of the world had been drawn together in the beginning by the hand of God. But what kept all the pieces of nothing together *now*, Grace wanted to know. Frank said she had it all wrong. "You can't get something out of nothing." But Frank hadn't opened things, so he didn't know. Grace thought about this until her head hurt and she had to lie down on the grass beside the rock, and that was the first time the bliss came. She came unravelled: her head did not hurt, her chest did not ache, and she forgot about her mother dropping things and her father crying in the garden. An empty white chill held her. Inside the bliss, time did not pass. Frank found her and shook her. "Wake up, Grace," he said, but she hadn't been asleep. She had been in a different place altogether. She hadn't wanted to come back.

In the fall, Grace started school. The first day, she was afraid, so Frank let her carry the pink pearl bride and her navy groom in her pocket. In the beginning, she liked going. Words were made of letters and letters were lines and lines were pencil marks that could be rubbed into pieces of grit and blown away. She liked numbers, too, because they were just one and one added, and if you took one and one away, you went back to nothing. But she had no interest in the equations of triangles or the wars of kings, and the teachers had to speak to her again and again. If they spoke too sharply, they would bring on one of her headaches, and she would weep until she vomited and they would have to send her home. Sometimes, she could not breathe and had to be sent home anyway. Finally, they let her sit at the back of the class and read. The bliss did not come at school; there were too many sounds—chanting and tapping and sniffling—and too many smells—wet wool and mould and chalk. But she was happy enough to read, because she could stay very still and no one bothered her with talk or questions, and sometimes she caught the bliss in between the words.

Their father came home from work one evening and did not go back. There was no work to go back to. He went quiet, speaking only to say yes or no or "Frank, fix some dinner for your sister." Frank said it wasn't just their father. Across the whole country, factories had been laying off and people were going hungry, and their father had been luckier than most, hanging on at the steel plant for almost four years. Frank was going to work at the tar plant. He would have to quit school, but at least he would be bringing something home. And Grace did not have to go to school anymore either, Frank said. It was pointless if she wasn't going to apply herself. She was twelve now, old enough to keep house for them. He left her a list of things to do, and sometimes, she finished the list, but other days, she went down to the creek, where it was very quiet, and lay in the long grass and let herself fade away.

Four years later, their father died. A sore in his gums went septic, Frank said, and the rust spread and poisoned the pathways to his heart. It poured the day of his funeral, and the neighbours stood under umbrellas and sheets of newspaper black with ink declaring war on Germany. "Poor Frank," people said. And "poor Grace," too, but mostly "poor Frank." Poor Grace was part of the reason they said "poor Frank." "Your brother will look after you, Grace," they told her. "And you should look after him, too." They knitted their eyebrows together and wagged their heads at her. They meant she must change her ways. She was sixteen years old; she shouldn't be running about all day in her mother's old clothes, her russet hair cut like a boy's because she never combed it. And Frank shouldn't be doing all the work in the house, especially after working all day in the tar plant. "At least you have each other," they said to Frank. "That is your comfort."

Someday, Grace thought, *all of us standing on the cold, wet ground will be under it. Ashes to ashes*. That was her comfort.

A few months after the funeral, Frank got a job at the steel plant. Things were picking up, he said, because of the war in Europe. He promised to explain the whole thing to Grace, but luckily, he started fixing the house and forgot. He painted the kitchen and the front room, and scrubbed and waxed all the floors. In the spring, he went upstairs and paced the four tiny bedrooms with a measuring tape. "These rooms are too small," he told Grace. "I'm going to join these two here, eventually turn the attic into another room. You'll help me, won't you, Grace?" Grace nodded and yawned. She let go of the measuring tape and went out to sleep under the cherry tree. The next day, Frank brought John Cherniak from the farm down the road to help him knock down the walls. Grace was supposed to help carry baskets of rubbish out to the backyard, but the banging and the dust made her head hurt. She sat on the wooden bench under the apple tree and watched John trudge across the yard and toss a bucket of plaster dust over the back fence. John was Frank's age, but he was bigger and broader than Frank. His blond hair was dark with sweat. "Are you just gonna sit out here while your brother does all the work?" he asked her. She nodded. He shook his head and said, "Jeez, Louise," but he did not sound angry. When he left, he lifted his cap to her and called, "Don't work too hard back there, Gracie," and she called back, "I won't."

One morning after the rooms upstairs were done, she found Frank washing the sheets from their parents' bed; the mattress was outside in the sun. "I'm getting married," he told Grace. "Her name is Vera. She's been working in town, keeping house for Dr. McCabe's family. She's coming tomorrow to meet you. You'll really like her, Gracie."

But Grace wasn't sure about this. Vera was all briskness and bustle; her brown striped dress was tightly belted, her fair hair was pinned back firmly, and she hadn't been in the kitchen five minutes before she started moving things around. "Why, this belongs with the sewing things!" she exclaimed when she found the tin button box beside the sugar bowl. She was unpacking some of her own things in advance of the wedding: a teapot, towels, a white leather Bible in a pearly cardboard case. Over the sink she hung her clock with a pale blue face and spiky black hands. "We have a clock," Grace said. No one had wound it in years. "This one's electric," Vera said. She squeezed Grace's hand. "Soon we'll be sisters. Now, would you like to help me with dinner?"

"No," Grace said, then remembered her manners. "Thank you."

Vera laughed. "You are funny! You can peel the potatoes over there while I see to the chicken." She didn't laugh, though, when she saw how Grace had peeled off ragged white lumps. "Grace, let me show you a better way," she said. "See, if you do it like this, you only take off the skin." She was perplexed that Grace wasn't looking. "Don't you want to learn, Grace?"

"No," Grace said, and she went to sit in the front room and looked for a quiet pond in her mind while Vera had a whispered consultation with Frank in the kitchen and the earth drank away the day's light. When Frank finally took Vera home, Grace retrieved the button box from the sewing basket and took it up to her room.

Lying in bed on those mornings when the sickness came, Grace waited until the nausea peaked. Then she padded softly down the stairs, lifted the latch on the kitchen door and ran to the outhouse at the back of the garden, her stomach tightening, her mouth full of saliva. In the cool dark, she threw up, then sat on the wooden seat, waiting for her legs to solidify again. Any minute now Vera would wake up. Grace had to be back in bed before Vera called her: "Grace! Get up! Honestly, Grace, I've called you twice already. You'd sleep all day if I let you."

It vexed Vera, this desire to sleep in the day. Vera could not abide things out of order. Besides, it was a sin to sleep during the day. "How?" Grace asked, and Vera promptly recited a list: "Pride, envy, gluttony, lust, avarice, wrath and sloth." Sleeping in the day was sloth.

"Rise and shine," Vera said, sticking her head around the door just as Grace was lowering herself back into the bed. "I want the garden weeded before the sun gets too hot."

"But we just did it," Grace said.

"And we'll do it again," Vera said. "You want to eat, don't you? Get dressed. Don't dawdle."

Grace pulled on yesterday's clothes, a long grey skirt that had belonged to her mother and a blue blouse that was too tight across the chest, the buttons straining out of their holes. Over the blouse she put on her mother's grey sweater, buttoning it all the way to the top, and then checked herself in the oval mirror above the oak dresser. She used to think she looked like a fox, with her cropped, reddish-brown hair and her pointed chin. Once, trying hard to think fox thoughts without human words, she'd brought the bliss on. Today, her small face looked puffy, and Vera would complain that she hadn't brushed her hair. "You could have lovely hair," Vera said, "if you would only work at it." Even hair was work.

Downstairs, Vera was filling the teapot. She had already laid out the buttered bread and sliced meat for Frank's lunch. This was Vera's method: before she closed any task, she opened another, creating an ever-continuing chain of never-finished work.

"Frank, your tea is here. I'm going down to the root cellar to get some eggs for a cake. We'll have barley soup for dinner. Frank, remind me to mend those trousers when you get home tonight. Grace, can you clear the table when your brother is finished, please?"

Grace said, "I'll do the garden now, Vera."

"After you clear the table," Vera said briskly.

Vera was still hopping mad when Frank came home in the evening. "Please talk to your sister, Frank. She went out to weed the garden after you left, and at noon I find her down by the creek, staring into space, and the garden not even touched. She's nearly nineteen years old. What's to become of her? What husband will put up with that?"

Grace was already in bed. Vera said if she couldn't help out, she shouldn't expect to eat. She could hear Vera downstairs, telling Frank she was at her wit's end. Frank murmured something in return. Grace crossed her hands across her chest and stared at the ceiling until the roof beams began to soften at the edges. Beyond the walls of the house, Grace heard roots swelling and curling through wet earth, and the faint sigh of fruit trees as they lost their soft white petals. Beyond the garden, crickets conversed with frogs and the creek gurgled and drained endlessly away. Down the road, in the graveyard, spiders dropped on silver threads from trees and the grass grew long around the tombstones. In her room, Grace grew lighter and lighter as the walls dissolved. Out of the silence and darkness, the gleam began, cold and bright and still. If she looked directly at it, it would extinguish itself, leaving her stranded in the night with nowhere to go except into sleep, as thin and worn as an old sheet. But if she was quiet, listening to nothing except the breath passing in and out of her, it would arrive, eventually, in full, and take her into itself.

This was where she went at night, when she was supposed to be asleep, and why she slept during the day, curled up under a tree. She could have the bliss during the day, as well, if Vera weren't always interrupting her. "What are you doing, Grace? For heaven's sake, you just woke up two hours ago. You cannot possibly be tired." She had to go all the way down to the creek, where Vera rarely came because she always ended up with mussed hair and mud on her shoes. But even at the creek, Vera's voice found her, calling her to come and bring in the laundry.

In spring and summer, every Wednesday morning Vera put on her good brown dress and hat and walked up the road and caught the bus to town. When she returned, she changed back into her housedress and sat in the garden with her knitting and told Grace the news from Mrs. McCabe. Mostly this concerned who was expecting, who had delivered, whose baby had colic or a weak constitution. Grace sat nearby, under the apple tree, where the grass was a deep green and the air was thick with the smell of the roses Vera had planted all around the house. "Shall I do your hair, Vera?" Grace asked. Vera often said no, but one day she nodded, and Grace went to fetch the brush.

"Well, Millie Henderson is going to have another baby," Vera said as Grace unwound Vera's golden brown hair and smoothed it with her fingers. "Mrs. McCabe is just beside herself." Mrs. McCabe was an investigator for the Children's Aid Society and the Mother's Allowance Commission, and oh! if people only knew what she had to deal with! The filthy children, red-eyed and coughing, the thin-as-a-rail mother who didn't know if she was coming or going, all crammed into one room, mattresses on the floor without sheets or pillowcases, a single threadbare towel to serve as face cloth and tea towel and baby blanket. Worse were the loose women, brazen types who spent their allowance on cigarettes, who had men over and then lied to Mrs. McCabe's face, even when she swooped in and found them together in the kitchen. "Her cousin, my foot!" Vera said. "Does she think Mrs. McCabe was born yesterday? It was probably whiskey in the tea cups!"

Millie Henderson wasn't brazen, just feeble-minded. Her husband was a no-good drunk who had run off three years ago, and Millie had only just qualified for Mother's Allowance when he showed back up. Now he was gone again, and the cupboards were stripped of anything edible or sellable, and Millie was pregnant, and she would have to wait *another* three years to qualify. "It's just a shame. Heaven knows, the last thing Millie Henderson needs is another baby. Ouch! Grace! Don't pull."

Grace hadn't been pulling. She knew why Vera was cross, though: she and Frank had been married for almost three years and there was no baby yet, only monthly troubles. Vera had gone to see Dr. McCabe last year and had come home with her eyes full of tears. "He said he couldn't say for certain," she told Frank. "He said only time would tell."

Grace separated Vera's hair into strips and began to plait it.

Vera sighed. "Mrs. McCabe is going to recommend that the baby be taken away. The Children's Aid can find a good home for it down south."

While Vera went on about Millie Henderson and bad blood, Grace was thinking that Vera had honey hair. Honey hair and hazelnut eyes and cinnamon freckles. Her brother, Frank, had dark russet hair, like tea, and tanned skin the colour of toast. "You and Frank will have beautiful children," Grace said. "Delicious cake-and-tea children."

"Don't talk foolishness, Grace," Vera said and fell silent.

"But why do you want children, Vera?"

"What a question!" Vera exclaimed, but she gave no answer. "Well, really!" she said when Grace persisted. "As if you don't know why people have children."

But Grace did not know.

"It's in the Bible," Vera said. "Go forth and multiply."

Grace wound Vera's hair back into a knot. Whenever you asked someone something they couldn't answer, they said it was in the Bible.

A few days later, she lifted Vera's Bible out of its pearly white box, and sure enough, there it was, right at the beginning. *What else is in this book?* Grace wondered. At first, it was all lists and warnings, but then she found a man who looked on the works his hands had made and saw that all was vanity and vexation of spirit. She slipped the Bible under her arm and took it down to the creek. This man came forth naked from his mother's womb and returned as he came, and could take nothing of his labour with him. He had laboured for the wind. All rivers ran down to the sea and yet the sea was never full. There was no profit under the sun.

Grace was electrified. She didn't get a chance to find out what happened to the man, though, because Frank was calling her.

Grace followed her brother upstairs to the attic, a long, empty space with a slanting roof and silvery light from the small, round windows at either end. Grace held the boards while her brother hammered. "Now listen, Grace, don't take Vera's Bible outside anymore."

Grace said, "I won't."

"That's one of the few things she brought from home. It was her mother's Bible."

"All right."

"Vera has had a hard life," Frank said. "Her father drank up everything. They were quite well off, but he just drank it all away. She doesn't mean to be hard on you, and truth be told, Grace, you should be helping her. You can't spend your whole life with your head in the clouds. And I don't like being in the middle. Hand me that board."

Grace stood in the middle of the room, where it was dark and cool. Up here, she knew, the bliss would be very strong. She might not have to come back at all. "I like it up here," she told Frank.

Frank sighed. "You would." He stood back to survey the wall. "Well, this'll be done soon."

But the house would never be done, Grace knew, because work begat work, just as fathers begat sons. That was a word she'd learned from the Bible.

At night, the bliss came briefly and departed. Grace pressed her hands against her stomach. This was how it had been since the sickness started: the bliss gleamed in the darkness and died out, doused by a sudden thirst or twinges in her gut, or else she simply fell asleep and was woken at dawn by the mounting nausea.

Today, when she awoke, the room was brighter than usual, and she had no time to think of her mother or anything else before she threw back the blankets and raced out. Her stomach was empty, but it still churned up bile. She wiped her face on her sleeve and stepped out of the outhouse, only to come face to face with Vera in her white nightgown, her hair spilling over her shoulders. "Every morning!" Vera cried. "Every morning! Did you think I wouldn't know? You—you whore!" She slapped Grace, a full, resounding smack. Then her hands flew up to her own cheeks, as if she herself had been struck. Her fingers clutched at her face, pulling it apart like dough; her mouth opened like a tear, and she wailed. The sound scattered the birds out of the apple tree and brought Frank out of the house, his face slack with fear. It was the worst sound Grace had ever heard in her life.

THE BABY

Vera called Grace for lunch. The whole morning had come flying apart. Vera had wept, Frank had shouted, Grace had thrown up again. The kettle boiled dry, there was no breakfast, and Frank was late for work. Grace went upstairs to sleep.

Downstairs, the day seemed to have knit itself back together. The clock above the sink chipped quietly away at time. On the table was a bowl of tomato soup and a plate of bread and cheese. Vera's hair was coiled into a bun at the back of her head, and her skin was milk clean. She folded tea towels while Grace ate.

"Grace, you need to tell us who it is." She cleared her throat. "The father."

Grace stared at her soup. Three months ago, she had been stretched out in the long grass beside the creek because the bliss was coming, and when she'd opened her eyes, he was waiting there, and that was the last time she had seen him.

The first time, it had been early spring, and when he found her by the creek, he frowned. "What are you doing down here?" he wanted to know.

She said, "I'm just sitting."

"Why don't you sit up in your garden?"

"I like it here."

"Why?"

She wished he would go away. Soon Vera would start calling for her, and she would have to go up and sweep the walkway. But he seemed to take her silence as an invitation to sit down and keep talking. When she finally stood up to go, he said, "Nice talking with you, Grace," even though she had said hardly a word.

After that, he seemed to find her almost every time she went down to the creek, and she didn't mind his talking because, unlike Vera, he didn't seem to expect answers; he didn't tell her to get her head out of the clouds, and sometimes she even found herself listening to what he said. His brother had gone to town to work at the plant, and his sisters had moved away when they married, and even though he did everything he could, his parents were old and the farm was still falling to pieces, and he didn't know why he bothered. He looked over at her and she found herself saying, "There's no profit under the sun." He nodded and said, "No profit whatsoever. Sell the whole thing, I keep telling them. Move to town. I'll get a job at the plant." But his parents wouldn't agree; they had put their lifeblood into the farm.

The last time she saw him, he looked worried, two small lines between his eyebrows and a pucker in his lip. "You shouldn't be sleeping out here, Grace," he said. His dark blue eyes looked sad. "I told you that before."

"I wasn't sleeping," she said.

"Well, resting, then. You should rest at home."

She smiled at him. He reached out and put a hand on her knee. It was heavy and warm, and she shivered. The bliss always left her cold. He licked his lips. "Go home now."

She said, "I don't want to go home."

"Well, you better go home anyway."

Under the hem of her dress, his thumb stroked the bare skin around her knee. "Please, Grace," he said. "Go home." He closed his eyes and took his hand back. The veins in his neck were like chords.

She sat up. His eyes flew open and relief spilled out of them. "That's—no. No, Gracie, don't." She was pulling up the skirt of her dress. "Touch me there," she said. "Like last time." Last time, he had covered her with his fingers, stroking her edges slowly and softly until she melted in his hands. "I liked it so much," she told him. It was different from the cold white castle of bliss. She had gone into ripples and the ripples grew into waves and the waves carried her across a dark, sparkling sea and left her, panting and hot, on the ordinary earth.

"We shouldn't," he said. He looked so miserable, she thought he might cry. "It's not right."

"Who says?"

"Well, the Bible, for one thing," he said.

Grace shook her head. "I looked in the Bible and I couldn't find it anywhere."

"It's there, all right," he said glumly.

"One more time," she said.

"Then why don't we get married?"

He had asked her that last time: "Marry me. The farm will be mine. I can look after you." She had seen his mother at church, the hard line of her mouth under a black bonnet, and his father, thin as a wire. She knew the grim house, tarpapered, with slits for windows, and the chicken coop and splintering barn and falling-down sheds and leaning fence and the fields across which the wind whirled in its circuits. She could see all the work that would have to be done; it would run through the days the way rivers ran down to the sea, carrying them all along with it. She shook her head.

"Well, if you won't marry me, I'll sign up," he said. He had also said that last time. Grace didn't see what one thing had to do with the other. "Don't you care that I might be killed?"

"Please, John. This one time." She lifted his hand and put it back on her knee. "I'll never ask you again."

And sometime after that, she began to wake up sick before it was light.

Vera stood up abruptly and began to wipe down the countertops. "Now you listen to me, Grace. Get your head out of the clouds and pay attention. This is important. First we have to know who took advantage of you." She scrubbed at a shadow on the wall. "If someone has hurt you—"

"No," Grace said. "It wasn't like that. I wanted to."

At the sink, Vera's face turned strawberry pink, and her hands were blurry and furious under the stream of water. "Well, it's all right, then. It's all right if you have a fellow. Tell us who he is. Frank'll go and talk to him."

Grace set down her spoon. *Talk to him and say what?*

"You can get married in the next week or so, and no one will know. Lots of babies come early."

"Get married?"

Vera turned off the tap and stared at her. "Grace, don't you understand that you're going to have a baby?"

"Yes, but I don't want to get *married.*"

Vera threw her hands up in the air, aghast. "But you can't have a baby without a husband! You don't . . . Grace, you can't . . . What will people say?"

As far as Grace could see, people would say the same senseless things they always said. She didn't care what people said. But Vera cared. Vera was beside herself. Vera said she would not have Grace under her roof. They had done their best, and this was how Grace repaid them, bringing shame down upon them all. If she was not going to put it right, she would have to pack her bags and go.

Grace looked up. This was an interesting idea. "Go where?"

"Exactly!" Vera slapped the table. "Where would you go?"

"I don't know," Grace said, bewildered.

Vera sent her out of the kitchen. That evening, Grace listened to the rise and fall of voices downstairs. Vera said Frank had to make her tell. He had to make them marry. Grace closed her eyes. John had signed up and shipped out already, but maybe they could make him come back and marry her. They could not, however, make her tell his name—that much she knew.

Then Frank said she could not stay. He said he had not looked after her properly after their mother had died. They would send her down to the nuns in Toronto or Windsor who had places for girls in trouble. She wouldn't be the first one to go down and she wouldn't be the last. The nuns would find a home for the baby, and maybe Grace would end up staying down there. She wasn't a bad girl. And when he thought about it, maybe the convent was the right place for her.

Grace turned over onto her side and squeezed her eyes shut to hold down the surging tears. She didn't want to go live with nuns in Windsor. She didn't want to have a baby. She tried to think of what she did want, but the only thing she was sure of, she knew she couldn't have. In this world, you weren't allowed to sit quietly and think your thoughts all day. You had to get up in the morning and straight away start working, and every piece of work you did just made more work until you were dead and laid to rest in the ground, asleep under the earth. Dust to dust.

Downstairs, Vera was quiet. Then she said, "Maybe we should let her stay here. We can take care of the baby. Everyone will know anyway. It's the first thing they say when a girl goes away. And there's no telling what kind of home they'll find for the baby, or even if they'll find one. Sometimes they can't."

Frank said, "That's true."

Grace curled herself around the pillow and fell asleep.

In the morning, Vera made Grace take a bath and laid out one of her own outfits, a dark green skirt and plain white blouse. "We're going to town," she said. Grace's limbs were heavy and stiff, and town made her more tired than anything, but it was easier to just do what Vera said. The bus let them off in front of Dr. McCabe's stone house with potted plants on the veranda. Dr. McCabe had iron grey hair and a heavy moustache. He called Grace to come in and said, "Well, young lady, what do you have to say for yourself?"

What an odd question, Grace thought.

"You're in trouble, your sister-in-law tells me."

"No," Grace said. "I'm going to have a baby."

"That's what I said. I hope you realize what your brother and sister-in-law are doing for you. There aren't many who would do it, believe you me."

Vera helped her undress, and Dr. McCabe pressed her stomach and her breasts and listened with his stethoscope. He spoke over her to Vera, asking about Grace's eating and sleeping habits, telling Vera that Grace seemed healthy enough and the baby would come in March or April. Vera helped her dress, repeating what the doctor had just said. "He says you're fine. The baby will come in the spring."

On the way home, they stopped at Friedman's for yarn and cloth. There were hats and sweaters and blankets to be knit, Vera said, and diapers and towels and flannel sheets to be cut.

As soon as Frank finished the attic room, he would make a cradle for the baby. Grace plodded behind Vera, wishing she could lie down at the side of the road just for a moment. When they got home, Vera surprised her by telling her to sit and rest. "You have to take care of yourself, Grace," she said.

Grace sat and rested throughout the autumn and the winter. She thought about pieces of white stone, broken into smaller and smaller pieces; she thought about a tree, adding and subtracting roots and bark and leaves, but never finding when exactly a tree started being a tree; she thought about a spoon being dropped, the clatter, the fading of sound into silence. All these things before would have brought on the bliss, but now they left her unmoved. Sitting in the chair or lying on the bed, she remained solid. The bliss had left her completely.

Vera gave her small things to do: a shirt to mend, a scarf to unravel for wool. She said Grace did good handiwork when she put her mind to it. Vera did the big things herself, the cooking and cleaning and doing down of beets and apple jelly, and she never complained now to Frank that Grace did not help, and in the evenings, she sewed and knitted for the baby: a white jacket, hat and booties, laced through with green satin ribbon; a stack of flannel diapers. She held them up briefly for Grace to see, and then wrapped them in tissue paper and took them upstairs to her room. When she came back from town, she had things from her sister: bottles and rubber nipples, a cup with a lid, three extremely small spoons. "Doll spoons," marvelled Grace, but Vera said, "Don't play with those. They're for the baby."

She also had pamphlets from Mrs. McCabe, which she sometimes read aloud, about the scientific method, with schedules and discipline and toilet training. "Because otherwise, you spoil the baby," she said, "and I don't know how many times poor Mrs. McCabe has had to deal with the results. Feeble-minded children, juvenile delinquents, you name it."

Grace fell asleep in the rocking chair and often woke up to the smell of cinnamon. "You have to eat," Vera said, bringing in a tray with another piece of raisin pie, and if Grace wasn't hungry, Vera ate it herself. Then she ate the rest of the pie, one sliver at a time, and the cinnamon rolls as well. Sometimes, they both fell asleep in the afternoon and Frank woke them when he came in. Under Vera's cinnamon freckles, her face glowed and grew rounder. She sewed a wide smock for Grace and let out her own clothes. "You look like you're going to have a baby too," Grace said, when Vera put on her loosened skirt.

"Don't be silly," Vera said. "I've just put on a little weight." But she pressed her hands against her thickened waist.

In March, there was a little thaw, and Grace's hands and feet grew puffy. She flailed in bed like a flipped-over bug and finally rigged a belt to the dresser so she could hoist herself up. She woke up one morning with a single sharp pain, and by the end of the day, Dr. McCabe was there. Vera held her hand while Grace writhed. She had no idea how long it lasted. In a way, it was like the bliss: the self dissolved, not into a marble castle, but into a dark place of pain. The pain was thick and solid, with streaks of darker pain. There was no room for thought. Time stopped completely and only started again when Vera sat her up and told her the baby was coming. "Push now, Grace," she said, and a wave towered over her and came crashing down, and at the end of the wave, she pushed and was torn open.

Vera said, "It's a boy! Oh Grace, it's a beautiful boy!" The doctor spoke, but she couldn't hear him properly. Her face and hair and nightgown were soaked, and she was freezing. She had to push again, and then it was over. Vera pulled her out of the tangle of sheets and stripped off her wet nightgown. Grace shivered and tried to stop sobbing. "It's all right now, Grace. It's finished. The baby's fine. He's with the doctor," Vera said, buttoning Grace into an old flannel shirt. She stripped the bed and remade it. "You sleep now," she said, and guided Grace back to bed. Grace felt blankets being piled on top of her, and she closed her eyes and fell straight into darkness.

Hardly any time later, Vera woke her. She put a loaf of bread wrapped in a white towel into Grace's arms. The bread was still warm from the oven. "He needs to be fed," Vera said, and Grace looked down, bleary-eyed. It was the baby. It had dark golden hair and a red, furrowed face, and it moved its head back and forth, mewling. "For heaven's sake, Grace, you have to—here, like this." Vera unbuttoned the flannel shirt and pushed Grace's nipple into the baby's mouth. Grace gasped when the mouth closed in on her. For such a small thing, it had a fierce hunger. When the baby finished, Vera lifted it out of her arms and told her to go back to sleep.

The sound of crying pinched her awake some time later. Vera was in the doorway. "Wake up, Grace." She waited until Grace was sitting up. "Hold his head properly." Grace moved her arm under its head. Its eyes were closed, but it sucked ferociously for a long time. Vera straightened the sheets and refolded the extra blankets. "Frank and I were talking about a name. We were thinking about Daniel."

Grace said, "Look." When she touched the baby's palm, it seized her finger.

"So that's settled, then," Vera said. "Daniel."

Grace tried to pull her finger out of the baby's fist but could not. She wondered how it knew to hold on like that.

The baby slept in the cradle in the front room, and Vera brought it upstairs when it cried. Grace fed the baby, and Vera fed Grace. She carried in trays of oatmeal, poached eggs and toast, milky tea and custard. In between feedings, Grace dozed. "I'm run off my feet," Vera told Frank happily. "But he's such a good baby!"

If Vera did not bring the baby right away, the crying made Grace's heart race; her hands and legs were jangly, and she squirmed and pulled at the bedsheets until Vera brought it, and Grace got her nightgown unbuttoned, and the baby turned its head and latched itself onto her. As soon as the crying stopped, the pins and needles in her limbs disappeared and she could breathe again. Vera said, "I'll come back and get him when he's finished."

Grace didn't mind this part. The baby was warm in her arms, and although her nipples had ached and chafed at first, they didn't anymore. She put her face close to its head and breathed in deeply. It had its own sweet smell under the smell of white soap. When Vera lifted the baby out of her arms, the place where it had been grew quickly cold.

Sometimes, her milk started running before the baby even cried. Something let go in her breasts, and just as milk began to leak out, the baby would cry. She wondered at this. She wondered about the baby. Sometimes, when the baby stopped feeding, she didn't call Vera right away. She examined its tiny fingers and ears and touched the strands of dark blond hair. It knew how to drink, how to hold on. If she touched the side of its cheek, it turned its face towards her hand. She wondered what else it knew.

She heard the baby crying, and when Vera didn't bring him, she got out of bed and stood at the top of the stairs. "Vera?" she called. "Where's the baby?"

"He's fine," Vera called back. "I just gave him a bath. Go on back to bed."

Grace's heart was hammering. She went downstairs and found the baby wrapped in white flannel in the cradle in the front room. His eyes were closed and his face was red; he was crying with all his might. "Vera?" she called. "Vera!" She could hear Vera rummaging in the root cellar. Grace drew in a tattered breath and lifted him up. Instantly, he stopped crying and pushed his hot little face into her breast. *He knows who I am*, she thought, astonished. Sinking into the chair beside the cradle, she unbuttoned her nightgown and the baby opened his mouth.

The door opened and Vera came in, a basket of empty jam jars in her arms.

"Grace! What are you doing?"

"He's hungry."

"You have to let him cry, Grace. You can't come to him every time he cries. That's how you spoil him," Vera said. "Next time, leave him be."

The baby stopped drinking and looked at Grace. His eyes were the colour of dark slate, and she could see that he already knew everything in the world.

DANNY

Danny smelled of sleep and milk and a lemony sweetness. His skin was white and pink, and more golden hair was coming in, soft and feathery. Just before he yawned, a tiny frown of concentration appeared between his eyebrows. When Grace lifted her shirt to feed him, he squirmed and kicked impatiently. His eyes looked for her, and when they found her, he smiled, and every time Grace laughed. She unwrapped his blanket, examined his feet and hands, kissed his fingers. She could not get enough of him. The cradle was in her room now—she had carried it upstairs herself, over Vera's objections—but most often he slept in the bed beside her. She fell asleep listening to his breath, and a prickling in her skin always woke her just before he cried.

Outside, the snow had melted away completely, and the light was warm on the windows. Grace was a whirl of energy. She did everything Vera asked. She swept the floor and beat the carpet so she could put a clean blanket down and settle the baby on it. She raked stones out of the soil and planted carrots and potatoes so the baby would have food when he was ready to eat it. She watched Vera cut out a pattern for a baby jumper and said, "Let me make it, Vera." Vera showed her how to fit the seams together, and Grace's needle flew in and out, making small, even stitches. Vera borrowed Mrs. McCabe's camera and Frank took their picture, Vera and Grace in front of a rose bush with Danny between them in the jumper they had made for him.

The moment Grace was done her work, she raced to where Danny was, usually on a blanket surrounded by pillows in the front room. If he was asleep, she lay down beside him and watched his eyes move under their lids. If he was awake, she carried him around the house, showing him things. He liked brightly lit places, but only if there was something dark as well, so that his eyes could follow the edges. He liked things that dangled, and reached his round little hands out for them, and things that moved, like curtains when the window was open. And he liked surprising sounds. Grace sneezed, and Danny let out a peal of laughter.

Vera said, "Close the window, Grace." Babies needed fresh air, but fresh air carried germs. They needed to be wrapped up against the cold, but they also had to be able to kick their legs. Their hands had to be free, but they weren't allowed to suck on them. They had to be fed, but on schedule, held properly but not too much. Otherwise, they would be spoiled. Vera was especially worried about spoiling. She told Frank, "I have to watch her constantly. She carries him around like he's a doll, and the minute she puts him down, he fusses. If she keeps this up . . ." She didn't finish. The booklets from Mrs. McCabe explained what would happen if Grace kept this up.

When Vera held Danny, her face changed, softening with the sheer pleasure of him, and she murmured and sang to him, and

Grace felt bad for wanting to keep her away from the baby. So she listened and nodded when Vera said, "Listen to this, Grace. This was written by a doctor. 'Babies under six months old should never be played with, and of kissing, the less the better.' Do you hear that, Grace? And here you are, playing with him like he's a toy and kissing him all the time. You don't want to ruin him, do you, Grace?"

"No," Grace said. She waited for Vera to leave the room before she kissed him.

"Listen, Grace: 'A really contrary infant might try for an hour, or even for two or three hours, to get the best of his mother by crying. She must never give in, provided she is convinced that nothing is physically amiss with the child. Habitual criers should be left alone most of the time; otherwise, they might become nervous.'" Vera looked up from the book. "You see? Do you want him to be nervous? Now put him down."

Grace put the baby down. The trick was to always be waiting, to be listening for that catch in his breath and watching for the shadow that darkened his face before he cried. The trick was to get to him just before he cried, whisk him away, upstairs, downstairs, wherever Vera was not, to feed him and rock him and kiss him, and then to put him back in his cradle before Vera got back. "You see how much more peaceful he is," Vera asked, "now that you aren't picking him up every minute of the day?"

It was hard to get to him, though, when Vera sent her outside to pick tomatoes. It was hard when Frank said, "Vera says you're spoiling the baby." It got worse when Vera found her in the root cellar, feeding Danny on the steps. "Grace! Have you gone mad? Bringing the baby down here?" Vera's astonishment grew into fury. "And you just fed him! This is why he won't stay on his schedule. Give him over!" But Grace would not give him over. She took Danny upstairs, leaving Vera yelling on the steps.

That night, when Frank came home, there was no dinner. Vera had been in her room all afternoon. Frank looked at Grace playing with Danny in the kitchen and rushed upstairs. Over by the windows, Grace could hear Frank's low murmur in the room above, but no matter where she stood, she couldn't hear Vera at all. When Frank came downstairs, he looked like all the air had been sucked out of him. "You've really upset her, Grace. Her nerves are shot." When she didn't look up, he said, "Grace. She just wants what's best for the baby. You know that."

Grace did know it. The problem was Vera's idea of best.

The next morning, the baby began to cry just as she started to water the beans, but when she hurried to the house, she found the door locked. Her skin prickled and her breasts were heavy. The prickling spread over her chest, up her neck, down her arms to her hands. She pounded on the door while the needles multiplied under her skin. "Please, Vera," she begged. Inside, Danny's cries grew louder. She ran around to the front door, but it too was locked. She had never heard Danny cry so hard before. Grace hammered the door with the palm of her hand and then kicked it furiously. "Let me in!" she screamed. Vera appeared at the window. "That is enough!" she hissed. "Stop it this instant or I'll leave you out there all day."

She slammed the window shut.

Danny cried and Grace threw herself to the ground under the sun. This was the place people meant when they said hell. Eventually, the door opened and Vera let her in. Grace pushed past her. "Don't you dare wake him," Vera said. Grace sat by the cradle and watched Danny sleep. His face was flushed and damp with sweat. "I'm sorry, Danny," she whispered. "I heard you crying, but I couldn't come."

At dinner, Frank looked up from his soup. "What happened to you, Grace? Your face and arms are covered with bites."

Grace said, "It's nothing." It was the needles that broke through her skin while Danny cried for her.

Vera looked at her closely. "Poison ivy. Don't touch the baby until it goes away. It's time he took the bottle anyway." Her voice was as flinty as her face.

Grace covered her eyes with her hands.

Vera showed Grace the bottles and rubber nipples, which had to be sterilized, and the powdered formula, which had to be mixed up with cooled boiled water. "He's six months old now. Formula is better for him," Vera said. "And it's so much more sanitary." But Danny would not take the bottle, sanitary or not. He pushed the rubber out of his mouth and cried and cried. Vera was not bothered. "He'll take it when he gets hungry enough."

Danny cried all day. Grace's face and arms were flaming red, her eyes swollen from crying. "What a fuss you make," Vera said. "Do you think I'm doing this to hurt Danny? Anyway, crying is how babies exercise their lungs. Stop that caterwauling, Grace." Finally, Danny closed his mouth around the rubber nipple and drank.

"You see how much better he sleeps now?" Vera said the next morning. "He didn't wake at all last night, did he?" But he had woken. And Grace was awake seconds before him. So for a few weeks, Danny drank from the bottle during the day, and Grace fed him at night, and Vera was happy until she turned on the light in the middle of the night and found them. She grabbed Danny and slammed the door behind her. In the morning, she said, "You think I'm being hard, Grace, but he has to have proper food. He's going to eat baby food now and learn to drink from a cup. Otherwise, he's not going to grow properly."

Grace said, "He *is* growing. Every day he gets bigger."

Vera brought out the booklet from Mrs. McCabe. "Look here.

Scientists have made this formula. Do you think you know better than scientists?"

Grace turned the booklet over. It had the same cover as the box of formula. She said, "But I'm right there at night. I can just feed him."

Vera had a solution to that. It was time for Danny to sleep in his own room. "Babies have to learn to be independent." She said the sewing room would be Danny's room, Grace's room would be the sewing room, and Grace could move up to the attic room. Frank moved Grace's bed and dresser. "You always said you liked it up here," Frank said. The room was big, the length of the whole house, with light at both ends. "And you'll have your privacy." But Grace didn't want her privacy. She wanted to scream. She squeezed her fists and pressed them into her eyes until the sockets hurt.

"Listen, Gracie," Frank said, then fell silent.

"She wants to leave him alone in the dark," Grace said. "She lets him cry." He was a *baby*. It made no sense.

"She worked for Dr. McCabe's family," Frank said. "She helped his wife with all their babies. Now, wouldn't a doctor and a doctor's wife know what's best for a baby?"

Grace dropped her hands from her face. "I know what's best for him."

Frank shook his head. "I don't think you do, and I can't be in the middle like this. Enough is enough. From now on, what Vera says goes."

What Vera said was, the baby would come with her to town in the mornings. Mrs. McCabe loved to see Danny, and so did Vera's sister, Anne. Grace wanted to come to town too, but Vera said no. Mrs. McCabe had a reputation to protect. Grace said nothing. She was afraid of Mrs. McCabe because of the Children's Aid Society. They took babies away from mothers without husbands. They had taken Millie Henderson's baby away. Vera said that the Children's Aid could come and make a visit. If they found Danny not being cared for properly, they would take him away. They could do that; it was their jurisdiction.

Grace was sorry she hadn't told them about John Cherniak. Frank would have gone over to talk to his parents, and when John came back from the war, he would have married her. They would have moved to town like he wanted, and even if they didn't, the farm wouldn't have been so bad. She could have worked in the house while Danny played on a blanket beside her. She could have worked in the fields while Danny slept in a basket under a tree. John's mother, with her black bonnet, wouldn't have cared how much she kissed her own child. John's mother had already had children, and her daughters in town all had children of their own. There would be lots of babies to go around. Then there were the things she and John had done by the creek—they could do those things any time they wanted, and she could have had brothers and sisters for Danny.

But it was too late for all that. No one would marry her now.

What she needed was a place of her own. At night, she transformed herself and Danny into foxes or blackbirds and found a place in the woods that Vera could not get to, and then she was able to sleep, but in the morning, she was ashamed. *You are not a bird*, she told herself angrily. *You can't live in a tree*.

What she needed was money, to pay for a real place.

What she needed was a job. But what jobs were there for women who didn't know how to do any jobs? She didn't even know who to ask, except Vera, and that was out of the question. Then, at the beginning of December, Vera surprised her.

GOING

"Well, Mrs. May's daughter is certainly doing well for herself," Vera said while they peeled potatoes at the kitchen table. Snow hissed softly against the windows. "Remember how she got in trouble last year and went down south? Now she has a job there." Grace did not remember, but her entire body went erect and a tremor ran through her fingers.

"She's making a good eighteen, nineteen dollars a week now."

"Where does she stay?" Grace asked. Her voice was uneven, but she kept peeling.

"She stayed at the YWCA at first," Vera said. "Now she's got an apartment with another girl. That's what they do, the girls. They get together and share a place."

"I wonder how she knew where to get a job."

"Advertisement in the paper. She got there on a Sunday night, and by Tuesday morning she was working." Vera sliced the potatoes and dropped them into a colander. "No one knows her down there; she can start fresh. She'll probably meet a fellow and get married."

Grace began to sweep the peelings into a pile. "What kind of job?"

"A cereal company. Mrs. May showed me a photo of the two of them, Bridget and her roommate. They were going to Niagara Falls for a holiday, and they had on the cutest hats."

"Did she know how to do that work before she got there?"

"Oh that," Vera said. "No. They trained her."

The potatoes were finished, but Vera and Grace sat at the table, the silence between them lengthening until Vera said, "If you wanted to do something like that, Grace, I'd be behind it."

Grace didn't look up, but her heart jerked and began to race. She could see them, Danny and her, in a little apartment, sitting together in the window seat, looking out onto the tops of trees. In her mind, she kissed the top of Danny's head and drank in the smell of his hair.

"I could talk to Mrs. May," Vera said. "Find out where Bridget is working. Maybe Bridget could introduce you at the factory. Would you like to do something like that?"

Grace said, "Yes."

"Well!" Vera looked surprised. Then she beamed. "Well, good! It might be just the thing for you."

"But I don't know how . . . I mean, how would I . . ."

"Oh, they just want decent, able-bodied people. They'll show you how to do the work."

"I mean, I don't know what I'd do with Danny while I was at work."

Vera blinked. "What you would do with Danny."

"Yes. If I found someone who could watch him—"

Vera's face snapped shut and she snatched the colander off the table. "And here I thought you'd finally gotten your head out of the clouds! You can't take Danny down there! A woman with a baby and no husband—they won't even look at you. And even if you did get a job, which you wouldn't, you'd have to pay some stranger to look after Danny while you were at work." She slammed the colander into the sink. "What you would do with Danny! Honest to goodness, Grace. I don't know what goes on in your head sometimes."

Grace went into the living room and squeezed in beside Danny on the sofa. He was asleep, his fists tucked under his chin, surrounded by pillows so he wouldn't fall. She studied the shadow his lashes made against his cheek, the arc of his mouth. Did Vera really think she could go live hundreds of miles away from Danny? *I don't know what goes on in* her *head sometimes*, Grace thought.

At supper, Vera and Frank talked about the war and which men were seeing action and whether anything good could come out of the alliance with Stalin. Grace cut her potatoes into smaller and smaller pieces. "Frank, do they hire women at the plant?"

"Sure, there are plenty of women working in the offices," he said.

Vera scowled at her. "They're educated women," she said. "They went to secretarial school."

"But in the plant part?" Grace persisted.

"There are some now," Frank said. "Why?"

Vera answered for her. "We were talking about Mrs. May's daughter this morning. She's got a job down south, and Grace said she wouldn't mind doing something like that. If you aren't going to eat, Grace, take your plate to the kitchen." Grace took her plate to the kitchen and stood behind the door, listening.

Frank said he didn't like the idea of Grace going away. He didn't see why she shouldn't try to find work here in Sault Ste. Marie. Not at the plant—that probably wasn't the place for her—but if she wanted to work, she could probably find something, and Vera could look after the baby in the day.

In the kitchen, Grace shook her head. Vera was already looking after Danny in the day; that was not the solution.

Vera said, "But she can't get a fresh start here, Frank. You know how people talk. If she goes down there, she can build a new life for herself. Look at Bridget May. She has her whole life ahead of her now."

Frank sighed and said he didn't know. He just didn't know what to think anymore.

Later, washing the dishes, Vera said, "Grace, you need to go away where nobody knows you. And you can't take the baby because you have to work."

"I could pay someone to look after him," Grace said, wiping the soapy tines of a fork. "I could find someone nice."

"You wouldn't make enough," Vera said. She wiped her hands and got out a paper and pencil. "Come here. I'll show you." Grace sat beside her and watched her write $80 at the top of the paper. "Let's say you make this much a month. This is how much you'd pay for rent. Then you'd have to pay for your bus fare. And groceries. And clothes for yourself."

"I don't need clothes."

"You'd need clothes if you were working. You can't go to work in your old housedress. And Danny needs clothes. Shoes. Winter boots. They outgrow things so fast. Plus other things—if he got sick, you'd have to pay the doctor. You'd have to buy medicine."

Grace looked at the paper. Vera hadn't finished. "Now you have to pay someone to care for Danny. Do you see?" There was less than no money left.

Grace saw. She was also suspicious. If there was no money left, how was Mrs. May's daughter buying new hats and going to Niagara Falls? She said, "I can't leave Danny."

"Why don't you just go down for a few months after Christmas and try it out?"

Grace said, "We'll see," which is what Vera said when she meant no but didn't want to discuss it.

Vera seemed to think it meant something else, though, because as Grace was going upstairs, she said, "And don't worry about your brother. I'll talk to him."

Up in her attic room, Grace sat with her head in her hands, trying to think of a way out, but all her ideas ended in rags and rooms with dirt floors and the Children's Aid Society at the door. If she stayed, at least she and Danny would have a roof over their heads. She would just have to avoid fighting with Vera. If she didn't fight with Vera, Vera wouldn't fight with Frank, and Frank wouldn't look pained and pinched when he told Grace to stop fighting with Vera. If she didn't fight with Vera, she could be with Danny, which was all that mattered.

But not fighting with Vera was hard. Not fighting with Vera meant she couldn't be with Danny anyway, because she was in the basement running clothes through the wringer or outside knocking icicles from the eaves while Vera took Danny to town and had his picture taken at Venini's Studio. Not fighting with Vera meant Vera decided what Danny could eat and when he should sleep, where he could play and whether he was too old for Grace to be singing nonsense songs to him.

Danny's legs were lengthening like crazy weeds; he climbed out of his pillow fortress on the floor and crawled everywhere, frowning at every object that came his way. When he recognized it, his face broke suddenly into radiance; then he put it into his mouth. "Danny!" Grace laughed helplessly, extracting the chewed-up leg of the woolly lamb. "You can't eat that." He babbled sweetly, just syllables, but sometimes, they matched what he saw. "Ba ba," he said to the ball. "Ma ma ma," he said to Grace.

At dinner, Vera told Frank, "Oh, and Danny called me mama today."

Grace pushed her chair back, her face suddenly hot and her hands trembling. "He did not," she said.

"Oh, for heaven's sake," Vera said. "He doesn't know the difference."

"He knows who his mother is," Grace said, her voice rising wildly. Vera told her to lower her voice, she would wake the baby. Grace wanted to weep and throw up all the words she had swallowed ever since Frank had said, "From now on, what Vera says goes." She wanted to stamp her feet and pull out her hair and hit Vera over the head with the casserole dish of scalloped potatoes, crack her skull like an egg. "He's my baby," she yelled, and she flung her plate over the table onto the floor. Frank shouted, "Grace! That is enough! Go upstairs and don't come down for the rest of the night." In the living room, Danny wailed, and Vera rushed from the table. Frank pointed to the staircase. "Go," he said.

Not fighting was impossible.

She took Danny up to her room and held him on her lap, stroking his dark blond hair. He played with her fingers and she told him that she had to go away for a while, to find work and a place to live, to see if it was possible for a woman with a baby to have a job and make a home. It would be unbearable for her, every minute, but she would endure it for him, and he must endure it for her. "Do you understand, Danny?" she asked him, and he wriggled deeper into her lap and nestled his head under her chin.

"Grace!" It was Vera at the bottom of the stairs. "Where's the baby? You better not be up there playing with him like he's a doll!"

Grace buried her face in her son's neck and wept.

It was unthinkable. It boggled the mind and broke the heart. It ran against the running of all things. It was not doable, and yet she was doing it. She was putting clothes into the straw-coloured suitcase. Fold, fold, tuck. She had to stop every few minutes because her chest would begin to burn and the room would grow dim, and she'd realize she wasn't breathing.

She looked around. "Now, make sure you have everything," Vera said every time she came upstairs. "Your comb, your toothbrush. Did you pack those new blouses I made you?" There was still the photo of Danny in the frame, but she would carry that in her purse. The cupboard drawers were askew, empty except for scraps of paper and yarn. Everything Grace owned and nothing she wanted was in the straw-coloured suitcase. The only thing that mattered to her was the only thing she would leave behind.

Frank said, "I don't agree with this. You don't *have* to go away, Gracie. You just have to try to get along with Vera. Work more as a team. Give and take. She just wants what's best—"

But Grace cut him off. "No, Frank. I am going." That silenced him. She didn't say that there was no give and take with Vera. Under her own roof, Vera would always win. She didn't say that she hated Vera with such a black, implacable passion that she was afraid to stay.

Frank went down to talk to Vera. "I'm not saying she can't look after her own child, for heaven's sake!" Vera said, her voice rising up through the vents. "But should I stand idly by and let her do what we know to be wrong? I can't do that, Frank. She has no idea, simply no idea."

Up in the attic Grace could hear the strain of the mattress springs as Frank sat down heavily. "Well, I can't fight both of you," he said, his voice thickening.

"It's the best thing for her," Vera said, softening. "The longer she waits, the harder it will be. And it will do her a lot of good to get out on her own, learn what the world is made of."

Grace already knew: the world was made of tiny pieces of nothing that flew together and stuck. One tiny granule met another in the great nothingness, and they longed for each other. There was no reason for it. No reason why one near-invisible fragment of glass in a plate should long for the other fragments, and why the other fragments should long for it, and yet it did and they did. If one fragment was lost, the plate fell apart in grief. It was pure desire that held everything together. Plates, rocks, trees, beetles, children. The world was made of pieces of nothing that desired to be together.

It was not necessary to leave to learn that. But there were other reasons to go. If a person had a child but no husband, a room but no house, a place but no home, a will but no way, and if a person was losing her son and herself, little by little, day by day, because she knew what she knew in her skin and bones but not what her sister-in-law knew in her books and pamphlets, then yes, it was necessary.

A FRESH START

Frank took her to the bus station in the dark. She didn't wake Danny; it would have killed her to say goodbye. Not that it would matter. She was dead already. The walking dead.

"Grace, do you have the ticket?"

"Yes." The talking dead.

"You look very nice, Gracie. That suit is very becoming on you." The dead wore new clothes, a navy skirt and matching jacket cut and sewn by the living.

"We wait over there," Frank said. The moving dead. The standing dead. The dead could swallow coffee from a paper cup, but they could not taste it.

"You have your wallet? Keep your purse in your lap at all times."

The dead could nod.

"Here's the driver now," Frank said. "Show him your ticket."

"I'm coming back for him as soon as I get set up."

"I know. I know you are. Don't cry now, Grace. You know we'll look after him like he was our own."

The dead could cry. Water droplets fell from their eyes, but they could not feel them.

On the bus, Grace sat with her purse in her lap, her hands and feet like rocks at the end of stick limbs. The bus rolled forward. Outside the window, Frank waved his hat, and then he was gone.

Out on the highway, the light was grey. Bare black trees stood in pools of icy water and lifted their aching arms to the swirling, empty sky. The road cut through rock face crusted over with ice. Inside her was a raging thing that swallowed and recreated itself endlessly. Crying was no relief from it. Thinking was no help for it. It would not be talked to, it could not be tricked. She had left her boy. It was unbearable. It had killed her, and yet here she was, sitting on a bus, getting off the bus, dragging a suitcase down a frozen sidewalk. The dead did what they had to do.

"Now, when you get to Peterborough," Vera had said, "you'll be able to walk to your place. Isn't that convenient?" She had drawn a map. "It's too bad Bridget May moved to Niagara Falls. The bus terminal is here, and apparently there's a bank right here, and then you turn here onto Brock Street. That's your street, where the rooming house is. Mrs. Barr's. Bridget May recommended it, and I've talked to the woman. She has a nice room ready for you."

Mrs. Barr's was a narrow wooden house painted an oily grey and surrounded by a wire fence. The walkway was treacherous with rutted ice. Grace knocked, and then knocked harder, and after a long time, a woman opened the door in a pink bathrobe and frothy pink slippers. "Why didn't you ring the bell?" she asked. "Jeez, you could have been standing out here all night." Her impossibly black hair looked like it had been whipped up into a confection of rolls and waxed. She blew out a long streamer of smoke. "I suppose you're Grace Turner?"

Grace nodded.

"Don't you look like a month of Sundays. What's the matter, you have a bad trip?"

I am dead, Grace thought, but she could only shake her head. Mrs. Barr said to come in already, her heating bill was going to go through the roof.

She took Grace upstairs to her room, which smelled of cold cream and cigarettes, pointing out that the smallest room was always the cutest. She explained the use of the hot water tank, the rules for making tea, the ban on gentlemen callers, the meal schedule, the bath schedule, the laundry schedule and the ledger in which the schedules were recorded. She watched as Grace hung up her clothes and observed that Grace sure hadn't brought much, and was she always this quiet? The other girls, Connie and Noreen, were a hoot. Grace would meet them at dinner. Grace said she was tired and if it was okay with Mrs. Barr, she would like to go straight to bed. Mrs. Barr shrugged. "No skin off my nose."

When Mrs. Barr was gone, Grace took the photograph out of her purse. She couldn't look at it. Instead, she lay down in her slip between cold, damp sheets and pressed the frame to her chest with both hands.

The dead could stay very still. If they thought no thoughts, they could eventually fade into sleep.

The problem with the dead was that when they woke, they had forgotten everything. They thought they were at home in their own bed, and they sat up, listening for their baby cooing or fretting downstairs. Instead, they heard someone telling Connie to hurry up already and felt a pain where the sharp edge of a picture frame had dug into their side. Then they remembered and had to suffer their death all over again.

The problem with the dead was they were not actually dead.

❦

The first place, a motor factory, said she was too late: they had just taken on three. The cereal company said to go see McGarry at the end of the hall, but when McGarry introduced himself as Dan, Grace burst into tears. Dan McGarry waited until she'd found her handkerchief, then stood up and walked her to the door. "Goodbye, dear," he said, and he called out, "Next." The third place was the red brick clock factory on a hill across the river. A woman with smooth, glossy braids wrapped around her head sat behind a window in the office. Grace leaned close to the glass and said, "Hello?" but the woman kept typing. Grace rapped on the window, more loudly than she had meant to, then pressed her hand against the glass to erase the sound. The woman looked up. Her eyebrows were two long black wings; one arched up sternly. "Please do not put your hands on my glass," she said.

Behind Grace, there was a giggle. She turned to see five women sitting on a long bench.

"If you're here about a job," the woman behind the glass said, and Grace shouted, "Yes! Yes, I am!"

More laughter.

"Take a seat with the others."

No one on the bench moved to make room for Grace, so she stood until the door banged open and a tall, sandy-haired man hurried in. "Hello, ladies," he said. He had worried eyebrows, and one of his shirttails was untucked, but his voice was full and dark and flecked with warmth. It reminded Grace of hot chocolate. "I'm Vanderburgh. Manager. This way, please." They followed him to another room and lined up at a desk. He asked where they were from and where else they had worked, and when it was Grace's turn, she said, "I worked at home," which made one of the other women snort, but Mr. Vanderburgh said, "That's fine." He had hound dog eyes, kind but sad. "Now Theresa is going to come in and give you an aptitude test," he said, taking a box out of the desk drawer. "She'll only show you once, so watch carefully." Inside the box, Grace could see screws and wheels and a clock face.

When Mr. Vanderburgh left, the woman in front of Grace moved to the back of the line. Grace, who had been third, was now second. The woman in first place looked at Grace and said, "I think I left my . . ." and then she too went to the back of the line. *They want to go last*, Grace realized, *so they'll have more time to learn to do it.* A slender woman in a dark blue coverall seemed to spring into the room on long legs. She wore a dark blue kerchief over her copper curls, which were the same colour as her freckles. Even her eyes were coppery. "All right, girls. Step up so you can see. I'm going to assemble the clock, starting with this piece here." Her hands moved quickly, laying out the pieces.

Grace remembered taking a clock apart after her mother had died, but she couldn't remember how anything fit. She drew a long breath, and when her lungs were full, she tucked the air in and held it. Theresa picked up a small, square box and attached a screw, a spring, a wheel. She snapped them together. Another wheel, the face, the hands, the front cover, a butterfly key. When she was finished, Grace breathed out.

"Let's start with you," Theresa said, pointing not at Grace but at the woman who had left her something or other at the end of the line. The others pushed closer to the table, but Grace closed her eyes and listened to the scrape and clatter of metal pieces.

"Next," Theresa said. Grace kept her eyes closed.

Next, next, next.

"Last one," Theresa said, and Grace opened her eyes. She moved to the table and picked up the small metal box. She kept her mind empty and let her hands remember. They found the pieces, turned and fitted and snapped them into place.

"Good." Theresa took the finished clock from her. "Thank you, ladies. You can go now." She tapped Grace's shoulder. "I'll take you to the office. Mrs. Thurman will have some papers for you to sign."

"To sign?" Grace's hands fluttered to her cheeks. "I have a job?"

Theresa laughed and pulled open the door for her. "You have a job."

On the way back from the factory, she stopped at a department store and spent a long time looking at the toys. She ran her hand over painted wooden blocks: Danny already had blocks that Frank had made him. She plucked the strings of a small wooden guitar and pushed a train along a track. Finally, she picked up an odd plastic shoe on wheels. She ran it along the shelf, and suddenly the top flew open and a soft brown dog popped up. Grace paid with the money that Frank and Vera had given her to hold her over. She already had a job. She could already buy something for Danny. She asked for a box and took the toy straight to the post office.

Back at Mrs. Barr's, she called home. "I have a job in a clock factory," she told Vera. "How is Danny?"

"Already? That's wonderful, Grace."

"Is Danny all right?"

"He's fine. He's sleeping."

"I sent him a present. It's a toy dog in a shoe. For his birthday coming up." It hurt her throat to say it when she wouldn't be there for it.

"Why are you wasting your money, Grace? He has toys. Here, talk to your brother."

Frank said, "Well, well. A working woman. Congratulations, Grace."

"How has Danny been, Frank?"

"He's been good! He was singing away in his crib this morning when I got up."

"What did he do today?" she asked. She needed to know what time he had woken up, what he had played with, when he had eaten, whether he had made that face when he ate his carrots, because sometimes he didn't. But Vera had taken the phone. "We'd better say goodbye," she said. "This is costing you a fortune. Write us and tell us how you are doing."

"I'm going to call later," Grace said, "so I can talk to Danny."

"Don't be silly, Grace. He's a baby. He can't talk on the phone."

Grace put down the phone and stood in the kitchen of Mrs. Barr's boarding house. Through the French doors, at the other end of the dining table, Mrs. Barr was making a note in a ledger. Today she wore a lime green robe, long and silky, with a matching scarf holding up her tower of black hair. Smoke trailed her cigarette. "Sign here," she said, and pointed to the entry under *Grace Turner: March 15: Telephone. Ten mins.*

Grace wrote her name. Her arms were heavy and she was afraid she would cry. She shouldn't have come. Danny was there and she was here. He would look for her and she would be gone. He wouldn't understand why, and she couldn't even tell him.

"Who's Danny?" Mrs. Barr asked, and Grace looked up, startled.

"You kept asking for Danny on the telephone." She twisted her lower lip sideways so that she didn't blow smoke directly into Grace's face. "Is Danny your fella?"

Grace laid the pen down and closed the ledger over it. Yesterday, Mrs. Barr had told Grace, "I treat my girls like my own," but Grace didn't want to be one of Mrs. Barr's girls. There were pillows of soft flesh under Mrs. Barr's eyes, but the eyes themselves were hard and glittery. Also, Grace knew she hadn't been on the phone for more than five minutes.

"No," Grace said. "I don't have a fella."

Mrs. Barr steered another line of smoke sideways. "Well, you certainly seemed worried about him, whoever he is."

Grace shook her head. "I'd better have a bath and get to bed so that I'm rested for tomorrow."

"Actually, it's not your bath night," Mrs. Barr said. "Your night is Tuesday. But I think Connie's out tonight, so you can have one if you want." She peered at Grace through the smoke. "Do you want to have a bath?"

She didn't want a bath; she wanted to get away from Mrs. Barr's flickering eyes. She said, "All right. Yes."

Mrs. Barr opened the ledger and wrote, *March 15: Bath.*

The morning before work was not as bad as the evening after work. The evening was bad because after she had washed out her underwear and sponged her coverall and brushed her teeth, there was only the dark tunnel of night and the deafening wind that roared through it. In the morning, she had breakfast at the table with Mrs. Barr and the other girls, which was unpleasant but not nearly as painful as the long, empty night. Grace said please and thank you; Connie and Noreen, who worked at the cereal factory, exclaimed at everything Mrs. Barr said. "You're the bee's knees, Mrs. B.," they said. "You're the cat's pyjamas." Mrs. Barr told them how she kept her hands so white and her skin so supple, and how all the fellas were stuck on her in her heyday, before she married Mr. Barr, god rest his soul. But her favourite topic was the horrible Ruth Ellis and her horrible boarding house. Ruth Ellis also rented out rooms, but she was an old maid who taught high school and had a very odd manner and went around in odd getups with her nose in the air; her boarders were hussies and floozies who went about in trousers and ran around with married men. Connie and Noreen had seen one of her boarders just yesterday standing outside in a short little nightdress up to here, talking to some man over the fence! Grace pretended to listen, eating as much as she could and folding an extra slice of bread and jam into her pocket so that she wouldn't have to buy lunch at the canteen. Every dollar she earned would go into the envelope under her mattress, and when she had enough to get a place of her own, she would go home and get her son.

The walk to work was not as bad as breakfast, especially if she walked fast. At work, she waited in the courtyard with the others, listening to their cheery calls and bird-like shrieks. One would start singing "My Melancholy Baby" or "Don't Cry, Baby" or some other song with a baby and a goodbye in it, and the others would join in, layering their voices in harmony. When the door opened for them, everyone groaned except Grace, who exhaled in relief. She hung her coat in the cloakroom and hurried to her place. Her mind was blank now, a long white field like the garden under snow, and her hands became eyes. She made clocks. Fit, snap, adjust, press. Snap, press, snap. At lunch, when the others rushed to the canteen to buy tea and ham rolls, she went to the cloakroom to eat the bread and jam she'd wrapped up at breakfast. She drank water cupped in her hand from the sink. Once or twice a day, Mr. Vanderburgh came through and nodded at them. "Good, good," he said in his chocolate voice.

The walk home was bad, because every step brought her closer to Mrs. Barr's dinner table. The dinner table was bad because Mrs. Barr wouldn't let her be: "What do you think, Grace? Are you listening, Grace? You know, when you knocked at the door, I thought you were a boy with that haircut. That must be the style in Sault Ste. Marie. Is that the style up there, Grace? Oh, I think Grace must be thinking of a fella—are you thinking of a fella, Grace?" Mrs. Barr flashed her eyes at Connie and Noreen, and they dabbed at their smiles with their napkins.

Most of all, dinner was bad because it ended with night.

Night was the worst. In the dark, panic came over her, pinning her to the bed until she lurched upright, struggling to draw in a complete breath over the galloping of her heart. *He is fine,* she told herself. *He's safe, he's warm, he's fed. He is asleep right now.* In her head, she walked down the stairs from her attic room to Danny's bedroom and sat by his crib. She saw the moonlight on his face and heard him breathe, and then she could fall asleep. Sometimes she woke up crying from nightmares. Danny was lost down by the creek; he was crying for her. She was on her way home to Danny, but she was on the wrong bus. She found the right bus, but when she got home, the doors were all locked. They had taken Danny and gone.

Danny, she thought, squeezing the hard picture frame to her chest. She was a tiny figure, standing below a towering wave of grief. Any moment it would come thundering down on her. Again. She was living in dread of drowning while drowning. *Danny*, she thought, *I'm coming.*

But how would he know that?

Frank wrote, just as he promised. Danny was walking now. He fed himself carrots and apples and chicken cut up into cubes. He was playing with his toys, his wooden blocks, the woolly lamb and the bear, but he really loved that dog in the shoe. When the dog popped up, he laughed and laughed. Dr. McCabe said he was the healthiest baby he'd ever seen, and Mrs. McCabe told Vera she had never seen such a good-natured baby. *We're taking very good care of him, Gracie, don't you worry*, Frank wrote. *He doesn't want for anything, I can promise you that.*

Every word of the letter cut her and healed her and cut her again. Danny could walk! He loved the toy she'd bought for him! He laughed and laughed! She carried the letter with her and couldn't stand to read it, couldn't stand not to read it, read it and wept.

Sometimes Frank's letters went on about nothing: April was coming in like a lion, Vera had gone for an x-ray for possible female troubles, Mrs. May's daughter had gotten married in Niagara Falls. Grace's eyes skittered over the paper until they landed on Danny's name.

The best time was while she worked, because there was only work. Then there were no letters to wait for. There was no envelope under the mattress, waiting to be filled. There was no needling Mrs. Barr, no sneering Connie and Noreen. There was not even a Vera, a Frank, a Danny, a Grace. There were only pieces of a clock, and then a clock. Pieces, clock. Pieces, clock. There was no time to think, because time was not yet assembled.

They were paid in the courtyard on the second Friday after work. Grace stood near the brick wall, listening to the others talk about the dance out at White Pines, the sale at Kinny's. Theresa appeared in the yard, her coat unbuttoned, her copper curls free of their kerchief. Grace had only seen her a few times in passing; she supervised another section. When she saw Grace, she worked her way through the crowd.

"Grace, right? How are you settling in?"

"Fine. I'm fine."

"You know, you're the first person who put the clock together the first time. Usually we have to do it twice to get one person. Were you good at making things as a kid?"

Grace shook her head ruefully. "I think I was better at breaking things."

Theresa laughed. "Where are you staying, Grace?"

"At Mrs. Barr's."

"I'm at Ruth Ellis's. Listen, you want to go to Mike's Lunch after and get something to eat?"

Grace was startled. "No, no, thank you," she said. "I mean, I can't."

"Are you sure? My treat."

Grace didn't know what "my treat" meant. "No, thank you," she said. She heard her name, and Theresa pointed with her chin at Mrs. Thurman. "That's you," she said.

Grace hurried over, and Mrs. Thurman handed her a clipboard and said, "Sign, please."

Grace found her name, G. *Turner*, and signed beside the number. Thirty-five dollars. When Mrs. Thurman handed her the envelope, Grace felt her face stretch strangely and realized she was smiling, perhaps crazily. "Thank you," she gasped, and she thought Mrs. Thurman smiled back, but it was so brief it was hard to tell.

Someone tapped her on the shoulder. It was Theresa. "Try not to let Mrs. Barr get all of it," she said.

In the end, Mrs. Barr got every cent of it and more. "I don't understand," Grace said. "My sister-in-law said the room would cost eight dollars a week."

"And so it does," Mrs. Barr said. She was sitting at her kitchen table with the ledger open. "But I advanced you the first two weeks, which you have to pay now, plus the next two weeks in advance, which is how I operate. Plus board and incidentals." Under Grace's name was the list of board and incidentals: *Tea, tea, bread and jam, dinner (extra potatoes), phone call, bath, bath, bread and jam, dinner (second helping), bread and jam, bread and jam and butter.*

"I thought it was included. Room and board."

Mrs. Barr laughed merrily. "Oh, Grace! Room and board

means room *and* board. If only I could offer room and board for eight dollars! No, it's all separate, because different girls want different things. Take Noreen, for instance. She has nothing but tea for breakfast. If room and board were included, like at Ruth Ellis's, then Noreen would be paying for food she doesn't eat. No, at my place, you pay only for what you use, which is much fairer, don't you think?"

Grace blinked hard to drive back tears. "I didn't have dinner the first night."

"No, but you didn't tell me in advance that you wouldn't be having it." Mrs. Barr patted her hand. "I'll tell you what. I'll give you $2 back so you have some pocket money, and you can pay it next time. I don't like to see my girls without pocket money."

Ruth Ellis's house, set behind a weathered wooden fence, was orange brick with creamy trim that reminded Grace of butter icing. On the front door was a knocker shaped like a snake eating its tail, with a brass plaque underneath that said, KNOCK AND THE DOOR SHALL BE OPENED. Beneath the plaque, someone had stuck a note: *Lucy, if you're reading this, it means you forgot.* AGAIN!!!!

Grace lifted the snake and knocked. The door opened almost instantly, and there was Theresa, looking surprised over a half-peeled banana. "Grace! Did you change your mind about Mike's?"

"Does Ruth Ellis have a room available?"

Theresa said, "No, not at the moment. But come in."

Ruth Ellis was a teacher. Her parents had also been teachers, and this had been their house. Ruth rented out rooms, Theresa said, not because she needed the money but because she liked the company and she believed in young women being independent in the world. Inside, books were stacked everywhere, on end tables and the floor, and the bookcases were full of carvings and masks and little stone statues of women with huge breasts and hips and no feet. On the dining table a glass bowl of water sat on a black cloth.

"What's that?" Grace asked.

"Lucy's homemade crystal ball. Here, sit here." She pushed a cat off an armchair. "Do you want some coffee?"

"No, thank you."

"Tea? A banana?"

"No, thank you."

"Are you sure? There's no charge for it," Theresa said.

Grace said, "You know that's what she does, charges for everything? Mrs. Barr?" It was odd to want to talk. Her sentences sounded like they were being shaken out of a sack.

"Everyone knows. She'd charge for the air you breathed, if she could."

"I won't be able to save anything," Grace said. "I have to find another place to stay."

"We're full here right now," Theresa said. "There's the YWCA, but that's also full. You could check the notice board outside the church, because sometimes people have a room. If I hear of anything, I'll let you know."

Grace stood up. "Thank you."

"Wait, are you sure you won't have coffee?"

Grace hesitated, then shook her head. She had to go over to the church and then stop at the grocery store to buy her own bread and jam. "Maybe another time," she said.

Buying her own bread and jam and having only tea for breakfast meant she could save three dollars a month. She didn't buy clothes, like Connie, or magazines and nail polish like Noreen, or go the hairdresser like the girls at work. When her hair started to fall into her eyes, she simply tied it back with an elastic band. She stopped taking baths and washed standing up at the sink, even though Mrs. Barr complained loudly about the backwards habits of country bumpkins. When a crack opened up in the sole of her boot, letting the slush seep through, she lined the inside with strips of newspaper and cardboard and wax paper snatched from Mrs. Barr's garbage can when no one was looking, and after a month, the snow was gone and the sidewalks were dry and her boot was fine. After another month, the trees unfurled luminous new leaves, and the forsythia bushes outside the factory were a blaze of yellow against the wall, and in the courtyard, the women talked about straw hats and sang "Oh, What a Beautiful Mornin'," and Grace had eighty-four dollars in the envelope under her mattress. At lunch, she went to ask if Theresa had heard of another room to let; she found her sitting on the floor of the cloakroom, her knees pulled up, crying into her hands.

"Theresa?" Grace crouched beside her. "What happened?"

Theresa shook her head but did not look up.

"It's me, Grace. Should I call somebody?"

Theresa's curls shook more vigorously.

"Should I go get Mrs. Thurman? Mr. Vanderburgh?"

"No!" Theresa wailed and looked up. Her face was wet and her eyes were red-rimmed and swollen.

"What should I do, then?"

"I wish I were dead." Theresa hiccupped loudly.

Grace said, "I'll be right back."

She raced to the canteen and looked frantically for the coffee urn. The girl at the cash scolded her for trying to take china out of the canteen when she should have used a paper cup. "I didn't know," Grace said. "I've never come in here before," and the girl said, "No kidding." When she got back, Theresa was standing at the sink, splashing her eyes with water.

Grace handed her the paper cup of coffee. Theresa sipped it

and shuddered. She handed the cup back to Grace. "Help me drink that, Grace. I was only kidding when I said I wanted to die." They passed the cup back and forth until it was empty. "I look a fright," Theresa said, running her hands through her curls. She looked at Grace in the mirror beside her. "I'm not pregnant, if that's what you were thinking."

"I have a baby," Grace said before she could stop herself. The words scorched her mouth, and she had to swallow hard to continue. "At home. Back home. With my brother and sister-in-law." She looked at Theresa's face, but it told her nothing except that she had been crying and now she was listening. "That's why I came down here," she said. "To earn enough money to get a place of my own. Being away from him is killing me. And Mrs. Barr is taking all my money."

"You poor thing," Theresa said.

Grace shook her head violently. She didn't want Theresa to say "poor thing," because she didn't want to cry. "I can't sleep because I miss him so much. I can't think about him, and I can't stop thinking about him."

Theresa sighed. "I know."

Grace stared at her. "Do you have a baby too?"

"No," Theresa said. "I have a bad boyfriend. I just make myself unhappy."

The whistle blew, and Theresa said, "Wait for me here after work."

Ruth Ellis was wearing what Mrs. Barr must have meant by an odd getup: loose pale yellow pants with a tight band of gold braid at the ankles, a long silky tunic and an orange scarf with tiny mirrors sewn into the hem. It was from India, Theresa said, where Ruth Ellis had travelled with her parents one summer. It was beautiful. As for her odd manner, it turned out that, unlike

Mrs. Barr, Ruth Ellis did not pepper people with questions that couldn't be answered or tell long stories about her heyday. She spoke because something needed to be said, and what she said always made sense.

She was putting together a bicycle on the front porch when Theresa brought Grace home. Theresa said, "Ruth, this is Grace," and Ruth didn't look up because her eyes were locked into the frame of the bike, but she said, "Hello, Grace. Theresa tells me you need a new place. Can you hold this wheel for me?"

Ruth Ellis asked her to stay for dinner, and afterwards, they took their coffee onto the porch and sat looking out over the lawn. On one side, an enormous maple tree cast a long shadow into the yard. One of the branches was low and sturdy enough to hang a swing from. The grass was green and soft; if a child fell off the swing, he wouldn't be hurt. "This is a nice place," Grace said. Ruth said the only thing she wanted to change was the fence: she wanted to tear it down and plant a hedge. "A flowering fence," she said, "instead of a wall. Nicer on the eye. What do you think, Grace?"

Grace said, "A wall would be safer."

Theresa explained why she had been crying: she was in love with Mike Vanderburgh. Grace said, "Mr. Vanderburgh?" which made both Ruth and Theresa laugh. Theresa said she couldn't account for it. He wasn't that smart. He was nothing special to look at, as Grace herself could attest to. And yet, whenever he spoke to Theresa, she just melted. "He does have a nice voice," Grace said, and Theresa looked radiantly happy for a moment. "He does, doesn't he?" Then she looked miserable again. She said she wanted to be with him so badly she felt sick, and she never really could be, because of Mrs. Vanderburgh.

"Maybe it's because of Mrs. Vanderburgh that you want him so badly," Ruth said. "Maybe if you could have him, you wouldn't want him."

"No," Theresa said. "If she dropped dead, I would marry him in an instant. But she's as healthy as an ox, and he won't leave her. Even though she does nothing but complain. He leaves his socks lying around. He chews too loudly. He forgets things and slumps in his chair at dinner."

"All complaints you might have if you had to live with him," Ruth said.

Theresa hunched forward, squeezing her freckled hands. "When I'm away from him, I know it's all wrong and I should end it, but when I'm with him, I'm convinced of the exact opposite. It's so hard to know what's true."

Ruth turned to Grace. "What do you think, Grace?"

Grace said, "I don't know. I only love my baby."

Theresa said, "That's not being *in* love, though. That's instinct."

Ruth said, "That's the best kind of love. It doesn't have to question itself."

Grace's head throbbed. "I left him!" she cried out. "He didn't even know I was going. He doesn't know where I am!" Ruth's arm was around her and Theresa pressed a handkerchief into her hand. "It's okay, Gracie," Theresa was saying. "We're going to help you get him back."

LAUNDRY

Mrs. Barr was furious. "You can't leave," she said. "You have to give notice."

"She just did," Theresa said.

"Advance notice! Six weeks!"

"Six weeks? Are you *insane?*" Theresa shook her head. "Let's get your things, Grace."

Mrs. Barr followed them up the stairs, talking to Theresa all the way. "I'll take her to court," she said. "I'll sue."

Theresa slammed the door of Grace's room and said, "Hurry, Gracie." Grace pulled her clothes off hangers and stuffed them into her suitcase on top of the photo of Danny. Her heart was a wild bird trapped in a cage. Mrs. Barr was hammering on the door, threatening to call the police, Clockworks, Grace's family. Grace froze at that. "Don't listen to her, Grace. She won't call anyone."

"I'll call her supervisor at work," Mrs. Barr yelled, and Theresa jerked open the door. "I *am* her supervisor at work," she said.

"I'll go to the manager. I'll have the money taken out of her paycheque."

"Have it taken out of your ass," Theresa said and closed the door. "Got everything, Grace?" Grace didn't know what she had; she only knew they had to get out. Theresa picked up the suitcase, and they pushed past Mrs. Barr and hurried down the stairs and out the door, which Mrs. Barr slammed behind them, yelling, "And don't darken my doorway again!"

"Gladly," Theresa called back.

"Will she go to court against me?" Grace asked. Her veins were full of syrup, and she could hardly move her legs. If Mrs. Barr went to court, they would take all her money.

"Of course not." Theresa opened the front gate for them.

Grace's heart was still trying to escape from her chest. Then it stopped beating altogether. She opened her mouth but nothing came out.

"What is it, Grace?"

"My money," she managed to say.

"You left your money?"

Grace covered her face with her hands. Now she would have to start all over. It was hopeless. She didn't know why she kept trying. Except that her other option was to tie a stone around her neck and walk into the river, and she couldn't do that, because she couldn't leave Danny twice.

Theresa pulled her hands away from her face. "Grace. Where did you leave it? In your room?"

"Under the mattress."

Theresa looked at the house. Her eyes moved up and down, back and forth. "Here," she said, handing Grace the suitcase. "Go knock on the front door and tell her you feel bad about leaving without notice and ask how much would she accept in lieu of six weeks."

"But she already has all my money upstairs!"

"You're not actually going to pay her. Just keep her talking."

"Where will you be?"

"I'll be around. Go on, Grace. Look contrite and keep her talking until I come back."

Grace walked back up the steps and knocked on the door. She looked for Theresa, but Theresa was gone.

"Mrs. Barr?" she called. "Mrs. Barr? It's me, Grace Turner. I'm very sorry. Please don't take me to court."

The door opened, and there was Mrs. Barr, smiling nastily. "Oh, so now you want to make amends."

"I just don't want to go to court."

"Well, it's too late for that. I just got off the phone with the judge." She peered through the screen. "Where's your friend with the mouth on her?"

"She went home. Please, Mrs. Barr. I don't want to go to court."

"It's too late. I've already booked a date and I'll have to pay to cancel it."

"How much does that cost?"

"Fifteen dollars," Mrs. Barr said. "So you'd owe that on top of the six weeks."

"All right," Grace said. They had reached the end of this conversation, and there was no sign of Theresa. "All right, but—"

"All right but what?"

"All right, but can we make it four weeks' notice? It's only I don't have enough for six weeks."

"Fine, but only because I'll be glad to see the last of you. Plus fifteen dollars. And I want it right now."

"All right," said Grace. "But . . . but I was just wondering, can we make it two weeks' notice?"

Mrs. Barr's face reddened. "Get the hell off my property," she hissed, "before I call the police."

Grace fled, banging the suitcase against her leg. Out on the road, she leaned against a tree and tried to catch her breath.

Theresa appeared from around the corner.

"Where were you?" Grace demanded. "I made everything worse. Now she's calling the police."

Theresa shook her head. "She's not calling the police, Grace. You have to stop being so afraid of people. Mrs. Barr has no power over you."

"She has my money," Grace said.

Theresa pulled an envelope from the waistband of her pants. "No, she doesn't."

Grace clutched Theresa's arm. "How did you get it?"

"Well, my idea was to go up the drainpipe—"

"You climbed up the *drainpipe* to the second floor?" Grace was aghast.

"No. The back door was open. Thank Christ."

Ruth and Theresa had already set everything up. Theresa had pushed her bed against the wall to make room for the cot and emptied out two drawers in the dresser, which turned out to be one and a half drawers too many for Grace's things. Grace put the photo of Danny on the windowsill beside a pot of geraniums.

"Let me see him." Theresa reached for the picture. "He looks like you, Grace."

"Do you think so?" A warmth went through Grace.

"Where is his father?"

"I don't know. He signed up and I didn't hear anything after that."

Theresa handed back the photo. "Were you in love with him?"

Grace thought for a moment. She remembered how John had squeezed her fingers and the heat of his breath. She remembered the sound he made when he pushed into her, like a small cat that wanted something. She liked that little sound. Was that "in love"?

"No," she told Theresa. "I didn't really know him."

"Did your brother and sister-in-law know him?"

"They don't know he's the father."

Grace touched Danny's face through the glass.

"Gracie."

Grace looked up.

"Do they know you're coming back for him?"

"My brother knows."

"I meant her."

Grace saw what Theresa was thinking. It was the thing that kept her awake and woke her when she did finally fall into sleep. One of the things. "She thinks I'll stay down here and forget all about Danny," Grace said. "She thinks she'll never see me again."

Ruth Ellis said she needed a plan. Moving out of Mrs. Barr's and sharing Theresa's room was only the first step. Theresa had asked Mike Vanderburgh to give Grace extra split-shifts, but when Danny was here, she wouldn't be able to work such long hours. "You need to think about how you are going to provide for Danny in the long term," Ruth said.

"Can't we stay here?" Grace asked. She loved Ruth Ellis's house. She and Theresa and Lucy were free to do exactly as they pleased: eat whenever they felt like it, read at the breakfast table, talk or not talk at dinner, try on all the outfits Ruth Ellis had brought back from her travels and then fall asleep in them on the sofa in the middle of a Saturday afternoon. Lucy was a pretty, dark-haired teacher from Saskatchewan who had ten younger brothers and sisters back home; she sent back money every month and knew about things like colic and croup. She and Theresa said Danny was the loveliest baby and asked Grace to read out Frank's letters. They would never say, "Put the baby down, for heaven's sake, you'll spoil him." In fact, Ruth Ellis said that in India and China, women carried their babies in slings *all day*. When she thought about bringing Danny to Peterborough, she thought about him here, in this house.

But it seemed Ruth Ellis did not. "Yes, of course you can stay, but that's a temporary fix. Danny's going to need his own room someday, and you need to know that you can stand on your own."

"I don't know if I can," Grace said.

"If you can't, you have no right bringing Danny down here. That's your job as his mother."

Grace closed her eyes.

"You need a plan, Grace. You need a place of your own, and you need a way to make more money. You also need a story for when people ask where Danny's father is."

"I don't care about that," Grace said. "What people think doesn't affect me."

"Thoughts give birth to actions, and actions do affect you."

Grace pressed the heels of her hands against her eyes. It was hard, talking to Ruth. She took your arm and started you in a certain direction, and she didn't let you step down until you both got to the destination. It would have made her head hurt if she let it, but she wouldn't let it. She could see that Ruth was right. Finally, she dropped her hands. "All right. Danny's father and I got married down at City Hall in Sault Ste. Marie," she said. "Two weeks after, he—John—shipped out. Two months later, I got the telegram." She looked at Ruth. Ruth nodded, waiting. "I didn't even know I was going to have a baby," Grace said, but still, Ruth was not satisfied. "My brother and sister-in-law said they would look after the baby until I got settled down here."

"What else?"

"And I came down here and . . . I don't know what else," Grace said.

"You lost your husband," Ruth said. "How do you feel?"

"Oh!" Grace brightened. "I'm sad. Very, very sad."

Ruth Ellis laughed. "That's good, Grace. But try not to look so happy when you say it."

The other part of the plan came to her in the courtyard at work, listening to the other girls; they reminded her of Vera in the way they listed everything they had to do before they did it. Unlike Vera, though, they could only do one thing at a time. They had to set their hair, so they couldn't iron their skirts; they had to iron their skirts, so they couldn't wash out their sweaters or mend their blouses, and they were simply exhausted. As a trial, she did Theresa's laundry, then Lucy's, and finally Ruth's. They proclaimed themselves satisfied. "Now, you have to advertise," Ruth said, and Theresa said, "You need to start going to the cafeteria, Grace. You need to be a little friendlier."

"But I can't spend money in the cafeteria," Grace said.

"You have to spend money to make money," Theresa said. "A couple of cups of that coffee might turn your stomach, but it won't break the bank. And you need to let Lucy do something about your hair."

"My hair?" Grace reached for the back of her neck, where her hair was tied in a clump with a shoelace. She hadn't had it cut since she'd left home, and it was too thick and wiry to be loose. "What does my hair have to do with laundry?"

"The less you look like my crazy Aunt Betty, the more people will want to trust you with their things," Theresa said.

So Lucy cut bangs into Grace's hair and curled the ends under, and Grace went to the cafeteria, and Theresa waved her over and introduced her to Myrna and Kathleen. "Grace is a whiz with laundry," she told them. "She does ours. She charges, of course, but I can't tell you all how much more time I have now."

Myrna said, "My mother does mine for free," but Kathleen said, "How are you with mysterious stains, Grace?" Kathleen had bought a new skirt, she explained, in the most beautiful cream-coloured Irish linen, and when she got it home, she found a brown stain right at the hemline. She took it right back to the shop, but the saleswoman refused to give her a refund. "She said she couldn't take back soiled merchandise. I said, 'No, you only sell it.' It's a beautiful skirt, but I can't wear it." She lowered her voice. "It looks like blood."

Grace said, "I don't know. That—"

"—won't be a problem," Theresa finished for her.

It was a narrow, rusty brown stain right at the bottom of the skirt. Grace tried a mixture of things: salt, cold water, warm water, laundry soap, hand soap, vinegar. She dabbed and wiped and squirted. Theresa yawned. "I'm going to bed, Grace. You'll just have to say you don't do mystery stains." Grace sat at the wooden table in Ruth Ellis's basement. Her fingers ached from the scrubbing and her feet were cold. This afternoon, when Kathleen had given her the skirt, she'd been elated. News would spread, customers would come, and soon she would be able to go home and get Danny. Now a stain on a skirt was ending her new life before it even began.

The furnace rumbled off, and in the stillness, Grace could hear the wind outside and the drip of the faucet and an insect chewing on something in a corner. She sat very still and what came over her was not the bliss but something akin to it. It was the bliss with eyes. She pushed back her chair and ran up the stairs.

In the morning, Theresa grabbed the skirt from the kitchen table. "Grace, I don't believe it. You got it out?" She inspected the cloth. "Amazing! It's completely gone. What did you use on it?"

Grace smiled. "Scissors."

Theresa's mouth dropped open. "You didn't."

Grace held up a thin strip of cream cloth. Theresa grabbed the skirt again and studied the hem. "Nice stitching. But what if she notices that it's shorter?"

"She only tried it on once in the store," Grace said.

Kathleen looked up from the skirt. "Beautiful," she said. She held it against her waist and swished it around her knees. "Just beautiful."

Grace collected the clothes on Tuesday and Friday in the courtyard. She worked briskly, thoroughly, braiding one task neatly into the next, just like Vera. In the evening, she sorted the clothes. While some soaked in whitener or hot water, she examined the others for holes and tears. She washed them at night, laying them over the backs of chairs and a clothesline strung between poles in the basement. In the morning, if the sky was clear, she put them out on the line. At lunch, she borrowed Theresa's bicycle and raced home to bring them in. In the evening, she ironed and folded. It was Lucy's idea to make everything into little packets. "And you need to wrap them in something to return them. Tissue paper," Lucy said.

"It costs," Grace said.

"But the girls will love it. You'll be returning all their old, worn-out things wrapped in nice paper, like brand new."

Grace bought the tissue paper and began finding little things to tuck inside: a crisp red leaf, a sprig of monkshood. In the winter, she could use a sprig of pine. In the spring, she would use wildflowers. She would have Danny by then, and he could help her pick them. On impulse, she bought some red satin ribbon to put around the packets of laundry, and after that, there was a lineup in the courtyard on Fridays.

MOMMY

Everything happened in February. Grace was collecting laundry from the cereal factory, the bank and Clockworks, and because she wasn't paying for her room at Ruth Ellis's, only board, she had to ask Ruth for a second envelope. When she asked for a third, Ruth made her go to the bank. Now she had a savings account and a wagon she pulled to collect. It was all done discreetly, at lunch and after work. Everyone had her own pillowcase with her initials or name written in ink (mostly) or embroidered (a few at the bank). She still used tissue paper when she returned the clothes, but the pillowcases kept things separate and didn't look unsightly in the wagon. She did more than wash and iron and fix loose buttons: she let out waistbands and sewed linings into skirts and replaced velvet trim with lace. "Give it to Grace to freshen up," Kathleen told Myrna, who had nothing new to wear to the White Pines dance, and Grace took Myrna's pale green dress home and recut the collar. Then she added a flounce with dark green satin that Marta at the bank had asked her to remove from a skirt. "Can you freshen this, Grace?" the women began to ask, and if nothing came to Grace when she sat at her work table in the basement, she would look through Lucy's movie magazines or Ruth's photo albums for ideas.

Theresa came home in tears because Mike Vanderburgh said he couldn't see her anymore and they had to pretend nothing had happened, or ever would. "As if we have to pretend that part," Theresa told Grace. He claimed his wife was suspicious, but he refused to provide details. Theresa said he was just trying to get rid of her. She couldn't stand to see him every day. She was going to go over to the motor factory and ask for a job. The next day, Mr. Vanderburgh fired her for coming in late, but she had only come in to get her things. She was due to start at the motor factory that afternoon.

Ruth Ellis told Grace about a place for rent. A coach house, it was called, with two small bedrooms, a decent kitchen, a sitting room and a bathroom, in the backyard of a house belonging to Mrs. Waverly, a widow whose son had just moved to Detroit. Mrs. Waverly's eyesight was going, and if Grace would be willing to go in once or twice a day and make sure the bed had clean linens and the dishes were washed, Mrs. Waverly would let her have the coach house for a very reasonable rent. There was no washing machine, but Ruth could help her with that. She had been meaning to buy a new one anyway, and Grace could have the old one. Grace said, "It's happening so fast," but Ruth said that Grace had brought her plan to fruition and it was time to start thinking about going to get her son.

"I still don't have anyone to look after him," Grace said.

"I think you should leave your job at Clockworks," Ruth said. "Do the laundry business full-time."

"I wouldn't make enough," Grace said.

"You'll make the same as if you stayed at the factory and had to pay someone to look after Danny."

"But what if people start doing their own laundry?"

"Then you'll have to figure out what else you can offer them."

Grace said, "I don't like this plan."

"Well, come and see the coach house first," Ruth said.

The walls were grimy, but Ruth said Grace could paint them. Watery light came in through the front windows. Two large oak trees stood between the coach house and the main house, bare now but "they'll create a nice screen in the summer," Ruth said. They went in to meet Mrs. Waverly, who was the oldest person Grace had ever seen. Beneath a waxy layer of age, though, her blue eyes were bright, and she gripped Grace's hand firmly. "I won't be any trouble," Grace said, and Mrs. Waverly said, "Nor will I." Grace liked the coach house, but Theresa loved it. "I'll move in with you, Grace," Theresa said. "That way, your rent will be even lower. I mean, if that's fine with you." She stopped and looked stricken. "And you, Ruth."

Ruth gave her a long look. "You think you can take up again with your Mr. V and I won't know because you're over here," she said.

"I will never take up with him again," Theresa declared.

"That's what you said last time," Ruth said.

"He didn't *fire* me last time."

Grace had planned to go back to Sault Ste. Marie in the spring, but Theresa and Ruth both said she should do it now. "You can borrow my car," Ruth said, but she wouldn't come with them. "Please come. She'll listen to you," Grace said.

"I'm not the one she has to hear."

Grace and Theresa left before dawn on Saturday morning and drove north, passing through the same frozen forests and fields Grace remembered from a year ago, only this time she didn't feel dead. She felt sick. When they got to Sault Ste. Marie at dusk, it began to snow, and Grace told Theresa to stop the car so she could throw up. They sat at the end of the road until Grace's stomach settled. Theresa squeezed her arm. "It's going to be fine, Gracie. You're just going home to get your baby."

The house was exactly the same: the leafless apple trees, the wooden trellis in front of the house, bare now, the rose bushes covered snugly in burlap. Warm yellow light filled all the downstairs windows. Grace was out of the car before Theresa had turned it off. Her legs had a mind of their own, propelling her to the back door so quickly she could hardly keep up with them. She knocked and then knocked again. Vera opened the door. She was holding Danny on her hip.

"Danny," Grace whispered, and her eyes filled with tears.

"Grace!" Vera said. "What on earth?"

Behind her, Theresa said, "Evening, Mrs. Turner. I'm Theresa. A friend of Grace's."

"Is everything all right? Are you sick? Did something happen at the factory?"

Grace could not take her eyes off Danny. He was gnawing on a wooden block. His blond curls had darkened, and he was longer and bigger. He had changed, but not so that she wouldn't recognize him. He had only become more himself, more Danny. He was not a baby anymore; he was a *boy*.

"Everything's fine, isn't it, Grace?" Theresa nudged her from behind.

"Yes," she said. "I'm fine. We came . . . we came . . ." She looked at Theresa for help.

"For a visit," Theresa said.

Vera took them into the living room. "Make yourselves comfortable," she said, "while I make you tea. Heavens, Grace, you should have let us know." She was still carrying Danny.

"Danny," Grace said. He looked at her and smiled shyly. "Danny. What do you have there?"

"This," he said and held out the block.

"I'll be right back," Vera said, and she carried Danny out.

But Danny came back on his own. "This," he said to Grace, and she took the block from him. "This?"

"This."

"Frank went over to the Cherniak place," Vera called from the kitchen. "They're selling it, you know. John just went back overseas. Frank went to look at their gardening things."

Grace slid off the chair onto the floor beside Danny. She picked up another block from the table. "This?" she said, holding it out, and he took it from her.

"Put this and this," he said, and showed her. She did what he said, and he nodded in approval. He scampered over to a wooden toy box in the corner and opened the lid. Grace followed him. Inside were more blocks, and the little brown puppy in the shoe. "Oh, you still have it!" Grace pulled out the toy. Danny took it out of her hands. "This," he said, showing her how to move the shoe until the dog popped out.

Grace looked up at Theresa, who smiled. "Clever," she said. "Like his mom."

Vera appeared in the doorway with a tray. "Danny, come over here so I can give them their tea. Grace, don't sit on the floor like that. You'll get a draught." Vera's face was flushed, and she kept pushing a strand of honey-coloured hair off her forehead.

"Can I trouble you for some sugar?" Theresa asked, and Vera said, "Oh! Of course! I'll be right back."

"Danny," Grace whispered. "Do you know who I am?" He squatted beside her and picked up another block. She wanted to kiss his chubby little hands, but she didn't want to scare him. "Do you remember me, Danny?"

Vera was back. "Now, Grace, don't be upsetting him. He's not good with strangers. Here's the sugar."

Theresa said, "She's not a stranger," and took the bowl from Vera.

"Well, you two enjoy your tea. I've got to feed Danny and then Frank should be back and we can all have a nice talk."

She scooped Danny up and hurried out of the room.

All of Grace's resolve drained out of her. She was not Grace who had her own place, Grace who had a job and her own business, Grace who had friends, Grace who lived in Peterborough and had saved her money to bring her son to live with her. She was Grace No One, Grace Nothing, Grace with Her Head in the Clouds.

"She won't give him to me," she whispered.

"You didn't come to ask her," Theresa said.

Grace shook her head rapidly. Theresa didn't know Vera. She didn't know what they were up against.

"Grace. Look at me." Theresa's face looked unbreakable, like a stone carving on Ruth Ellis's bookshelf. "He's your child."

Vera came back. "I was thinking you might like to walk over to the Cherniak place and fetch your brother, Grace."

From the kitchen, Danny called out, "Mommy?"

"Just a minute, Danny," Vera called back.

Grace stood abruptly. "I've come to take Danny back with me. I've got a place of my own and I have a business. I've saved enough money and I can look after him now."

Vera's eyes went round. Grace could see the panic in them.

"I—I'm very glad you could look after him while I got set up," Grace said. "You were a big help to me."

Vera's face turned pale and then very quickly red. "Your tea is getting cold." She left the room.

Grace took in a long breath. Theresa put an arm around her shoulders. "That was great, Gracie. Here, sit down for a minute."

Grace sank into the armchair under the lamp. "I used to sit with my mother right here," she told Theresa. *And when she got sick*, she thought, *I lost her and I turned into a little bird and tried to fly out of the world.*

"I think you should go upstairs and start to pack Danny's things," Theresa said. "I have a feeling this is going to get difficult."

Going to get difficult? Grace thought. She wanted to laugh or cry, she couldn't tell which.

Upstairs in Danny's room, she rolled his clothes up and put them in a pillowcase. Downstairs, she could hear Vera questioning Theresa. Did Theresa work as well, and how did she know Grace, and where was she from, and who were her people. "Where did Grace get to?" she heard Vera ask, and then the door opened downstairs and Frank called out, "Who's here, Vera?"

When she came downstairs, Vera was whispering to Frank in the kitchen and Theresa was sitting with Danny in the living room. Grace handed the pillowcase to Theresa, who put it under the chair. Vera called out, "I've got to put Danny to bed. Grace, your brother's home now."

Frank kissed her cheek and held her hands and said she looked different, completely grown up. It was good for her, the move down south. "I've come to take Danny back," Grace said, and he looked away. "I know," he said. "But let's have some dinner first."

At the table, Theresa and Frank did most of the talking. Theresa told them about Peterborough, Grace's little coach house with oak trees in the yard, Grace's successful laundry business. This made Frank smile proudly. "So you started your own business, Gracie. Well, well." He told her that people were moving closer to town, but also, town was moving closer to them. They were building houses for when the men came back. Some of the men who signed up were coming back in bad shape. John

Cherniak from across the road, Grace might remember him, had come home on leave and Frank didn't even recognize him. Oh, he looked fine, physically, but there was something different in his face now. The things the men saw over there . . .

Grace cut her meat into small pieces, but swallowing was painful, and Vera kept getting up to get something from the kitchen. By the end of the meal, there were two plates of bread and a collection of salt shakers on the table. "How long can you stay?" Frank wanted to know. Grace said, "We both have to get back," and Theresa said, "We can come for a longer visit in the summer." Frank said that would be ideal.

Vera went to make up the bed in the attic room for them.

In her old room, Grace sat on the edge of the bed while Theresa opened and closed drawers. "Do you have anything you want to take back?"

Grace shook her head. She wanted to creep downstairs to where Danny was asleep and lift him out of the bedclothes and carry him out to the car, but she couldn't bring herself to do it. It was like stealing. Worse than stealing. She was afraid Vera was having the same thoughts. She might try to take Danny away, hide him somewhere, maybe at Mrs. McCabe's. She would not sleep the whole night.

"What's in here?" Theresa asked, her voice muffled inside a cupboard. She brought out a red tin box and shook it. Something inside clattered.

"My mother's button box!" Grace took it from Theresa and opened it. "The bride and groom buttons."

Theresa put the box in Grace's bag. "Give it to Danny when he's older. He can keep his toy soldiers in it."

After Theresa went to bed, Grace sat by the window and listened. She heard the sound of the creek, and she remembered the feeling of the bliss hovering over her. She had told Ruth Ellis about the bliss once, and Ruth had shown Grace a photo of the whirling dervishes and another of a man sitting cross-legged under an enormous tree. "They want to escape the world," Grace said, but Ruth said no. "They want to know it directly, without the filter of thought."

Grace stared into the darkness. She could still feel the mark of the bliss, in the quietness behind her eyes and in her hands, but she no longer yearned to dissipate into it. She didn't want to escape the world. She was bound to it now that Danny was in it.

In the morning, Vera smiled at them, and her face was milky smooth again. Frank was still upstairs. Danny was in his high chair in the kitchen, and when he saw Grace, he waved his bottle at her and said, "This! Where my this?"

"Would you like tea or coffee, girls?"

Theresa said, "Coffee, please," and Grace said, "We have to leave, Vera. It's a very long drive."

"Of course. I'll pack you up some sandwiches. How's that?"

"We'll need Danny's bottles as well," Grace said. "I've already packed his clothes and toys and things."

"Yes, I know. I found them and put them back. You know very well you are not taking that child anywhere," Vera said. Her voice was mild.

Theresa leapt up from the table. "I beg your pardon," she said, "but Danny is her child and—"

"I beg *your* pardon," Vera said, "but you don't know the first thing about it. She gave him to us. She—"

"I didn't!" Grace said. "I left him here so I could get set up."

"You left him here because you couldn't look after him. You wanted to start fresh down south!"

"I wanted a fresh start with Danny."

"You don't know how to look after him! You don't know the first thing about raising a child."

"I'm his mother."

In the high chair, Danny's face creased and he started to cry. "Look how you're upsetting him," Vera said, whirling around and picking him up. His foot caught under the tray, and he cried harder.

"Give him to me, Vera."

"Leave him alone."

"Give him to me!" Grace tried to pull him out of Vera's arms.

Danny sobbed and hid his face in Vera's neck.

"Over my dead body," Vera said.

The kitchen door swung open, and Frank said hoarsely, "Let him go."

"Listen to your brother, Grace!" Vera said triumphantly.

"Let him go, Vera."

Vera turned to stare at him.

"She's his mother," Frank said. He looked sick.

Vera's eyes overflowed and the tears splashed onto Danny's head. "Grace," she croaked. "You can have another baby. Please don't take him away from me. Please."

Grace knew the size of that grief, how it obliterated the world and left you a blind, naked, howling creature. "I'm sorry," she said and opened her arms for her child.

Theresa said everything for her. She said that they were doing the right thing, that Grace talked about nothing but her little boy and how much she wanted him back. She said that Grace was doing very well on her own and that she had good friends who would help if she needed help. She said Frank and Vera should come down to Peterborough to see them, and she would drive Grace and Danny back up in the summer for a visit. She said this to Frank. Vera had gone upstairs. They could hear her crying.

Frank went up and came down with a bag of Danny's clothes and added some of his toys. They looked, but they couldn't find the dog in the shoe, and finally Theresa said they'd better start back. Frank carried Danny out to the car. Danny had his arms around Frank's neck and was playing with his collar. When Grace reached for him, he hung on to Frank. Frank kissed him and unhooked his hands from his neck and handed him to Grace. "You go with your mommy now," he said.

"Mommy!" Danny cried out, reaching for Frank. "Mommy."

"Take good care of him, Gracie," Frank said, his voice quivering. He turned his face away as they climbed into the car.

Danny cried in her arms and would not stop. "It's all right, Danny, it's all right," she kept saying. He flailed and wailed and choked on his tears. She held him and tried to kiss him, but he writhed and twisted and pulled away. "Mommy, mommy, mommy," he cried.

"He'll be all right," Theresa said. "It's going to take some time."

They turned onto the highway, passing through Garden River and Bruce Mines, and still Danny cried. Grace cried, and even Theresa had to stop driving to blow her nose.

"Stop, Theresa," Grace said finally. "Stop."

Theresa manoeuvred the car onto the side of the road. Danny had stopped flailing and screaming, but he was still crying in Grace's arms. "Mommy," he said. His voice was broken into pieces by hiccups and sobs. "Mommy, mommy." Grace stared ahead, blinded by tears. This was worse than when she had left. It was worse than all the nights without him. It was worse than anything she had ever felt.

"Grace?" Theresa asked softly. "Grace, what do you want to do?"

DAWN

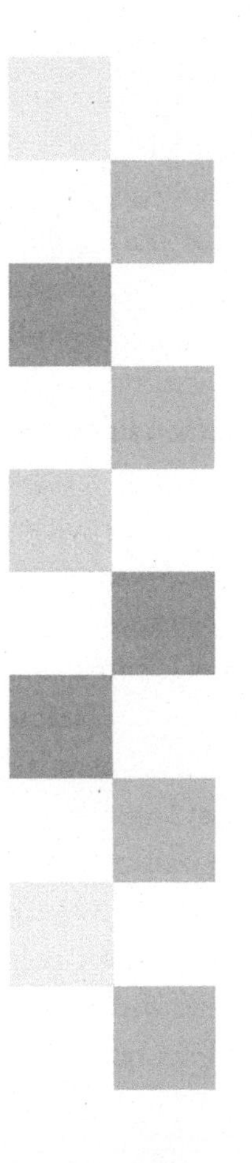

YELLOW BRICK ROAD

While the beginning was still ending, before the real ending began and everything fell to pieces and went to hell in a handbasket, there was a brief period when it seemed their luck had changed and things were going to work out after all. Dawn came downstairs one morning to find Geraldine and Jimmy murmuring over a jar of grape jelly. Geraldine smiled at her over Jimmy's tousled blond head and said, "The day has Dawned." She hadn't said that in a long time.

Jimmy said, "Look, Dawn. A secret message." Inside the jar, a small patch of white gleamed. They tried to dig it out with a knife and then a fork, and finally they emptied the thick purple mass into a bowl and Geraldine plucked out the paper and opened it. She burst into laughter.

"What is it?" Dawn and Jimmy yelled.

She showed them. It said, *Boo*. Geraldine was still laughing. "Your father," she said. She kissed them both on the top of the head and made them jam sandwiches for lunch, singing, " 'When you're near, there's such an air of spring about it. I can hear a lark somewhere begin to sing about it.' "

"That was a nice morning," Jimmy said on the way to school. But Dawn thought it was more than that, and by the end of the day, she had proof. First, Dean announced he wouldn't be going away on business anymore because he was opening his own business, right here in town, and if they would give him their full and undivided attention for a moment, he would tell them all about it.

They were eating a double supper: the Kentucky Fried Chicken and fries that Dean had brought home and the pork chops, peas and mashed potatoes that Geraldine had already cooked because apparently Dean had never heard of this new invention called The Phone. Dean said it was great that she had cooked, because now they could have an all-you-can-eat buffet feast, and he even set it up like a buffet, using all the bowls and serving platters they had. He loaded their plates: a mashed potato volcano spilling peas, with chicken and pork chops like houses at the base and a forest of fries climbing the slopes.

"Dig in, kids," he said, "and I'll let you in on The Plan."

The Plan was this: downtown, a few doors from the Sunset Café, Dean was opening a club the likes of which this town had never seen. "Club" meant nightclub, where grown-ups went at night to talk and listen to music.

Jimmy said, "You mean a barroom?"

Dean laughed. "No, Uncle Frank. Not a *barroom.*" It didn't look like anything now, because the carpenters were ripping it up and stripping it down, but in a few weeks, when the lights were installed and the round mahogany bar had been built, oh man, the bar was going to be the centrepiece, the showpiece of the whole place, right in the middle of the main room.

"Who's paying for this?" Geraldine asked.

"The investors," Dean said. "They're really excited—"

Geraldine snorted. "*The investors?* Dean, you're getting in over your head with this guy."

"This is nothing for Del. Peanuts. With all the deals he's got going, this is small change."

Geraldine sighed.

Dean said, "Don't worry, Ger, I've got him just where I want him."

Dean hadn't come up with a name yet, but he was open to suggestions. He leapt up and played a drum roll on the table with his index fingers. "Ladies and gentlemen," he said, "guys and dolls, cats and chicks, Turner Enterprises is pleased to present, all the way from Toronto—"

"Donny Osmond!" Dawn said.

"The Jackson 5!" Jimmy said.

Dean sighed. "Well, that's not quite the *calibre* I had in mind, but who knows, maybe we'll bring them up to do a special concert and you two can emcee." He drew the room for Dawn and Jimmy with some cutlery, the salt shaker and a straw. "The whole place goes completely black. Then a single ray of light cuts through the darkness. It hits the edge of a guitar . . ." He stopped and shook his head. "All I can say is, minds are going to be blown."

Dean put his arm around Geraldine, and she leaned against him, and that's when Dawn saw that things really were going to be different. Because Dean wouldn't be away on business now, so Geraldine wouldn't have to do everything by herself—work all day and then come home and look after the kids, make dinner, wash the clothes, do the shopping—and the club would be a smashing success and make bushels of money so Geraldine wouldn't have to worry about the bills on top of the fridge (and Dawn wouldn't have to stand on a chair to count them), and things would finally get back to normal and start to come true.

And then, more luck: at school Dawn made a new friend. Brenda Nolan (Big Brenda or Beluga Brenda) had watery eyes and white-blond hair. Her father owned a grocery store and they had a swimming pool in the backyard. Brenda said she and Dawn would have pool parties in the summer while Marlene from their class and all her stupid friends sat around on their front steps with nothing to do except fan themselves with their hands and bore themselves to death.

Aside from the promise of pool parties, the main advantage to being friends with Brenda was that Dawn had someone to eat lunch with. Plus, it was nice to be able to say things like, "I'm going over to my friend Brenda's" or "My friend Brenda has a pool." Normal things that normal kids said. The main disadvantage was that anyone who was friends with Brenda could never be friends with Marlene or anyone Marlene was friends with, and Mike Harrison called them Laurel and Hardy and sang whenever he saw them: "Fatty and Skinny went to bed, Skinny blew a fart and Fatty fell dead."

"How can Fatty *fall* dead if she's already *lying* in bed?" Brenda yelled.

"She was *sitting* in bed, cutting her big fat toenails and eating her toe jam," Mike yelled back, and Marlene laughed so hard she cried. Or pretended to.

Still, Dawn felt fortunate to have a friend, especially considering that the change in luck had stalled at home. Now when Geraldine came home from work, she took her swollen hands and feet straight to bed. She got up and drank water straight from the tap, then went back to bed, one hand on the wall to steady herself. Her eyes, slits in her moon face, looked the same whether she was awake or asleep. Too sick to get up and yell, she threw things against the bedroom door if Dawn and Jimmy made too much noise. Mostly they were things that thudded, but once, something shattered. Dawn only hoped it wasn't a mirror. So she took Jimmy to Brenda's after school almost every day, and Brenda didn't mind that she couldn't come to their house. That was the other advantage to Brenda: she hardly ever minded anything.

On Saturdays, they went to help Dean with the club. He often needed skilled assistants for special missions. "Yep," he said, inspecting Jimmy's eyes with an imaginary magnifying glass. "Eagle eyes. Perfect for the flea market."

"We're going to look for fleas?" Jimmy asked.

"Not fleas. Funk. Your mission, should you choose to accept it, is to find little pieces of funk. There's a fine line between junk and funk, but I believe you two will be able to discern it."

The flea market was row upon row of wooden tables inside a big barn-like building. Dean showed them funk: a handful of old-fashioned keys, a fan made out of feathers, a tiny green bottle with a rubber stopper. Then he showed them junk: an ashtray with an Algoma Steel logo, a book called *Teach Yourself Typing*. Jimmy found a pair of sparkly red shoes with bows, and Dawn found a framed photo of someone's great-grandmother, looking stern and stiff in a long black dress with a white lace collar. Dean said they had the knack, the eye, and they would be amply rewarded.

The club, which was going to be called Tangerine—or maybe Pipe Dreams in honour of Vera, who said Dean was full of them—was a series of interconnected rooms on the main floor, with bathrooms and an office in the basement. In the main room, Antoine was doing the mural. Short and bald, Antoine had apple cheeks, wire-rimmed glasses and a tangle of feather and leather pendants dangling from his neck. He reached into the basket at his feet and pulled out an earring and a silver spoon. With his other hand, he dipped a paintbrush into a can of glue. He worked fast, painting and sticking and then drying the glue with a hair dryer. A path of doll shoes led to a lake of blue glass surrounded by paper umbrella trees. An eye painted on a saucer cried a pearl. A sunburst brooch rose out of a teacup.

Antoine shrieked when he saw the shoes. He dropped his brush and grabbed Dean by the shoulder. "Yellow," he said. "I need yellow. I need a lot."

Dean said sure, he would keep an eye out for yellow pieces.

"No, no," Antoine said. "I need yellow now. Right now." He was clutching the shoes to his chest, and his round blue eyes were huge and blinking frantically. "You won't be sorry." He began prying pieces of his mural off the wall. "Go! Yellow!"

So they went back out, and at the Sally Ann they found a white scarf with yellow flowers, a gold belt and a plastic banana. "Not enough," Dean said. Jimmy had to pee, so Dean drove them home. He took a dollar out of his pocket. "Whoever collects the most yellow gets this." They kicked each other getting out of the car. "And whoever wakes up Geraldine gets a spanking," Dean called as they raced inside. "I'll be back in an hour."

Dawn found a bottle of Sunlight dish detergent, a plastic lemon in the fridge and a bar of yellow soap. Jimmy found some pencils, several pieces of plastic race track and a picture of a yellow dress in Geraldine's box of photos.

They both spotted the phone book at the same time, but Jimmy reached it first. They were ripping out the yellow pages and hissing when Geraldine came into the kitchen. Her stomach was a basketball under her purple bathrobe. "What is this?" she asked, looking at the mess on the floor—snips of paper and a slick of dish soap. "We need yellow things for the mural," Dawn told her. "Look at all the stuff we got."

Geraldine pretended to look in the bag before opening the fridge. Then she turned back to them. "Let me see that bag again," she said slowly.

When Dean came back, they were waiting outside with their hats and boots on. He said, "There is a surprising shortage of yellow in the world, kids . . . What happened?" Jimmy was still sniffling.

"He cut up a picture of Geraldine's sister in a yellow dress, the only picture she had—"

"She made a mess with dish soap—"

"Get in the car," Dean sighed.

Jimmy won the dollar for the pieces of race track but kept sniffling because Dean wouldn't go back to let them get Professor Pollo. They spent the rest of the afternoon eating butter tarts from Mike's Lunch and watching Antoine stick pieces of yellow on the wall.

The following Monday, Dawn's luck at school improved even more dramatically. Brenda was home sick, and Marlene invited Dawn to sit at her table in the lunchroom. "I wanted to ask you something," Marlene said. She had a heart-shaped face and pierced ears and shiny brown hair in a bouncy ponytail. Dawn thought, *Maybe Brenda and I were wrong; maybe she's not stuck-up at all.*

"Who's that lady who came to pick you up last week? I think you called her Geraldine?"

"That's my stepmother," Dawn said, swallowing.

"Oh," Marlene smiled sweetly. "You have a stepmother?"

"Yeah," Dawn said. "My dad got married this summer. Last summer. I mean just this past summer."

Marlene nodded. "Dawn . . . I hope you don't mind if I ask, but . . . where's your real mother?"

"My real mother," Dawn said, and her voice sounded strange in her ears, dusty and withered, like something that had fallen behind a dresser. She swallowed to lubricate her throat. When she looked up, she saw that they were all leaning towards her—Marlene, Charlotte, Jessica, Lisa. Their eyes were soft and shining with sorrow, their brows furrowed with tender concern. She was so touched that her own eyes filled up with tears. "She was beautiful and kind. I hardly remember what she looked like. She had long blond hair and blue eyes. She looked like a movie star." She swallowed hard. "She died when I was five."

The others murmured in alarm and sympathy, and Charlotte offered Dawn a napkin. Dawn wiped her eyes and cleared her throat.

"How did she die?" Marlene asked softly.

A series of deaths flashed before her eyes. A last-minute trip to the store to buy medicine for the sick baby, the car spinning out of control across an icy bridge on a dark night. A woman in a long white nightgown breaking free from a fireman's grip: "My children! My children are in there!" The nightgown disappears into the roaring flames, appears a moment later at a window to drop two tiny bundles into the firemen's net below, then disappears as the house collapses.

Dawn blinked hard, sending more tears down her cheeks. The other girls pressed closer, trying to outdo one another in consolation and wisdom. "It's too hard for her to talk about it." "Oh my god, poor thing." "What are *you* crying for, Charlotte, your mother's not dead." "She's got a mental block; she probably can't remember. Can you remember, Dawn?"

That's how she became part of Marlene's group. Even girls from grade eight knew her name now. They whispered when she went by, and she straightened her shoulders and bowed her head, putting on one of the various sad and stricken looks she practised in the mirror at home. Dawn still went over to Brenda's after school, because she wasn't two-faced. She wasn't going to stop being Brenda's friend just because she was Marlene's. Also, she had to bring Jimmy wherever she went, and she couldn't bring him to Marlene's. But she ate lunch with Marlene, and when the teacher said, "Find someone to work with," Charlotte and Lisa both turned in their seats to catch her eye. Brenda said nothing. *I can't help it,* Dawn thought. *I can't make Marlene and everyone like her.* There was nothing she could do, and nothing Brenda could say.

But it turned out there was something Brenda could say, after all. One day she approached Marlene's table at lunch. "Did you want something, Brenda?" Marlene asked smoothly.

Brenda stuck her chin out at Dawn. "Her mom's not dead. That's a big fat lie."

Everyone looked at Dawn. "I think," Dawn said, as loudly as she could, although her heart was flapping and fluttering like a trapped bird against her breastbone, "I think I should know what happened to my own mother."

The others agreed, "Yeah, Brenda, she should know," but Dawn could feel their belief cracking and splitting, and the story she had been rehearsing in her head about her memory breakthrough slipped through a crevice and disappeared.

Brenda said, "My mother worked with her mother. She knows the whole story. Her mother's not dead. She ran off with another man."

DEAN

THE LIGHT BULB TRICK

Wharton said if Dean didn't bring the money a week Friday, he'd pound the living daylights out of him. He'd do it, too. With his tree-trunk neck and hams for hands, he'd thump Dean into the ground, next Friday and every Friday until he had the money. Nothing, no talk or walk or turn of phrase would change that, no slide or glide into a new place where suddenly Dean's arm was around your shoulders and everyone was laughing, including you. Wharton came from the same distant place as Dean's parents, the City of No, whose inhabitants rarely laughed, and suffered a perplexing imperviousness to Dean and his talk. (Town Motto: We Don't Want Any.)

At home, Dean rifled through pockets, groped under the chesterfield cushions and emptied out his mother's change purse. Funds found: $0.82. Funds outstanding: $9.18. Likelihood of a pounding: very likely.

All because of a light bulb. "Horseshit and bullshit!" Dean

shouted into the stillness of the house. Outside, in the four o'clock gloom, it began to snow. His father wouldn't be home from work for a couple of hours, but his mother, having her hair set by Mrs. May down the road, could interrupt his search at any time. He stood in the doorway of his room, his mind a whirl. Pointless to look in here. He carried his money in his pocket, when he had it, which wasn't often, because his parents confiscated any cash that found its way into his hands. It had to go straight to the bank, they said, so he wouldn't spend it. "Money doesn't grow on trees, Dean." *Well, obviously*. "You can't have your cake and eat it too." *What's the point of cake you can't eat?*

The whole point of money was to spend it. It was its own trick and story. Without money, you were sitting by yourself outside the corner store on a flat, grey day in the kingdom of tedium; with money, six kids you'd never met before were sprawled around you on the steps, sipping happily from their individual bottles of Coke, freed by an unexpected act of generosity and talking like they'd known each other all their lives.

He threw himself onto his bed. A fourteen-year-old in another family might be able to ask. Some other kid might be able to explain to some other father, who would say, "Betting's a foolish thing to do, son," and this other kid would agree, "I know, I *know*," and he *would* know, too, and the father would say, "Well, it's a lesson learned" and open his wallet. Dean's father would not open his wallet for a bet, even if Wharton came over with a signed IOU, a priest and a pistol. He would have to say he needed it for sports equipment or something, and then, inevitably, a week or a month later, they would discover the truth and all hell would break lose. Hell and rhetorical questions: Did he think they wouldn't find out? Did he think money grew on trees? Did he think he was too old for a strapping?

Then the exchanged glances and a week of sighs and forecasts of doom: What would become of him if he kept this up? They didn't know. They. Just. Didn't. Know.

Might be better to just take the pounding from Wharton. It would be over quicker.

The light bulb trick was a recent addition to his repertoire: the toilet paper blizzard, a midget in the closet, pennies from heaven, Magillicutty's ghost. His parents called them antics and acting up. He called them pieces and tricks, although that made them sound like common magic, of the now-you-see-it, now-you-don't variety, which he despised. There was actually no word for what he did. Someday, though, he would record the details in a black leather book with only his last name in raised script on the cover; he would make sure just enough people saw it to establish its existence so that when it went missing, they would tell their kids, and their kids would tell their kids, and people would look for the Turner Black Book forever.

Rumours would circle him and reporters would follow him out to his limousine, clamouring to know what he had planned next and was he was the one behind the Christmas baskets hung in the trees outside the orphanage, and where did he get his ideas. His parents wanted to know the same thing, only they phrased it differently.

"What is putting this nonsense into your head?" his mother demanded when he was sent home from school for climbing out the detention closet window, sliding down the drainpipe, sprinting back into the school and slipping into his seat before Mr. Harrison had finished writing quadratic equations on the board.

"It was about a thousand degrees in there," he began, "so I opened the window to get some air, and—"

"But why were you in detention in the first place?" she'd cried. (Spitballs, but he wasn't going to tell her that now.) "Why do you always have to act up?"

The truth was, the ideas just came to him, he didn't know from where, in flashes, all joy and bedazzlement, burning away that queasy, uneasy feeling he had so much of the time. Working on a piece made him feel sharp and bright, like when you brush against the radio and the thin film of static you hadn't even noticed disappears. "I guess it's in my blood," he told her, which made her mad as hornets.

Some of his pieces still needed practice, but the light bulb trick was perfect. Last year he'd made five dollars at the church social. How it worked: you stood at an open second- or third-storey window looking reflective, and then you said, like it had just come to you, "You know, I'll bet I can drop a light bulb out of this window in such a way that it will hit the pavement and not break."

"Sure, if you wrapped it in a pillow," someone would say. "And it landed on a mattress."

"No, I mean a naked bulb. There's a way of holding it so that when you drop it, when it hits the pavement, it doesn't break."

After the jeers and snorts, you narrowed your eyes and said, "Uh . . . anyone care to bet?"

That afternoon, Wharton had stepped forward right away, bet ten and unscrewed the bulb from the cloakroom himself. Everyone else went silent, and Dean felt their faith waver. He should have known right then and there that something was up. No one would bet ten bucks straight away like that.

Dean held the end of the bulb with his thumb and forefinger. "This is the trick," he told the crowd. "It's all in the grip. This way, the wind currents act as a buffer." He licked a finger and held it up, frowning as he calculated. This was the part he loved: when the tide began to turn, waves of disbelief curling helplessly against the incoming current of desire. Their doubt was drowning in their hope, their longing for a story they could take away with them: guess what Dean Turner did today.

He shook his head and asked for something to practise with, a pencil, a comb. They watched the comb fall and bounce, and that was the signal for Dave Stanghetta downstairs, pressed against the wall with his baseball glove, to get ready to catch the bulb, hold it half an inch from the pavement and let it drop with the smallest clatter.

But Wharton must have heard about it from someone. He sent his goons to waylay Dave, and upstairs, they all listened to the bulb explode on the frozen concrete below.

It wasn't the money that got to him; it was the wave of disappointment that went through his crowd. They had believed, and nothing had come of it. Dean Turner had collected their hopes and tossed them out a window.

And now he was lying on the bed, staring at the ceiling like an idiot while his pounding ticked ever closer. He leapt up. Options: attic or the parental bedroom. Nothing in the attic except old furniture and the Christmas decorations, plus it was always freezing up there. Their room was his best bet; he was certain they had money socked away. They would miss it, of course—Dean would bet ten bucks that every single penny in this house was accounted for, including the eighty-two cents he had just scrounged up—but he'd worry about that later. He fetched his flashlight from his bedside table.

He'd been through their room countless times before, not always looking for money, just looking, and he knew the smells by heart. The wooden trunk at the foot of the bed exhaled a cheerful whiff of forest, followed by the stench of mothballs. Nothing in there except the good linens and knitted baby hats and boots threaded with green ribbon. His mother must have put them away for the next baby, but no baby had ever materialized. Once he'd asked for a brother for Christmas—an older brother; he thought you ordered them from the catalogue—and his mother got something caught in her throat and left the table, and his father told him angrily to hush with that kind of talk. They were embarrassed, he thought, at the possibility of having to explain the facts of life to him—or the impossibility, given their use of directions to refer to body parts (down there, backside). He replaced the baby things and started in on the closet (more mothballs, laced with lavender).

Behind his mother's Sunday dresses and his father's one good suit, against the back wall, were the hat boxes and shoeboxes containing receipts and sewing patterns. He ran the beam of light over the shelves, wondering what he could turn a pounding into that people would be talking about years from now.

Nothing came to him, but he saw, for the first time, that the wall under the last shelf was a different shade of plywood. His heart sped up. He knocked against it. *Hello?* He yanked the plywood away and aimed his flashlight into the dark. Metal glinted back. *Hello!*

It was an ordinary tool box, except it was locked, which was a good sign—actually, it was great, because a lock could only mean money. Not only that, but it was a puny little lock, easily snapped off. And not only *that*, but having just searched the house, he knew where there was another lock just like it. He flew down to the kitchen and then back up with a pair of pliers and the lock's twin brother. *You want your ten bucks, Wharton, you'll get your ten bucks.*

Smiling at how easily the lock yielded, he threw open the lid. Spit filled his mouth. Nothing! A bunch of papers. He pawed through them angrily. Not a dollar, not a single goddamn dime. What the hell was so important that it had to be locked up? Bank statements, his parents' wedding certificate. The deed to the house. Maybe he could pay Wharton with that. *Here you go, Wharton. Keep the change.*

A faded photograph of his mother, younger and thinner, with her hair in a bun, and some other woman with short hair, in front of the rose bushes out front, holding a baby between them. He turned it over, but the back was blank. A yellow envelope with a card inside from the Province of Ontario. *Certificate of Birth. Required Surname: Turner. Registered Given Name: Daniel. Mother: Grace Turner.* Who was Grace Turner? Some relative he'd never heard of. *Father: Not Given.* He knew what that meant. Poor kid was a bastard. No wonder he was locked up.

From the bottom of the box, he lifted out a brown folder. Inside was a long, cream-coloured paper with heavy black print. He saw the title at the top of the page, with its ornate, curling A, and his name typed in plain letters at the bottom. He tried to read the document, every *hereby* and *wherefore* and *on this day*, but it made no sense. His ankles gave out under him and he sat down hard on the wooden floor.

Downstairs, the back door opened. His mother. He threw the papers back into the box and snapped the lock into place. He had barely made it to his room when she called up the stairs. "What are you doing up there, Dean?"

"Nothing."

"Well, you should be doing your homework. I'm going to start dinner."

"Okay."

He actually took out his science textbook and stared at the blur of black lines. His chest was an iron-banded barrel. He couldn't count how many times he'd been through that closet. How many times he'd been within a foot of that metal box. *So that was what I was looking for all along.*

The plan was to wait until after dinner, until they were sitting in the front room, his father reading the paper, his mother knitting. *Either after dinner or never*, he told himself, but he couldn't eat. He sat watching them butter their bread and pass the potatoes and chew their food. His mother's light brown hair, freshly set in pincurls, gleamed in the yellow light. She was telling his father that Mrs. May's sister-in-law was actually related to them, because she was a Butler and the Butlers and the Turners were related.

Dean's father helped himself to another pork chop. "What are you waiting for, Dean? Your dinner is getting cold."

Dean squeezed his hands into fists in his lap.

His father said, "Are you sick?"

His mother said, "Are you in trouble?"

Dean said, "Am I adopted?"

For a moment, all he could hear was a storm of blood, whirling and rushing in his ears. Then a clatter of cutlery. "What on earth!" his father exclaimed, and his mother cried out, "What kind of talk is that?"

He kept his eyes on his plate and took shallow breaths through his mouth. The blue clock above the sink tapped out the seconds. The refrigerator hummed. He would wait all night if he had to.

When he looked up, he realized: *they* were waiting for *his* answer.

What kind of talk is that.

Oh, he could tell them: it was the talk of the metal box at the back of the closet, the talk of a flashlight in the dark and a twisted-off lock. It was the typed and signed certificate talk: hereby, wherefore. He could tell them, but he would not. The whole thing had gotten turned around: he should be the one with his arms folded and his mouth set in a straight line and sparks shooting out of his eyes; they should be the ones with sore throats and cold, wet hands, their limbs weighed down by thick, dark dread.

He gave them another chance. "Am I?"

"Of course not," his mother said. "What put that idea into your head?"

Whereby, on this day, I saw my name filled in.

If he said it, he could never take it back. But if he didn't say it, it could still be untrue, and everything could be sorted out. He swallowed hard. "The teacher was talking about it at school today. A kid in my class was adopted."

They looked so relieved, he wanted to cry.

"Well, you most certainly are not," his mother said.

His father picked up his knife and fork.

"Eat your dinner, Dean," his mother said.

"Do as your mother says," his father said.

Your dinner. Your mother. Everything looked the same—the red and white tablecloth, the blue-faced clock against the yellow wall, his mother and his father in their places—and yet he was seeing it all for the first time. He was sitting at the table, but he was also watching himself from somewhere else, crouched in dark, tangled underbrush, the wind howling all around him.

Dean picked up his fork and began to shovel potatoes into his mouth. "I need ten dollars by next Friday," he said. He did not look at either of them. "I made the hockey team, and I have to buy all the equipment."

HALLUCINATIONS

He had to wait until they went to church without him on Sunday morning. He had to say he was sick on Saturday night. Not that it was difficult to convince them. He had hardly touched his food all week. He could see them looking at each other. They were still wondering. *Who at school did you say was adopted, Dean?*

New kid. Name of Macowski. You don't know him.

They were going to take him to Dr. McCabe if he wasn't back to himself by Monday morning.

Back to himself. Now, what self would that be?

He heard the sound of the car engine fade, but he didn't move for twenty minutes. It was hard to drag himself out of bed. He banged his knee on the edge of the oak dresser, then just stood there, staring at himself in the oval mirror. It couldn't be true. He *looked* like his father. They had the same dark hair, the same cowlick. When he smiled, he had a dimple, one of his mother's two. And anyway, something like that could not have been kept from him for fourteen years. There would have been signs, clues. He would have known.

He'd made a mistake, he'd read it wrong, he wasn't thinking straight.

He just needed to go back into the closet and open the box and see those papers again to make sure.

Inside the closet, he pushed his way through the clothes and knelt on the floor, pulling aside the plywood panel and aiming his flashlight into the darkness. The beam cut straight through to the cement wall.

The box was gone.

He sat on his heels.

Now what?

He didn't know what. His brain was frozen. The spaces between things seemed distorted, like in a nightmare. A daymare. Maybe he had hallucinated the whole thing. Maybe he had been so worked up over the light bulb fiasco that his brain had cooked up this story, a little mental abracadabra, to distract him. *Poor guy,* his brain thought. *He doesn't realize there are worse things in the world. Being blown to smithereens by the A-bomb, say. Getting rabies. Being adopted.*

And it had worked beautifully too, thank you very much, brain of Dean Turner. He didn't give a goddamn straw about Wharton now.

He felt a small surge of hope. It was one possibility.

The other possibility: they had moved the box.

"Bastards," he whispered fiercely.

The box was gone, and he knew it was gone, but he couldn't stop looking for it. He passed his hand through the empty space; he knocked on walls and banged on shelves. Coats fell off their hangers; a shoebox fell, spilling receipts. Bastards, bastards. They would be home soon and would find him here among the coat hangers. *The criminal always returns to the scene of his crime*. His father had told him that. *Except he might not be my father*. Dean shivered. What if his real father was a bank robber who cracked safes for a living, and that's why Dean found it so easy to break into locked boxes? What if what he got from his father was not a cowlick but bad blood?

He stuffed handfuls of receipts back into the shoebox and yanked the coats back onto their hangers. Everything was crooked. He didn't care. A black fury had risen in him. He choked on tears and spit and unzipped his fly and pissed into the back of the closet.

Back in his bed, he fell asleep and had strange dreams: feverish dreams in which ball bearings rolled through his head and his limbs turned to grey rock with lichen growing on them. He surfaced from one dream into another, aware of the watery afternoon light through his eyelids. He must be sick: his mother never allowed him to sleep during the day. He twisted in the sheets and his body turned into a long creek, curling through the fields and murmuring to itself. Fish flickered deep in his veins.

He woke when his mother called him for dinner. "You look better, Dean," she said when he came downstairs. He expected it to be dark outside, but it was still afternoon; they ate early on Sunday. The whole house smelled of roasted chicken. "Do you feel better?" She laid a cool hand on his forehead. He felt hollowed out. He ate two servings of buttery chicken and mashed potatoes in pools of golden gravy. It was Sunday dessert as usual, apple pie and praises to the Walinski boy: parents lacked the proverbial pot but boy studied every night in a broom closet, put himself through law school, and look where he was today.

"A lawyer," his father said, "with a big house in the east end."

The familiarity was almost comforting.

After dinner, he announced he was going for a walk. His mother protested, but his father said the fresh air would do him good. Outside, night was summoning itself under the branches of the apple trees. He headed to the creek, inching down the snowy bank to the ice. This had been his domain since he'd caught his first fish, at age six, standing on this same flat rock, with a rod he'd made himself. Now he had a proper rod, and since his birthday last year, a Mitchell reel (he had almost cried to see the glossy red box sitting on his breakfast plate, the exact model he had asked for instead of the flimsy approximation he had expected); he was down here every day in the summer, and even under snow, he knew every turn in the creek, every secret stone and hollow.

He stepped out onto the ice. It creaked, protesting his weight, but he knew it would hold. Above him, the lights of the house blazed against the darkening sky. He trudged down the frozen, snow-covered creek, listening to the rhythm of his boots and his breath, past the first bend, the fallen log, the wide turn, the narrows. By the time he got to the white pine that leaned out over his favourite fishing hole, an old, waxy moon was rising. It threw down enough light for him to keep going, but back at the house, he knew, they would be starting to worry.

Would they be so worried if he were not their kid? Would his father buy expensive Mitchell reels for someone else's kid? Would his mother make butter tarts just because they were his favourite if she didn't have to?

The thing was, he had no actual proof, beyond what he had seen by flashlight, in a closet, in a hurry, and what he *had* seen was like a dream fragment now: it shifted out of sight whenever he tried to look directly at it. And people did hallucinate, staggering around the desert or on the battlefield. He had done it himself: once, a bat hanging from the beam in his room had resolved itself into a sock; another time, rehearsing pennies from heaven in the attic, he thought he saw a ghost. Now he could add the time he thought he was adopted.

It made sense. Or it made more sense than being adopted and then lied to for fourteen years. Because it wouldn't just be the am-I-adopted, no-you-are-not lie. It would also be the how-we-named-you lie (his father wanted to call him James, but his mother had her heart set on Dean), and the you-have-your-father's-cowlick lie. Every day would have been a lie, and they just weren't the kind of people who could pull that off. Plus, he had seen his birth certificate. Dean Turner. Born April 1944 in the city of Sault Ste. Marie. You couldn't make a birth certificate lie.

There had been other papers in that box, and he hadn't looked at them properly. He had been stunned, cold with shock, stupid with fear—there was no word for what he had been. But those papers probably explained the whole thing. He had a cousin somewhere who was adopted. Big deal.

Standing under a fringe of white pine, he rubbed his gloved hands and stamped his feet and huffed, waiting for the clouds to open and release the moon. This was his own fault. Had he not been showing off with the light bulb trick, he never would have found the box in the first place. His parents were right: he needed to settle down, stop acting up, be more like the Walinski boy.

It was either that or go home and tell them he had opened the box.

He turned back and trudged home through the darkness. It was time to turn over a new leaf.

OPERATION NEW LEAF

He got off to a good start, waking before his mother called him, and in the hour before breakfast, he actually studied for a history test. This earned him a 94 and a trip to the principal's office, courtesy of Father Croce, on charges of cheating, but Father Dougherty merely asked him a few questions on Roman history and released him, satisfied. It was insulting but also kind of amusing to watch Croce twist himself into a muttering fury ("Studied, my ass!"), trying to figure out how Dean had done it. That evening he cleaned his room and took out the garbage without being told, and asked his father to bring home some iron ore from the plant so he could start his science project ("The Making of Steel"), even though it wasn't due until April.

He found he could forget the box. Not forget, exactly. But he could live with it. The unanswered question, the questionable answer. He didn't have to figure it out in order to go to school in the morning, or watch *Gunsmoke* on Saturday night, or eat hot, gooey butter tarts straight out of the oven, or taste the oily, bitter homemade wine that Dave smuggled out of his father's garage in a jam jar. He didn't have to figure it out to ask Rita Vachon to the dance, or to neck with her after. He could walk over it, talk over it. He could skate on top of it. The truth, whatever it was, was lying deep in cold, dark water, with a layer of opaque ice over it. He was up here. Skate, skate, skate. What did he care what was down there?

The only glitch was that ideas still went off in his head like flares or opened like sudden secret doorways, difficult (impossible) to ignore. He could have just paid Wharton, for example, but in the middle of math class he had an idea so irresistible that he skipped lunch to go to the bank. Back at school, he made a few bets on whether he could infuriate Wharton simply by paying his debt, and then, surrounded by a crowd of whispering, grinning onlookers, he fed ten dollars in nickels through the grille of Wharton's locker. He found Wharton in the cafeteria. "Hey, Wharton. I left the ten bucks in your locker."

Wharton sneered. "How'd you leave it in a locked locker?"

"Slipped it through the air vent at the top." He smiled as Wharton lurched to his feet. "Don't worry," he called out. "It's all there. Every last nickel."

People said after you could hear Wharton's roar all through the school.

That led to another idea, and he spent the next two months getting people to bet on Wharton. He bet he could make Wharton challenge him to a fight and then back down. He bet he could get Wharton accused of stringing a cheesecloth bag full of pennies above the principal's office and rigging it so the coins dribbled out every time someone went in or out. He worked through George Gerard and Dave Stanghetta, providing the script, coaching them on the exact ratio of audacity to nonchalance. By the end of it, Wharton was looking at Dean with a wary respect, or something close to it, Dean had won back his ten dollars, and Rita Vachon had agreed to go steady with him. All in all, he thought Operation New Leaf was going extremely well.

Then, just after he turned fifteen, as the creek thawed and black water soaked through the ice, and the snow dissolved, revealing bare yards and mud slicks, he had a series of setbacks. First, he was invited to leave Barb Fox's house and never return after Mrs. Fox walked in on them on the sun porch while his hands were inside Barb's shirt. Dean hadn't known that Mrs. Fox and Mrs. Vachon were sisters, which made Rita and Barb cousins, and although Rita said their kinship had nothing to do with why she never wanted to see him again, he was sure it hadn't helped. In his misery, he forgot about a history test and Father Croce literally tripped over himself in glee to hand back his failing paper. Father Harrison called his parents to complain that he was creating a disturbance in math class (if you could call throwing your voice a disturbance), and in the course of the conversation, his father found out that Dean hadn't actually been on the hockey team. His science project, now overdue, was still a bag of rocks.

He sat in his room, trying to balance a piece of slag on a piece of coal. Downstairs, the good china was piled neatly on the dining table, and the house smelled of almond cake and floor polish. It was Institute Night, which meant he was banished to his room for the evening while the Institute ladies drank tea and yakked downstairs.

"You're to go upstairs and stay there," his mother said crossly before he'd barely taken off his coat.

"I know," he said. "Jeez."

"I mean it," she said. Her voice was cold and hard. "None of your acting up."

His face grew hot at the memory of it. Before, he had been able to shrug it off, but now he was worn right through. He talked too loudly; he had a one-track mind; he couldn't settle down; he didn't apply himself. Everything he did was some class of acting up. Creating a trick that would amaze and amuse? Wearing his hat at an angle? Acting up. Even laughing was acting up! The things he loved best were weeds to be uprooted, or fires to be stamped out. Not only did they not understand him, they didn't even *like* him.

Downstairs, the Institute ladies began to arrive. They'd been coming to the house twice a year for as long as he could remember, making a terrible racket, all talking at once and cackling, and then suddenly hushing: someone had heard so-and-so's (indistinct) was (inaudible), and someone else had been found with (indecipherable, followed by shocked silence).

Sometimes he got more of the story when they came upstairs in pairs to use the bathroom. (Mary Beth's husband was running around on her, Dr. McCabe's daughter was caught drinking rum at the bootlegger's). He usually threw open his door to greet them, calling them "Ladies" and bowing gravely. They always fluttered and cooed, and after he had gone back into his room, they'd say to each other, "Gosh, Vera's boy is getting big. And handsome. A real charmer." Tonight, he kept his door closed (bowing to the Institute women = acting up), but he could still hear them in the hallway.

"You should talk to Vera," one of them said. "She had one."

"When did she have hers?"

"I can tell you the exact date. January 7, 1944. The day she went into the hospital, that was the day we heard my brother lost his leg in France."

In his room, Dean tossed the iron ore and slag back into their bag. Once they started in on who lost what limb in which war, there was no chance of hearing anything even faintly interesting.

"But what should I say?" the first woman was saying as they passed his room. "I can't just go over and say, 'Oh, Vera, I hear you had a hysterectomy.'"

"Well, not like that. But—"

Dean waited until they were all the way downstairs before he pulled the dictionary off the shelf. He knew what it meant. He just wanted to make sure.

Hysterectomy: surgical removal of the uterus.

January 7, 1944. Months before he was born.

Adopted. Even the word was ugly: cutting and gaping. Shame ran through its syllables and dripped out the end. *He* was that thing. That word meant him.

This was why he worried them and baffled them and caused them to go about with lined foreheads and pursed lips.

In his room, he paced. If he thought hard enough, he might remember. The oldest picture in his head: he was on the floor in the living room holding Brownie, the dog in the shoe. He was what, two? Three? Before that, nothing, but no one remembered anything before that. He opened his door and listened—teaspoons clinked against the good china downstairs and a woman said, "Oh, for heaven's sake, Bess, you're on my skirt again"—and then he went to the cabinet in the hallway where she kept the photo album. Back in his room, he opened it at random and lifted the tissue paper from the stiff black page. There he was, sitting on the floor, toy trucks lined up around him. He slipped the picture out of its mounting corners and turned it over. *Dean, 3 years, 6 months*. Turning the pages, he saw *Dean, 2 years*, standing in diapers beside the armchair, *Dean, 20 months*, tottering with a bottle, *Dean, 12 months*, sitting on his father's knee. That was the start of the album. He closed the cover, irritated. The pictures told him nothing.

Except that you weren't here for the first year of your life, a voice in his head said, and Dean bolted up, chilled. It wasn't the voice that announced the Cities of Origin, or the Smart-Ass Voice that so enraged his teachers. It was an older, colder, careless voice.

He understood what it was saying. He imagined some old stone building with draughty hallways full of unwanted kids. Orphans and runaways and bastards. The adults came and looked at them through a window and pointed to the one they wanted. The babies wouldn't know anything, but the older kids probably combed their hair and stood up straight and tried to look like they came from the City of No Trouble. That was the problem right there: you couldn't actually tell where they were from. You didn't know what you were getting.

His mother used to say what a good baby he had been. Never cried, never fretted to be picked up. She could put him down and he would stay there. She thought she was getting a good, quiet child like the Walinski boy. By the time he started to show his true colours, it was too late. No returns.

He pushed his hair back from his forehead to see his whole face in the mirror. Years ago, he had asked his mother, "Do I look more like you or dad?" He *remembered* this. Jesus! And she'd said, "More like your dad. You have the same cowlick."

A cowlick that was not his father's. A mother who was not his mother. "What am I going to do?" he whispered.

Find out, the voice said. The sound of his own bad blood speaking.

At a loss, he started at the library, standing in front of a row of encyclopedias. Where to even begin? A for adoption, O for orphan, C for children, P for parents? It would take all day. He glanced over at the librarian gluing something into a book behind a wide, polished desk. She looked old and cranky and nosy. He approached with caution. "I have to do a project on adoption," he told her. "Do you have any books on it?"

"Adoption!" she exclaimed. He saw that she was actually young. But still cranky. "What kind of project?" And nosy.

"Just a project for school."

"What kind of topic is that for a project?" she said. "What school do you go to?"

"Central Tech," he lied.

"What kind of information do you need, exactly?"

"Anything on adoption agencies."

She gave him an odd look, but he held her gaze. "Well, the Children's Aid Society usually handles adoptions. I don't know if we have anything, but I'll have a look," she said. She walked over to another desk, and he turned and walked out.

In the phone booth outside, he asked the operator for the number of the Children's Aid Society and dialled.

"Children's Aid. Good afternoon."

"Do you have children for adoption?" he asked.

"I beg your pardon? Do we—?" the woman asked.

"Have children for adoption. Do you put children up for adoption?"

The woman said, "This is the Children's Aid Society. To whom would you like to speak?"

Dean hung up and waited ten minutes. He called again and in a deep, ponderous voice, he said, "May I please speak to the adoption department please?"

"Young man," the woman said, "we have work to do here."

"My name's Clark. My wife and I want to adopt a child."

The woman hung up.

At school, he decided to talk to George Gerard, whose habit of reading things unnecessarily had given him a head full of facts and an irritating but interesting way of poking holes in what people thought. He'd say, "See, that's where you're wrong," and suddenly you *would* see. They were sitting under the football bleachers, sharing the last of George's cigarettes. Dean blew a sloppy smoke ring and said, "Hey, you ever meet anyone who was adopted?"

George nodded. "Cousin in Sudbury."

"Does he know?"

"That he's adopted? Don't know. Only met him once. We had to share a bed one Christmas when we went up there."

"He must feel terrible. If he knows."

George considered this. "Why? It's not like it's his fault."

"True," Dean said. He hadn't thought of that. He lit a match and watched it burn down. "Only he doesn't actually know who he is, your cousin. What if his mother was a whore or something, and his father was a gangster?"

"Look!" George had produced a perfect smoke ring. "Top that, Turner."

"He'd inherit that bad blood," Dean persisted.

George shook his head. "That's an old wives' tale. There's nothing in blood. It's just blood. That's how they can do transfusions."

Dean took the cigarette from him and inhaled. George was right. There was nothing in blood. Good old George. He exhaled a misshapen smoky oval and rubbed out the butt in the grass. "You wouldn't feel weird if you found out his real dad was serving time for murder? Come on. You'd think twice about sharing a room with him again."

George laughed. "I'd think twice, anyway, because the little bastard pissed the bed." He passed Dean the last cigarette.

"But it goes against nature," Dean said. He was dragging up everything now for George's cross-examination. "I mean, look at animals, right? It's instinct. No animal just walks away from its young, unless there's something wrong with the kid."

"Our cat did that once when its kitten was deformed," George said. "With people, I think it's more like something's wrong with the parents and the government takes the kid away. For its own good, like."

Dean watched the smoke twist up from the cigarette and curl around his fingers. Something wrong not with the kid but with the parents. Another idea he hadn't thought of. "Yeah, but if there's something wrong with the parents, there's probably going to be something wrong with the kid, eh?" Dean passed the cigarette to George and waited for him to say, "See, that's where you're wrong."

George thought a moment and said, "You mean they're going to pass it on, like hair colour. Yeah, I see what you mean."

"So it is bad blood, then," Dean said coldly.

George shrugged. "I guess." He handed the end of the cigarette to Dean. Dean knocked it away. "For fuck sakes, Gerard, I don't want the butt."

"All right. Don't take my head off."

Dean spat and stood up suddenly. "Where'd you get these cigarettes, anyway? They taste like the bottom of an old lady's handbag." He kicked at the cigarette pack, just missing George's hand.

George stared at him. "Jesus, Turner. What's wrong with you?"

"Nothing," he said. Everything.

Finally he went to see his English teacher. Brother Nick looked over his silver half-glasses and told Dean to take a seat. Dean still owed him a descriptive essay on one of the seasons. "What can I help you with, son?"

Dean said, "Well, I've got this cousin, see, who has this dilemma about his parents." He looked up to see how Brother Nick was taking this. Brother Nick was frowning ever so slightly.

"He's actually my second cousin," Dean added, for that extra whiff of veracity. "He thinks he might be adopted."

Brother Nick raised a furry grey eyebrow. "What makes him think he's adopted?"

It came to him so fast, it was scary. "Both his parents have blue eyes, see. And my cousin has brown eyes. And he just learned in science that's impossible."

Brother Nick leaned back and considered this. "Has he spoken to his parents?"

"Well, that's what I said. Why don't you ask your parents, and he said, oh, I could never do that, and I said, well, is there any other way to find out, and he said—"

Brother Nick broke in. "All right, Dean, let's stop right there. It sounds like your cousin needs to speak to his parents immediately. Or his priest. This is quite serious. If he doesn't speak to his parents, you have to tell your parents."

Dean nodded vigorously. "Exactly! That's what I was thinking I should do. But he said he's going to call some office, the Children's Society or something—"

"The Children's Aid Society? Here in town?"

Dean nodded.

Brother Nick shook his jowly head. "Oh no, no, no. That's not . . . they can't . . . they wouldn't be able to tell him."

"Maybe he meant another office, like a headquarters?"

"The main office is in North Bay, but that's not the point. Even the North Bay office wouldn't tell him anything."

"Why not?"

"They aren't allowed to. It's the law."

"Oh."

Brother Nick shifted his bulk in his seat. "I've heard of cases like this before. This has to be nipped in the bud."

Dean wanted to snort. Now he was a *case*. "I'll talk to my

parents as soon as I get home," he said. "Anyway, my cousin's probably going to just forget the whole thing."

"That's not the point," Brother Nick said, and he laid out the point, the problem and the solution: the point was God's guidance, the problem was that we thought we knew better than God, and the solution was prayer, because no matter who our parents are, we have One Father, the Lord our God, and one Mother, Mary, and we have to trust in their divine love, and if we did, then all would be well.

It took Dean another ten minutes to extricate himself. He kept his forehead furrowed to convey seriousness while his brain whirled and whistled. So they wouldn't tell him anything. They weren't *allowed* to by law.

The law, huh?

It came to him in one backlit image, what he would do, how he would do it. He wouldn't need much. A car, of course. That was the hard part. Everything else was simple: a crowbar, a hammer and a flashlight for reading papers in the dark.

DISAPPEARING ACTS

Even the car turned out to be easy. He'd put it in his black book under "Disappearing Acts." Instructions: Say good night to your parents at the usual time. Lie in bed, fully clothed, until they go to sleep. Wait. Wait some more. Then down the stairs (avoid the creaky step). Pick up the key from the basket on top of the fridge. Fetch the bag you hid earlier in the basement. Open the door, slip out into the darkness. So long "Mom." So long "Dad."

He put the car in neutral and pushed it out of the garage. The crickets were making an awful racket. Upstairs, the windows were completely dark, but just to be sure, he pushed the car all the way to the end of the driveway. At the end of the road, he turned right. The streets were empty, the houses dark. The steel plant blazed like a house on fire, but everything else was silent and still. When he got to the highway, he braced his arms against the wheel and gunned her.

He'd left no note. Eventually, it would leak out. *Did you hear?* he imagined people saying, *Dean Turner is gone. Really? Where? No one knows. He just disappeared in the night. Stole his parents' car. Right out of the garage.* They'd all be jawing over it for weeks, trying to figure it all out, cooking up one wrong story after another.

He didn't care what they came up with, because he wasn't ever coming back.

Now you see him, now you don't. Common magic had its uses, after all.

Half the town must have known he was adopted. You couldn't just come home with a kid one day and say it was yours. It was old news to everyone except him. He had always thought people looked at him differently, too closely, at church, walking down Queen Street, at the doctor's office. All this time, he'd thought they were saying, *That's Dean Turner, who climbed out a window at school after the teacher locked him in the detention room. And when the teacher turned around, there he was, sitting right back in his seat.* Now he knew. All this time, they had been turning to each other, telegraphing their knowledge with raised eyebrows (*Did you know? Oh yeah, I knew*), while he blathered and boasted and carried on, oblivious.

YOU ARE NOW LEAVING SAULT STE. MARIE, a sign said.

"Good riddance," Dean replied.

Easiest thing he ever did, until the first complication: the car ran out of gas, a few minutes outside of Sudbury. The sun was just coming up, a pink stain on the horizon. He let the car sigh to a stop on the side of the road and made a mental note to add to his instructions: Before you leave, check the gas.

He fetched his bag and an empty jerry can from the trunk and headed to town, rehearsing the lines in his head. "My dad and I ran out of gas. Just down the road a bit. He said I should go on account of I'm young and my joints aren't acting up yet."

A delicate layer of frost covered the brown fields and the still-bare branches of trees along the road. He walked faster. From somewhere, a rooster crowed. The jerry can smacked his leg, and the hammer and chisel in his bag bit into his hip. The gas station was dark and silent. He kept going. In town, outside the Empire Hotel, he stopped at a row of cars and began pressing his face against windows, peering into the dark interiors. He saw nothing of interest until he came to a dark blue Packard: the owner had left a pair of leather gloves on the dashboard and a tweed cap on the passenger seat. Not his style, but useful additions to the currently empty disguise compartment of his bag of tricks. Dean slid in and fitted the cap onto his head. "Not bad, old chap," he said to the rear-view mirror. If only he had a pipe. He was wriggling his fingers into the leather gloves when he noticed the keys in the ignition. He shook his head. "Oh, that's very kind of you, but really, I couldn't." The key turned easily and the engine cleared its throat and began to murmur softly. "Well, if you insist," he said, shifting the car into gear. By now the sun had hoisted itself above the barren hills and was glaring at him through the windshield. Dean pulled down the sun visor, and an unopened packet of cigarettes fell into his lap. He smiled. "Don't mind if I do."

It was mid-morning when he reached North Bay, the early spring sun appearing as polish along the tops of everything. He parked the Packard outside Delilah's Grill and checked his face in the rear-view mirror: he was pale, with dark wells under his eyes and in the hollows of his cheeks. He smoothed back his hair and got out. Inside Delilah's, he ordered bacon and eggs, toast and chocolate milk. The waitress had fluffy blond hair pulled back from her face with a blue hairband. Her name tag said ROSE. She called him honey and said he looked tired. He said he had been driving all night and waited to see how she reacted. She didn't look surprised or say, "What? Aren't you kind of young to be driving all night by yourself?" She just nodded and asked if he wanted coffee as well. When she brought it, he told her he was on his way to meet his real mother for the first time. "She gave me up when I was a baby because she was too sick to look after me," he said. "But she's better now."

"Oh, that's terrible," Rose said, and she looked like she meant it. "What did she have?"

"TB," Dean said.

"And she's had it since you were a baby?"

"There were complications," Dean said.

"So you've never seen your real mother, that you can remember?"

"No," Dean said, and his eyes filled up with tears. Rose gave him an extra plate of toast on the house, and he wanted to leave a whole dollar tip, but then he thought better of it. He was on his own now; he needed to save his money.

His plan was to drive by the office and case the place in daylight, but out on the street, two policemen were standing beside the Packard. They appeared to be just talking, not looking specifically at the Packard, but Jesus! Cops were a complication he definitely did not need. Dean ducked into a stationery shop and pretended to study the pens in a display case near the window. The cops crossed the street and went into Delilah's Grill. Dean bought a newspaper and hurried out of the store and got into the car as fast as he could without appearing to run.

Turning off Main Street, he looked for a strip of quiet, respectable houses where a Packard would not be out of place. He finally parked under a tree at the end of a dead-end street lined with old stone houses, and set out with his newspaper and tweed cap to find a park bench. He needed to keep some distance between himself and the Packard until darkness fell. He also needed a nap.

❧

The front door was solid glass, but at the back of the building was a row of windows at eye level. He put on the leather gloves, lifted his hammer and chisel, and went to work. The idea was to separate the frame from the wall and slide the whole thing out, neatly, silently, cleverly. He wanted to go in like a ghost, disturb nothing, put the window back on his way out. Do it with style. After a half-dozen attempts, he'd made only a small incision in the wood; he was sweating now in spite of the cold, and his arms ached from holding the chisel at such a weird angle. *To hell with style*, he thought, and raised the hammer. The night shattered into a thousand sudden pieces. Using the chisel, he knocked out the jagged pieces of glass. Then he laid his jacket over the ledge and hoisted himself in.

He was in some kind of nurse's room—a cot covered with an olive green army blanket, a metal desk, a white chair. The night had reformed itself into a black, silent block. He stood very still, straining to hear above the noise of his own heart. At the sight of the bed, he was overcome with sleepiness. He wanted to lie down. Just for a minute. He had a blanket just like that on his bed at home. "No," he told himself sternly. "If you sleep now, you won't wake up till they find you here in the morning."

He headed for the red EXIT glow at the end of the hall and ran up the stairs to the fifth floor. He would start at the top, work his way down. The office doors were all open. He peeled off his gloves and pulled the flashlight out of his back pocket.

At first he was neat. He opened filing cabinets and shut them quietly, ran his hands lightly over folders. He loved the idea of leaving nothing ruffled or ajar, not a paper clip out of place. He would take what he came for and no one would know a thing. The window he couldn't help, but he'd leave a rock inside and they'd think some kids had done it.

He slid a folder out of a cabinet drawer and opened it. It was an adoption file, all right. *Mother: Marie Louise Pacquette. Age: 18 years. Promise of Marriage: No. Previous trouble: No. Putative father: James William Black. Unmarried. Is a declaration of paternity made? No.* It was dated December 4, 1959. Last year. Everything was recent, and some drawers had nothing but notices and government letters and letters from lawyers. He went faster, and as he went faster, he got messier, and as he got messier, he got madder. It was going to take all night to go through every cabinet and cupboard. He slammed drawers and didn't bother when they flew back open and jammed, folders sticking out.

He was coming out of the stairwell on the fourth floor when they caught him.

There were two of them, Doran and Parks. They were very casual, telling him how they'd been driving by and had seen the Packard and stopped to investigate. As they were calling it in, they just happened to look up and see a spot of light moving on the fifth floor. They were so friendly that he had to ask them, "Am I under arrest?"

They escorted him to the cruiser parked out front. Doran told him to watch his head as he got in. They hadn't bothered with cuffs. He thought briefly about making a run for it, but it would be so damn undignified if they jumped into their car and caught him before he got to the end of the road. At the station, they took his wallet and escorted him into an office and told him to wait while they contacted his parents. He was disappointed it wasn't a cell. A cell would make a much better story. Not much he could do about it, though, and anyway, the real story he had to worry about was the one that would explain why he had been rifling through files in the Children's Aid Society office at three in the morning. He could use part of the story he'd told Brother Nick: he was doing this for his cousin, guy just found out he was adopted and he was so upset he was threatening to kill himself, so Dean came down here to try to find something out. Yeah, it was wrong, bad, against the law, but for crying out loud, what would *you* do if you looked up from your egg salad sandwich to see your cousin practising noose knots with his school tie?

The door opened and a man came in with Frank's hammer and chisel. He said, "Dean Turner. Sergeant Cooper." At the sight of him, every thread and shred of Dean's story vanished down a deep hole. Dean recognized Cooper instantly as an inhabitant of the City of You Think This Is Funny? Town Motto: This Is Not Funny.

He had a colourless brush cut and bulging blue eyes in a big, florid face. He also had a way of pausing and blinking every few words. As if his words were so dense they needed an extra few seconds to be absorbed. He said Dean had committed very serious crimes (pause, blink) for a fifteen-year-old boy.

"But I didn't take anything," Dean said.

Blink. "You ever hear of breaking"—pause—"and entering?"

"Yeah, but people usually break and enter to steal something. What was I going to steal in an office building?"

Blink. Blink. "You tell me."

"Actually, sir, my question was rhetorical," Dean said. "Translated roughly, it means there is nothing to steal in an office building. Hence, breaking and entering for the purpose of theft would be null and void."

"You think this is funny?" Cooper pushed back in his chair and aimed his hard-boiled egg eyes at Dean. "Let me tell you why I do not think this is as funny as you do. Charge one: breaking and entering." Pause. "Charge two: grand theft auto, two counts." Blink. "Charge three—"

"Grand theft auto?"

"Your parents' car, which they told us you took and which we assume you left outside of Sudbury before—"

"I don't think you can charge a person with stealing their own family car," Dean said.

"—*before* you picked up the Packard which was reported stolen yesterday morning."

"What Packard?"

"You didn't steal the Packard from outside a hotel in Sudbury?"

"No, sir."

Blink. "Then how'd you get here?"

"I hitchhiked."

"And the thief who stole the Packard just happened to leave it outside the office you broke into?"

Dean shrugged. "Weird, huh?"

Cooper gestured to the tools. "You steal these?"

"No."

Blink. "You just happened to find them under a smashed window?"

"I brought them from home."

"For the purpose of breaking and entering."

For the purpose of sticking them up your ass, Dean thought. A wall of fatigue rose up, and he crossed his arms and settled down behind it. This conversation was over.

Cooper left the room and Dean slid down in the chair. "Don't show weakness," he told himself, but he was tired in a way he'd never been before. He was tired of all his thoughts, and they were tired of themselves. They just lay there in his head, limp and flat and disconnected from everything. If Cooper came back and said Dean was going to spend the rest of his life in prison, he'd shrug and shuffle off to his cell.

He must have fallen asleep, or into that grey in-between place, because when Cooper came back, he could see by the splashes of light on the floor that it was much later. Cooper stood there waiting for Dean to look up. Dean could feel him blinking.

"Your parents just got here."

"They're not my parents," Dean said.

"Really? Who are they, then?"

They're liars, Dean thought. He didn't answer.

"Well, they sure drove a long way for someone else's kid."

Dean said, "I was adopted."

"I gathered that," Cooper said, and sat down at the desk.

"Why?" Dean straightened in the chair, alert again. "Did they say something?"

"No," Cooper said. "But why else would you be going through files at the Children's Aid?" He opened a drawer, fiddled around with something, closed the drawer. "I was adopted myself," he said.

Dean smirked. "Sure."

Cooper said, "It's true. My cousin told me. We were arguing over something. I was eleven. I said I was going to tell my dad, and she said, 'That's not your dad, anyway. You were adopted.'"

Dean studied Cooper's face. "Did you believe her?"

"No. But I went in and asked them. My mother said no and my father said yes. So I knew it was true."

Wow, Dean thought. That was as bad as *What kind of talk is that?* "Did you ever find your real parents?"

"I did."

Dean leaned forward. All his thoughts had come awake, and hope was flickering and humming just off to the side. "How? Where?"

Cooper was playing with a paper clip. He straightened it out and then bent it into a V. "Where did I find them? I'll tell you where I found them."

The hope flickered out.

"I found my mother in the kitchen, making my lunch for

school. I found my father in the backyard, fixing my bike. I found them every day when I came in the door. Every time I sat down at the table to eat the food they had bought and cooked for me."

Dean slid back down in the chair.

"Look at me, son," Cooper said, and Dean looked up, his face aflame.

"I may be adopted, but I sure as hell am not your son." Although as soon as he said it, he realized Cooper could very well be his father. Just about any male past the age of thirty on the whole goddamn planet could be his father.

Cooper straightened the paper clip again and it snapped in two. He placed the pieces carefully on the blotter. "I know you're thinking about the woman who gave birth to you and the man who made her pregnant, and you're wondering who they are and why they didn't keep you."

Wrong, Dean thought. *I'm thinking that you are the biggest ass I've ever encountered in my long and varied history of encountering asses*.

"But the truth is, those people out there in the waiting room, they're the ones who wanted you. They're the ones who are bringing you up. They're the ones who didn't sleep a wink after they found out you were gone."

Dean turned to look. He saw only their backs, but he recognized them immediately. His mother's wide back, his father's thin one. His mother's dark brown hat. His father's battered grey fedora. A feeling of tenderness and longing opened in him, and his throat and nose itched furiously. He averted his face. He didn't want to bawl in front of Cooper so that Cooper could later claim it as victory. *Yep, finally got through to the kid. Had him in tears by the end of it*. The wetness in his eyes had nothing to do with Cooper.

"Think of what you're putting them through," Cooper said.

A surge of anger drowned the longing. *Think of what they put me through*, Dean wanted to shout.

"The thing is," Cooper went on, "those other folks, they aren't anything to you. They gave you up because they had to, and that's the whole story. It wasn't personal."

Dean stared at him. It wasn't *personal*? The people who were supposed to want you for the most indispensable, irreducible, unquestionable reason of all—because you were their own flesh and blood—*didn't* want you and they gave you away to people who, when they saw your true colours, didn't much want you either, and it wasn't *personal*? Dean swallowed hard. "Yes, sir," he said. "I understand now."

Cooper missed the sarcasm completely. He nodded and stood up. "You think you want to know, but trust me, you don't. They keep those records closed for good reason."

"Oh, very good, sir. You're very wise, sir."

Cooper glared at him. "There's no need to get snarky with me, young man."

As he was closing the door, Dean called out, "It's not personal."

He watched Cooper talk with his parents in the hallway. Cooper had probably been the kind of kid his parents wanted. A homework-doing, Mouseketeer-cheering, old-lady-helping kid who didn't have to always be showing off or playing the fool. A colourless kid who would stand between them at church and think good thoughts instead of wondering how hard it was to get into the sacristy and whether the wine in there would be worth the effort. Then they were walking towards him, Cooper in the middle, and Dean remembered the photograph of Vera and another woman and a baby between them. There'd been another birth certificate. *Mother's name: Grace Turner.* A relative he'd never heard of, a woman hidden in a closet for having a baby before she got married.

His mother.

UNDERCOVER

He wouldn't put it in his book, because he hadn't developed it himself, but he knew how to make another person disappear. Remove photos of said person from all albums (don't forget to check cardboard box of miscellaneous pictures). Go through the house and collect personal effects: clothes, shoes, monogrammed gloves, alphabet key rings. Check books for the person's name written in fading ink on the flyleaf. Shake out books just in case the person left something pressed between the pages: a letter, an address written on a slip of paper. Never, under any circumstances, mention the person. That wouldn't be hard once all physical traces had been removed. And even removing the physical evidence was probably not so hard after you got rid of the actual person.

He had no idea how they'd accomplished that part. He could only say that there was nothing of Grace Turner in the house.

Their only oversight had been leaving the photo and the birth certificate in the box in the closet. And they'd corrected that.

He kept his investigations to himself. It wasn't difficult. When adults wanted you to be something badly enough, they'd take anything as a confirmation that you were becoming it. They wanted you to be a doctor, you got 87 on a biology quiz, and bing, bang, boom, you were on your way to medical school. Never mind that Mrs. Agnew had been using the same biology tests for five hundred years and anyone could get a copy with the answers for a quarter and, in fact, you yourself were selling the copies this year. Or they wanted you to have settled down, and weeks passed where nothing happened except you came home and did your homework, and on Saturday you raked Mrs. May's lawn and she sent you over to her sister Mrs. Murphy's house to do some yardwork, and lo! you had settled down. Never mind that you were undercover the whole time, taking notes and cracking codes. They wanted you to put this adoption business behind you; you said you would, and be-bop-a-loo-bop, you had put it all behind you.

He had slept in the back seat all the way home from North Bay, waking to the crunch of Vera closing the passenger door. For a few moments, it was just him and Frank listening to the engine click and sigh. Frank took off his glasses and began cleaning one lens with a handkerchief. "It's hard for her to talk about," he said.

Hard for her *to talk about?* Dean thought. *Think of what you're putting* them *through. How could you do this to* us*?*

Frank looked at him in the rear-view mirror. "We didn't tell you because we thought it would be better for you not to know. We couldn't have children of our own. We tried, but she had to have an operation, and—"

Dean didn't care about any of that. "Where did I come from?" he asked. "Who are my real parents? Where are they now?"

Frank breathed on the other lens and began to polish it. Dean wanted to grab the glasses and throw them out the window. He was reaching for the door handle when Frank spoke up. "The woman couldn't keep you. She was young and not married. That's all I can tell you."

"That's all you know or that's all you can tell me?"

"That's all we know."

Dean's face tightened into a mask. They should know better than to lie to an expert.

Frank said, "The best thing is to just put it out of your mind. Don't let it be a monkey on your back."

"Fine," Dean said. He knew how to play that game. He got out of the car. "I'm going in."

Vera was in the kitchen, breaking eggs into a mixing bowl. He opened the refrigerator and stood peering in. From the corner of his eye, he could see that she had put down her wooden spoon and was looking at him. Even though it was too late, because he was on his own now and there was almost nothing she could say to change that, he waited. The clock ticked; on the stove, the coffee pot began to burble.

"Don't stand with the fridge open," she said. "And wash your hands."

It was Mrs. May who told him. "Grace Turner? Why, that's your aunt. Your father's sister. She went to work down south." Her sister Mrs. Murphy told him even more. Sometimes, he was sure he was two steps away from unravelling the whole thing. Other times, what seemed like a brain-swelling, throat-choking revelation shrank into some scrap of common information by the time he got to the next clue. The hardest part about being undercover was that he had to pretend he knew nothing and wanted to know even less. It took him almost two years to put it all together.

But Cooper might have been right about one thing: *You think you want to know. But you don't.*

He had started his detective work by knocking on Mrs. May's door and asking if she had any yardwork he could do. She had babysat him when he was a kid, on the rare occasions Frank and Vera went out. Her children were all grown up and her husband had died years ago. She would be lonely, he thought. She would welcome the chance to talk. And she had to know something; she'd lived at the end of the road, in the small white house with blue shutters, for years. But she turned out to be discreet; she'd stop mid-sentence and say that she had already told him too much, after spending twenty minutes telling him nothing at all.

He had much better luck with Mrs. Murphy, who lived in a much bigger house with a bigger yard across town. The sisters had nothing in common except that they were both fat, and not even that was the same. Mrs. May was the soft kind of fat and called him "Dean, dear" and always sounded breathless. Mrs. Murphy was the hard kind of fat, addressed him as "Boy" and had a voice like a can of nails. Her house had a complicated system of eaves and gutters and mouldy waterspouts, and there was no one to help her with the upkeep. Her children were ingrates, her neighbours were criminals, and her husband was dead—poisoned, Dean was fairly sure, by Mrs. Murphy herself, although a cast-iron frying pan over the head was not out of the question.

"You just do your work there and don't listen to her," Frank had advised the first morning Dean set out on his bike. But it was impossible not to listen: she talked constantly, and swore more inventively than he did.

It was easy to get her to talk. All he had to do was mention a person and she went off like a firecracker. *Father Croce*. Father Croce was a drunk, and Dean couldn't tell her he hadn't smelled the goddamn drink on him. *Father Dougherty*. The principal of

Dean's school had his finger up his arse. (He agreed with her on that point, even though he wasn't sure what it meant.) *Dr. McCabe*. Dr. McCabe had been screwing his secretary all these years, and Mrs. McCabe knew it, but that didn't stop her from flouncing around in her silk this and her fur that.

Vera. Well, Vera certainly did well for herself, considering what she came from. Vera's father had been a drunk, hawked everything he owned for the drink and even sold the pots and pans when there was nothing else left. Vera's sister had married a man just like him, only he was well off, so she kept her pots, but Vera got lucky. What was Dean doing with the leaves over there? He was going to walk through them and scatter them all over hell's half-acre. *Frank*. Now there was a sad story. Frank's mother had died of creeping paralysis, and Frank's father had died of septic shock. And Frank had to bring up his younger sister, Grace—

"My dad has a sister? Really?" Dean said. "He never talks about her."

"Well, I'm not surprised."

Dean stopped raking. "What do you mean?"

"She got knocked up and had to go down south. Why are you holding the rake like that?"

Dean bent down and pretended to free something from the end of the rake. If she got onto the subject of his crappy workmanship, he might never be able to steer her back.

"Where down south?"

"Oh, I can't remember. It was a long time ago. Peterborough or Kingston."

"And then what happened to her?"

"How should I know? I had enough worries of my own with that lout I was married to."

"She, Grace, wasn't married?"

"Why do you think she went down south?"

"Who was it . . . the father, I mean?"

"What do I look like, the FBI? Watch what you're doing there. If I wanted the leaves smeared around, I'd let the wind do it for free."

When he'd tried pressing Mrs. May for more information, she said, "Oh, I'm not one to gossip, Dean, dear. You'd have to ask your mother and father about Grace. She was a sweet girl. She used to pick flowers over in the field where Donaldson's store is now. I hardly remember her."

But Mrs. Murphy said, "I remember her, all right. She was soft in the head."

He almost dropped the rake. "What do you mean?"

"What do you think I mean? Are you soft in the head yourself?"

Dean scowled at the ground. "I mean, was she crazy? Stupid?" He didn't know what he would do if Grace turned out to be retarded or something. *Those records are sealed for a reason.*

"No, no." Mrs. Murphy waved him back to work impatiently. "She was just *off.*"

He held on to the "just." Just off. Like milk. You could still drink it. It had just been left out too long. He started to ask about the baby, but Mrs. Murphy said she'd seen enough of his leaf-arranging, thank you very much; the Pronger boy two streets over did a much better job.

At home, he searched for her again and again in the bookcases and the cupboards, in between cookbooks and among the spice jars. She had been here. She had grown up here with Frank, who was not his father but his mother's brother. She had touched these walls and sat under these lights and walked through these doors. But they'd erased every trace of her, or else she'd taken everything with her. She had left nothing of herself behind. Except him.

He waited several weeks after Mrs. Murphy dismissed him before he brought up her name to Frank. They were in the basement, painting two wooden benches Frank had built for the front lawn. Dean said, "Mrs. Murphy says I have an aunt named Grace." He watched Frank carefully.

Frank smoothed another band of dark green paint onto the pale wood. "My sister," he said.

"Where does she live?"

"Down south. She went down there to work during the war. She got a job in a big clock factory. Watch what you're doing there, Dean. You're dripping everywhere."

"How come she never visits us?"

"She has her life down there, I guess."

"But she's your sister."

"Well, to tell you the truth, she and Vera didn't get along very well. They were like chalk and cheese."

"Does she ever write to you? Does she know about me?" Dean asked. His hand was shaking. He put down his brush.

The door to the basement opened and Vera called down, "Frank, bring me up some potatoes."

Frank said, "Bring your mother some potatoes. And Dean, don't mention Grace to her. It upsets her."

I'll bet it does, Dean thought. In the root cellar, he counted out potatoes. All the pieces of a new plan were whirling around in his head. He didn't have to break open sealed records; he only had to find a big clock factory in southern Ontario, and how many big clock factories could there be?

KNOCK AND YOU SHALL FIND

He went to Marie, the bank teller Frank and Vera usually went to. "Hello, Dean," she said, smiling warmly. "We haven't seen you in here in a while. And you used to be one of our regulars!" This was true: they used to bring him in once a week, dressed up in his church clothes, his hair slicked back. Vera had often pressed a spit-dampened handkerchief to his chin and cheek at the last minute. What would people think if he went into the bank looking like a ragamuffin? (*Sit down. Be quiet. Stop that. What would people think?*)

And all this time, what had people been thinking? There goes Dean Turner. His mother was odd, off, something wrong in the head, his father was unknown, name Not Given, a drifter, a grifter, a butcher, a baker, a candlestick maker, a thing that went bump in the night.

"I think the last time I saw you, you needed all those nickels, remember? For the school bingo? That was a couple of years ago. Are you still doing that?"

"No, that was a one-time thing."

"How's your mother, Dean?"

Did she know? Maybe every time she saw him with Frank and Vera, she wondered. She was waiting, like everyone else, to see how he would turn out, what would show through, the face of his real mother, the bad blood of his father.

"She's still sick," he said. "My father was looking after her, but now he's starting to come down with it."

"Oh, the poor things."

Dean pulled the cheque from his front pocket. "He's down at Maniaco's, getting chicken to make soup. He sent me to cash this. Should we wait for him, though?"

"No, no," Marie said. "Did he sign it? As long as he signed it."

Dean turned the cheque over. *Frank Turner*, small, neat n's and r's. His best work yet. Marie took the cheque and stamped it. "Did he give you his bank book, Dean?"

"No, he left it on top of the fridge. He was going to go back for it, but he wanted to get the soup made before my mom woke up."

Marie nodded sympathetically. "It's hard when the woman of the house is sick, isn't it? Everything is topsy-turvy." She counted out the bills. "Now, how are you going to carry this down to Maniaco's?"

"Oh, I have my wallet," Dean said, showing her.

Marie laughed. "Well, won't you feel like Mr. Rockefeller for two and a half blocks!"

Dean smiled. Maybe she didn't know. It was possible. The town wasn't that small.

"You give your parents my best wishes," Marie said.

"I will," Dean promised.

When she called him back to the counter, his knees wobbled. Had she compared signatures? But she only wanted to give him a pen with the bank logo printed in smeary ink: YOUR BUSINESS IS OUR BUSINESS. He put it in his pocket with his Rockefeller-thick wallet.

He wore his black winter coat over his school trousers and white shirt, and packed his tie and grey sweater into his rucksack. This time, he took the bus. On the bus, you were just a guy going to visit your Aunt Jean and Uncle Walter, or going down south to look for work like so many people before you. On the bus, you were unremarkable, unidentifiable if anyone asked, just one of several male passengers of average height, all in dark coats. *Now, did he have a hat? Jeez, I can't remember.* Cars were trouble; they led to cops. A rule for his book. He'd never have anything to do with a stolen car again.

He took the night bus so he wouldn't have to pay for a room. There was no way to know how long Frank's paycheque would have to last. Also, the less of it he spent, the more of the original amount he would have when he was ready to pay it back. *Dear Frank and Vera,* he would write. *Here is the money I borrowed. I wouldn't have had to do it this way if I had my own money, which is in a bank account I don't even know the number of. Speaking of that, you can keep that money as payment for all you have spent on my room and board all these years. I appreciate everything you have done for me. Yours truly, Dean Turner.* He fell asleep in the darkest part of the night and awoke as the bus was lumbering off the highway into the town of Peterborough at dawn. He'd left the Soo in winter and arrived down here in spring. The snow was gone, and tiny buds glowed on the branches. The main street had a small square with benches and a clock tower, and stores with blue-and-white-striped awnings. They were still shut up, but beside the bus depot, a coffee shop was open. In the men's room, he rinsed his face and ran his wet hands through his hair.

He ordered coffee, black, and eggs, sunny side up, but he couldn't eat. The coffee stripped his tongue and turned to acid in his stomach. The waitress told him how to get to the clock factory. If he was looking for work, though, he was probably out of luck; they weren't hiring. "I'm going to meet somebody," he said. "Grace Turner. Maybe you know her? She's been living down here for a while."

The waitress shook her head. "Never heard of her."

But that didn't mean anything. In the Soo, the waitress at the Adanac Diner wouldn't know every single person who worked at the steel plant. Grace Turner might be a person who didn't eat in diners. Frank and Vera never did: why pay an arm and a leg for something you could just as easily and far more cheaply make at home? He hoped she wasn't like Frank and Vera, though. He hoped she was more like him.

Outside, he followed the waitress's directions: down to the clock tower, walk to the river and follow the road up the hill until he came to the factory. "You'll know it when you see it," she said.

At home, the light was still hard and cold; here, it was lemon-coloured and smelled of earth. He liked the look of the place, like a holiday town with those awnings and the benches. There were more people out on the street now, men and women in coats and hats, a police officer (Dean nodded to him politely), a few cars. He kept his head up as he walked, scanning faces. His mother was here somewhere. She lived on one of these streets. She took her paycheque to the red brick bank on the corner, shopped across the street at the department store. Maybe she was walking to work right now. All he had was a faint image of a faded photograph; he couldn't bring the face to mind. But he believed it was the kind of memory Brother Nick had told them about, where you cannot produce the answer independently but you can recognize it in a list of options. In a multiple choice test, he would know her when he saw her.

He recognized the factory from the picture in the library book. The librarian who had been suspicious of his adoption project had shown considerably less interest in his essay on industry in Ontario, waving him over to a shelf of cardboard-bound reports with barely a glance. He found Clockworks in Peterborough almost immediately. But Mrs. Murphy had said Peterborough or Kingston, so he called the operator: there was no clock factory in Kingston. And now here he was. Just inside the factory entrance was a wall of clocks. He was startled by one with a pale blue face and delicate black hands: it was the same as the clock hanging above the sink at home.

He found that he was counting the clocks on the wall.

You don't have to, he told himself, putting his hand against the metal door. *You can go back. Or go in. It's up to you.*

He hadn't thought of what he would say, beyond the initial question. He had been expecting her to know him instantly, and only now did he wonder what he would do if she said, "Yes, I'm Grace Turner," and then just stood there like she was waiting for him to produce a telegram or a ticket. He needed to give her a clue, something like, *I can see why you might not recognize me, it's been seventeen years*. Or even *I'm from Sault Ste. Marie*.

That's all he'd give her. If she didn't recognize him, he would never forgive her, but at least he wouldn't be standing in front of her stammering about a locked box in the closet.

Inside, he approached a glass-fronted office. Behind the large window, a woman sat at a desk, surrounded by filing cabinets. He studied her profile: her grey hair was coiled in a braid around her head, and she wore wire-rimmed glasses. She sat straighter than he had ever thought it was possible for a human being to sit. She hadn't looked up from her typewriter, and he hadn't knocked on the glass, but she called out, "Can I help you?"

"I'm looking for someone," Dean said, and felt the words bounce off the glass. The woman kept punching keys. He bent his head so that he could speak directly into the slit at the bottom of the window. "I'm looking for someone. One of your employees. A woman—a lady—her name is—"

"You're getting fingerprints on my glass," the woman said.

Did she have eyes in the side of her head? He pulled his hand away from the window.

"Her name is Grace—"

The phone rang and the woman picked it up. "This is Mrs. Thurman," she said. "No. Yes. That is correct. You are welcome. Goodbye."

Dean straightened up, cleared his throat. "Uh, ma'am?"

Mrs. Thurman pulled the sheet of paper from her typewriter and held it up. Satisfied, she laid it beside the machine.

"Her name is Grace Turner? The lady I'm looking for? She works here." The woman was rolling another sheet of paper into her machine and still gave no sign that she could hear him.

He tried to slide the window open all the way, but it was clamped with something. "Hello? I'm looking for Grace Turner. It's a—an emergency. Her brother is sick."

"Hands, please," the woman said.

She *could* see out the side of her head.

"Is she here today?"

"She is not."

His mouth opened, but no sound emerged. He had found her. She wasn't here today, but she was *here*.

"Well, can you tell me where she lives?"

"I cannot."

"But it's an emergency. Her brother is very sick. I came all the way from Sault Ste. Marie."

"Then I am sorry for you, young man. But I cannot tell you where she lives."

Anger, hot and sour, flooded up from his gut, past the hard knot in his throat, and coated his coffee-burnt tongue. *Easy*, he told himself, and tried to breathe normally.

"I'm sorry to trouble you. I can see you're quite busy, but why can't you tell me?"

"She doesn't work here. She hasn't worked here since the war."

Dean dropped his head, struggling to clear his throat of the painful blockage. He had lost her again. She'd been here behind the wall of clocks, and as soon as he asked for her, she'd disappeared. Just as she'd been hidden in a box all those years until the moment he had discovered her. The closer he got, the farther away she slipped.

But this woman had known her. This woman had worked with her, had probably seen her every day for years. She was real, Grace Turner, and she had been here. "Do you know where she works now?"

"I do not."

"But do you know where she lives, then? Does she live in the same place? Could you check your files?"

"We wouldn't have those files now. It's been fifteen years since she worked here," the woman said.

"But I need to find her," Dean said. The anger was gone, replaced by a dark, shameful urge to weep. "It's an emergency."

The woman frowned at her typewriter. Dean lifted his hands and pressed them against the window. They were good and sweaty. He smeared them up and around. Behind the now streaky glass, she got up, fetched a small spray bottle and a square of newspaper and came to the window. She widened the opening and passed them through. She said, "Ruth Ellis's boarding house. Wellington Street. That is all I can tell you, because that is all I know. Now I'm going to ask you to please remove your fingerprints from my window, and then we will say good day."

"Whoa, whoa. Ruth Who? Wellington Street. What's that?"

"Last known address."

"But does she live there now?"

"I don't believe so. Window, please."

He sprayed the window and wiped it down. She took back the spray bottle and paper and said, "Thank you."

He got to the door before he realized he didn't have a street number. "Excuse me, but do you have the address? On Wellington Street?"

She was back at her desk, rolling another sheet of paper into the evil black typewriter. She said, "Knock and the door shall be opened."

"*What?*"

"Seek and ye shall find. Good *day*, young man."

"Good day," he said, and added under his breath, "old bat."

He found it right away. It was the first house he went to, a large house of orange brick with freshly painted trim behind a hedge that was all covered in burlap. He opened the mailbox at the gate: two letters addressed to Miss R. Ellis, one to Marcy Cole. On the veranda, he examined the knocker: a snake swallowing itself. The wind lifted, and from the rafters above him came the sound of small bells; he craned his neck and saw a row of wind chimes. He grabbed the knocker and rapped sharply. Just then, he noticed the plaque underneath. KNOCK AND THE DOOR SHALL BE OPENED. Maybe this was the town motto. A plump young woman with long brown ringlets answered the door. Ruth Ellis, she said, was in the hospital, but when he said the next name, her face lit up.

"Grace Turner! Oh, she moved to Toronto a long time back."

He wanted to collapse right there on the porch. Toronto. Again she'd slipped away. Still, this was another person who knew her. "But you knew her? She lived here?"

"Oh, yes. Only I didn't know her, of course. She was before my time. But Ruth keeps in touch. She keeps in touch with all the women of the house. She'll have that address in here somewhere. Come in and I'll try to find it."

It was the weirdest house he'd ever been in. He was afraid to move for fear of knocking over a pile of books or bumping a picture off the wall, and it wouldn't be an ordinary picture, either, but a photograph of three people, men, women, who could tell, whirling around in white skirts and tall hats, their heads thrown back, or a painting of a blue-faced man with an extra eye in his forehead, wearing a skirt and playing a flute.

"I'm sorry," said the woman, looking up from a drawer. "How did you say you knew Grace?"

"I'm her—nephew," he said. "My father lost touch with her, and I was passing through Peterborough and thought I'd look her up."

The woman kept talking to him while she rummaged through a cabinet. Her name was Marcy, she was a teacher, like Ruth used to be, and in fact, Ruth used to be her teacher, oh, a long time back, and what a teacher she was, she had opened their eyes to the world, all their eyes to all the strange, precarious, blinding beauty of the world, and now dear Ruth was laid up in hospital and they didn't know—they didn't think—here Marcy had to stop looking for the address and begin to look for a handkerchief. When she regained possession of herself, she offered him coffee and strawberry-rhubarb pie, milk and chocolate cookies, a bowl of soup. She couldn't find the address.

"I know it was Baldwin Street—that much I do remember—because I mailed letters for Ruth, and I remember Baldwin Street, Toronto, clear as day."

She said she would write it down for him. She did not remember the number, she was sorry.

"It's okay," he said, taking the paper. "I'm getting used to that."

"I'll ask Ruth. When I go to the hospital this afternoon," Marcy said. "You call back this evening and I'll have it for you. If Ruth's awake. Sometimes she's not. Sometimes she's—" Marcy broke off and cried quietly into her handkerchief.

Dean said he would come back later. As he was leaving, he said, "But did Ruth ever say anything to you about Grace? About her being—you know, off?"

"Off to where?"

"No. Off like odd or something? Not very smart?"

"What a strange question. No. Not at all. Grace started her own business, I believe."

He gave her his most brilliant smile. "Thank you! Thank you so much." He flew back through the town, over to the bus depot. He had no time to wait for street numbers. *Knock and you shall find*, he said to himself. "One ticket to Toronto," he said to the clerk.

He fell asleep on the bus and dreamed he was standing outside a house on Baldwin Street. He knocked and a voice from inside called, "Who is it?" "I'm here to see my mother," he tried to say, but his mouth wasn't working properly. "Muther," he said. "Buther." He knew with inexorable dream logic that he was at the wrong house. At the next house, no one answered his knock, but the handle turned freely in his hand. He went in and he was in his living room at home, the same brown carpet, the same reading lamp, Vera knitting in the armchair, Frank on the sofa reading the paper. From deep in the stillness of the house, a clock ticked. He had gone home by mistake.

He opened his eyes. The bus had pulled into a station, and a stout woman in a rust-coloured coat was arguing with the driver about her ticket. Dean squirmed in his seat and peered out the window. In a parking lot across the street, a man in a suit got out of a gleaming white Cadillac and ran around to open the back door. A huge puff of white skirt billowed out, followed by the rest of the bride. Her hair was a dark three-tiered cake decorated with thin loops and bands of icing. Dean watched the man and his cake-headed bride walk up the steps to the banquet hall. He hadn't thought about this possibility: Grace, married. She could very well be married, with other children, kids that she'd kept, that had turned out. Her husband wouldn't know about the baby she'd left behind. And now Dean was going to show up on her doorstep and tell everything.

She wouldn't want to see him. She would try to close the door, beg him to go away. "It's nobody," she would call out over her shoulder, and when she turned back to him, her voice would go hard and cold. "I don't know you. You're nothing to me. Get out of my sight."

He wouldn't be able to bear it. He would throw himself off a bridge.

He wiped his mouth with his sleeve. It might not happen like that, he told himself. Her hands might fly to her cheeks. She might cry out and welcome him in. She would tell him that she'd waited so long. There would be an explanation, a reason why she had left him there in Sault Ste. Marie with his aunt and uncle. It would all make sense, and she would put her arms around him and say, "At last, at last." She would introduce him to her husband, and he would shake Dean's hand firmly and warmly. She would say, "Come and meet your brothers and sisters." They would be shy at first, but then they would come forward and want to show him their rooms and their stuff.

Or he would not find her at all. And then what? He didn't know what. He was too tired to think about then what.

Outside, fields were flowing by in the dying afternoon light. He was thirsty and hungry. He wanted to eat three of Vera's golden butter tarts, drink two glasses of cold milk and then lie down in his own bed, in his own room, in his own house. No. What he really wanted was to go back in time: he wanted to know nothing. What you didn't know wouldn't hurt you, unless you found out that you didn't know it. Then it was like a wildcat trapped inside you, slashing and scratching and howling to be let out. Nor did letting it out help: it just clawed and bit you and made a mess of things. He wanted to go back to the day of the light bulb trick. He would realize that Wharton was on to him and he'd substitute another trick. He'd go home with Wharton's money in his pocket and wait for his mother to get back from Mrs. May's. He wouldn't open a box or steal a car or forge a signature on a cheque. He'd be Dean Turner, son of Frank and Vera. He'd ask them no questions, they'd tell him no lies.

BALDWIN STREET

The plan was to buy a map at the bus station kiosk and sit down with a bottle of Coke and figure out where he was and how far he was from Baldwin Street, but as soon as he stepped off the bus into a cloud of exhaust, he was jostled into a fast-moving crowd and carried along for blocks. The city soared up all around him in walls of concrete and glass and stone. People poured out of buildings, pooled at corners, trickled down side streets. He tried to memorize the street names—Yonge, Queen, Bay, University—so that he could find his way back, but then he stopped thinking and just walked and looked. He could feel the city's pulse in his veins. It pulsed with traffic and with something else. Everything was lit up like a Christmas tree, even though Christmas was four months gone: everywhere something twinkled or blinked or buzzed, inviting him to use Kodak film, have a coffee, buy tickets, cut keys, visit the future, drink a milk-shake, come in and see the show: *The Guns of Navarone* or *West*

Side Story or *Splendor in the Grass* or five others he had never heard of. Every movie in the world was playing here.

The city pulsed and now he was pulsing too.

From around the corner, a man appeared with a wooden signboard around his neck. He stopped in front of Dean and rapped the top of his board, where the writing started off huge—*THE DAY OF THE LORD IS AT HAND* and then got smaller and crazier until Dean couldn't make out anything. Something was coming and it wasn't good, was the gist of it. The man rapped the board again and Dean said, "Yeah, yeah, I got it." The man moved on.

A young woman in a short fur jacket walked past him, and then turned and looked him up and down. He winked, and to his amazement, she winked back. Then she, too, was gone.

A woman and a man stumbled out of a doorway, laughing. The man caught the woman's hand and spun her around. Her lipstick was a dark, glossy red.

Finally, Dean slipped out of the stream of walkers and leaned against a wall, his rucksack forming a cushion against the cold concrete. He had no idea how to get back to the bus terminal, and he didn't have a map. It was probably too late to start searching, anyway. He would find a place to stay for the night. A hotel. A nice one. He'd have a shower, order a steak dinner, get a good night's sleep. Why not? He had the money, and he couldn't stand against a wall all night. Although here, he probably could. In the Soo, if you were propped up outside a building for too long, someone would want to know who you were waiting for and who you were related to and if it was hard work, heh heh, holding up the building. Here, no one even glanced at him. People moved at a fierce clip. He searched faces as they passed him, but no one except the woman who'd winked met his eye. Their eyes were fixed on some distant goal. They surged across intersections and disappeared, replaced by the next wave.

The sky was dark now. There were no stars, but who needed pinprick stars in this electric blaze? Dean finally pushed himself off the wall and stepped off a curb, and a car slammed on its brakes, stopping not an inch from him and honking long and loud. The man behind the wheel rolled down his window and leaned out. Dean patted the hood of the car. "I'm all right," he told the man. "You didn't hit me."

"Eejit!" the man said. "Get the hell out of my way or I will."

Eejit! Dean burst into laughter. He did a quick jig and tipped an imaginary hat. The man merely rolled up his window and drove on. Dean looked around: people had *seen*, but no one was *watching*. No one would report to someone who would pass it along to someone else who would mention to Vera and Frank that Dean had been seen acting up downtown, holding up traffic and dancing around like a leprechaun. He was in the City of Toronto. Town Motto: Act Up All You Want, Just Stay the Hell Out of Our Way.

He turned and found himself on a quiet road. The pulse of the city was harder to feel here. He stopped at the next intersection to read the street sign.

God*damn*. It was impossible.

Baldwin Street.

He wasn't ready to find it, but he turned left onto Baldwin Street anyway. His feet kept lifting and planting themselves. They stopped, rotated him a quarter of a turn and dragged him up the walkway of the first house. When he reached the door, there was nothing to do but knock. No one answered; the house was in complete darkness. He tried the next house. A man in an undershirt with a halo of greying hair shook his head. No one here by that name. At the next house, a tiny elderly woman answered. "Other side of the street," she said.

A sudden plummeting. He reached for the banister to

steady himself. "Are you sure?" he said. "Grace Turner from Sault Ste. Marie?"

"Oh, I don't know where she's from, but Grace Turner lives on the other side. Now is it 67? I think so."

His stomach was cramping painfully, like he had swallowed pins and staples and nails.

At the other end of the street, the houses were joined together in twos. Number 67 was dark, but he went up the stairs anyway and stood on the veranda. It was clean and empty—not a plant or a chair or even a welcome mat. He knocked, and jumped at the sound of a window sliding open. He almost bolted, then realized it had come from the house next door. Someone there was trying to find a radio station. A phone rang. A dog started barking. Another dog started barking. Dean knocked more loudly. Next door, a man yelled, "Aunt Theresa! Phone!"

Dean knocked again. "Hello?" he called. He put his hand on the doorknob and twisted. Locked. Next door, the man yelled louder for Aunt Theresa. A woman yelled back, "Tell him I'm not home."

"Why doncha tell him yourself?"

"Ha ha. Close the window, Danny, it's freezing in here. And don't tell your mother I took this call."

Yes, for god's sake, close the window, Dean thought. He put his ear to the door: nothing. (Although it was hard to tell with the racket next door.) He leaned as far as he could over the railing to look into the front room, but he could see nothing except curtains and the back of a sofa. Kneeling, he lifted the mail slot and peered through.

No use. Not home. Again.

Back on the sidewalk, Dean appraised the house. No glimmer of light came from any part of it. The front door of the next house opened, and two dogs bounded out and went straight for

Dean. He froze, and they circled him, barking happily, all aquiver with excitement. "They won't bite," someone called. Dean looked up. A tall young man with dark blond hair was coming down the walkway. "Sorry," he said. "They're complete lunatics. My mother rescued them from the pound years ago, and they still can't believe their good fortune." He scooped up the squirming dogs, one under each arm. "I saw you from the window. Are you here about the guitar?"

Dean said, "No." He could hardly hear himself. "No," he said more loudly. "I was actually looking for the person next door."

"The Hanleys? They're at the hospital."

"Will they be back soon, do you think?"

The guy shook his head. "Probably not. Their kid has polio. We've hardly seen them the last couple of weeks." The guy looked at him more closely. "You okay?"

"Stomach ache," Dean said.

"You want to come in for a minute? Use the bathroom or something?"

"No, thanks," Dean said. The guy nodded and went back inside, one squirming dog under each arm.

The Hanleys. Grace Hanley. It was worse than he had suspected. Not only was she married with a kid, but her kid had polio. She'd need a visit from her long-lost son like she needed a hole in the head.

Except, he realized, he wasn't long-lost, and the realization made him stop right there on the sidewalk. She had *always* known where he was. If she had wanted to see him, she could have. And she hadn't. Which meant she didn't want to. For some reason. For what reason? The same reason she left him in the first place. He was a fool, on a fool's mission, running around the province, prowling around strange cities, looking for someone who didn't want him, who had never wanted him, for *whatever* reason.

He hurried back towards the city's pulsing core and asked the next person he passed for the name of the city's nicest hotel.

The Royal York was full, except for a suite that cost twenty-eight dollars. The clerk looked younger than him, with oily hair and a face to match. He looked for Dean's luggage and then said, "There are rooms at the YMCA if you—"

"I'll take the suite," Dean said coolly. He counted off the bills quickly.

The clerk hesitated. "Do you have some—some identification, sir?"

Dean raised one eyebrow. "Are you kidding me?" He pushed the bills across the counter. "The airline misplaced my luggage. Please send it up as soon as it is delivered."

The room was thickly carpeted, with gold plush chairs and a sofa and a television built into a heavy mahogany cabinet. The canopied bed was in an alcove behind French doors. Dean pushed back the heavy maroon curtains: one set of windows looked out over a net of sparkling lights; the other, a vast darkness. *The lake*, he thought. The United States was on the other side. Land of the free, they said. He had money; he could cross the border and join them.

He stripped, showered and sat at the desk in a towel to order dinner. Tomorrow, he would go down to the bus terminal and get a ticket. New York or California. He would get a job, find a place to stay, start a new life. Meet women who fell out of doorways laughing. He would be the mysterious stranger. Where did he say he was from? a woman with dark, glossy lipstick would ask, and the other woman would say, *I heard Montreal*. Someone else would have heard Moldavia. He could write a new history for himself, and it would be true. He would live at hotels like this one, as the founder, president and voice of Turner Incorporated.

He would go downstairs to the breakfast room every morning; he would eat in a different restaurant with a different girl every night of the week, except for when he was tired. Then he would do exactly what he was doing now: stretch out on the sofa in a towel and wait for the discreet knock at the door that signalled the arrival of his steak and baked potato and bottle of wine.

He wouldn't spend any more time trying to find the mother who had left him behind, given him up, passed him along—*Here, take this*—or the father who probably never even knew he existed. Tonight, he would sleep with an emblazoned city, an entire continent, at his feet, and tomorrow, he would wake up in his new life.

He slept until noon and woke with a headache. He shaved, put on his tie and grey sweater. His clothes looked cheap and schoolboyish in the gilt-edged mirror. He checked his wallet: sixty-eight dollars left. He'd have to go easy until he found work. At a diner a few doors down from the hotel, he ordered toast and coffee. A few blocks farther, he went into a department store, and before he knew it, he was trying on suits. He turned in front of the mirror, eyeing the line of a charcoal-coloured jacket from over his shoulder. Italian wool, the clerk said, finest wool in the world. He pinned up the sleeves and said, "Our tailor can do this for you right now, sir." Dean slipped off the jacket and said he needed to make a trip to the men's room before he made his selection.

Downstairs, he ordered a milkshake in the cafeteria and counted his money again under the table. If he took a night bus, he wouldn't have to pay for a hotel room. He didn't need a new jacket to ride the bus, and anyway, Italian wool would be too hot in California. His headache was only a faint thumbprint against one corner of his skull. He leaned his head back against the vinyl headrest, closed his eyes and allowed himself to come unmoored.

He was already in California sitting on a lounge chair overlooking the ocean. The sun warmed his upturned face, the breeze lifted his hair. When he looked up, he would see palm trees, and a woman would say silkily, *Excuse me, is this seat taken?* Instead, he heard Vera say, "Sit up straight."

Dean's eyes flew open.

In the next booth, a tall, large-chested woman with orange lipstick and a fur cape was talking to a girl with long light brown hair. The girl had her back to Dean; he could only see her hair and her shoulders in a cream blouse.

"You look like the wreck of the *Hesperus*," the woman said.

She didn't look so hot herself, Dean thought. Her brown pincurls looked like half-melted candies.

The girl said, "Mom, can I have french fries?"

Her mother said, "You'll have the salad plate."

Dean ordered another milkshake and shifted into the corner of his booth so he could see the girl's profile. She was pretty. The woman noticed him then, or rather, her eyes stopped on him briefly and then flicked him away. He shifted back out of her sight.

"I just don't know," the woman was saying. "I thought he would be better today. They said he was better. But he's exactly the same. Didn't you think so?"

"I thought he was a little better," the girl said. "He didn't look so tired."

"What are you *talking* about? He looked terrible!" the woman said. "I can't see that they're doing him any good in there. You know what that place does, Laura? It encourages him. They mollycoddle him." She took a compact out of her purse and studied her face. Dean slipped farther down into his seat. *Laura*, he thought.

The waitress brought their salad plates. He listened for as long as he could. Laura was not eating properly. Why was she holding her fork like that? She was slouching. She was picking at her food. When he couldn't stand it anymore, he went to the men's room. When he got back to his seat, the woman was fastening the buttons on her cape. "I mean it," she hissed.

The girl was shaking her head. "I can't help it," she said, and hiccupped.

"I have had it up to here with you," the woman said.

"All right, okay. Just a minute," the girl said, but she didn't move. It sounded like she was crying.

The woman snapped her purse shut and marched to the front cash. Dean waited until she had disappeared out the door, then got up and slid into the seat across from the girl. She had a round face, ivory skin, delicately arched eyebrows over closed eyes. Her cheeks were wet. Her mouth was the pale pink and the texture of a rose petal. Her eyes opened; they were very dark.

"Hi," Dean said.

She wiped one side of her face and left the other side wet. "Hi," she said back.

They looked at each other. Dean raised his hand and waved at the waitress. "One order of french fries," he said, and the girl looked wonderstruck. Her eyes were still leaking, so he said, "You wanna hear something crazy?"

She nodded.

He told her a story. A boy found out he was adopted. There was a photograph and a birth certificate in a box. There were clues. He followed the trail, but when he got to the end, to Baldwin Street, he found nothing. He had knocked, and the door hadn't been opened. He had sought, but he hadn't found. She didn't move the entire time, but her eyes radiated, as if she were listening through them. They warmed him and steadied him. "Is this a true story?" she asked when he was finished. He tapped his chest just above his heart. "True story," he said. "Now you tell me one."

Her story wandered all over the place but ended with her father in a mental institution with a nervous breakdown. Her face flushed darkly when she said it, and her eyes were skittish.

He was a welter of wants: he wanted to reach over and take her hand, he wanted to kiss her rose petal mouth, he wanted to slide into the seat beside her and put his arm around her protectively, he wanted to take her back to the hotel suite and lay her down on the bed and undo her cream-coloured blouse. He wanted to run away with her. They would leave behind their missing, mean, broken, lost, sick, soft-in-the-head, odd, off, criticizing, crazy, disappointed parents and start a new life together. He leaned forward and touched the back of her hand.

"Listen. Do you wanna come with me—" he began.

"To Baldwin Street?"

He laughed. "No, Quick Draw McGraw." Baldwin Street didn't matter. Baldwin Street was crumpled paper in the bottom of his rucksack. Tonight he would get on the bus and cross the border, and his new life would start; he didn't have time to waste on Baldwin Street. He said, "I have a better idea. Coming?"

He could see the answer in her eyes before she said it. She was from the City of Yes. Town Motto: Yes.

DAWN

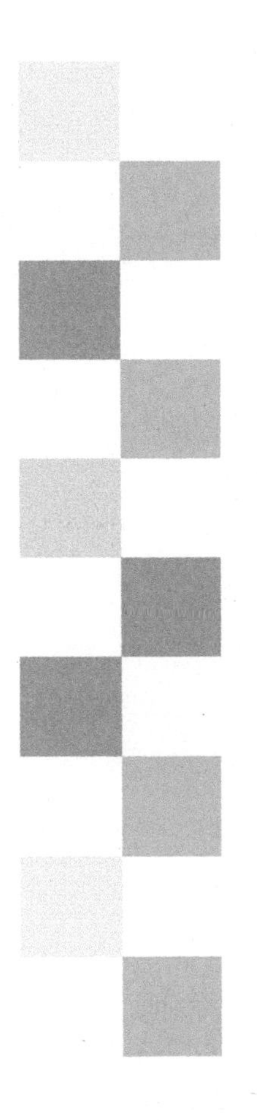

MRS. KRAUS

It was hard to tell when the ending actually arrived, partly because it came disguised as a series of new beginnings: a bag of money, a sparkling clean house, baby Amy, Opening Night. For a while, Dawn blamed the bartender at the club for the whole thing, because if he hadn't taken Professor Pollo and stuck him behind the bar like some kind of ornament, Dawn wouldn't have left Jimmy unattended, and Jimmy wouldn't have ended up in the hospital having his stomach pumped, and the police wouldn't have come to the house and found a stolen car in the garage.

It was Jimmy who found the bag of money. He appeared in Dawn's room one afternoon, gesturing crazily, with a look on his face like he had to pee really bad. She followed him to the spare room, which was going to be the baby's room but which was latched and locked because Dean said there were rusty nails sticking up out of the floorboards, and he was going to clear it out and paint it, and Dawn and Jimmy were going to help. Someone must have gone in there earlier, though, and left in a hurry, because today the lock was hanging open off the latch. "I already went in," Jimmy whispered. "There are no nails."

Dawn pushed open the door. Inside was a bed with a naked mattress, a lamp without a shade and a bunch of empty cardboard boxes. Jimmy told Dawn to sit on the bed, hold Professor Pollo and make a wish. His eyes were so bright, Dawn felt spooked. She sat down and accepted the Professor. "All right. I wish for a million dollars. There. Happy?"

Jimmy was wriggling and wiggling all over. "Yes! Yes! Now look under the bed."

Dawn looked, then got down on her knees and pulled out the garbage bag. When she saw what was inside, she gave a little scream.

Jimmy said, "See?" He plopped Professor Pollo down on top of the bag and said, "Whaddaya think of that, sunshine?"

They stared at the bag for a long time. Then Dawn said, "Jimmy, you know what we have to do?"

Jimmy nodded. "Go to the store."

"*No*, Jimmy. No. We have to count it."

They were still taking out handfuls of money when Geraldine called from downstairs, "Dawn? Jimmy? Are you up there?"

"Coming!" They stuffed the money back and barely got themselves out of the room before they heard Geraldine start up the stairs. Dawn was so terrified, she clicked the lock shut, and they both collapsed on the floor and pretended to be playing with Professor Pollo. "What are you two doing up here?" Geraldine asked. "Why are you sitting in the dark at the end of the hall?"

"We're just playing," Jimmy said.

"Well, come downstairs for dinner."

They watched her waddle back down the hall. "Why did you lock it?" Jimmy whispered. He was furious. "That was so stupid!" Fat tears rolled down his face.

"She was gonna see the lock was open. Then she'd know we were in there."

"So? *So?* Who gives a care if she saw?"

"We'll get back in, don't worry. We will, Jimmy. We will."

They looked at each other. Jimmy wiped his eyes. "I know how it got there, too," he said.

"How?"

"Bank robbers. They hid it there."

But that wasn't it at all. Dawn had just figured it out. She told Jimmy about hermits: rich old geezers who didn't trust banks and hid their money under their mattresses. They ate stale bread and reused their tea bags and saved every last penny.

Jimmy said, "Are Vera and Frank hermits?"

"No, they believe in the bank, see. But hermits hate banks. This house belonged to a hermit. He lived here all alone, and he had no family, so no one knew about the money. He died and no one thought to look under the bed."

Jimmy wanted to know how he died.

"He choked to death on a chicken bone."

"You said he only ate stale bread."

"And chicken wings. He got them cheap from the grocery store." She considered telling Jimmy the rest—the old man's body had been partially eaten by his cats—but Jimmy was really too young for that.

Every day the next week, when they came home to find Geraldine sleeping, they searched the house for the key. It was most likely on Dean's big key chain, but Dean was working every day and night at the club, and when he did come home, he was a whirlwind of instructions: "Jimmy, go upstairs and get me a clean white shirt." "Dawn, pour me a glass of orange juice, please." "Geraldine, I need the phone book. Hurry up, hurry up, I haven't got all night, they're putting in the bar and I have to get back."

Then something so surprising happened, they forgot about the money, or at least Dawn did, at least temporarily: they came home from school to find the whole house clean. The bathroom sink gleamed, the kitchen floor was light blue again, all their clothes were neatly folded in their drawers. Even the garbage pail was scrubbed white and smelled like a Christmas tree. They hadn't seen the house like this since they moved in. It was even better than the day they moved in, because the beds were made.

Geraldine was awake and sitting at the kitchen table. "There's something special for you guys in the fridge."

It was a tray of yellow cupcakes with thick orange icing. Geraldine asked them to get her a pencil and paper. She wanted to make a list of things they needed: new shoes, underwear, jeans, sweaters, whatever. Dawn asked if they could afford all this, what with the baby coming and everything. She didn't want to mention the bills on top of the fridge. Geraldine said she had been given a bonus at work. "Now, get your coats on," she said. "We're going shopping!"

They wore their new outfits to see the finishing touches being put on the club. In the green-walled room, crescent-moon seats encircled high round tables. This was Emerald City. Another room was red: plastic red flowers hung from the ceiling, and red flowers with black centres were painted on the walls. There were no chairs in here, only benches against three walls, and a stage. The mural in the main room was almost finished; through the middle, a road made of yellow funk wound its way to the sparkly red shoes Jimmy had found at the flea market. In the centre of the room, like an island, was the showpiece: a circular bar.

Antoine was finishing the ceiling in the women's bathroom. On the black surface, he was painting silver stars around a black-and-white picture of a surprised woman's face.

"Why is I Love Lucy here?" Dawn asked.

Antoine said, "This is a different Lucy. This is Lucy in the Sky."

But anyone could see that it was Lucy from *I Love Lucy*. Dawn said, "It should be Dorothy."

Antoine said, "Well, you can call her Dorothy. How's that?"

That, thought Dawn, was just stupid. But instead of answering, she went to find Jimmy. He was in Dean's office, a windowless room under the stairs, trying to open the safe behind the desk. He was still looking for the key to the spare room, even though Dawn had told him over and over to forget it—the lock, the key, the bag of money. She wasn't even sure she believed in the money anymore. It seemed so unlikely that it might have been a mirage, like on Bugs Bunny. She suggested this to Jimmy.

"Come on, Dawn," Jimmy said scornfully. "It was a *bag* of money."

From the doorway, Dean said, "What bag of money?"

Jimmy looked to Dawn for help. Dawn said, "It was on TV."

Dean looked from one to the other. "Get your coats," he said. "We have to go home."

Things were very bad because of the money. Dean stamped up the stairs, yelling his head off for Geraldine to get her ass up there right now. When he came out of the spare room, his face was pale and sweaty. "Go get it," he said. "Right now."

Geraldine stomped downstairs to the basement and came back up with an almost empty garbage bag. She threw it at him.

"Where's the rest of it?"

Geraldine pulled Dawn and Jimmy out of the doorway of Dawn's room. They stood side by side in the hall, Geraldine's hands on their shoulders. She started softly. "Where is it? Where *is* it? Your kids are wearing it. It's in their closets. It's in the medicine cabinet. It's in the goddamn fucking fridge. That's where the rest of it is." By the time she got to "the goddamn fucking fridge," she was screaming.

There was more screaming and door slamming, until Dean went back to the club, yelling over his shoulder, "It wasn't my money, Geraldine! It wasn't my money!" Jimmy couldn't find Professor Pollo, and Dawn couldn't find the Finding Stick. Jimmy's eyes were wide and blank, and Dawn knew he wouldn't sleep without the Professor, so she made a new stick out of a ruler and two pencil crayons, but it didn't work. "He'll turn up," she said. "He always does." Jimmy was sitting cross-legged on the bed, rocking a little. He had stopped crying, but his face was wet and his nose was running.

"You know what I wish?" he said.

"You could find Professor Pollo?"

He shook his head. "I wish we could go back to Grandma and Grandpa's."

Dawn went cold. His voice had throbbed when he said it. She didn't know if she could counter the effects of that kind of wishing. She wasn't even sure she wanted to.

Sometime shortly after that, Amy was born. At the hospital, Geraldine showed them how to hold the baby, who was wrinkled and red but otherwise perfect, and they took turns, sitting next to Geraldine on the bed. When Dawn laid her finger on Amy's palm, Amy made a tight little fist around her finger and hung on for dear life. *She knows who I am*, Dawn thought. "Hi, baby sister," she whispered, and kissed Amy's cheeks. She loved her completely already.

Dean had a diaper bag full of balloons, pop, cupcakes, plastic cups and a bottle of champagne. They pulled the curtains around Geraldine's bed and everyone climbed on. Geraldine was giggling. "The lifeboat," she said. "Dean, move your big fat feet." Dawn blew up the balloons and Jimmy handed out the cupcakes and glasses. Dean took out the champagne and then held up his hand for silence.

"Now, here's the situation, kids. You know they don't allow champagne and cupcakes in the hospital, right?"

Dawn and Jimmy nodded.

"You know why?"

They shook their heads.

"Because only the very worst-tasting things are available in the hospital, right, Geraldine? Oatmeal, tapioca, etcetera. If something tastes good, it isn't allowed. That's why we've got the curtains pulled. But here's the problem." He lowered his voice even more, and they all had to lean close to listen. "When I open this bottle, it's going to make a big pop. Then the nurses will come and we'll all be booted out of here on our backsides. All of us except Amy. So when I give you the signal, you three have to make a sound. Like a big cough or something—"

Jimmy said, "I know! I know! A big sneeze!"

"Even better. A big sneeze. Are you ready?"

They had to wait for Geraldine to stop laughing. "Okay, ready? One, two, three—"

They all fake-sneezed and the champagne cork shot up to the ceiling. Dean poured fast, but champagne still ran down the sides of the bottle and soaked into the sheets. He gave Dawn and Jimmy a dollop each in their glasses. They were all giggling and shushing each other.

Dean raised his glass. "A toast," he said quietly.

Dawn raised her glass. Dean said, "Welcome to the family, Amy." A tear ran down Dawn's face and plopped into her champagne, and she was sure she could taste it, a tiny bubble of saltiness swimming happily in a million bubbles of sweet.

The house felt weirdly empty after Geraldine and Amy came home. Geraldine and Amy spent most of their time sleeping. Jimmy didn't want to play anything because Professor Pollo was still missing. And Dean was hardly there because of Opening Night. The quiet got on Dawn's nerves.

A band from Toronto was coming for Opening Night, and Dean was going crazy with the arrangements. The printer had screwed up the posters, the bartender he had hired as a favour to Del Cherniak didn't know a highball from the highway, and Antoine's mural was coming off the wall in bits and pieces. Dean even looked like he was going crazy: his eyes were bloodshot and his hair was standing up. He had slept at the club the last two nights to supervise while the electricians redid the goddamn wiring. He'd come home to take a shower, and he hadn't been in the door five minutes before the phone started to ring. He lit one cigarette, put it down, turned around and lit another. "No," he barked into the phone. "No. I don't care if they have to run the wires out the window and down the street! *No!*" As soon as he hung up, the phone rang again. "Yes, I told them to reprint. Why? Because it's Yellow *Brick* Road. Not *Bricks*! For fuck sakes!" He left the phone off the hook when he went to take a shower.

Geraldine knocked on the bathroom door and asked him if he had a minute. He opened the door and said, "Geraldine, I do not have a minute. I do not have a second. Do you not understand how much I have riding on this?" He stormed past Geraldine. Dawn stood in her room, peering out through the crack in the door.

Geraldine said something Dawn couldn't hear, but she heard Dean's response as he pounded back down the stairs. "Because if I don't clear eight grand, I'm *fucked*, thanks to you."

Dawn went through the house, putting out the cigarettes.

Dean was taking them to Opening Night. Not at night, because it was a bar, but the day of, so they could watch the band rehearse, which would be like their own private concert. The Yellow Brick Road was full of people. The mural was fixed now, and a red velvet rope kept people from leaning against it. Dawn sat at the bar while Dean took Jimmy to the bathroom. She was studying the bottles when she saw a familiar brown foot. Behind the cash register, on an upside-down ice bucket, sat Professor Pollo. She climbed up on her stool and reached for him, but the bartender grabbed her hand. "Hey, hey, little girl. That's not yours."

Dawn stared at him. Was he crazy? "It's my brother's." She was so angry, she had trouble speaking clearly. "We left it here by mistake."

"I don't think so," the bartender said.

"It is so my brother's! Ask my dad!" Dawn slid off the stool. "Never mind. I'll ask him myself." Didn't this guy know her dad *owned* the place?

She found Jimmy eating brownies in Dean's office. "Want one?" he asked.

"No. Where's Dad?" she said. "I have to tell him something."

"He went across the river with Antoine to buy some kind of light you can't get here." He bit into another brownie.

Dawn stood, chewing a hangnail. If Jimmy saw Professor Pollo behind the bar and the bartender didn't hand him over, he'd go crazy. On the other hand, maybe Jimmy going crazy was just what that jackass out there deserved. Just then, a guy stuck his head in the door. "The band is going to rehearse." He saw them. "Where's Dean?" He didn't wait for them to answer.

Everyone stopped working to hear the band. Dawn didn't know why; they were so loud, you could hear them no matter where you were, even in the bathroom downstairs, under I Love Lucy, with your fingers stuffed into your ears. Dawn kept imagining how angry Dean would be when he came back and she told him about Professor Pollo. He would fire the bartender on the spot. "Do you think my daughter doesn't know her own brother's toys?" he would say. "Do you think my daughter would lie?" Dawn went back upstairs and circled the bar, glaring at the bartender. *Just you wait*, she thought.

The band rehearsed for at least an hour, and they still didn't sound any better. Dean still hadn't come back, and Professor Pollo was still behind the bar. Jimmy appeared beside her and grabbed her arm. His eyes were filled with tears. "It's okay," she said, "I'm going to get him back." She had to turn her head so he could yell in her ear. "I don't feel good, Dawn," he said. She made him sit down at a table and told him she'd bring him a drink. "A drink and something else that will make you feel a whole lot better," she said. When the bartender went to the other side of the bar, she climbed up on a stool and snatched Professor Pollo from the upside-down ice bucket. But when she got back, Jimmy was gone. It took her a moment to realize he was under the table. He had thrown up all down his shirt. His eyes were open but mostly the white part was showing. The band finished their cacophony and Dawn realized she was screaming.

The bartender drove them to the hospital and carried Jimmy in. He told Dawn he was going back to find Dean. Dawn was weeping. A nurse came out and wanted to know what Jimmy had had to eat or drink that day. Dawn tried to swallow her sobs. "He had

Alphabits for breakfast." She could hardly speak. "A hot dog for lunch. And brownies. He's allergic to strawberries."

A different nurse came out. "Who brought that boy in?" she said.

"I did. He's my brother."

The nurse frowned at Dawn from over her half-moon glasses. "Where are your parents?"

Dawn stared back at her. "My dad went over the river to get some lights."

"What about your mother?"

"My mother?" Dawn was confused by the question. She thought it was a test, to see if she would lie.

The nurse shook her head. "All right, come with me." She left Dawn in a small room with a desk and two chairs. "Someone will be here shortly," she said.

Shortly seemed to take forever.

"Is my brother all right?" Dawn asked when the nurse came back.

"He's having his stomach pumped. He'll be okay. This lady would like to have a few words with you."

The woman behind the nurse wore a grey pantsuit, black-framed glasses and a black velvet hairband in her straight, chin-length grey hair. She carried a square black briefcase instead of a purse and sat in the chair beside Dawn. "What's your name, dear?"

"Dawn Turner."

"Dawn, I'm a social worker. My name is Mrs. Kraus. I need to ask you some questions about what happened."

Looking back, she could see why it was hard to pinpoint the exact beginning of the end. So many things had seemed new, even the bad things: talking to a social worker, seeing Jimmy in a hospital bed sipping ice water from a plastic cup, going home and finding the driveway blocked with police cars and police officers coming in and out of the house and garage. Everything was like the start of something, if not something good, then at least something different, and yet when it was all over, Dawn and Jimmy ended up right back at Vera and Frank's, where they'd begun.

LAURA

GIRLS LAND, BOYS LAND

The baby bleated, and the birds of terror fluttered awake. Even through layers of sleep, Laura could feel their scratchy wings against the inside of her skull. *Please, please stay quiet,* she begged the baby silently. Burying her face in the hot pillow, she searched her memory for something to fall into, something still and dark, like an inky lake at nightfall, and finally found the Pointe.

The Pointe was a protective arm of land with two cottages set in its crook. To get there, you had to drive through Sunnyside, a wide beach with a marina and tennis club and dozens of dark, glossy cottages clumped together like Licorice Allsorts. At the Pointe, there was only the summer place Laura's parents rented and the bungalow belonging to the Shells, who lived there year-round—Mr. Shell, a writer, Mrs. Shell, who worked in a surveyor's office, and their daughter, Sue Ellen. Behind the two houses was a wilderness threaded with trails and beaded with mysteries:

a shrub with a sandy floor inside, a ring of oak trees around a table-like stump and, in the middle of nowhere, connected to nothing, three mossy concrete steps—a portal into another dimension, according to Sue Ellen.

Sue Ellen could shimmy up trees, jump hurdles over chairs and swim across the bay. She had once rescued a stranded baby deer and fed it with a bottle until the Humane Society came and took it to the zoo. She had a real bow and arrow (with which she once shot a squirrel by mistake), and a way of describing something so that it came true. When she discovered that she and Laura were reincarnated Egyptian princesses, Laura felt her insides thrum with ancient syllables. When she said boys were spying on them, the hedges rippled with shadows and whispers. When she pointed out the border between Girls Land and Boys Land, Laura could see it as clearly as if there were a fence with watchtowers.

That last summer, Laura and her mother went to the cottage alone. A few months before, Laura's father had stopped going to work. He sat at home in his chair, and if Laura or her mother asked him anything ("Dad, do you want some soup?" "Richard, just how long do you intend to sit there?"), he would tell them the whole thing all over again from the beginning: it was all the fault of a man by the name of Marcus Findley, who had insinuated and laid traps, who pretended to be one thing and then revealed himself to be in cahoots with others. The bathroom was mentioned, and a key, but they couldn't figure out what had actually happened. It chilled Laura, but her mother muttered, "Oh, for god's sake, Richard. Be a man!"

Laura's mother said they wouldn't be going to the cottage if her father didn't get off his backside and get another job. Anyway, Laura's mother was tired of the cottage—you had to drive to Sunnyside for any kind of company, unless the Shells were your cup of tea, and they were not hers. For one thing, Mrs. Shell went around in baggy shirts and rundown shoes, and she had a big, seesawing laugh that Laura's mother called unseemly. (Laura's mother had a low, rippling laugh, and she was always smartly turned out; even at the cottage, her lipstick matched her sundress and the scarf in her hair.) And Laura's mother was sorry, but she just didn't believe in mothers going off to work. The war had been over for ten years! Sure, some mothers still did it, but that didn't make it right. If you were a wife and mother, that *was* your work. And what kind of writer was Mr. Shell anyway? Laura's mother had never heard of him; he couldn't be a very *successful* writer, which was probably why Mrs. Shell had to work in the first place.

Laura prayed that her father would get up and get a job. Instead, he started to cry in the mornings (without sound, just tears slipping down his face and into his now grimy shirt collar), and Laura's mother said, "I'm at the end of my rope. I really am." She called and reserved the cottage for two weeks. When Laura asked how they would pay for it, she said, "That is your father's responsibility."

They arrived at the cottage before lunch. Laura's mother gave her two cupcakes and said, "If they ask over there, just say your father stayed in town to work."

Laura raced across the lawn, calling for Sue Ellen. Sue Ellen dropped down in front of her from a pine tree, wearing a headdress made of willow wands over her short, sun-streaked curls. "What weapons hast thou brought this annum, Mighty Huntress?"

"I have brought my keen eyes and ears," Laura said. She extended her hand. "And supplies."

"Excellent," Sue Ellen said, taking the cupcake. "But we cannot talk here." She tilted her head at the hedge between the cottage and her house and whispered, "We have a situation."

They stopped in to say hi to Mr. Shell, who was smoking cigarettes and reading a magazine at the kitchen table. When he saw Laura, Mr. Shell stood up, bowed, shook both her hands, kissed her cheeks and twirled her around in a little do-si-do. "Greetings, City Girl," he said. "How are things in the bright metropolis?"

Sue Ellen said, "Dad, I have to debrief Laura on a situation."

Mr. Shell bowed again. "Of course," he said solemnly. "I will not detain you."

The situation was serious: the whole Pointe was a war zone between Girls Land and Boys Land. At Girls Land Headquarters in the bramble bush, Sue Ellen explained how they had to patrol the borders twice a day and check for traps and secret messages. The Boys were ruthless, relentless; they could not let their guard down, not even for a minute.

For the first few days, Laura's mother sat in front of the cottage with a stack of magazines, refusing Mrs. Shell's invitation to dinner and Mr. Shell's plea for distraction from the terrors of the blank page. Then, one afternoon, she was sitting on the Shells' patio, drinking gin and tonic with Mr. Shell, a magazine open on the table between them. "I had no idea you wrote for them," Laura heard her saying. She waved her unlit cigarette in a gesture of wonderment. "I don't know why I didn't make the connection earlier." Mr. Shell leaned forward with a lighter. He proclaimed himself a mere hack, which made her laugh, and Laura was relieved: her mother wouldn't have to drive to Sunnyside for company, after all.

Mr. Shell was the perfect gentleman, Laura's mother declared later that night as they cold-creamed their faces in the cottage's tiny bathroom. "And it's completely wasted on Mrs. Shell, I'm sure," she said.

"Dad's a perfect gentleman too, isn't he?" Laura said, and felt a pang in her throat for her father, sitting at home in his chair.

He might have sprouted a fine layer of dust now, like the ornaments on the mantel.

"Of course," her mother said, and Laura's throat hurt even more.

Each day, Sue Ellen and Laura got closer and closer to victory over the Boys of Boys Land. It was Sue Ellen's best game yet. But when Laura related their latest feat to her mother, her mother didn't get the point. "Why don't you invite some other kids to play?" she said, frowning at the white plastic flower on the strap of the new swimsuit she had just bought in Sunnyside. "I mean, wouldn't it be better with real boys?"

She meant the Sunnyside boys who played basketball at the marina and tore up and down the road, hooting and hollering on their bikes. Boys Land Boys never hollered: it would give away their position. They were silent, narrow-eyed, stone-hearted soldiers who would risk their lives to defend their territory and carry information back to their Leader, Michael Pierce. They were a different breed of boy altogether.

Something *was* wrong with the game, though, and it took Laura a while to figure it out. The problem was that every gain had to be countered by a small loss. The game advanced, but without conclusion. How long could it go on before it lost its flavour?

When Laura tried to explain, Sue Ellen said, "We're on the verge of defeating them once and for all. That's the whole point."

But when they won, the game would be over, so defeating the Boys for good could not be the point. The point, Laura thought, was not to win but to be caught. At least, that's how they played it at Laura's school: when a boy chased you, of course you ran, but if he didn't catch you, you might as well have not been pursued at all.

Sue Ellen was good at war, but she hadn't read the books Laura's mother kept in the top drawer of her night table, bulging paperbacks written by women named Violet and Evangeline, with titles like *Love Asunder* and *Rogue Heart*. Also, and worse, the Shells didn't have a television and there was no theatre in Sunnyside, so Sue Ellen had seen almost no movies. Maybe that was why she didn't know what came next. Hostilities were always followed by contact, danger by rescue, separation by reunion. In a proper story, everything ended with love.

Laura had even worked out the perfect beginning: on a reconnaissance mission, she would be waylaid and taken into Boys Land, where Michael Pierce would hold her hostage. Sue Ellen would try to rescue her, but she, too, would be captured. They would be held in separate cells and have to tap messages through the walls. Some Boys would become their allies. Michael Pierce himself might even fall in love with one of them. (She would not tell Sue Ellen this part just yet.) Hundreds of possibilities would open up; they could play forever.

They were sitting outside Headquarters when she laid it out for Sue Ellen. The sun was hot and sharp on her bare arms, and she could almost feel the rough rope against her wrists. (She did not tell Sue Ellen the details, how she would kick and punch her captors and how Michael Pierce would stare at her, astonished. "You fight like a Boy," he would say, and she would spit in contempt, which would make him laugh. He had black hair and piercing blue eyes, and wore a buckskin jacket and a knife in his belt.)

Sue Ellen thought about this. "We *could* raid their Headquarters when they're all out spying. Break in, get information, get out."

Laura said, "I guess."

Sue Ellen narrowed her eyes. "I mean, it's not like you *want* to be captured, right?"

"No," Laura lied. "No!"

"Well, it sounds like it," Sue Ellen said. She was clearly annoyed. "I have to go home. I'm supposed to remind my dad about his deadline."

When Laura caught up with her, she was standing at the hedge between their properties. Mr. Shell and her mother were sitting at the picnic table on the Shells' veranda, and from the hedge, it looked like they were holding hands, but then she saw they were just playing cards. "Dad!" Sue Ellen yelled. "Deadline!" Her father waved at her, drew another card and slapped his forehead in despair. Laura's mother's laugh rippled out towards them.

Sue Ellen scowled. "My father has to work, you know. He can't work if she's over there every day."

Laura said, "What do you mean?"

"I mean his work!" Sue Ellen said loudly. "He has to write!"

But Laura meant it wasn't her mother's idea to go over; it was Mr. Shell who invited her. Laura's mother was just being neighbourly.

That night Laura was woken by low voices and for a moment, she thought the Boys had really come. But it was her mother and Mr. Shell, talking on the other side of the hedge. Laura sat up and pressed her face against the screen, but she couldn't see anything. She opened her mouth, a technique Sue Ellen had taught her, and then she could hear: "Oh, yes, do that." "This is *crazy*." "Shh, shh." "Oh my god, I love you." "I love *you*." "No, don't, you'll wake the whole . . ." "Shhhh."

After a while, Laura lay back down and pulled the blankets over her head. Her mother and Sue Ellen's father were . . . *in love?* How could it even be true? Laura's mother always said, "The moment I laid eyes on Richard, I knew he was the one for me." But assuming it was true, then what? Would her mother and Sue Ellen's father have to get married? That would mean a divorce, which Laura's mother said she didn't believe in (and *that* was in reference to Marilyn Monroe—Laura wasn't sure if regular people could get divorced). But they would have to divorce in order to marry; she didn't know how else it would make sense. It would still be awful, though, even if it made sense, because what would happen to her father? And to Mrs. Shell? (Maybe her father and Mrs. Shell would get married? No. That was probably going too far.)

She was awake most of the night trying to figure it all out. One thing she knew for sure: she could not tell Sue Ellen. But she told her anyway, almost immediately, while they were out on first patrol the next morning. She finished by saying, "But it's okay, Sue Ellen, because don't you see? We'll be sisters." But Sue Ellen's eyes turned to stone. She said, "What are you *talking* about" and threw down her bow and arrow. Then she disappeared into the bush.

Laura sat on the mossy concrete steps, wishing she could disappear into another dimension, or at least back into last night (she would cover her ears, she would bury her head, she would not wake up). She sat there until the sun was high overhead and she was light-headed with hunger. When she got home, her mother was packing. "Go say goodbye to your little friend," she said. Her voice was flinty, but she cleared her throat and it softened. "We have to get back. I'm worried about your father."

Laura walked along the border of Girls Land, but without Sue Ellen, it was just a thin path through the bush. She cut straight through Boys Land territory and got into the car, and they were back in the city by lunchtime.

At home, Laura's father had moved from his armchair to the bed. That fall, he moved to the hospital, the first of many extended visits, and Laura's mother got a job in a doctor's office. By herself, Laura was free to play the game the way she had wanted to. The Boys came at night, all stealth and speed and strength; they lifted her out of bed and carried her over the border, deep into Boys

Land, into the very chambers of Michael Pierce. He touched her hair and told her she was his now, and nothing could change that. The force of his declaration made her weep with gratitude. This was what she had wanted all along.

But once she was his, the game fizzled out. She tried to imagine what would come next; logically, they would get married and have children, but somehow, this storyline never took her very far. It was a constant mystery, why there was nothing left to play after the declaration, that moment of shattering happiness so perfect it shattered happiness itself.

SIGNS

She lifted her head from the pillow and in the gloom saw the empty crib. Her mother-in-law must have taken the baby downstairs. Her little girl was already down there, in a booster seat at the kitchen table, with a pink plastic bowl of animal crackers and her little white juice cup. Her mother-in-law would be shaking her head, her lips pressed thin, thinking, *What kind of mother?* What kind of mother goes to bed right after she wakes up and comes unravelled at the sound of her own baby's cries? No kind of mother. That's the kind she was, hiding up here in the dark tower with no prince on the lawn below calling her name to break the spell. She fumbled for the lamp on the bedside table and cried out at the sight of herself in the oval mirror across the room: an old woman stared back, her scalp showing through her thin white hair, her face yellowed and mottled with age. A hundred years had passed.

Well, what did you expect? her mother-in-law said from the other side of the door. *You said let you sleep, so we let you sleep.*

"Where is the baby?" she called out, but no one answered. The light in the room was dissolving, and she fell back through the depths to where there might be a hatch, a portal that would open onto a different life or carry her backwards through time to the Turning Point so that she could turn and turn away.

She had been eighteen when she wished for Dean Turner. That afternoon, in the cafeteria at Eaton's, with a storm of tears about to overtake her, she had closed her eyes and prayed, "Please give me a sign."

She meant a sign that she would not cry today, would not take after her father, was destined for love and happiness and dreams that came true and did not run out abruptly like the end of a movie reel flapping noisily on the projector. "Let something happen," she pleaded silently.

She opened her eyes: her mother was gone, and Dean was sitting in her place.

Somewhere inside her, the course of time shifted. A turning point.

Light came off him when he talked. Sparks, she wasn't sure from where: his dark eyes, maybe, or his teeth, which were very white. When he smiled, a dimple formed on one side of his mouth, like he was about to tell her something he shouldn't. He talked like people in movies, the words spooling out so fast that, in the beginning, she was always a half-sentence behind. He raised his hand and a waitress appeared with a plate of french fries. He leaned back and draped his arms over the back of the booth. He had broad shoulders and long fingers. *Who* are *you?* she thought, and just at that moment, he stuck his hand across the table and introduced himself. "Dean Turner," he said. He was from the City of Northerly Bore, also known as Sault Ste. Marie. He was staying at the Royal York Hotel. He was adopted.

She couldn't even imagine telling it: how he appeared out of nowhere, an adopted boy who travelled on his own and shed sparks when he talked. He had come to Toronto to find his mother, he said, and now, after all his travels and travails, he didn't want to meet her, as crazy, as batty, as loop-de-loop loopy as that sounded.

"Nuts-and-bolts screwy," Laura agreed, and his eyes glinted. "Whacky-shack whacky."

Except she knew what he meant. She always yearned to see her father, right up until they got to the visitors' room and the door opened, when her yearning suddenly spiked and transformed into its opposite, because the person who came through was not her father. He looked like her father, but he was clearly a stand-in. He was gaunt, and his lips were badly chapped, and even though she held her breath as he leaned in to kiss her cheek, she could smell sour sweat and metal and something unspeakable. Her real father had gone somewhere, and even the stand-in was waiting for him to come back: he kept asking them the time and looking back at the door that led to the ward. Sometimes it was just easier to miss someone.

Dean Turner was looking at her so intently she felt she was dissolving into him. He touched the back of her hand, and a long, powerful quaver went through her. This happened to other people, she thought—in books and movies—and now it was happening to her.

"Come with me," he said, and she went, just like that. He took her arm and they strolled through the store, stopping in the luggage department so Dean could tell the clerk they were going to Timbuktu on their honeymoon, and was this material heat- and dust- and camel- resistant? In electronics, they looked for the largest, loudest TV ever made as a hundredth birthday present for their half-blind, half-deaf great-grandmother. At the glove counter, they needed sunglasses because Laura, the daughter of someone who could not be named, was being followed by ("Don't look") that guy in the black coat by the stairwell. In front of the mirror in ladies' wear, Dean lifted a strand of her hair and said her mother was wrong: it wasn't mousy, it was *burnished.*

Then he checked his watch and announced that he was taking Laura to dinner. "What's the best restaurant in Toronto?"

Laura didn't know. They only ever went to cafeterias and diners. "But wherever it is, we aren't dressed right." He was wearing grey pants, a white shirt, black loafers. She was wearing the pleated navy skirt and blue boat-necked sweater she always wore to the hospital. "We look fine for Eaton's," she said. "But you'd need a jacket. And I'm wearing these," she said, kicking up her foot so he could see her white sneakers. "We won't even get in the door."

"Is that so?" Dean narrowed his eyes and wriggled his eyebrows at the same time.

"Yes, it is," she said, giggling. "Why? What are you going to do?"

In the men's section, he walked straight to a rack and lifted a dark grey jacket off a hanger, just as if it were his. He slipped it on, and they stood side by side in front of the mirror. She lifted the tag on the sleeve and gasped.

"Italian wool," he said, and she rubbed the material between her fingers. "Finest in the world."

The salesman wanted to pack it in a box but Dean said he would wear it. "Next stop, shoes," he told Laura.

She looked down at his feet, but he shook his head. "Not for me," he said.

"I don't have any money," she said.

"I know," he said. He grabbed her hand and they ran back upstairs.

"These," he said, picking up a pair of black patent leather pumps with a thin strap high across the instep.

"You can't buy shoes for me, Dean."

"Why not?"

Laura thought about what her mother would say if she came home in these shoes. If she knew that Laura was running around Eaton's with a guy she'd just met in the cafeteria. She shook her head.

"Okay," Dean said. "We won't get them. But try them on. Just to see how they look." The clerk who had been hovering took the shoe into a back room and came out with a box.

She peeled off her socks and slipped her feet in, rising up on the heel to become a tall and slender Laura. "Do you like them?" he asked.

"I love them."

She walked over to a mirror and twisted her burnished hair into a chignon. Her cheeks were flushed. She looked like someone else.

Dean appeared behind her. "Beautiful," he said, and her face went even pinker. Dean handed her a cardboard box. "For your old shoes," he said.

"You can't buy these for me, Dean."

"I already did," he said. He waved at the clerk behind the sales desk; the clerk waved back.

Laura bit her lip. "Okay, let me buy you something now," she said. "But I only have a dollar."

"Buy me a pen," he said, "so I can write you secret messages." In the stationery department, she bought him a ballpoint pen and he uncapped it and wrote her name and address on the inside of his arm.

They went several blocks, racing, skipping, ducking out of the way of annoyed adults. Everything was funny. A woman told them to act their age, and a police officer asked them if they'd been drinking. They couldn't stop laughing.

"Here," Dean said, stopping. They were outside Barberian's Steak House.

"It looks expensive," Laura said.

"Exactly," said Dean.

Inside the wood-panelled room, the maître d' looked at them crossly, but as soon as Dean started to speak, the man rearranged the expression on his face and listened intently. Laura thought it was all in the way Dean looked at you. His eyes flashed, like he had just taken a picture of you, like he really *saw* you. And it was the way he talked, of course. He didn't sound like an adopted boy from Sault Ste. Marie. He sounded like someone famous, someone who lived in California and drove a convertible and had a wallet full of cash. The maître d' led them to a table at the back. They ate dinner rolls and read the menu while waiters refilled their water goblets. Dean told her about the book he was writing about his life so far. He told her about a trick with a light bulb and a shower of pennies. He told her this was not the first time he had run away. The first time, he had stolen a car. This time, he had stolen a cheque. There. What did she think of him now? She thought he was an unredeemable degenerate, didn't she?

"I don't even know what that means!" she exclaimed, laughing, but he was serious. "It means no good. Everybody knows I have bad blood." He was staring at his empty plate, his face suddenly blank and lightless.

"No," Laura said, her face growing hot with indignation. "You are the most wonderful person I've ever met. I wish the world was filled with people like you." He wouldn't look up at her, so she beamed her thoughts into him. *I love you*, she told him silently. *I just met you, but I love you.*

Under the table, he reached for her hand.

The waiter came and lit the candle in the lamp at their table and asked if they were ready to order. Dean waved him away and then called him back and asked for another basket of bread. He said, "I can see the candlelight in your eyes," and that long, trilling thrill ran through her again. They were finishing their third basket of bread when Dean realized loudly that they were going to miss their train. He stood up abruptly, dropping his napkin to the floor, and signalled frantically. Two waiters helped them collect their things, and Dean pressed a folded bill into one's palm as he led Laura out.

Dean took her hand and they ran, laughing, down the street. He pulled her under an awning and kissed her. She was alive in every limb and joint and cell, a conduit for something immense and undeniable. The universe was flowing through her, in all its goodness and sadness and craziness, unimpeded and undiluted, and no matter what happened next, it would be the right thing.

He framed her face in his hands and they kissed again. *He loves me too*, she thought. It was crazy, but it was true.

His face crumpled and he began to weep. "Dean!" she cried out, and then put her arms around him. He pressed his face into her neck. "Laura," he said, and her entire chest ached at the way his voice wavered. She kissed his ear and his cheek and told him he would find them someday, and even if he never found them, it didn't matter. She knew who her parents were and mostly she wished she didn't. He straightened up and wiped his face. She felt powerful; she had brought him back from the edge of the storm, the same way he had brought her back when he appeared across the table at Eaton's. They walked a bit farther in silence, and then Dean pointed to a crowd of people in front of a windowless brick building. "What's going on in there?" She wanted to keep walking with him, just the two of them, through the dark streets forever, but he led her through the crowd, down a staircase and into a dim, smoky room. It was a nightclub of some sort, jammed with men in turtlenecks and women in tight pants and sweaters.

Laura felt like a kid in her gingham skirt, but Dean seemed to recover a little of his sparkle. When the band came on, the room went completely dark, and Dean reached for Laura's hand. A single narrow beam of light cut through the room and fell on the neck of a guitar. Another beam caught a raised drumstick. Another splashed a pool of light under the microphone. The singer, dressed completely in black, stepped forward into the pool. Dean looked transfixed.

Halfway through the song, he turned to her, and she saw that the light had come back to his face. The hurt was still in his eyes, but it had shrunk to a splinter. When the band left the stage, they squeezed themselves through the crowd and out into the night, Dean talking a mile a minute. Had Laura noticed how the lighting made the musicians look like they were floating in the dark? Didn't she love the circular bar? Laura nodded, thinking, *Please kiss me again.*

He stopped talking and did. Not even in the best Michael Pierce scenarios had she felt so cherished. He wound her hair around his hands, and his voice, silky and soft in her ear, said he was so glad to have found her, and she had to promise, *promise*, not to leave him or let him go. She promised. Then he sighed and said he should be getting her home now.

They took a taxi, and she wished they could drive through the night, side by side, their arms and hands entwined, her head on Dean's shoulder, but the driver said, "Broadview and Mortimer," and they had to climb out. They stopped between street lights to kiss in the shadows. Dean said he would call her in the morning and blew a kiss from the end of the driveway before turning and jogging into the darkness. Her mother yanked open the door, hissing furiously, but Laura, insulated by the warmth of Dean's invisible arms and the imprint of his mouth on her lips and neck, hardly heard her. Upstairs in her room, she lay in some joyous state between dream and memory for the rest of the night. At last she understood why things had happened the way they did: why her mother's new shoes had pinched on the way home from the hospital, why Dean had stood outside his mother's house and decided not to knock, why Dean had been adopted and why Laura's father was in the hospital in the first place. From the very beginning, their paths had been winding and striving towards each other. This was how happiness worked: it disguised itself as a series of accidents and disappointments, and then you looked up one day and there was the love of your life.

Except he didn't call in the morning, and when she finally dialled the hotel, the clerk said Mr. Turner was no longer their guest. It was just like the day she had come home from school and her mother said, "Your father was taken by ambulance to the mental hospital." They were like dream words that made no sense when you woke up.

Her mother made her take the shoes back.

She waited for him to call from wherever he was, and then she waited for him to write with the pen she had bought, and even though she didn't like this twist in the plotline, she knew this was how the stories generally went. She wasn't *meant* to understand until they came together again and everything was cleared up in a tumult of kisses and tears. She was supposed to sigh and fret and wander along the path near the Don River, pale and sick at heart, until he stepped out of the shade of the willow tree, as pale and feverish as she was, having risked everything and lost everything to find her again, or at least until he sent her a postcard from the hospital where he had been taken after being conked on the head or run over by a bus.

"It's just like *An Affair to Remember*," her friend Winnie sighed.

Everything happened for a reason. She just had to have faith.

After six months, her faith began to disintegrate: it seemed they were not meant to meet, fall in love, separate and reunite, get married and all the rest, happily ever after, the end, amen. Maybe there was no reason for the way the whole universe had liquefied itself and poured through her veins that night. It was not an affair to remember but a random encounter, without repeat or resonance.

Winnie said, "I guess it wasn't meant to be, after all," and Laura said, "I guess it wasn't." She could say it, but she couldn't make herself believe it entirely.

Even three years later, when she was working at the bank and seeing a lot of her co-worker, Warren Haddon, she sometimes thought about Dean Turner. When Warren kissed her, he felt like a wooden block in her arms, and when he put his hands into her blouse or between her legs, his touch was faint, as if he were stroking her through a quilt. Her mother said Warren was a perfect gentleman, and he was. He always stopped after a moment or two and removed his hand and straightened up and said he guessed he should be getting her home now. He walked her to the door and kissed her good night under the porch light. Sometimes, terrible thoughts knifed their way into her mind and she imagined saying something shocking to him just at that moment, something cruel and obscene. She didn't know what was wrong with her.

After years of on-and-off attempts and weekend visits, her father was home full-time. He wasn't the father she had mourned as a child, but he wasn't the stand-in either, and in truth, she hardly remembered that other father now, the one before Marcus Findley and the breakdown. They never talked about the hospital, but sometimes, in the middle of a sentence, her father's face would go blank, and Laura would search her mind for something to say to bring him back. After a couple of seconds, he blinked and returned, whether she spoke or not. Still, it was alarming.

Laura asked her mother, "Do you ever notice how Dad disappears sometimes when you're talking to him?"

Her mother said, "Why do you always have to see problems where there aren't any?"

Laura didn't know why. Her father was fine; he was working as a clerk ("assistant manager," her mother said) at a hardware store. Her mother was fine; she continued to work at the doctor's office because, she said, she had never been one of those women content to sit at home and polish the silverware; she had practically pioneered the way for married women to work. And Laura was fine. She had a steady boyfriend and a job, and her hope chest was filling up with tea towels and embroidered pillowcases. She had learned to sew and was putting together a grown-up woman's wardrobe: a sky blue skirt and quilted jacket, a shimmering pale gold flapper-style party frock, a forest green suit. There was no reason whatsoever for the storm clouds to be gathering just out of the corner of her eye. There was no reason for her to drop her head and pray, *Please let something happen*, but she did, and that winter, Warren got down on one knee in her living room and opened a little black box and said, "Laura, will you marry me? Will you be my wife?"

It wasn't the something she had meant. But then, what else could it have been? Dean Turner was not going to walk through the door singing "You Belong to Me." *This* was what came next. At least it would mean her own house, away from her mother, who still told her to straighten up, smarten up, stop moping and daydreaming, and away from her father, who sometimes went somewhere in his head and someday might not come back.

They set the date for July 14 and booked the hall, and her friends at work threw her a shower, and she argued with her mother about the dress and the invitations and the flowers. Her mother said they couldn't afford the kind of wedding Laura seemed to want, but Laura found a flaw with everything, expensive or not, and couldn't decide on anything, and it was making her mother crazy. "You're going to end up with no wedding at all," her mother said, and Laura burst into tears and slammed her bedroom door.

In May, Warren called and said he had some very exciting news for her, something that would make her very happy, and could she be ready in fifteen minutes? At the Cherry Pie Diner, Warren told her he had been offered a promotion. "Manager," he said gravely, but he couldn't completely suppress his smile. The youngest manager in the bank! It was a small branch, but still, it was a tremendous opportunity, and Laura wouldn't have to worry about a transfer because Warren didn't expect her to work after they got married. As manager, his salary would be more than adequate.

"That's wonderful," Laura said.

"And I have a cousin up there, so we would have some family already," Warren said. Laura didn't know where "up there" was; she had missed that part. The position would start in August, Warren said, right after the honeymoon. He had negotiated that himself. They were sending him up at the beginning of June to meet the staff, and he would look for an apartment or house to rent. He leaned back in his chair and smiled. "Not many start their married lives in such a good position," he said. "And Sault Ste. Marie is a nice place to raise a family."

A bolt went through her. "Sault Ste. Marie?"

Warren looked irritated. "Laura. Haven't you been listening?"

Everything inside her lifted and tilted precariously, and she had to clutch the bottom of her chair to keep herself from sliding off. *Don't be foolish, Laura*, she told herself in her coldest, hardest mother-voice, but her heart had already galloped off.

Later that night, she called Warren. "I want to go with you when you go up."

"Oh," he said. "Well. That probably . . . They won't—"

"If we're going to live there," Laura said, "I want to see it. I want to know what I'm getting myself into."

"But it's so close to the wedding," Warren said. "You'll have so much to do."

"Everything's mostly done," Laura said. "And don't you want me with you when you look for a place?"

So it was settled. Laura would have to pay for her own ticket, of course, and she would stay at a hotel while Warren stayed with his cousin. Her mother said it was a useless extravagance at a time when they should be saving money, but Laura barely heard her. She could barely think at all.

EVERYTHING TURNS OUT IN THE END

A door opened and a voice said, "Mommy? Are you waked up now?" Laura heard herself groan. *Get up, Laura,* another voice said sternly, but it was only in her head. That voice said all kinds of things: *Get up; don't move. You're not to blame; this is all your fault. You're on the right path; you took a wrong turn; you would have ended up here, no matter what. Everything is all wrong, but somehow it will work out for the best in the end.*

The voice could not be trusted. She pulled the sheet over her head. At the bottom of the dark pool, the voice could not even be heard.

Sault Ste. Marie had made her eyes hurt. The ache began when they landed at the tiny, windy airport and deepened on the long ride into town, where she and Warren used her room to freshen up. At the bank, where Warren introduced her as his fiancée, her eyes kept darting off, left and right, and by the end of the day, she felt like she was separated from her body by a thick, transparent sheet of pain. Back at the hotel, Warren said, "Jeez, Laura, you look *terrible*," and she said, "I know. Do you mind if I don't come to your cousin's? I have the most terrible headache." Warren said he would explain to his cousin, kissed her forehead and told her to get a good night's sleep. She watched from the window as he climbed into the taxi and disappeared.

There was no phone in her room, so she went down to the lobby. He might not even live here anymore. He might not remember her. He might be married. Even if he still lived here and remembered her and wasn't married, he might merely say, "Well, have a good visit and thanks for calling." Anyway, she was engaged. The wedding was two months away. The hall was paid for, and the gilt-edged invitations that she had fought for so ferociously had been sent out, and the dress was hanging in a plastic shroud in her closet.

She just wanted to make sure. Plus, if she was going to be living here, she didn't want to run into him by chance and have to bumble through introductions and explanations.

The operator had only one listing, for Turner, Francis. She called, and a man answered on the first ring. "Wharton, for crying out loud, I said I'd be there."

"Hello?" Laura said.

"Hello," he said after a pause. "Who's this?"

"Is this Dean Turner?" She knew it was him.

Another pause. "Well, now, that would depend on who's asking," he said. His voice had gone dark and silky.

"It's Laura."

"Hello, Laura," he said warmly, but she could tell he didn't know who she was.

"You probably don't remember me," she said, and her words slopped against each other, as if she were a little drunk. "We met a couple of years back. In Toronto."

He didn't say anything, so she took a breath and charged on. "We met in the cafeteria at Eaton's, remember? We . . . we went shopping and then we had dinner—"

"Where are you calling me from, Laura?" She couldn't read the tone of his voice.

"I'm in town. I'm with my—I work for the bank and I'm in town for a few days and I thought I would—"

"Where are you staying?"

"At the Algonquin Hotel. I just wanted to, you know, say hi. I remembered that you were from here, and I . . ." She couldn't think how to finish. Why wasn't he saying anything?

"Listen, Laura, I have to make a call, because some guys are expecting me, but—"

Her hand was trembling. "Yes, of course. I mean, I have to go now too because my—I just wanted to say hello. It was nice talking to you."

She hung up and made it to the stairwell before the tears seeped out of her eyes. Oh god, she was a fool. What had she been hoping for? That he would say, "Laura! At last! I've been looking for you everywhere!" No, not that, but that he remembered her, at least. That a part of him was always wishing for her, the way a part of her was always hoping for him.

She knew what her mother would say to that. *Why do you imagine these things? God, Laura, you remind me of your father before the hospital.*

Her mother would have also said, *What is wrong with you? You're engaged to be married! Why are you calling men you don't know?*

She slumped into a chair in her room, hands dangling between her knees, too perplexed now for tears. She had everything a girl could want, and she didn't want any of it. Something *was* wrong with her. She *was* like her father before the hospital: telling the same story over and over, crying over nothing, unable to let go. Constitutionally flawed. But from now on, no more. Enough was enough. She would marry Warren and settle down and be happy and stop going around with tears in her eyes and her head in the clouds.

She washed her face, brushed her teeth and went back downstairs to call Warren at his cousin's.

Warren's cousin lived in a shabby apartment on the third floor of a house. A secretary at the *Sault Star*, Deb McKenna was what Laura's mother would have called homely: she had a broad face and big hands and dark, wiry hair straining against the wave it had been set into. They sat on Deb's worn sofa and drank canned orange juice with a splash of rum and listened as Deb recounted her bad dates with reporters. "You're lucky," Deb said to Laura. "You're lucky to have my cousin, that's all I can say." Laura linked her arm through Warren's and agreed.

Deb's roommate wandered in wearing a vivid yellow silk shirt over a pair of man's pyjama bottoms, and waved at them on her way to the kitchen. Deb said Geraldine was waitressing at the Gold Room while she looked for a better job. Laura called out, "Do you have any clerical experience, Geraldine? Because Warren is going to be the manager at the Royal Bank." Warren shot her a warning frown, but Geraldine said she was waiting for a call back from the steel plant. Warren said that a plant secretary probably made more than a bank teller, anyway. Geraldine came out of the kitchen, eating peas straight out of a can. "I might have to start off as a secretary," she said, "but I'm going to end up *in* the plant."

"Oh, don't say that," Laura said. "I'm sure you won't end up in the plant." But perhaps she had misunderstood, because Geraldine laughed and shovelled another spoonful of peas into her mouth. Laura looked at the mismatched chairs, the faded HAPPY NEW YEAR 1963 streamer still taped above a closet door, the egg-stained plate on the windowsill, and she thought, "This could be me. If it weren't for Warren, I'd end up rooming with a homely girl and a weird girl who eats peas out of cans, hoping to be noticed by someone like Warren so that I could start the rest of my life. I *am* lucky."

The next evening, Laura wore her flapper-style dress, the pale gold fringed sheath, to dinner with Deb and Warren and Warren's new colleagues and then to the Cinnamon Lounge, where Warren discussed housing prices and neighbourhoods, and Deb told Laura about a guy she was seeing last fall who'd popped the question and then called her up the *next day* and said he'd changed his mind. Laura shook her head in disbelief. Warren said, "That's a ridiculous price. Listen to this, Laura." People at the next table got up to leave in a flurry of chairs, and on the other side of the room, Dean Turner put his arm around a girl whose red hair was falling out of its beehive. He was talking, and everyone at his table was laughing. Laura stood up suddenly, knocking over Warren's drink, and excused herself.

In the bathroom, she dabbed at the Coke stain on her dress, her breath coming in spasms. She was trying to remember if that table had been empty when they came in, but her thoughts kept colliding with each other. The headache threatened to start up again, an ominous pulse above her left temple. She reapplied her lipstick, but it looked garish against her pale skin, so she wiped it off. *I don't know what to do*, she thought. But there was nothing *to* do, except go back out and sit down with Warren.

Out in the corridor, she almost walked straight into him. He smiled at her and made a little bow. Her ears filled up with a thrashing noise, and her throat felt suddenly coated with ice. He didn't recognize her.

And then he did. “Hey!” he said happily. “Laura! I called you at the hotel last night, but they said you’d gone out.” He leaned back and appraised her. “Wow. You look even more beautiful than I remembered.”

She said, “I’m here with my fiancé.” The cold in her throat was spreading.

“Fiancé? Where?” He leaned in, and she could smell alcohol and aftershave. She shivered. He placed his hand over his heart. “Tell me it’s not so.”

Lies! she wanted to shout. She wanted to slap him. Instead, she said, “Excuse me, I have to go.” The cold had reached all the way to her feet, turning them into chunks of ice in her gold kitten-heel shoes.

“Wait, wait,” he said, catching her arm and steering her into an alcove at the end of the hallway. “Listen. I was really glad to hear from you last night.”

She shook him off.

“Can’t we talk?”

“Why didn’t you write me if you wanted to talk? After that night.”

“Write you?” He looked bewildered. “I didn’t even know your last name.”

“It was on your arm,” she hissed, but he still didn’t get it. She pushed past him and then whirled around. “You wrote my address on your arm! You said you would call me the next day!”

Back at the table, Warren was shaking hands with everyone. “Ready to go?” he asked her. She was.

Forty minutes later, something pinged against her hotel window, once, twice; then something harder clanked against it, but when she looked out, she saw nothing. Then Dean stepped out from behind a tree on the lawn below, and her heart somersaulted in her chest. She slid the window open and pressed her face against the screen. He whispered something that was lost in the night air.

"I can't hear you," she said, struggling to raise the screen.

He whispered it again, this time with gestures.

"What?" She couldn't hear a word. Finally she managed to lift the screen and stick her head out. "What? What do you want?" she called down.

He squeezed his head in his hands theatrically and said loudly, "I'd like to announce my intention of sneaking up the back stairs of this hotel to see the girl named Laura who is hanging out a second-floor window. Unfortunately, the front desk clerk refused me entry, and even more unfortunately, the girl herself appears to have gone deaf, so my nefarious plan to have her sneak down and open the back door to let me in will, in all likelihood, never come to fruition."

She was frozen in place.

"I've already woken up two other guests," he said. He touched his hand to his heart. "Please, Laura. Let me come in."

She raced downstairs and opened the back door at the end of the hallway. He slipped in. "Go up first," he said quietly. "Wait, what's the room number?"

A few minutes later, he stepped into her room and closed the door behind him. He said, "I always wondered if I'd see you again."

He was not even touching her and her skin was fizzing and sparking.

"I do remember," he said. "I remember the restaurant. I remember when we kissed outside that bar." His eyes were burning into her. "I still have the pen. At home in my room. It's white. It says YOUR BUSINESS IS OUR BUSINESS." For a minute, she tried to remember if the pen had said anything (had it even been white?), but then he leaned over and kissed her, and it was exactly the same, the feeling of stars and oceans and flowers moving through her.

"I called the hotel the next day," she told him. "You were gone."

"I made the mistake of calling home," he said, "and they talked me into coming back. By the time I got here, the address had rubbed off."

She took his hand and led him to the bed. He sat down and reached for her, but she stepped back and reached behind to unzip her dress. He smiled and leaned back on his elbows. She pulled down the satin straps and stepped out of her dress and pulled off her nylons and dropped everything on the floor at her feet. She raised her hands over her head. "Take me," she said. The words came from nowhere. She didn't even recognize her own voice.

In the morning, he said, "Come with me," and for the second time, she did. It was a chaotic, breathless rush. She took too long writing the letter to Warren (her hands were shaking, and she wrote "Warrent" and "wring"), and then Dean wouldn't let her pack her clothes. "No time!" he said, waving her purse at her. "You said he was picking you up at eight o'clock, and he looks like the kind of guy who's twelve and a half minutes early for everything."

"I don't know what to wear!" she protested. She was standing in her bra and nylons.

Dean picked up her fringed dress from the floor and shook it out. "Wear this," he said. "This is the world's best dress."

"But it's a party dress," she said, stepping into it.

"We'll buy new clothes," Dean said, zipping her up.

"But my clothes *are* new," she protested, thinking of how painstakingly she had sewn the forest green suit, the sky blue skirt and quilted jacket. She was chewing a hangnail, laughing and crying. "I'm only going to be ripping them off you," Dean said, wriggling his eyebrows and snapping his teeth. She let him wrest the empty suitcase from her. They flew down the back stairs and out to where his car was parked in an alley, right under a NO PARKING sign. He started the engine, checked his rear-view mirror and said, "Ready, Freddy?" Out of breath, she nodded. But instead of driving, he climbed out of the car, checking over each shoulder. "Just wait here," he told her. She slid lower in the seat, imagining Warren appearing at the end of the alley. Moments later, Dean was back. He gunned the engine as he pulled out of the alley. "Our disguises," he said, handing her a paper bag. Inside were two pairs of sunglasses.

At the top of a hill, he pulled over to the curb so that he could show her where he worked. The steel plant sprawled beneath them, a tangle of wire and smoke between black towers and girders and rusted cylinders. "Every time I go in there," he said, "I walk under something that could crush me and crisp me and grind me to dust. You'd think I'd feel some sort of fear, right? But it's all just clanking and wheezing and the goddamn whistle. Boredom is what finishes you off in the end."

"You don't belong in there," she said, laying a hand on his cheek.

He kissed her. She parted her lips and let his tongue fill her mouth. He pulled her hair back and kissed her neck. A car behind them honked and he released her to drive, but a few minutes later, he reached over and slipped his hand under her dress and stroked her through her white cotton panties. Wetness had already bloomed through. She shifted and opened her legs so he could get his fingers under the elastic, then threw her head back. "Stop the car," she said.

He kissed her and slid his fingers in and out of her until she came with a shudder. When she opened her eyes, he smiled into them. "God, you're fantastic," he said.

He drove with one hand on the wheel, one arm around her shoulder. The wind blew soft and warm. They crossed the bridge and were welcomed to the United States of America by a large sign and detained by a customs agent who knew Dean from some kind of all-night poker match. "Remember dead-eyed Jack?" he kept saying to Dean, who shook his head and said, "Poor old Jack."

"Who's dead-eyed Jack?" Laura asked when they finally got away.

"I have no fucking idea."

They stopped for breakfast at a place Dean knew—"The best hash browns you'll ever eat," he said—and then they bought a giant box of fudge and sat on a bench at the river's edge. He put his head in her lap and fell asleep, and she stroked his hair and watched the sky fill with clouds. When he woke, he said it was too late to go anywhere. "Anyway, we need to pick up a few things."

In a department store, they bought a small suitcase, a yellow sundress and a sweater for Laura, and a long-sleeved shirt and a pair of dark trousers for Dean. Across the street in the drugstore, he filled their basket with toothpaste, a razor, perfume and after-shave, a comb, Cracker Jack, Coca-Cola and a small box of cigars.

Back in the car, he removed the gold rings from two cigars and took Laura's hand. "For the motel," he said, sliding one ring onto her finger. "Sometimes they ask." Laura remembered the ring she had left in the envelope in the hotel room. Warren would have called her mother by now. Her mother would be sitting at the kitchen table, smoking and making a list of people to call and things to cancel. Her father would sigh and shake his head and say just enough to show he knew what was going on and agreed with the consensus. She would never be able to go home, even after she had a real ring on her finger and was Mrs. Dean Turner.

Dean let go of her hand. "Or we could just go back. It's not too late."

"Of course it's too late," she said. It came out more sharply than she intended. She slid over and tucked herself into his arms. "Do you think I want to lose you again?"

Between them, they had enough money to get all the way to New York, Dean said, where they would both find jobs within five minutes of their arrival, but in fact, they ran out of cash almost right away because they spent the next night in Saginaw so that Dean could look up a guy he knew who would be able to set him up with another guy who had connections in New York, only "look up" meant take the guy and the other guy out for drinks and dinner and more drinks and pay the tab, which came to thirty dollars, which was all Laura had in her wallet. Dean said it was worth it, though, for the names of New York high flyers and nightclub owners who wouldn't look at you unless you came with a recommendation. "I promise you, Laura," Dean said, "you will never say to me, 'Gee, that dinner in Saginaw was a waste of money.'" Meanwhile, though, how would they get to New York?

Dean said, "Don't you have money at home?"

"You mean in Toronto?"

"Yes."

"Yes, but I can't go home, Dean."

"No, I know you can't go home. But you could go to the bank, right?"

She gasped. "Warren works at that bank!"

"So?"

She teared up. "Dean!"

He put his arms around her and told her he understood: he never wanted to see Warren again, and he'd only ever laid eyes on the guy from across the room. It would be easier if they had more cash, but they could get jobs right here.

Only it seemed there were no jobs in Saginaw, and after two days of walking the main street and one night sleeping in the car, Laura said she would go to Toronto. They drove back over the border at Detroit, and in the late afternoon, she walked into the bank in her dark glasses and withdrew all her money. Charlene accepted her bank book and withdrawal slip and counted out her money without looking at her. Everyone else behind the counter stared at her. The entire transaction seemed to take hours. Warren's desk at the back was empty.

"Thank you, baby," Dean said when she slid back into the car.

She nodded. A tear slipped out from under her glasses. She said, "Can we go now?" She was afraid someone would come running out after her, call her a tramp, a slut. She was afraid it would (somehow) be her mother.

The plan was New York, New York, but somewhere along the way, in a pretty little town with a white courthouse and cobblestone streets, they would get married. They would know the place when they saw it, and Dean would pick Laura's bouquet himself. They would arrive, husband and wife, Mr. and Mrs. Dean Turner, to begin their real lives in the world's truest city. But the towns they passed through had ugly, modern courthouses, or they smelled of sulphur or sewage. In the meantime, Dean bought a box of rubbers at a drugstore because they couldn't have a baby until they were well settled in their new lives.

Then there was a new plan, which was to have no plan. You couldn't plan for life, anyway; you had to be open to whatever came along. If they had wanted a planned life, Laura would be married to Warren right now and Dean would still be working at the plant. The new plan was to hit the road and see where it took them. It might take them to New York or California or Timbuktu, for all they knew.

Laura hated the new plan. In the eight weeks since they had fled Sault Ste. Marie, the road had taken them to Scranton and then Bridgeport, and their money was running low again. Then it ran out, and they both got jobs at a motel in Atlantic City, where Laura developed a rash from the cleaning fluid and Dean developed a broken nose in a fist fight with the man who ran the gas bar. Things improved in Ocean City, where they rented a cabana on the beach and Laura got a job typing up invoices at a car dealership and Dean went out every day to look for work. At night, she lay in his arms and listened to the surf roll in. The cabanas around them were empty; it was too rainy for tourists. "Much better this way," Dean said. "No one can hear us make love."

She wanted to talk about what came next. Dean said, "Next what?"

"We can't live here after Labour Day," she said. "We need a plan."

"Okay, Planner McSpanner," Dean said. "Here's the plan: At the first sign of frost, we get back on the road and drive clean across the country to lovely, luscious, sunny California."

But she woke the next morning nauseated, and the morning after that, she threw up. "It was that pizza," Dean said from bed. "Remember I said there was something wrong with it?"

Laura opened the bathroom door. The nausea had already begun to rise again. She said, "It wasn't the pizza."

Everything turned out in the end. It turned out differently from what they had planned and not planned, but they were together, which was why they had run away in the first place and what was supposed to happen all along. They went back to Sault Ste. Marie and got married at City Hall. Dean talked himself back into his job at the steel plant, and Laura got a job at another bank. She called her parents, but her mother refused to come to the phone. "Are you happy, sweetheart?" her father asked, and Laura wept. "I am, Daddy. I really am."

Frank and Vera said they would help. They were lovely people, Frank and Vera, although Vera was a little stern. More than a little, actually. "Don't let Vera scare you," Dean said. "No matter what you do, you're going to disappoint her. The thing to do is not even try." But Laura wanted to try. Both Vera and Frank said they hoped she would have a good influence on Dean, that he would settle down now and turn over a new leaf. They wanted Dean and Laura to stay with them, rent-free, until they had saved enough money to buy a place of their own. And in truth, Laura didn't mind this idea; the house on Sylvan Avenue was big enough, a mansion compared to the little bungalow she had grown up in, and she liked the gables and dormer windows and the rose-laded trellises. Plus, it would give her a chance to get to know her in-laws, now that her own parents were so far away (and one was refusing to speak to her, in any case).

But Dean was adamant: they were not living under Frank and Vera's roof, thumb or prison rules, no way, no how. He promised to find Laura the perfect apartment, but every place they looked at had something wrong with it—it was too small or too close to a schoolyard, or the downstairs neighbours were Nosy Parkers. In the end, the one they took had the flaws of all the other places combined. Dean said, "It'll give us time to find something better," but Laura liked the apartment, with its cupboards tucked cleverly into the wainscoting and little leaded windows overlooking the backyard where the Angelinis grew tomatoes. The first morning, while Dean slept, she changed into a blue skirt and white blouse and went to get groceries at Philomena's down the street so that she could cook a big breakfast for Dean. But when she got back, he was gone *on a mission necessary for the future well-being and happiness of* Mrs. *Turner*, according to the note. She made the bed and picked up his clothes, and then sat in her kitchen, sipping coffee from one of the cups Vera had given her. My *home*, she thought. *Our home*. The home of Mr. and Mrs. Dean Turner. She didn't care that they weren't in New York or California; she didn't care that the apartment had thick vinyl folding doors for the bedroom and bathroom and all the closets. She had told him that last night, when he fell into a melancholy mood after sex and said he was a terrible husband for not being able to give her the kind of home she wanted. "You are all I ever wanted," she said. "From the first time we met." She kissed and smoothed his forehead until he stopped scowling and put his arms back around her. And now he was out getting a surprise, for her.

She got up and washed and dried the cup. Then she opened all the windows, reorganized the contents of the cupboards and drawers, scrubbed the floors and washed the curtains. Mrs. Angelini brought up an armful of gladiolas from the garden, and Laura put them in the crystal vase that had been a wedding present from Mrs. May, a neighbour of Frank and Vera's. When the pot roast was in the oven and the potatoes were boiling on the stove, she looked around and hugged herself. She was a woman of leisure until her husband got home from wherever he was. Where was he, anyway? It was getting dark outside.

EVERYTHING HAPPENS FOR A REASON

She had slept for too long, and when she woke up, Dean was gone. She tried to call him, but her fingers kept misdialling. They were supposed to meet at four o'clock, but she had gone to the wrong station and now he would leave without her. *Dean, Dean,* she sobbed. *Wait for me, I'm just getting a jacket.* She opened the closet door and plunged her hands into the coats, a navy raincoat, a fur-collared camel hair. These were her old coats, in her childhood home in Toronto. In the kitchen, her mother was sifting flour into a bowl. "Help me with these cookies before your father gets home from the hospital," she said, pushing the blue mixing bowl towards Laura. Laura looked down and gasped: the bowl was full of dirt and the dried husks of wasps.

She woke, this time for real. Across the room, her own face looked back from the oval mirror, shadowed in the winter twilight. She had slept all day. Her mouth was full of ash. She could hear the rough murmur of adult voices downstairs, then the high, bright voice of her daughter, like a sudden yellow streamer glimpsed through grey branches. She would go down and help with dinner. She would say, "Much better, thanks," when her father-in-law asked how she was, and it would be true. There was nothing the matter with her.

Downstairs in the kitchen, potatoes were boiling on the stove, and the table was set. "What can I do?" Laura asked Vera.

"Everything is done," Vera said, her mouth a straight, colourless line. She did not approve of sleeping in the daytime. It was worse than lazy: it was giving in.

"Well, I'll do the dishes after," Laura said. Vera did not answer.

In the living room, the baby was sucking on a plastic ring and gurgling in his playpen. Laura dropped onto the sofa, and Dawn climbed into her lap. "Let's play king and queen, Mommy." The king and queen had different ways of doing things. The king slept on his back with his arms straight by his sides, the queen on her side with her hands folded delicately under her cheek. The king ate with a soup spoon, the queen with a dessert fork. "You be the king," Dawn said. Laura was always the king. "Now, this is how they eat their oranges," Dawn said, demonstrating. The king broke his orange in half and peeled segments off with his teeth. The queen laid out segments in a line and ate them one by one.

"Do you like this game?" her daughter asked.

Laura said, "Yes." She didn't have to do anything except lie down with her arms by her sides, or remove orange sections with her teeth.

From the doorway, Vera said, "Why are you letting her eat that? You'll spoil her appetite."

Laura took the orange from her daughter's hand and folded it into a tissue. "Let's save this for dessert."

Dawn said, "Do you know how the king dies?" She stretched out on the floor, extending her arms to make a T. "This is how the king dies."

"I see. And how does the queen die?"

"She dies like this." Her daughter pulled her arms down by her sides.

"Isn't that how the king sleeps?" Laura asked.

Her daughter sat up and pushed her hair out of her eyes. "Yes," she said solemnly. "The queen dies like the king sleeps. When the king goes away, she has to die. But then she wakes up."

The fog came rushing back. It dried up Laura's eyes and the inside of her mouth, but she knew anything she drank would be heavy and metallic against her tongue. "I have to go lie down for a minute," she told her daughter. "Stay down here with Grandma."

Back in bed, she stared at the ceiling, afraid of sleep. If she could sleep and not dream. If she could sleep and not wake. Lying there, she wondered where she had gone wrong. A woman and a man met, they fell in love, they got married. Certainly, there had been deviations, the jilting of Warren and the running away, the "getting in trouble," but they had been in love and were going to get married anyway; she wasn't the first girl whose baby had arrived early, and she wouldn't be the last. Aside from that—maybe even including that—it was a typical story.

But the storyline began to falter a few months after they returned to the Soo. He went to work and she went to work, and when she came home, she sewed new curtains and waited for him and when he came home, he changed his shirt and went back out. She was happy because she was married to the man she loved. He was angry because he was out of cigarettes or the liquor store was closed or the Angelinis downstairs kept playing that goddamn ancient Perry Como song *over* and *over*, it was driving him out of his fucking *mind*.

People said the beginning was the hardest. Dean would settle down after the baby arrived. He would come home at night instead of going out with Will Wharton and the rest of them, thudding up the stairs at three in the morning with a new leather jacket that cost a week's worth of groceries. And when Dawn was born, Dean did seem transformed. He bought two dozen roses and carried the baby around and around the hospital room, introducing her to the flowers and the window and the world outside. His face shone. He was a father! He was the luckiest man in the world, married to the most beautiful woman in the world, with the sweetest daughter, and 1965 was going to be the happiest year of his life. But on the day they were discharged, he forgot he was supposed to pick them up, and she had to call Vera and Frank for a ride home from the hospital.

She swallowed her anger and her worry about his absences and the money, and they burned away slowly in a vat of acid in her stomach, because this was what marriage meant. It meant sacrifice and hard work, especially in the beginning. But how long was this beginning going to last? Even after Dawn turned one, Dean still went out with Will and the guys, none of whom were married, none of whom had any reason to be anywhere at any particular time. They were a bad influence on Dean, calling him up at all hours, keeping him out late. Was it too much to ask of a husband that he go to work in the morning and come home in the evening to where she was sitting, dressed up, made up, the smell of roasted meat beginning to seep from the oven, the whole place spotless, and their daughter bathed and dressed in fresh pyjamas? All he had to do was walk in the door at 6:00 and take off his coat and hang it in the closet and say, "Hi, honey, what's for dinner?" instead of slamming the door open at 9:45, dropping his coat on the floor, calling out over his shoulder as he changed his shirt, "I need my other jacket," and then rushing back out into the night, leaving her sitting in a deeply creased linen skirt, her carnation lipstick flaking, the Swedish meatballs shrivelled in a tray on the stove.

If he would come with them on the weekend to the park, where Dawn toddled after the pigeons, clapping excitedly when they lifted off the ground in a fluttering blur and settled a few feet away. If he would call her from work and say, "Honey, let's leave Dawn with her grandparents. I'm taking you to dinner. Do you remember when we went to that restaurant and ate three baskets of bread and then ran down the street, laughing our heads off?"

If he would remember that they had an appointment to have a family portrait taken at 3:00 on Saturday afternoon instead of forgetting and then claiming he had never agreed to meet them there and then asking why they didn't go ahead without him.

If she could have more of those moments after sex, when he came back to her and put his arm around her and made her laugh so hard she had to press her face into the pillow so she wouldn't wake Dawn. And more of those afternoons when he came home singing, and scooped up Dawn and whirled her around, and kissed Laura and told her she smelled delicious. Or waltzed with the three of them around the kitchen.

When it was good, it was very, very good—that line kept starting itself up in her head. It set her teeth on edge, and she had to snap her fingers in her ears to chase it away. The question was, if it could be that good in those moments, why was it so wrong the rest of the time?

In the evenings, in his absence, the apartment looked vaguely sinister: the brown vinyl couch looked oily; the rag rug looked like a stain; the armchair looked like it was ready to snap shut, trapping whoever was sitting in it. *Stop it*, she told herself, and shook herself vigorously, slapping her cheeks and bare arms. She told herself, *I don't have to wait for him. I'm not going to sit here and count the minutes*. To prove it, she picked Dawn up and ran with her, squealing with laughter, around the apartment, until she was breathless and collapsed onto the bed, where Dawn burrowed into the sheets and Laura pretended to find her and lose her and find her again. But when she checked the clock, only eleven minutes had passed. "Do you want to go see Grandma?" she asked Dawn and put her in the stroller. On Sylvan Avenue, she drank tea with Vera in the kitchen, trying to keep her eyes off the blue clock above the sink. She had to be careful with Vera. Vera would notice if Dawn's sweater was missing a button, or if there was a trace of dirt between her fingers, and she'd get up in the middle of whatever Laura was saying and get out her sewing kit or a washcloth. She also had to be careful in her answers to Vera about Dawn's schedule: Vera was a fierce defender of fixed mealtimes and early bedtimes; she would be horrified to know that Laura kept Dawn up with her on those nights Dean didn't come home, and then let her sleep beside her in the bed. On the whole, it was best to steer Vera away from the here and now.

But she had to be careful with the past, as well. Once, shortly after Dawn was born, she had started to tell Vera how she and Dean had met in Toronto. "When he was looking for his real mother," she'd said, and Vera had dropped her teaspoon with an angry clatter. "I am his mother!" she said.

Laura said, "No, no, I know. I meant—"

Two tight pink circles had appeared on Vera's cheeks. "I've put up with that nonsense from the time he was fourteen. His real mother, his real father. We wanted him! We raised him! And what do we get? *Frank and Vera*."

Laura was shaken, seeing Vera on the verge like this. It was impossible to imagine tears, but there were other kinds of breakage.

Even if the conversations were sometimes fraught, sitting in the house where Dean had grown up steadied her and quelled the startling ideas that flew around her head when she was alone with Dawn in the apartment. Like the idea that Dean wasn't ever coming home. Like the idea that he wasn't even real. Crazy ideas. How could he not be real when she was married to him and sitting right here beside his mother?

If she didn't visit Sylvan Avenue, she walked around the apartment, picking up toys, straightening the furniture. She didn't have to wait for him, but what else was she going to do? Without him, the story didn't make sense. The story was Laura and Dean and their daughter, Dawn. The story was that they were a family, that Dean was her husband, and husbands went to work in the morning and came home at night, and if they were going to be late, they called, and if they weren't going to come home, it was because they were away on business, not because they had offered to drive some guy they'd just met in a bar and his sister to Sudbury. The story was not Laura and Dawn, alone in the apartment. It was not Dean yanking the folding closet door so hard it came off its hinges and yelling, "Jesus Christ, I hate this fucking shitty apartment."

In which case, Laura thought, his misery was understandable: he was cooped up in a tiny apartment he'd always hated. So she called Mr. McCleary at the bank, and he offered her three days a week; then she called Vera and asked if she would watch Dawn during the day. "We want to buy a house," she told Vera. She didn't tell her that they were behind in their rent. She told Dean she was going back to work, and he told her he was going to quit his job at the plant and sell advertising time for the radio station on commission. "No, Dean," she said. "Don't do that." At least at the plant the paycheque was guaranteed. But it was too late. What he'd meant to say was that he had already quit. With his first paycheque from the radio station, he went out and bought a white Thunderbird. "See?" he told Laura. "I told you I'd make a fortune." A month later, when he missed a payment, the dealer called. It was an oversight, Laura explained, and the dealer said he'd *thought* so. He called again the next month, apologetic but firm: "Laura, I'm sure you understand—" Of course she understood: when you bought a car and didn't pay for it, they would call and send letters and then lawyers until they got their money. What she didn't understand was why Dean didn't get this; why, when she said, "The bank called," his face darkened and he said, "Those fucking bloodsuckers"; and why, when she tried to explain, he said she was just like them, a banker, a bloodsucker.

Then Mr. Angelini came up and said they had to go. "Just one more month," Laura pleaded, and he said, "One more month, one more month. Is that the only song you can sing?"

Dean didn't come home that night, and she lifted Dawn out of her crib and carried her out to the taxi and knocked on her in-laws' door until Vera came down in her bathrobe, her hair in pincurls. Together, they put Dawn to bed in Dean's old room. Laura tried to make it seem like a momentary trouble—they had overextended themselves, it seemed, even though both of them were working—but Vera saw through it. "It's not your fault," she said grimly. "I know that."

Relief coursed through her. She'd been afraid Vera would blame her, would think she was out spending money on new clothes or having her hair done. But Vera said, "He's never had an ounce of sense when it came to money. Spends it hand over fist and then wonders where it went." She shook her head. "I thought he would settle down after he got married."

Laura said, "Oh! He has settled down. I mean—" She didn't know what she meant. She didn't want Vera to think that she had failed to make him turn over a new leaf.

Vera said, "Well, you can always stay here. Until you get back on your feet."

Dean would hate it, but Laura didn't see that they had much of a choice. Mr. Angelini said he would change the locks if they weren't out by the end of the week. And maybe if they were here, Dean wouldn't feel so free to disappear for long stretches, or yell when she asked him where he was going, or push over the kitchen chairs because he couldn't find his car keys. His parents would help her set him straight. And it was just for a while, until she could sort out the car loan and the other bills.

Plus, she was pregnant again.

She took a second job as a typist two days a week at the *Sault Star*, working alongside Deb McKenna, who claimed to have forgiven Laura for jilting her cousin, because hey, these things happen, right?, but who showed far too much interest in the state of Laura's marriage, never failing to mention that she had seen Dean on his way somewhere at some odd hour, jeez that guy is always on the go, isn't he, Laura? Laura put up with it, though, because she had no choice, the same way she put up with Will Wharton, who made deliveries of paper and ink to the *Star* and always made a point to come in and say hello to the wife of his good buddy Dean. Once, pretending to nearly drop his stack of invoices, he brushed his hand along her backside and then pretended nothing had happened. Surely, then, Dean could put up with living at his parents', and if he hated it so much, he might come to his senses and return the car and start saving money so that they could move out and be in their own place before the new baby was born.

Frank and Vera rearranged the whole house for them, moving their own bedroom to the sunroom downstairs and leaving them with the second and third floors. They moved Dean and Laura's couch and TV into the attic room, which felt cold and hollow no matter how many throw rugs and doilies Vera brought up. "At least we'll have our privacy," Laura said, coming to sit next to Dean on the couch and taking his hand, but he pulled away and looked at her with ugly eyes, flat and dull like old pennies.

She missed their old apartment with the little balcony overlooking the fruit trees and tomato plants, and Perry Como's "Prisoner of Love" soaring up from downstairs, but she had money now to pay some of the bills that had piled up. She ate with Frank and Vera most evenings, and it was easier, not having to cook after she had been running around at work all day, and at least when Dean did not come home for dinner, she didn't have to eat alone. Vera didn't like the way Laura let Dawn suck her thumb, or how Laura let her fill up on milk and spoil her dinner, or how on the weekends Laura disrupted the routine Vera had worked to get Dawn into during the week. But Vera meant well, and it was only temporary, and what choice did she have, anyway?

Then a black fog started to overtake her, and she wanted to sleep all the time. When Dawn cried, her heart started to race. The doctor said it was nothing. Pregnant women got tired. She should eat properly and get a good night's sleep.

The night before Jimmy was born, Dean came in early and found her crying on the sofa in the attic room. He took her hands away from her face and wiped her eyes very gently. "Hey, hey," he said. "Look at me. Laura. Look at me."

She looked at him and hiccupped. "I feel so bad," she said.

"I know. I know. I'm sorry." He put his arms around her and rocked her. He said everything would be different from now on. He would be a better husband and a better father. He was turning over a new leaf.

"You always say that," she hiccupped.

"I know," he said, "but it's different this time. I promise. I promise. You'll see."

Jimmy was an angelic baby, white and pink and gold, with fine hair and round eyes. Dean looked stricken when he held him for the first time, and Laura thought, *Of course. He wanted a son. All fathers want a son.* This time, he remembered to pick them up at the hospital. He had a bag of toys—trucks and a baseball glove and a little beanbag monkey with a straw hat and a pipe. He'd bought things for Dawn, too, and told her how lucky the baby was to have such a good, smart, strong big sister. He carried Dawn on his shoulders and the baby in his arms. Dawn tugged at his ear and said, "Giddyup, Daddy," and Dean neighed and pretended to bite her leg while Dawn shrieked and held on.

It was good. Dean came home at night. He took Dawn out so that Laura could have some peace and quiet. They came tumbling back in, waving balloons, fencing with pussy willows, sticky with grape juice. On Saturday mornings, he practically destroyed Vera's kitchen making pancakes. He fell asleep on the sofa with Jimmy on his chest.

When it was good, it was very, very good.

Everything happens for a reason, Laura thought, watching Dean show Dawn how to hold the baby. "Thatta girl," he said. "See how he's looking at you? He knows you're his big sister. He knows you're always going to look out for him." The unhappiness had hollowed her out so that she could hold more joy. Things had finally turned around.

ALL THE KING'S HORSES AND ALL THE KING'S MEN

Within three months, things had turned back. Dean was coming home late again. He said sales were slow; he wasn't making enough on commission, but he would be damned if he would go back to the plant. It meant they had to keep staying at Vera and Frank's. It meant Laura had to go back to work at the *Star*. (The bank had let her go. "Take time off. Put your feet up. Stay home and look after your kids," Mr. McCleary said, pretending he was doing her a favour.) The black fog crept back. When the baby cried, she was terrified, and she couldn't say why. Shocking thoughts came to her, and she lacked the strength to keep them out. *I hate my life. I hope I fall down the stairs and die.* In the mirror, her eyes looked sticky and her lips pulpy. *Hideous.* She put her hands on her stomach, gripping the apron of excess skin that hung over it. *Fat.* She felt feverish, and strange pains ran up her back and into her chest. *Sick.*

She kept trying to pinpoint the exact place she had gone wrong. Should she not have married him? But that's what people in love did. Should she not have fallen in love? But how could that be helped?

That night in the Algonquin Hotel, he had said he loved her. He had said he was crazy about her. She was the only one for him. He'd lost her, but then he'd found her, and he was never going to let her go. He wanted to spend the rest of his life, etcetera, etcetera.

So why wasn't he happy?

He said, *Tra la la, tra la laa*. He said, *Doo wop ditty, da doo run run*. Or he might as well have, because what he actually said made no sense. He protested and promised. He talked in circles. He loved her, of course he loved her, he was happy, she was happy, the children were happy, they were all happy, yes, for fuck's sake, he loved her, why did she keep *asking* him that?

She kept asking because she'd overheard two women in line at the grocery store. "What, is he still running around on her?" (Still?) "With that little bit of a blond thing?" And then they had seen Laura and had a desperate need, both of them, to paw through their purses. Because a woman had called and asked for him, pretending to be a clerk from Davis Men's Wear at 10:30 at night. And because Laura herself had seen him one evening, talking to some people at the entrance of McSweeny's, his arm slung around a woman's neck. She didn't know the woman, but she wasn't a little bit of a blond thing at all, so maybe he was running around on the woman he was running around with, and maybe that meant these women meant nothing to him, they were a phase, and he would pass through them and come out on the other side. It had to mean that or something close to that, because it made no sense otherwise.

She didn't want to have made an unfixable mistake, and in fact, the mistake was easy to fix. All he had to do was stop seeing that other woman, or women. All he had to do was go to work in the morning and come home at night. Come home and stay home. Stay home and be her husband. It wasn't too late. As long as they loved each other, the story could be saved, because nothing was more powerful than love.

She overheard Deb McKenna in the employee lounge ("Well, she wanted him, she got him") and stumbled outside to stand in her shirt sleeves in the raw wind, too numb to feel the frost in the air. Will Wharton drove up in his truck and saw her standing there. "Jeez, Laura, aren't you cold?" He offered her a cigarette, and she took it from him. He was talking to her, and she talked back without understanding anything either of them said. Will didn't seem to notice. "You're a great girl, Laura," he said. "I always liked you. You know that?" He stroked her arm and then, when she didn't pull away, he pulled her close and pressed his mouth against hers. She let him kiss her, and then she went back inside. From her desk, she could see Will outside, finishing his cigarette. She didn't care that he had kissed her, or that anyone might have seen it, because it didn't make any difference. Nothing she did could make a difference. Only Dean could change things.

Vera was irritated with her because she was helping less and less in the house. "But I'm sick," she protested, and Vera snapped, "Then see a doctor." She made an appointment, and the doctor seemed to know exactly what she was talking about. He nodded as she ran through the list of symptoms, and handed her a prescription. *So I am sick*, she thought. The pills filled her head with a different kind of fog. She watched thoughts appear out of it (*I should get up and see why the baby is crying)* and fade back into it.

She wanted to be a good mother. She wanted to pick up the baby, oh her sweet, fair boy, with his plump little hands, his face nestled against her shoulder. But the sweet moment never lasted;

there were bottles to be washed and clothes to be folded and now the baby was crying and wouldn't be soothed, and her daughter wanted Jell-O "Right now, Mommy, right now," and why was this all her fault and her responsibility? The only relief came from putting her face into the pillow and forcing herself down into the well of sleep.

A door opened and a voice said, "Shh, shh," and the baby's cries faltered and stopped. *He prefers her*, Laura thought. He smiled and kicked his legs when he saw Vera, whereas he fussed and squirmed when Laura picked him up. Even Dawn said, "I want Grandma to cut my pancakes. You don't do it right."

She wondered how many more pieces she could separate into, and whether it was the sickness or the medicine that was dissolving the shell that held her together. All the king's horses and all the king's men. She used to read that to Dawn. Now her father-in-law read to her daughter while her mother-in-law rocked her son to sleep. An egg fell off the wall, then curds and whey got spilled, but that might have been a different story. The pills mixed up her thoughts. But if she didn't take the pills, she wouldn't sleep, and the birds of terror would be flapping and shrieking all night long. She lifted her hand off her face. It was four o'clock. It was always four o'clock. She would not go down for dinner. She was sick. The name of the ailment was uncertain. Headache. Stomach ache. Separation of self into parts. Tomorrow morning, she would have to get up, wash and dress herself, wash and dress the children, bring them downstairs for breakfast, find her purse and keys, and be out the door by eight o'clock. She would be drained and dead-eyed before she even left the house. But if she stayed home, there would be no money. If there was no money, the bills would not be paid. If the bills were not paid, the calls would start again. The people who called were polite, toneless. Mrs. Turner, we require. Mrs. Turner, we must have.

They didn't even bother asking for Dean anymore.

She didn't know how much was still owed. It was better not to add it up. They didn't know, downstairs. They thought things were under control, that money to buy a house was flowing into a savings account. She couldn't tell them that a river of debt was sucking them under. If she told them, something would have to be done, and she didn't know what could be done. They would say, "We don't blame you," but they would. She couldn't keep her husband home. She couldn't manage the accounts. She couldn't look after her children.

They would blame her, or worse: they would tell Dean to shape up or ship out, and Dean would choose the latter. Frank had already hinted at this. "You can always stay here," he'd said one evening when Dean had failed to come home for dinner and Vera had gone upstairs to put the kids to bed and it was just the two of them, sitting over remnants of chicken pot pie at the dining table. "You and the kids. If things don't work out with him, I mean. We can tell him to go."

Laura had leapt up from her chair, rattling the plates on the table. "I'd better start clearing up," she said, grabbing the gravy boat and some glasses. In the kitchen, she ran the water and tried to breathe through the pain in her lungs. It was the cruellest thing she had ever heard. *We can tell him to go*. It was like offering to cut off someone's head because they had a headache, she thought, and a gasp like a laugh escaped her.

If things didn't work out with Dean, they didn't work out. Without him, it was all wrack and ruin.

She went to work in the morning, and she came home sick and went to bed. The name of the ailment could not be said with any certainty, but she knew something was wrong, at the very core of her.

"What, sleeping again?" Vera said. Laura showed her the pills. Vera read the label and said, "Nerves. I told you it was all in your head."

All in my head, Laura thought. *Just like my father.*

Vera said she had to fight it off. Pull herself together. Snap out of it. "I had it too," she said. "After my operation. The doctor gave me medicine."

"What operation?" Laura asked, although she had already guessed.

Vera said, "A tumour. In my uterus. That's why I couldn't—why we adopted Dean."

"Did the medicine help?" Laura asked.

"I didn't take it," Vera said. "I just put my foot down. I said, 'I'm not going to feel like this anymore.' And that was the end of it."

"I'm trying," Laura said, her eyes hot with tears that could not be shed.

"Well, you need to try harder," Vera said. "That's all there is to it."

The name of the ailment was failure and shame. There was no cure.

She called home. Her mother answered. They had started speaking again after Dawn was born, and for the last three years, Laura had been telling her how wonderful it all was, her handsome, dashing husband, her beautiful little girl, her kind, loving in-laws, her angelic little boy. Now Laura told her mother she was thinking about coming home with the kids.

"Oh, at last!" her mother exclaimed. "Dean will drive, I suppose?"

Laura said she was coming alone. With the kids. To stay for a while.

Her mother said, "What do you mean?"

What Laura meant was, she was leaving Dean. She would take the kids and go home, and then he would realize. He would come to his senses. She said, "I need to come home, Mom. Just for a bit." Then she was crying, and in the sweet relief of it, she told her mother everything.

Her mother's voice was gentle. "Laura, honey, I wish you'd told me sooner."

"I know, Mommy. But I thought it would get better."

"It will get better, honey. It will. You just have to work at it. You'll see."

Laura blew her nose. "I *am* working on it, and it's not working. I need to leave him."

"Laura." The gentleness was gone. "Listen to me. You cannot leave your husband. You have two kids. How on earth would you manage? Believe me, I know. It was hard enough for me with one—"

"Mom, if I stay here, I don't know what will happen to me. I don't know what I'll do."

It was the wrong thing to say. Her mother said, "Laura, you sound just like your father." Then she said, "Your father is better now, and I won't have you upsetting him. Can you imagine—if you show up with Dawn and Jimmy? What would people say? After the stunt you pulled the first time?"

Her mother said no, absolutely not. She said Laura's place was with her husband and her children. She said Laura would have to work at it. That's what marriage was. Did she think it was all flowers and candles and a stroll in the park? It was no picnic, but you didn't jump ship when things got difficult. Laura's mother hadn't left Laura's father, had she? No, she had stuck by him, through thick and thin.

"I don't want to leave Dean!" Laura cried. "I want him to come back to me."

"Honestly, Laura," her mother snapped. "I can't talk to you when you don't make sense." She hung up.

Dean came in just as the sun was coming up. "Where were you?" Laura asked quietly from the chair she had been sitting in all night.

"At Wharton's.

"Don't lie to me."

He yawned. "I'm going to bed."

"What about work?"

"I'll call in sick."

"They're going to fire you."

He shrugged and dropped his shirt on the ground. "I don't care if they do."

"You don't care if they do." She leapt up. "I've been breaking my back working and you—you're out until all hours with god knows who. You have a wife and two kids living with your parents. You can't even—"

The lamp came flying across the room and broke against the wall.

She staggered backwards with a cry. "Oh, calm down," he said, climbing into bed. "I didn't throw it at you."

"But you threw it," she whispered. A deep, wrenching sob shook her. *When it was bad, it was horrid*. "Why do you behave like this? What is wrong with you?"

He lifted his head off the pillow to look at her. "I don't want to do this," he said.

"Then why don't you call to say where you are? Why can't you—"

"No! *This*! I never wanted any of this." He gestured wildly at the room.

"If you hadn't quit the plant, we wouldn't have to live here."

"Will you *listen*? I never wanted to get married and live in this shit town and punch a clock. *You* wanted this. This was your idea." He turned his back to her and pulled the blankets up to his neck.

Laura stood in the middle of the room, her arms hanging uselessly by her sides. "What do you mean?" she asked. "Are you saying you don't love me?"

"No, okay? No. I do not love you."

There it was, the truth, shaped into words and launched into the air at last. And even though she had known, it still came at her like a punch in the head; she saw flickering lights and felt an implosion of blood in her temples. "Are you leaving me?" she asked him. "What are you saying?"

He made a snorting sound. "I'm not saying anything. Now let me sleep."

Laura went into the next room, where Dawn and Jimmy were curled up in their cot and crib. Something dense and enormous had crash-landed in the middle of her head, and it was impossible to think around it. Half her thoughts were on one side of the blockage, half on the other; the beginning and ending of sentences didn't match up.

He hadn't wanted to marry her. But he had loved her. He hadn't wanted a wife and kids. But he had married her.

He didn't want to be married. But he was married.

He wasn't leaving. But he wanted to leave.

He never wanted this. But she hadn't wanted this either—living with her in-laws, paying bills that were never paid off, waiting for her husband to come home and stay home. The black fog, the birds of terror. She hadn't wanted any of it, but she was going to be stuck with it.

She could hear the kettle being filled in the kitchen. In a few minutes, the kids would be awake, and she would have to take them downstairs for breakfast. She stood up and began to dress for work, pulling on nylons, a black shirt and a white blouse. It took her a long time; her hands seemed to be very far away from the rest of her.

Downstairs, as she was shoving her feet into her boots, Vera said they were running out of cereal for Dawn. "I'll bring some home tonight," Laura said. Her voice came bouncing back off the kitchen tiles and echoed in her head, but Vera didn't seem to notice. "Not that expensive kind. Get puffed rice," she said, setting down a plastic bowl in front of Dawn.

Dawn chanted, "Get puffed rice! Get puffed rice." Laura pulled on her coat. Dawn waved her spoon gleefully. "Bye, Mommy!"

At 3:30, she was sitting motionless at her desk when Will Wharton came by with a load of paper and ink and told her she looked awfully pale. A tear burned a track down her cheek. Will said, "Jeez, Laura. Let me drive you home." She shook her head, but he insisted. "Go on, get your coat," he said.

She walked across the room on shaky legs. No one said anything, but she saw them watching her as she pulled on her beige woollen coat and boots. "Going home early?" Deb McKenna asked. Laura didn't answer. Will Wharton held open the door, and she walked out into the stinging cold.

He helped her into the truck and then got in and turned on the heater. She was crying silently, just tears and snot. Will handed her a crumpled tissue. "It's clean," he said. She held it limply and continued to cry as Will told her that Dean was a son of a bitch who didn't know how lucky he was to have a woman like her, and if she had been his wife, he would have made damn sure she wasn't sitting in a parking lot crying her eyes out like this. When he put his arms around her, she made no effort to push him away, and when he started to kiss her, she let him. He rubbed himself against her, jamming his hands under her coat, squeezing her breasts, groaning in her ear, "Laura, Laura." Finally, he shuddered and sat back and said, "Jesus . . . You wanna get a room or something?"

Laura pulled herself upright and buttoned her coat. "Can you take me to the bus terminal?"

"The bus terminal? Why? You wanna go somewhere?"

"Toronto."

He was silent for a while, and then reached for the gear-shift. "You know what? I'll drive you. What the hell. It's Friday. I wouldn't mind getting out of town for the weekend."

SECOND LIFE

Will Wharton dropped her off on Saturday night, after spending Friday night in a motel room in Sudbury trying to convince her to come away with him. They would drive to Buffalo and keep going, get as far as they could with the company truck before it was called in missing on Monday morning; they could get a place, get jobs, start new lives. She said no. She had heard this story before. Will sulked. He was still sulking when they reached the driveway of her parents' home in Toronto. "You could at least invite me in," he said. She shook her head. He said, "Well, I'm gonna keep going. I'm—"

"Goodbye," Laura said and climbed out of the truck.

For the next three days, she did nothing but sleep, waking only to stagger to the bathroom or sit up and drink the cool, milky tea her father brought her. When she finally got up, he talked about the smallest of things: the book he was reading about birds of Ontario, the strange badger-like creature he had seen in a field at Don Mills. He said he was going to paint the kitchen a very light green. He asked her if she wanted a slice of toast.

He didn't ask her why she had left, or tell her that she had to go back. She leaned back against the pillows and closed her eyes. The fog was gone, and the strange pains in her limbs. Her insides had been completely hollowed out. She was almost weightless. She had come through something terrible, but she was too weak to look back and see what it was.

After her mother left for work in the morning, her father asked if she wanted to go for a walk. She had to wear her old camel hair coat and a pair of her mother's boots from the front hall closet. Her father held her arm and guided her down the street to the corner. The air was sharp and clean, and her breath formed wet circles on her wool scarf. "Shore lark," her father said, pointing to a small bird on a fence. "They like the snow." They stopped to watch the small bird with its little cap and scarf of dark feathers. Laura pulled her fingers out of the ends of her gloves and balled them up against her palms for warmth. Her wedding ring was loose on her finger. When she pulled off the glove, it dropped into the snow. "Did you lose something?" her father asked. She shook her head.

Inside the house, she sat in the dusty-rose armchair by the window and watched the branches wave in the wind. "I should call them," she told her father, but she didn't get up. She wanted him to be sick with worry, with fear and shame and regret. She wanted him to wait by the phone, jumping every time it rang, pacing in front of the window, listening for a car in the driveway, footsteps up the walkway. She looked at her father. He patted her hand and asked if she wanted a boiled egg.

In the afternoons, she watched the branches, and in the evenings, she watched TV. When her mother asked her how long she intended to sit in the armchair, she said, "Until I feel like getting up." Her father said, "She's okay, Margaret. Let her be." Her mother muttered, "Oh, for god's sake," and went to bang pots in the kitchen. Laura could hear her but found that she didn't have to listen. She didn't care what her mother thought or said or did. She was warm and comfortable in the chair by the window, and when she grew tired of sitting, she walked with her father around the block or to the park, where he pointed out the birds and told her about their migration patterns.

After two weeks, when her father was out shovelling the driveway and her mother was taking a bath, she went into the kitchen and picked up the phone. Dean answered.

"It's me," she said. "I'm at my parents' place. In Toronto."

"I know."

"How do you know?" Her voice was clipped, flat.

"Your mother called us when you got there."

She waited for him to go on, but he said nothing. Finally, she said, "I'm not coming back."

"Okay," he said. "What do you want to do about the kids?"

The rage that rose in her was hot and ferocious and blinding. For a moment, she thought she was going to pass out. "They're your kids," she said. "You look after them." And she hung up the phone.

The rage remained, a conflagration burning behind her. She couldn't think her way back through it. But she was awake now, and she could think forward. She woke every morning and made a list of things to do. By the end of the day, every item was crossed off. In this way, she found a day job in a law office and a weekend job at the Canadian Cancer Society, registered for night classes in management and marketing and finance, moved into a room in a house full of working women, opened her own bank account and bought a second-hand car.

It was amazing, she thought, how much she could accomplish simply by not caring what other people thought she should do or said she was overlooking or in danger of becoming. She was able to visit with her father by not caring how many sighs her mother heaved or how often she shook her head and claimed not to understand this new world where women swore like men and men grew their hair like women and everyone seemed to be sleeping with everyone else, and now, thanks to Mr. Trudeau, you could get divorced at the drop of a hat and marriage meant nothing to anyone anymore and people could get up from their obligations as if they were pushing back their plates at a restaurant. Laura let the words pool and flow around her. She didn't have to answer unless she felt like answering, and mostly, she was content to talk to her father about how to build an aviary or the photos of herons he had seen at the library.

Her mother asked her when she planned to see her children. "You do remember that you have two kids, don't you?"

Seeing the children was not on her list. Laura said, "I have no plans to see them. If he wants to send them to see me, he can. He knows how to get in touch with me."

Her mother huffed and sputtered and threw up her hands. "It's not their fault you two couldn't get along. Why should they be punished?"

"They're not being punished," Laura said. "I'm the one who was punished. I upheld my end of things, all the way up to the end. I did nothing wrong."

"Laura, they're your children."

"They're his children too. He was going to walk out the door and leave me with them, and I guarantee you, no one would have said, 'Dean, what about your children? How could you have left your children?'"

"You don't even think about them," her mother said.

Laura said, "They're fine where they are. They don't need me." She got up and put on her coat. It was true: she didn't think about them. She couldn't. They were on the other side of the fire.

"You can't just walk away! You can't erase the past," her mother called after her.

But she could. She could walk, she could erase, she could bulldoze everything and start again. With nothing except her own will, she would build a second life, because the first one was untenable, unbearable, irreparable, a mistake from the very beginning. Every piece of it, every action and reaction and relationship, had grown out of a tragic error. Thinking that it could be fixed or would get better was foolishness, the kind of fantastical thinking that had led her into error in the first place and left her stranded in marriage to a man who didn't want her and couldn't provide for her, with two small children she couldn't look after, with in-laws whose help would have erased her completely, in a story that made no sense. The only chance she had was to step out of the story completely and start again, wanting nothing that she couldn't give to herself. She wasn't waiting for the phone to ring or her wish to come true. She was done with waiting and wishing.

She finished her courses, and the Canadian Cancer Society offered her a full-time job, and then a promotion. She moved into her own apartment. No one at work knew that she'd been married. Whenever someone asked if she had plans for the weekend, meaning a man, she always said she had no time. She studied on weekends and swam lengths at the Y. And in the evenings, she took more courses.

Three years and two months after Will Wharton had dropped her off at the end of the driveway, her mother called to say a letter had arrived from Sault Ste. Marie. She stopped by after work and opened it in her parents' kitchen. It was from a lawyer, notifying her that Dean was filing for divorce and would retain custody of the children. She signed everything and mailed it back on the way home. One less thing she would have to do herself.

Three days after she sent back the papers, she was standing in the kitchen of her apartment, reaching for a bowl, when she remembered Vera telling her to bring home puffed rice and Dawn waving her spoon. *No*, she told herself sternly, but the image stayed there. *Bye, Mommy*. After that, she woke up to the fog. She kept working, but she stopped eating. At work, she was given the highest employee performance evaluation possible and another promotion. She was determined to wait it out. *It will pass*, she told herself every morning.

Her father took her out for lunch, and the waitress took away her untouched chicken platter while her father stared out the window. "Laura," he said, "you need to see a doctor."

She said no. "It will go away on its own."

"Maybe," her father said. "But it won't stay away. You need to talk to someone."

"Did talking help you?" she asked. She'd said it sarcastically, but her father nodded. "Eventually," he said.

"And you're all better now."

"I've made my peace with my choices," he said.

Laura watched him stir sugar into his coffee. "Do you remember when we used to come and see you? In the hospital on Saturdays? You were always looking at the door or the clock."

Her father rubbed his mouth with the back of his hand and nodded. "I felt ashamed. Guilty."

"What did you feel guilty about?"

"Being sick. Being in there. Not being home to look after my family. But it was also the ailment. I felt overwhelming guilt over everything. Ants I killed as a boy. A girl I once called ugly and she heard me. Anguish over something I once said to my father in anger. That's the nature of depression."

So the ailment had another name.

His hair had gone completely grey, and his jawline had softened and sagged. Laura remembered him lifting her up onto his shoulders so that she could wave her hands through the branches of a willow tree. That was the father she had lost the summer he had sat in his chair and wept. The summer of Marcus Findley. He had gone away and never really come back. And yet here he was, his eyes saddened by her sarcasm, his forehead lined with worry, his hand reaching for his wallet to pay for the lunch she had not eaten.

She knew what would happen if she talked to someone. Her whole second life would come apart. And it would come out, eventually, that a second life was not possible unless it grew out of the first life. The person would tell her what she already knew: that you cannot step out of the story and start a new one. It was all one story. Then she'd have to go back. She'd have to do battle in order to make peace, and it would be a hard and joyless peace. She said, "Do you know someone, then?" He said, "I'll find someone."

It took another two years to get back, to find a new job in Sault Ste. Marie, to find an apartment and get set up, hire the lawyer who met with their lawyer to negotiate. Her lawyer, George Gerard, turned out to be a childhood friend of Dean's. He reminded her that the chips were stacked against her. It wasn't Dean she had to do battle with. Dean wasn't even in the picture. After his second marriage had fallen apart, he had slipped out of the frame, leaving behind a dozen variations on a theme: he had been arrested as one of Del Cherniak's confederates but talked himself out of a conviction, he had been convicted but escaped from jail, he had been jailed but new evidence was discovered and they had to let him go. He had gone to Toronto, or New York. The club was closed up. He was never coming back, or else he was coming back this weekend. The usual Dean Turner stories. The kids were with Vera and Frank, who would, George said, argue against any further disruption to their lives. "What can I get?" Laura asked.

"Visitation, most likely," George said. "If you want custody, you'll have to fight."

She could not fight Vera. She could not go to court and hear what a terrible mother she had been. How she'd lain in bed all day. Then one day upped and disappeared. Left her own children, drove off with a man in a delivery truck. It was easier just to take what was offered, and maybe that's all she deserved. She said, "Visitation, then."

George agreed to act as a go-between for the first visit, to pick up the kids and bring them to her apartment. She watched them approach from the window overlooking the parking lot. They were so much bigger than she had expected. Dawn was wearing a brown cord jumper and a white blouse. Her dark hair had been pulled up into a ponytail that Laura could already see was too tight. She held on to her brother's hand. Jimmy was wearing dark green pants, a white shirt and a bowtie, and was holding a stuffed animal of some sort. The wind lifted his hair and the edge of Dawn's dress. She couldn't hear their voices, but she could see that they were beautiful and whole. They were coming to visit. She was going to see them at last. Her daughter and her son.

DAWN

SHIPWRECK

At Frank and Vera's, Dawn woke in the night and couldn't remember where she was. "That happens to everyone at night, Tinker," Frank assured her when she confided in him. But she got confused in the day, too. One minute she was walking past the Pacinis' lopsided fence on her way home, the next she was in a completely foreign neighbourhood. Not a single house or car or front yard looked familiar, and she couldn't hear anything over the alarm clanging in her head. Then the houses seemed to undulate and she was in front of the Duchamps', on Sylvan Avenue, three doors from home. The alarm took a long time to wind down.

As her former life deteriorated in her head, the way dreams did, leaving only the gist of things, she felt a throbbing compulsion to see their old house across the street from the park. She asked Jimmy if he wanted to come, but he didn't see the point. Dawn said it was to remember better, but Jimmy didn't see the point of that, either. That was probably because he never thought people were really gone. For Jimmy, you practically had to be dead to be gone, whereas Dawn saw that there were stages of going, degrees of gone. Take Geraldine and Amy, who now lived in a townhouse on the other side of the city. Dawn and Jimmy still saw them a few times a year, when Geraldine called Vera to schedule a visit, so according to Jimmy, they weren't gone, but if Dawn wanted to see Geraldine or just hear her voice, she was out of luck. She could call, but that would be weird, because people always wanted to know what you were calling for. Also, Vera would ask who she was talking to. "Don't be bothering Geraldine," she'd say. "She has enough on her plate." So, even though she still saw them sometimes, she had to say that Geraldine and Amy were mostly gone.

At first the club was just closed (going), then it was closed down (going), then it was Gary's Pizza (gone). Del Cherniak, who had actually owned the club, was also gone, although his name was still in the news: "Cherniak Charges Piling Up"; "Police Step Up Search for Cherniak." He had been running a drug lab outside of Wawa and a stolen car racket in the Soo, and the club had been a front to launder the money. In court, Dean swore he hadn't been part of the criminal operations, which would have been more believable if there hadn't been a stolen Cadillac in his garage. At least, Dawn thought, there hadn't also been a garbage bag of money in his spare room. Dean didn't know where Del Cherniak was, but he didn't expect him to be caught anytime soon. Del had connections in Detroit. Del Cherniak was long gone.

Dean himself left in stages. During the trial, he was staying with friends downtown because it was helpful to be close to the court-house. After he was given a suspended sentence, he was staying with friends in Toronto while he checked out the club situation.

He wrote his number on three pieces of paper, one for Dawn, one for Jimmy, one for backup. He would come and get them as soon as he was settled. Jimmy said "away." Dawn said "gone." The operator said, "The number you have dialled is not in service."

Not everyone was gone. Frank and Vera never went anywhere. They didn't believe in running hither, thither and yon when there was work to be done, storm windows to be put up, at home. And some people who had been gone had come back: their mother had returned and she wanted to see them. "Over my dead body," Vera said, and the case had almost gone to court. Now there was a visitation clause in the custody agreement, so Dawn and Jimmy saw her on the first Saturday of every month.

It was a lot to get used to.

At least at Frank and Vera's, once you got used to something, you never had to get used to it again. Even after Dawn started high school, or when Jimmy had to go to H.M. Robbins for grades seven and eight because he and Tommy Palumbo had smashed all the windows at St. Francis, nothing on Sylvan Avenue seemed to change. The old boxy brown armchair was replaced by a new one, slightly less boxy but still brown. The new blue Chrysler was nearly the same shape as the old blue Chrysler. The free insurance calendar changed from flower gardens to puppies in baskets, but the dates remained fixed. Monday, Dawn, piano, Wednesday, Jimmy, ball hockey. First Saturday, Laura's. Easter Monday and Amy's birthday, Geraldine's. On Tuesday, Vera cooked spareribs, Minute Rice and canned peas. On Friday, they had fish. Dinner was at five, and bedtime was at least an hour before anyone else in their class had to go to bed, no matter what was on television. When they got up in the morning, they made their beds before they went downstairs for breakfast, which did not feature Pop-Tarts (too expensive) or notes in the jam jar (foolishness). No one woke them in the night to see a meteor shower, but no one forgot to pick them up after swimming class, either.

Vera wrote all their appointments in the calendar. She didn't like unexpected requests or cancellations. She didn't like it when Dawn and Jimmy came back from somewhere all riled up, either. Usually, this meant from Geraldine's, where, Vera claimed, they were allowed to run wild, which was more or less the case. At Geraldine's, kids wandered in and rummaged through cupboards, or rushed in to announce that Alex down the road was building another bomb out of a can of deodorant. It was hard to come back unriled.

But Vera didn't like it if they came back too quiet, either, like when they returned from Laura's, which was the least riled-up place they had ever been. Everything in Laura's apartment on Riverview Drive was white, black, heavy, thick and still: white sofa and carpet, black table, heavy drapes, pictures of snow-capped mountains in thick, heavy black and white frames. There was no clutter either: no bundles of coupons or baskets of socks to be mended. Nothing was old or patched or spliced together. It was even quieter in Laura's bedroom, which was the lightest possible shade of grey before white. The bedspread was silver-grey satin. It was like an apartment in a spaceship.

At Laura's, they always started at the kitchen table with apple juice and muffins and the day's itinerary: lunch, library or a movie, skating, shopping for school clothes. The first time, there had been no itinerary. Dawn and Jimmy had sat side by side on the white sofa, looking at their glasses of grape juice on the polished black tabletop. Laura asked them about school, who their teachers were, what subjects they liked, and leaned forward when they answered, like she was waiting for them to go on, but after "Miss Eliot" or "gym," they didn't know what else to say. "You must be wondering why I left," Laura finally said. "I know you were too young to remember, but you're old enough to understand now."

Dawn's head was suddenly cold. Just her head. It was the strangest thing. A picture of a snowbank came into her mind. She blinked, but the snowbank didn't move. The cold moved from her head into her throat.

Laura said she wanted to explain a few things. It had been very hard on her, she said. She had been very young. She had been overwhelmed. She had had no support. And their father had not kept his side of the marriage contract. He had not upheld his end of things. She had entered in good faith and she was left holding the bag.

Dawn was listening and not listening. The snowbank vanished, replaced by a bag, a bulging black sack tied at the top, like a cartoon bag. Something was squirming inside the bag, and it made her feel sick. She didn't want to see the bag. She tried to think about something else, but the only other thing was a snowbank. Was she going crazy? She was afraid of a bag and there wasn't even a bag. Now she started to feel faint as well as cold.

Laura said, "But I want you to be part of my life now. And that's really all I have to say. Is there anything you want to ask me?"

Dawn shook her head frantically.

Jimmy put up his hand. "Can we watch TV?"

Later, Jimmy spilled grape juice on the carpet, and Laura leapt up and opened a bottle of club soda over the stain. When they left, the stain was covered with a thick layer of lavender-tinged salt. After that, Laura served apple juice, and they always had an itinerary.

She told them to call her Laura. "It's probably easier for you," she said. Her name was in the paper sometimes for her job. Laura Turner, executive director of the Children in Crisis Foundation. Dawn always cut out the articles, even though she didn't have a place for them and they ended up creased under a dictionary or folded into a music book. Seeing her mother's name in the paper was like seeing her on a day that wasn't a Saturday: she would catch sight of Laura outside the mall or going into a flower shop, and a jolt would go through her. She would think, "That's my mother." No other thoughts followed.

Sometimes, Laura told them about her work, especially if she talked to a millionaire. Jimmy was interested in the millionaires, one of whom had his own helicopter. That was her job, basically: talking to rich people, convincing them to donate money to the foundation. She went to conferences and, in the evenings, gala events. Dawn was interested in the gowns or almost gowns, cream or silver swathes of cloth. Laura had matching shoes, strappy sandals with high heels, and beaded bags, all hanging in protective slots in the closet.

The fridge was another marvel of order and elegance. Inside, everything was small and singular. A miniature jar of mayonnaise, a carton of milk. One apple, one bun. There would be no shipwreck at Laura's place. Shipwreck was what Vera made to use up leftovers. She layered mashed potatoes, pieces of meat, beans, peas and noodles in a pan and baked it for the afternoon. It was covered over with gravy made from a packet. Jimmy liked shipwreck. Or rather, he liked gravy, and that was all you could really taste. Dawn hated it. She wanted to eat what her mother ate: a chicken breast, a green salad with translucent slices of radish. Food that stayed separate on the plate.

After dinner, Laura gave them each ten dollars for their allowance. Frank and Vera didn't believe in allowance; if you needed something, you asked for it, and Frank and Vera took you to Kmart after dinner, which meant you always had new underwear and winter boots, but never Pop Rocks or Pet Rocks or the soundtrack to *Saturday Night Fever*. Laura said, "This is for you to save or to spend on whatever you want." Luckily, Laura and Vera didn't talk, except to confirm dates and times, so Dawn and Jimmy were able to prevent the automatic allowance confiscation and redirection into the bank.

Then it was time to go home. Stepping out from the lobby after a few hours inside the apartment, Dawn was always surprised by the clatter and patchiness of the outside world. That's why she was quiet when she came back from Laura's. She didn't know why Jimmy was quiet.

What really riled them up, Dawn thought, was when Dean called. Even Vera got riled up. She would start cleaning the inside of the stove or the floor behind the refrigerator as if her life depended on it. Her face would be flushed and damp, and if you asked her the wrong thing (anything, basically), she would yell at you for asking foolish questions when she didn't have time for foolishness and then give you a list of jobs as long as your arm.

Dean usually called to say that he was coming to see them: in just a couple of weeks, or months at most, just as soon as he could get away. Better yet, he'd send them tickets and they could come down to Toronto.

It would be better if he sent the tickets, because Vera said she wouldn't let him darken the door.

"I'm not stopping him from visiting you two kids," Vera said, scrubbing the baseboards furiously, "but I won't have him in this house. Not after all the trouble he's caused us." She and Frank had paid all his lawyer's bills, and all the other bills too, after Dean went to Toronto.

When Dean finally came to visit, he saw Amy first, and then Dawn and Jimmy went to see him in his hotel room. They ordered room service and watched TV, and then Dean took them out on a Secret Mission that involved the Clue of the Dented Fire Extinguisher and a lot of running up and down the emergency stairwells. Dawn didn't enjoy that part as much; she was thirteen—too old to be playing Secret Mission. But Jimmy said it was the most fun he'd ever had in his life. He said, "Grandma would never let us play that at home. I hope he stays at a hotel every time." Still, he thought it unfair that Vera wouldn't let Dean into the house. "Imagine, she hates her own son," Jimmy marvelled, but Dawn wasn't so sure. Once, Dean had called and asked Dawn to put her grandmother on the phone. It was such an astonishing request that Dawn hid behind the dining-room door to eavesdrop. There wasn't much to hear. Vera said, "No. No. No, I won't. No, I can't. It's too late for that. 'Sorry' doesn't help." Then she hung up. Dawn peeked into the kitchen and her knees turned to jelly. Vera was leaning over, her hands over her face, making a sound that was either crying or choking or throwing up. "Grandma?" Dawn whispered, but Vera didn't move. Then Jimmy came loping down the stairs, and Vera straightened up, emptied a can of peas into a saucepan and told Jimmy to get his nose out of the fridge. Her voice sounded almost normal.

The next time Dean came up, they still went to the hotel, but they didn't play Secret Mission. Instead, Dawn and Jimmy sat on the big bed, pillows on their laps, while Dean paced and talked and wrapped them in silky grey ribbons of cigarette smoke. Growing up, he said, he had always known something wasn't right. The way people looked at him, there was something . . . Then he found the box with the adoption papers and it all made sense. All he wanted from Frank and Vera was the truth, but they wouldn't admit the truth. Number one: when he found out, they denied it. "Am I adopted?" he asked, and they said, "No, you are not." Two, when they couldn't deny it any longer, they said they didn't know who his parents were. Three, they said they got him from the Children's Aid. But he had seen a birth certificate and a photograph, and he had done his own investigation. His real name was Daniel Turner, and his real mother was Frank's younger sister, Grace, who had left home and left him behind and never come back. He had gone looking for her, but then he realized she didn't want to be found; she was married with another child and didn't want a stranger to show up on her doorstep and disrupt the whole set-up. The thing was, he wasn't certain. It made sense that she was his mother, but he didn't know for sure. It was pointless asking Frank and Vera, because of the lies. His whole life with them was a lie. He turned to Dawn and Jimmy. "At least you know who your parents are."

They leapt up and ran to him. "It's okay, Dad, it's okay," they said, throwing their arms around him. All this time, Dawn thought, she had been feeling sorry for herself because her parents were gone in various degrees, but it was true: at least she knew who they were. Her poor father! Later, they went to pick up Amy, and when they were eating banana splits for dinner and hamburgers for dessert at Dairy Queen, Dawn made up her mind to find out the truth. She would search for clues and keep notes in a little book, and then she would type everything up and send it to her father. She would call it "The Whole Story" and maybe someday it would be published in the newspaper. "Teen Detective Solves Family Mystery. Whole Story on Page Two." But after Dean had gone back to Toronto, and her search of the house turned up no documents or photographs, her determination began to dissolve. She couldn't think what to do next. Asking Vera was out of the question. Frank was a possibility, but every time she tried to ask, her tongue twisted inside her mouth, and no matter how she started out, the words always veered off into another question altogether and she'd end up listening to Frank explain the steelmaking process or the difference between direct and alternating current. Even if she could get the question out, more than likely he would just say, "Now, now. Don't be bringing that up. It will only upset your grandmother."

She gave up on the idea of the book, but still, she hoped for something, a clue or a phone call, maybe. Not the kind that made Vera double over and choke, but from someone who could make all the locked-up, rusted-over pieces of the past ease open. Someone who had been there at the beginning. The long-lost, long-gone, gone-for-good Grace Turner, maybe.

Four years later, there came a different kind of phone call, and even things on Sylvan Avenue began to change and go haywire. Things with ugly names, like "tumour," rose up out of nowhere and ran around smashing into other things—ordinary things like the china cabinet, but also other things with even uglier names, like "addiction." Schedules were disrupted and beds went unmade and things fell apart where they always did, where they had been falling apart for years.

CHEMO

"Jimmy!" Dawn stood at the end of the creek path, hollering into the trees. "Jimmy!" A breeze lifted the pale new leaves, and their undersides shimmered in the damp morning light. A bird called, two long, melancholy notes. "Time for church!" Dawn yelled. She didn't want to have to edge her way through the buggy thickets and clouds of gnats down to the creek. "I know you're down there, Jimmy," she called. Something buzzed near her freshly washed hair, and she slapped at it furiously. *Asshole.* Why did he have to pull this every Sunday?

She found him under the chokecherry tree, sitting at the fort. It wasn't really a fort, just a big, flat rock at the edge of the creek. Although the creek didn't technically belong to Frank and Vera, she and Jimmy still thought of it as theirs, especially since the city had fenced off both ends of the path, making their backyard the only way in. When they were younger, they had spent most of their summers here, making maps for buried treasure, daydreaming at the fort. Now Dawn hardly ever came down here except to find Jimmy.

"Oh, hi, Dawn," Jimmy said, faking surprise. "I didn't hear you calling."

"Then how did you know I was calling?" Dawn stood on the bank, her hands on her hips. "Grandma says get ready for church."

"I'm not going."

He said this every Sunday. He said he was an atheist. He even said it to Vera, who said, "I'll atheist *you* in a minute."

"What does that even *mean*?" Jimmy muttered to Dawn, but they both knew: it meant he was going to church.

Dawn studied her brother's face. He had changed so much in the last year that people said he looked older than Dawn; they said he looked seventeen and she looked fourteen. His jaw was long and hard, and his blondish curls had straightened and darkened into long brown feathers that fell into his eyes.

"Just come on, Jimmy," she said. "Grandma's freaking out because you aren't ready."

"She's always freaking out," Jimmy said, but he got up. "Go," he said, gesturing. As she turned and climbed the bank, she saw him push something farther into a pile of leaves with his toe. She could only see the cap, but she knew it was a bottle.

Up at the house, Vera was waiting for them at the door. "You two make me mad as hornets," she said. "You know we leave for church at 9:30. You know your grandfather is sick and I have my hands full."

"We'll be ready in two minutes," Dawn said, and they were. It didn't smooth out the crease between Vera's eyes, though.

In church, Dawn knelt and prayed. Let Grandpa get better. Let the chemo work and let him go into remission and let him live a long time. Let Grandma stop worrying. Bring my dad back and let Grandma be happy to see him and let him in the house, and let him find his mother, and let everyone start talking to everyone else again. Also, please don't let my brother turn into an alcoholic and don't let him buy any more drugs off Tony Danko.

Jimmy said the problem with prayer was contradictory requests. "Like two teams are praying, *Please let us win*," he said, "and God just randomly answers one team's prayers and not the other's? It makes no sense."

He had a point, but Dawn couldn't bring herself to stop praying; now that she had outgrown wishing on stars and candles and dimes in fountains, it was all she had left. And anyway, his point wasn't applicable in her case, because surely no one was out there praying, *Please let Frank Turner's tumour get bigger*. There was a very small possibility that Tony Danko was praying, *Please let me sell all this acid and pot and pills*, but she doubted it. She'd met Tony Danko; he wasn't the praying type.

What would be nice, she thought, would be someone to talk to while waiting for these prayers to be answered, like a guidance counsellor, only not Mrs. Ditmars, whose only concern was whether you were having S-E-X and who recited warnings like a robot even when you said absolutely N-O-T. Someone like the young woman with the crinkly eyes who had handed her a pamphlet in the mall last month for something called Lighthouse. Counselling, philosophy, friendship, the orange and yellow pamphlet said. But Vera must have come across it and thrown it out, because she couldn't find it now.

Dawn crossed herself, sat back in her seat and glanced at Jimmy. He smelled of Listerine. "What?" he hissed at her, and she shook her head. While God was taking care of the cancer, she might have to take care of Jimmy. After church, she would go down to the creek and empty out the bottle. If she loosened the cap and left the bottle tipped onto its side, it would look like an accident.

When they got home, Vera sent Jimmy to clear the cucumber patch and Dawn to do the laundry. Aside from taking Frank to chemo, and going to the pharmacy and counting out his pills, Vera spent all her time trying to get him to eat. She puréed vegetables into soup, laid slices of toast around a poached egg. Frank ate a spoonful of soup, took a sip of tea, then said he was full. Vera pleaded with him to keep his strength up. Last week, he had lost his balance and pitched forward, knocking his elbow into the china cabinet and smashing cups and saucers to the floor. He looked terrible, Vera said, all skin and bones.

Frank said, "I was always on the thin side."

But Dawn agreed with Vera. Her grandfather looked like a skeleton in a cardigan.

She unloaded the wet sheets from the washing machine and hung them on the line. Then she began peeling potatoes for dinner. When Jimmy came in, he said, "What's that smell? Like medicine."

"I don't smell anything," Dawn lied. It was a combination of metal and blood, dust and rust. She smelled it when she kissed her grandfather good night. It came off his skin. Up close, it was very faint, but somehow it accumulated in the air. The whole house smelled of cancer.

Jimmy sat across from her and picked up a potato.

"Don't peel it like that," she told him. He was cutting away thick slabs. "You're wasting it." She hated the bossiness in her voice, but she couldn't help it.

"You do it, then," he said, dropping the potato and knife. He leaned back in his chair and stared up at the ceiling. They could hear Vera pleading with Frank to have one more bite.

Dawn wished that tomorrow was a Laura day. At Laura's, the past did not carry over, and she could be a better Dawn, someone who didn't squabble with her brother or cry for no reason. She could become a different person altogether: pretty, popular, normal. “I wish we could live at Laura’s,” she said, reaching for another potato.

“Yeah, but where would we sleep?”

Dawn sighed. It was true: there was no room for them in the spaceship apartment. “Anyway,” Jimmy said, “I’m going to live with Dad in Toronto.”

“Oh, Jimmy,” she said.

“What?” He scowled at her. “Oh, Jimmy, what?”

“Nothing,” Dawn said, reaching for another potato.

The last time they’d seen Dean, a year ago, he took them out for dinner at Rossi’s and told them he was looking for a new apartment and, as soon as he moved, he’d send them their plane tickets in the mail and they would come down for a long visit. They’d have their own rooms, a hundred dollars for walking-around money and the city at their feet. “When?” Jimmy asked, and Dean had taken out his red leather address book and calendar. Happiness surged through Dawn: maybe this time it would come true.

Dean said they could come in May.

Dawn’s gaze fell to her plate, where the juice from her steak was congealing into splotches of pale, speckled fat. She said, “We have school in May.”

Jimmy glared at her.

Dean waved school away. “You can take some time off. Or come in June.”

Dawn knew then that they were not going to Toronto in May *or* June, but Jimmy was still waiting for the tickets. “I’m pretty sure he’s going to call this weekend.”

Dawn nodded.

Upstairs, they could hear Frank throwing up.

Jimmy said, “I’m going to clear the cucumber patch.”

“I thought you already cleared it,” Dawn called after him.

Vera came downstairs with a pill bottle in her hand and stood at the calendar, counting days. "That pharmacist is cheating us," she said. "Next time, I'm going to count the pills right there in front of him." She turned and inspected the colander of potatoes. "Dawn, you're not peeling those right. You're wasting half the potato! If you can't do something right, don't bother doing it. Where's your brother?"

"In the garden," Dawn said. Vera went back upstairs, and Dawn looked out the kitchen window. The garden was empty. She didn't remember the bottle until she was falling asleep, and when she went out in the morning before school, it was already empty. She walked through the cucumber patch on the way back, weeds whipping her bare ankles.

Dawn began to wake up at three in the morning and had a hard time going back to sleep. Sometimes she trembled with cold, no matter how many extra quilts she piled on, and even during the day, a chill lay over her. Normally she would tell Vera, who would slap a mustard plaster on her chest, but Vera was busy with appointments and pill bottles, and anyway, Dawn didn't think a mustard plaster would help. She didn't know what would help.

She fell asleep in math class. It wasn't really sleep, only a grey, watery substitute, but Miss Minelli kept her after school, and by the time she let her go, Dawn had missed the school bus and had to drag herself to the city terminal on Queen Street. People were walking around with their faces tilted upwards and their jackets tied around their waists, but even in the direct spring sunlight Dawn still felt cold and sick.

She stopped in front of what had been the Yellow Brick Road, then Gary's Pizza, now Coming Soon, Consumers Distributing. The building had new white stucco walls and large glass doors, and inside, workers in navy overalls were installing racks where the circular bar had been. She would want to tell Jimmy when she got home, but he never wanted to talk about the past. "What do we have to reminisce about?" he once asked. "'Remember the time Geraldine punched a hole in the wall?' 'Remember the time I ate hash brownies and had to have my stomach pumped?'"

Dawn said, "But there's so much we don't know. Like what happened to Vincent. Remember Vincent, who was with us when we lost Geraldine's money in the snow? Where did Del Cherniak go? And whose brownies were they?"

Jimmy said, "Who cares? Knowing doesn't change anything."

Then why was she standing on the sidewalk, wondering if a strip of Emerald City or scrap of mural remained inside the soon-to-be Consumers Distributing? Maybe a worker was in the women's bathroom right now, looking up at the starry ceiling and wondering what *that* was all about. She could tell him, "That was for Lucy in the Sky with Diamonds. This was my dad's club, the likes of which this town had never before seen." Except he wouldn't really care, because who was she to him? He'd just repaint the ceiling and then go out and have a smoke in the parking lot.

The building next door had a new paint job as well. The storefront was now orange, and the large window was lined inside with a translucent white curtain. In the bottom corner, a familiar-looking yellow sun radiated long, curly arms to the far edges of the glass. On the door, the word "Lighthouse" danced in black letters. Below, a neatly handwritten sign said, *Peace. Freedom. Counselling. Come in, friend.*

Her hand grew a mind of its own. It reached out and opened the door. Inside the big room, mismatched chairs lined the walls, and the air was heavy with a sweet smell Dawn could not identify. Underneath that, she could smell paint.

"Hello?" she called. She had expected a desk, a rack of brochures, a receptionist. *Do you have an appointment?* At the back of the room was an orange plaid sofa and a closed door. From behind the door, Dawn could hear a kind of chanting or singing, she couldn't tell which, in short rising, falling lines. Then the singing stopped and a bell rang, and chairs scraped over a wooden floor. She considered running out to the sidewalk, but it was too late. The door opened, and a guy with loose blond shoulder-length curls came out. When he saw her, he beamed. "Hey!" he said. "Hi!"

Dawn glanced over her shoulder to see who he was talking to, then blushed.

"I'm Justin," he said. "Welcome to Lighthouse."

She started to explain that she had just been walking by, but something caught in her throat and she started coughing. Hard. Her face flamed and her eyes watered. Justin disappeared into the back room, and Dawn put her arm over her mouth and coughed into her sleeve. Every time she thought she was finished, a deeper cough rattled up from the bottom of her lungs. Her chest began to burn.

Two girls appeared. They took her by the arms and led her over to the sofa. "It's okay," they said. "Just breathe." Dawn tried, but she could only cough.

Justin reappeared and handed Dawn a glass of water. "It's the paint fumes," he said. "Everyone's been coughing."

One of the girls handed her a tissue. Dawn wiped her eyes. They were bent over her, looking at her with concern. She tried to say "Sorry" and "Thank you," but the coughing started again. "It's okay," one of the girls said. "Don't try to stop it. Let it come."

The girls sat on either side of her, stroking her arms and patting her shoulders. Justin pulled a chair around in front of her and sat with the tissue box in his hands.

It's almost like I'm crying, Dawn thought.

The two girls, Annette and Cassie, looked like sisters, with the same auburn hair pulled back into complicated braids that reminded Dawn of pastry, but they weren't related. Annette had crinkly eyes. "You gave me a pamphlet," Dawn said, and Annette said, "At the mall? I remember you." Perry had a scraggly ginger beard and invisible eyelashes and was studying forestry at college. Dawn thought they were all twenty or twenty-one, except for Krista, who seemed older, maybe even thirty. "We've just finished a session," she told Dawn. She had straight ash blond hair to her shoulders, a pale, serious face and small, unwavering blue eyes. Her voice was low and clear and cool. "Why don't you stay and have tea?"

Dawn didn't drink tea, but they were all so nice that she said yes, and besides, she was starting to feel better. The tea was not the thick, brown, bitter stuff Vera drank, but clear and golden and faintly sweet all on its own, without sugar. It was called Radiance. "It assists in opening the third eye," Cassie said. "It comes from India."

They didn't explain what a session was, and didn't ask her why she had come in, which gave her no opening to ask about counselling. They asked where she went to school and what she was taking and what she had for homework, and when she said math and made a face, Perry said, "Let me see. I'm good at math."

He looked at her homework and saw immediately what she was doing wrong. "Here," he said. "Write x + 2 here. Then this becomes –4."

Annette and Cassie said their hair was in a French braid and offered to do hers, so Dawn sat in a chair while Cassie worked on her hair and Perry went through her homework on the floor, and the others laughed and talked, springing up from their seats like grasshoppers to pour each other tea. They reminded Dawn of the Waltons: they all had apple cheeks and clear skin. Maybe it was the tea, she thought.

"Oh, let Dawn have it!" Annette said when Justin called out from the back room that there was still a sandwich left from lunch, and he waltzed out with the plate balanced on top of his head and presented it to her with a bow and a flourish. The late-afternoon sun came in through the white curtain, and Dawn sipped her tea and felt warm for the first time in a long time.

"Come back tomorrow," Krista said. "We can take you through the pre-steps."

"Pre-steps?"

Justin touched her arm. "Preliminary steps. To join Lighthouse," he said. "We'd love to have you, Dawn."

"Thank you!" Dawn said, but then she remembered: tomorrow was a chemo day. She had to be home to start dinner. And keep an eye on Jimmy. "Tomorrow I can't," she said. "Maybe Thursday—no, wait." They waited, their faces kind and patient. "My grandfather's sick," she explained, and they all murmured soothingly and understood completely.

"Here," Krista said, pressing a card into her palm. "When he's better, call us. We'll be here."

On the bus, Dawn traced the embossed sun on the card. She could still feel the imprint of Justin's touch on her arm. By the time she got home, the imprint had faded and she was cold all over again.

PROGNOSIS UNKNOWN

When the final round of chemo finished in November, the garden was nothing but pale, broken stalks and wet black leaves, and Frank was almost translucent. Maybe it was because the chemicals had bleached his insides, or maybe it was because there was so little left of him that the light shone straight through. He said the prognosis was unknown. "The doctors said we just have to wait and see."

Vera said they could finally get back to normal now that they didn't have to run down to the hospital every other week, but "prognosis unknown" didn't sound like the road to normal to Dawn.

Plus, she was still worried about Jimmy. Last year, he had been eager to tell her what he was trying and what it was like. *Pot*: everything was much more interesting, you could climb into an idea and stay there for hours. *Acid*: time stopped, spaces stretched and contracted, then all the colours came out. *Some pills Tony*

Danko got from a guy in Sudbury: floating in a little golden boat surrounded by mist, and nothing could touch you, nothing would ever bother you again.

Finally, Dawn told him he'd better stop. "Stop, Jimmy. Stop, or else—"

"Or else what?"

"I don't *know* what, just *stop*, Jimmy, I mean it!"

But he had only stopped telling her what he was taking, and she knew it was something, because his eyes were often red or glazed, and he disappeared for hours at a time. She had found no more bottles at the creek, but she couldn't stop looking. She checked the toy box, his hockey bag, the back of an old TV set in the basement. She searched his room when he was out. Between the bureau and the wall, she found an oblong blue pill, exactly like the ones Frank had been taking. It might have fallen out of Vera's pocket. She couldn't believe that Jimmy would take Frank's medicine. She couldn't believe the pill had fallen out of Vera's pocket, either. Nothing ever fell out of Vera's pockets. She decided to have a talk with Jimmy, but only when the time was right.

One Sunday after the first snowfall, they took their skis out and made long trails up and down the frozen creek. At the rock, they sat side by side, making patterns in the snow with their poles. *Now*, Dawn thought, but she blurted out the wrong words, and Jimmy turned on her in a fury.

"Jimmy, are you still doing drugs?" he repeated in a nasty, mincing voice. "Oh my gaaaawd! Drugs are so baaaaaaaad."

"Well, are you?"

"Fuck off, Dawn." He grabbed his poles and skied to the bend in the creek before turning around. "Just fuck off and leave me alone," he yelled. Then he disappeared around the corner.

She took that as a yes.

The other sign they were not on the road back to normal was that Dawn couldn't sleep, even though she was as tired as it was possible to be, and every day, she got more tired than that. Sometimes, she would turn off the light and sleep would start lapping against her, soft and warm and ordinary, but then it changed without warning into a deep, icy, black hole and she would have to tear herself away and turn on the light. If she fell into that hole, she would never wake up and never get out. One night, she jolted awake and felt an evil presence hovering in the dark just above her bed. Her thoughts flew to *The Exorcist*, which Vera hadn't let her watch, but which her friends had related to her, scene by vile, shocking scene. She lay awake, saturated with cold, dark panic. In the morning, she was afraid to look at herself in the oval mirror above the oak dresser in case she saw a face that was not hers. Sleepiness began to overtake her at school, but even when she kept her eyes open, the lessons came pelting towards her and then bounced off harmlessly. She was falling behind in several classes, and if she didn't keep her grade thirteen marks up, she wouldn't get into university, an idea she had discussed at length with Laura. Her grandparents wanted her to go to Algoma University, where she wouldn't have to throw away money on residence fees and where they could keep an eye on her. But Laura said she needed to leave the Soo to get a good education, and she needed a good education so she could be independent and lead her own life and never have to rely on anyone (i.e., a man) to support her. In fact, Laura had already set up a savings account for Dawn to go away to school. She showed Dawn the bank book. "Four thousand *dollars?*" Dawn said, her eyes widening. Laura nodded happily. "I've started one for Jimmy, too. All you need to do is keep your marks up." The problem was, every time Dawn sat down to do her homework, she was overcome by a mixture of prickly dread and sleepiness. They cancelled each other out, leaving her in a cloud until Vera called her to go start dinner. The other problem was, she was either possessed by the devil or going crazy, neither of which was helpful in remembering the timeline of the French Revolution.

All her life she had wanted to get back to normal: to live in a house where no one had secrets or cancer, to eat dinner every night with parents who had not deserted her, then go to bed without surges of terror and sleep soundly until morning.

At the bottom of a page of math homework, she wrote,

Frank was not frank,
Vera was severe,
Jimmy jimmied open a bottle of pills
And it was always darkest
Before the Dawn.

Then she forgot it was there and handed it in. Luckily, the teacher didn't notice. But still: *not normal.*

One Friday after supper, the phone rang and it was Tony Danko. "Your brother's here and he's pretty fucked up," he told Dawn. "You better come and get him."

Dawn looked over at Vera, who was sewing a button back on to Frank's cardigan. "On page 52," she said. "The diagram of the paramecium?"

"The fuck?" Tony said. "You hear me?"

Dawn's face burned, but she continued, "You have to label it." Vera got up to get more thread, and Dawn said softly, "I'll be right there."

When she got to Tony Danko's, Jimmy was lying on the sofa in the rec room, staring at the ceiling. He blinked when Dawn talked to him but didn't move his head. Tony Danko said he would drive them home, but Dawn said to take them to Riverview Drive. It took twenty minutes to sit Jimmy up and put his coat on and half-drag him into the car. They got out at the park outside Laura's apartment and sat on a bench facing the building. "We'll just sit here until you feel better," Dawn told Jimmy. Jimmy said he was coming down, but Dawn thought he was still going up. "Less go home," he slurred.

"In a minute," Dawn said.

"This Laura's? Why're we at Laura's?" Jimmy tried to sit up straight.

Dawn said shh, she was trying to think, but now Jimmy wanted to talk. "'Member the first time we came here?" he said.

"I remember."

Jimmy said, "An' I spilled grape juice on the carpet 'n' she got so pissed?"

"She wasn't pissed, Jimmy," Dawn said.

"Oh my god, Dawn, you are so . . ." His head flopped over and he swallowed the rest of his words. She reached over and moved his head so that it looked less uncomfortable. A car crunched quietly over snow somewhere behind them, and overhead, the sky glittered with stars.

Jimmy lifted his head and mumbled, "It's what kids do. They spill their fuckin' juice."

Dawn patted his arm. "It's okay, Jimmy. She wasn't mad at you."

"Well, fuck her if she was. Why'd we have to go there, anyway? One Saturday. Why only one Saturday?"

Dawn didn't know. The arrangement was for the first Saturday of the month, from nine until five. Vera said it was what was proposed and what was agreed to, and Dawn had never thought to ask who had proposed and who agreed. Their whole lives had been a series of arrangements she hadn't agreed to. People made decisions, and even when they told you why, you didn't really understand. You just said, "Oh, okay," and went to get your jacket.

"Dawn," Jimmy said. "I wanna go home."

To distract him, she asked him what he had taken.

He said half a twenty-sixer of vodka and then the pills.

"Why did you take them both?" Dawn asked. Why wasn't it enough to be drunk *or* high? Why was it never enough until it was too much? "Where do you get the money?" she asked.

"Allowance," Jimmy said. "I'm cold."

"We can't go home yet," Dawn said. "It's only 8:30. Grandma and Grandpa will still be up." Even if Frank weren't still recovering from the chemo with an unknown prognosis, she couldn't bring Jimmy home like this. Frank and Vera hated alcohol, but they became hysterical at the mere mention of drugs. All drugs came under the category of Dope, and all Dope was lethal. If you didn't die of an overdose on the spot, you would end up killing a little old lady for her handbag. Her grandparents would be beside themselves if they saw Jimmy like this. She needed a different kind of grown-up.

"Stay here," Dawn told Jimmy. "I'm just going to the pay phone over there." Across the street, she placed the icy receiver against her ear and dialled Laura's number. The story came out jumbled, but at least Laura got the basics. She said, "Dawn, honey, that's terrible. I'll call you a taxi right away. He needs to be in bed."

"I *can't* take him home," Dawn said, exasperated. She had just gone through all that. "That's why I brought him here."

"But I can't do anything for him that your grandparents wouldn't do," Laura said. "And they need to know he was drinking. In case it happens again."

"Again?" It came out too loud. The start of a shriek. Across the street, Jimmy slumped over and then curled up on the bench. "It happens all the time," Dawn said. Her voice was full of holes, and the holes were filling up with tears.

"Well, that's what I mean. They have to know. I mean, what can I do for him? He doesn't live with me. I can't ground him."

"Can't he just stay for a while, until he's sober enough to go home?"

"I can't have him here, Dawn. Your grandmother would have a fit. Plus, I have people from the foundation coming here for dinner in less than an hour."

When she got back to the bench, Jimmy lifted his head. "Dawn, I'm so tired. I gotta lie down."

"You are lying down."

"I mean in a bed."

"Soon," she promised.

In an apartment on the other side of the building, facing the river, her mother would be arranging a platter of vegetables and dip. She would be wearing a silver-grey dress and putting out black and white coasters.

Dawn's eyes grew hot, but she refused to cry. These things happened and it was stupid to cry. Her brother was in a drunk, stoned stupor and her mother was having a dinner party for work. It was just bad timing. Frank had cancer and Vera was stricken. That was just bad luck. Her father lived in Toronto because the Soo suffocated him, and Geraldine lived on the other side of town and didn't call very often because she and Vera didn't get along, and Laura could only see them one Saturday a month because that was what had been proposed and agreed to, which meant there was no one to help her now, but it was no one's fault. Nothing was deliberate, so it was pointless getting all worked up about it.

But what *would* Laura do, Dawn wondered, if she just showed up? If she just went over there and knocked? Dawn saw herself pounding on the door with her fist, slapping it with her palm. When her hand got tired, she kicked the door. Up and down the hall doors opened and closed, but Dawn did not stop yelling: "Open the door! Open the door!" Her hand ached, but she did not stop pounding. She *was* possessed. She was on a rampage. "Open the goddamn fucking freaking door," she yelled. Beside her, Jimmy sank down onto the hallway carpet. "Stop it, Dawn," he whispered. "Just stop." A sinkhole of dread opened in her stomach. She wasn't dreaming it. She had no memory of walking across the street or getting into the elevator with Jimmy.

There was a click, and the door opened. Laura was in a bathrobe, her hair dripping wet. Dawn pointed to her brother. "Help him," she said. She didn't recognize her own voice. "Okay," Laura said. "Okay."

After Laura called an ambulance, she called Vera and Frank. "I made an executive decision," Dawn heard her say. "Well, I did. Meet me at the hospital." At the hospital, Laura didn't know Jimmy's health card number. Dawn sat in a hard plastic chair and tried to think if this was the same chair she had sat on when Jimmy ate the hash brownies and if everything in her life was going to repeat itself. Would a social worker show up next?

Vera and Frank arrived, and for the first few moments, the discussion was surprisingly courteous and smooth. Frank said, "Thank you for calling us," and Vera said, "I just can't believe he would do something like this," and Laura said, "I know, I know. It's a terrible shock," and they all stared at the floor. Since it was going so well, Dawn decided to tell them the rest, the bottles and pills and Tony Danko. Vera put her face in her hands and Laura said, "Let me get you some water." The nurse came and said Jimmy was fine, he was asleep, they would keep him overnight for observation. Everyone thanked the nurse, Frank thanked Laura again, and Dawn thought, *That went really, really well.*

Then Laura said, "We should probably talk about how we're going to handle this." She squeezed the fingers of one hand and then winced, as if she had hurt herself.

Vera said, "He's not going to see that Tony Danko anymore, for one thing."

Laura said, "I want to ask my colleague to consult with us, maybe tell us what programs are available. She's a social worker."

Dawn thought, *I knew it.*

Frank said, "Programs?"

Vera said, "He doesn't need a program. He needs a shorter leash."

"Like counselling," Laura told Frank. "Or maybe even a prevention program for addiction."

"Addiction! He's fourteen years old, for heaven's sake!" Vera said. "You tell a kid he's got a problem like that, and the next thing you know, he'll have a problem like that."

"But he does have a problem," Dawn interjected.

Vera told Dawn to keep her nose out of it. She told Laura that Jimmy did not need any of that nonsense.

Laura looked like she had been slapped. "Why is it always nonsense to you? You said the same thing to me when I was depressed and suicidal."

Frank said, "Let's not go into all that now. That's all over and done with."

Laura's voice rose. "It's not over and done with. I have to face the consequences every day of my life."

"You made your bed," Vera said, her voice climbing over Laura's. "Don't blame us for your mistakes!"

"I had no support, no understanding—"

"We supported you! We put a roof over—"

The nurse came over and asked if they could please keep their voices down. Dawn was mortified. Vera said, "We were just leaving. We'll pick Jimmy up in the morning."

Laura called down the hall after them. "You'll be hearing from my lawyer."

On the way home, Vera said she would fight tooth and nail on this one. Social worker! Prevention program! She would not put up with a stranger coming in and telling her how to handle the child she had raised practically from day one. Who was Laura to say she knew best for him when she had walked out before he could talk? "People think they can leave their kids with us and then come back and get them like they're picking up laundry!" Vera said.

Frank said, "I know, I know. But she's still his mother," and Vera burst out, "Frank! I cannot do this again!" and in the back seat, Dawn listened to the strange silence that drifted over the three of them like snow. *When I was depressed and suicidal. I cannot do this again.* The more she found out, the less she knew.

Vera pulled into the driveway and turned off the engine, but no one got out. In the back seat, Dawn waited for Frank to sigh and say nothing, which would mean Vera had won, end of that story, but he said, "She wants to help—"

"Well, why didn't she help when he had bronchitis? Where was she when he was throwing up in the middle of the—"

"And besides," Frank said, "who knows what our situation will be a year from now?"

It was Vera's turn to say nothing. They all got out of the car. Dawn looked up through the bare branches and watched a thick, slow-moving cloud extinguish a line of stars. A dog barked down the street. It was horrible to think that there was a situation worse than this one.

UNIVERSAL CONSCIOUSNESS

Vera and Frank brought Jimmy home from the hospital, and there was about an hour of quiet before the fighting started. Jimmy fought with Frank and Vera. Vera fought with Laura. Laura's lawyer fought with the principal of Jimmy's school. Every time the phone rang, someone was yelling at someone. Vera yelled at the social worker who called to say that Jimmy had an appointment scheduled on Wednesday, which turned out to be the same day Frank had a doctor's appointment, and then Jimmy yelled at Vera that he wasn't a goddamn baby and could go to an appointment by himself, and then Vera yelled at Laura for scheduling appointments without consulting anyone. Dawn and Frank listened from the living room. "Everyone's fighting," Dawn said.

"Well, they're talking," Frank said. "That's something."

He might have been right, because previously unthinkable conversations seemed to be happening behind Dawn's back.

Vera came into the living room and said, "Geraldine says she can pick Jimmy up after his appointment. It's two blocks from her place." Dawn's mouth popped open in surprise. When had Vera talked to Geraldine?

"I didn't," Vera said. "Your mother called her."

A few days later, Vera said, "Your mother wants to know if you want to visit her this Saturday. If you do, then call her." When Dawn pointed out that it wasn't the first Saturday of the month, Vera held up her hand and said, "I've got enough to keep track of. You're old enough to make your own schedule."

Vera and Frank went to an appointment with Jimmy's therapist, and when they came back, Vera said the most unthinkable thing of all: "Dawn, do you have a number for your father?"

Dawn brought out all the numbers, and Vera dialled every one, but either no one answered or it was the wrong number or the person hadn't seen Dean in ages.

Vera said, "Well, we tried." She said it was time to start dinner, but neither of them moved. The phone rang, and they both jumped. Dawn reached for it shakily, but it wasn't Dean. It was the doctor, asking to speak to Frank.

When she arrived at Lighthouse, only Justin was in the front room. "Dawn! Welcome back! Is your grandfather better?"

"Yes," she lied.

"The others are in session," Justin said. "But I can take you through the pre-steps." He patted the chair beside him, and she sat down, feeling fluttery and clumsy.

Don't babble, she commanded herself. She was sorry now that she had worn her good blouse, a ruffled yellow affair with flounces at the wrists: it looked prim and teacherly next to Justin's light denim shirt and jeans.

"Ready?" Justin said. She nodded.

First, he said, Lighthouse was not a religion. It took readings from the Vedas, the Sutras, the Koran, the Bible and teachings from all the great philosophers—Nietzsche, Maharishi Mahesh Yogi—but it was not a religion *or* a philosophy. It was a path, and this path was based on the recognition of a basic spiritual truth called Universal Consciousness, or UC. Everyone was already on the path to UC, whether they knew it or not, but some people were moving along the path faster than others because they had jettisoned their baggage and overcome the obstacles, the main ones being judging and fearing.

"I mean, when you're afraid, you're not free, right? When you're afraid of what other people will say about you or how they'll judge you, it's like being in a prison of their expectations."

His eyes were brown with gold flecks, Dawn noticed.

People who are afraid, Justin said, try to elevate themselves by judging others. And their judging makes others afraid. And the cycle continues. However. Using a scientifically developed method called Psymetrics, Lighthouse helped people drop their fear and overcome the obstacles and move freely on the path to UC. That was all. It wasn't a religion. It wasn't a cult. It was a philosophy.

Dawn had missed something. "But you said it wasn't a philosophy? Or—or is it?"

Justin said, "Oh fuck. Sorry. I'm totally screwing it up."

"No, no," Dawn protested. "It's me."

He tapped her knee. "No, it's not you, Dawn." He was looking straight into her eyes, which made her feel slightly woozy. "That was my fault, okay?"

Dawn nodded.

"Don't tell Krista I messed up."

Dawn was unable to suppress a smile. "Why? Are you afraid of being judged?"

Justin threw back his head and laughed. She laughed too, astonished by her own temerity.

"Touché," Justin said.

"Touché," she said back, which was totally the wrong thing, but before she could even begin to berate herself inwardly, Justin said, "We should have clinked glasses there or something." They smiled at each other for a bit, and then Justin cleared his throat and said, "So . . . anyway. Does what I said make sense to you?"

"It does," she said. Parts of it did. The fear part, anyway.

Justin nodded. "I knew you'd get it." He said she could start coming tomorrow for regular sessions.

A session started with meditation. They sat in a circle on straight-backed chairs in the back room. Krista, the facilitator, said, "Close your eyes. Breathe in, breathe out." Dawn sat as still as she could, but parts of her itched and twitched and her eyelids fluttered. After an interminable amount of time that turned out to be twelve minutes, the bell rang and they all opened their eyes. Krista then read a teaching about how, with commitment, the obstacles were pulverized into the dusts of time, leaving only the brilliant luminosity of Universal Consciousness. At the end of the session, Krista said, "Let go of your fear," and everyone said, "No fear."

"Let go of your judgment."

"No judgment."

"Where is the Light?"

"The Light is Within."

"Then be a beacon," Krista said, and rang the bell.

After that was open floor. Anyone could say anything that was on their mind without fear. Speaking openly without fear was a cornerstone of Psymetrics. Mostly, people were so afraid of being judged and rejected, Krista explained, that they said what they thought they should say instead of what they actually thought. The hair on Dawn's arms lifted. That was exactly what she did! If her friends at school said that punk rock was obnoxious, she said it was obnoxious. If they changed their minds, she changed her mind. Practically every exchange she had was a lie. Even at home. She said she was fine when she was not fine. She said she understood when she did not understand. She said things didn't bother her when they bothered her *all the time*.

"Dawn?" Krista said. "Do you have something?" They were all looking at her. She said, "I—I have a lot of fear," but she couldn't go on, because if she said any of it out loud, it would all become true and irreversible.

After a moment, Krista said, "I think I'd like to spend a few minutes with Dawn alone."

It was dark when she got home. Vera was furious, banging pot lids and pans as she did the dishes: Dawn hadn't called, and now her dinner was cold.

"Sorry, Grandma," Dawn said. And she was. She was sorry that her grandmother was so afraid, because Vera could be free any time she chose. Anyone could be free. Anyone could choose. They were all born with the knowledge, but it grew cloudier and fainter as they grew up. "If the doors of perception were cleansed," Krista had said, "we would see everything as it is: Universal Consciousness."

Lying in bed that night, Dawn went over all the things Krista had told her. She wasn't possessed by the devil, and she wasn't going crazy. "How do you know?" she'd asked Krista, and Krista had reached over and taken her hand. "There is no devil, Dawn," she said. "These feelings are your own feelings." Dawn nodded, her throat aching with the terrible truth of it.

Krista also said these feelings were understandable. "My god, Dawn. Your mother left. Your father left. Your stepmother left.

Your little brother is coping with his problems by drinking. Your grandfather has cancer. You can't talk to your grandmother. Who wouldn't feel like they were going crazy?"

Dawn had suffered losses, Krista said, but there was good news. First, on the path to UC, nothing was ever truly lost, because UC contained everything and once you were connected to UC you were connected to everything. Second, Dawn was already farther along the path than many people who had been studying for years. She was already a beacon. And finally, Krista said, "You're not alone anymore, Dawn. We're here for you."

In her room, Dawn lifted a strand of her hair to her face and sniffed; it still smelled faintly of jasmine incense. She drifted into sleep and stayed asleep until her alarm woke her in the morning.

Dawn went every day after school. Annette and Cassie, whose shifts at Rossi's didn't start until 6:00, were usually there already. Perry arrived a few minutes after Dawn. They both took out their homework, although Dawn didn't actually do hers and Perry's seemed to consist largely of highlighting passages in *Introductory Forest Science*. Annette brought sandwiches or banana loaf, and someone would make tea, regular or Radiance. Around 4:15, Dawn would go to the bathroom to check her hair and reapply her lip gloss. Justin always arrived at 4:30. She was happiest when he slid into the chair next to her; if his arm brushed hers or his knee bumped against her, she would feel the warmth of it for hours. But even when he sat across the room, she was happy. They had their own greeting: "Touché." Sometimes they just raised imaginary glasses to each other.

If Krista was there, they talked about Lighthouse projects: pamphlets and an open house and fundraising strategies. Krista had been planning to go to Montreal, but her cousin had this commercial property in Sault Ste. Marie, so Andre told her to take Lighthouse to Ontario. Andre had been Krista's psychology professor in California. He had developed the core UC teachings and was already conducting sessions when he realized the university itself was full of professional judgers and fear-mongers, so he left and opened up the original Lighthouse. It began as casual meetings of friends, but Andre noticed that people who just dropped in very soon dropped out. You could not dabble your way to UC. Plus, it cost money to run Lighthouse and spread the message. So now there were fees for membership and meetings. Krista waived these fees for Dawn. "You contribute in other ways," Krista said, and everyone nodded in agreement.

If Krista was not there, they played charades. At first, Justin and Dawn were on the same team, but they got separated after Dawn gave the signs for movie and four words, and Justin said, "*The Wizard of Oz*."

"It's true," Justin said, "I *can* read Dawn's mind." He put his fingers to his temples and closed his eyes. "I'm getting . . . wait . . . becoming clearer . . . She thinks you're morons and sore losers. Am I close, Dawn?"

If they weren't playing charades, they just talked. Dawn liked it best when she and Justin had the couch to themselves. He always wanted to hear more about her family, and she ended up telling him everything: how Laura had left when Dawn was three and her brother was a baby and then had returned, years later; how she and Jimmy had lived with their grandparents, then their father and stepmother, then their grandparents again. Justin killed himself laughing over Vera's expressions, but he especially loved hearing about the time with Dean and Geraldine. "Whoa," he interrupted. "Whoa. There was a *stolen* car. In your garage."

She had to laugh at how he spat out the words. "Come on," she said. "You don't want to hear this. Or . . . tell me about your family."

"Are you *kidding* me? You wanna hear the absolute worst thing that happened to me growing up? My father didn't assemble my swing set properly, and I fell off and broke my wrist. That's it. Oh, and once my mother had too much Baby Duck at Christmas and burned the gravy. We are the most boringly normal family you will ever come across, kiddo."

Sometimes he called her that. She liked it better when he called her Delta Dawn, like the song. When she sat beside him in session, she wished with all her might that he would slip his arm into the space between their chairs and hold her hand. She imagined other things, too. She hoped he couldn't read her mind.

When she was at Lighthouse, all her dread melted away. Even concrete fears were shown to be faulty and insubstantial. If she said, "I'm afraid that I'm going to fail math," the others would point out the flaw in her thinking. This was a technicality. Technicalities were conjured up and thrown down by the ego to impede progress along the path. So what if she failed math? So what if she did not graduate with her peers? So what if she didn't get to go to university? School offered facts; Lighthouse offered truth. Yes, it was true that her mother had left and her father was gone, but everyone had to walk their own path to UC in their own way. Yes, it was true that her grandfather might die, but everyone died. Those who did not understand death could not understand life. At Lighthouse, she was floating down a river of light and warmth, and everything was really and truly all right.

The problem was after the meetings. At home, there was a new word, the ugliest word of all: "metastasize." It meant the tumour was shedding in Frank's veins, seeding itself in new places. The prognosis was no longer unknown. The prognosis was six months.

But Vera said the doctors didn't know. People had been told six months and had gone ahead and lived for six years. Mrs. Klukay's brother, for example. They opened him up and it turned out he didn't even have cancer. She saw him just last week buying spice cake at the A&P. "It just goes to show," Vera said to Dawn. She was washing the dishes; Dawn was drying. "Half the time, they just don't know."

Furtively, Dawn scraped burnt onion residue out of a pan before drying it. Every day she took dishes out of the cupboard that were flecked with dried food. The kettle boiled dry so many times the bottom burned out. It made Dawn feel queasy.

Vera's hands were motionless in the soapy water. "The first time we met, we were standing in line for the bus, and I saw him and thought, *That is a good man.* I just knew. And I was right. I was right." Her eyes were far away. "All the years went by overnight."

"Those who cannot face death cannot understand life," Dawn said.

Vera's hands jerked out of the dishwater. For a moment, Dawn thought her grandmother was going to slap her. But she only hurried out of the room.

Dawn picked up a spoon and dried it carefully. She wished she could live at Lighthouse. Sitting in the circle with her friends, she would be completely connected to UC and nothing could hurt her, not even her grandmother's serrated sobs.

The path was graded. The facilitator noticed where you were blocked and when you were ready to move up a level. Then you went into a closed-door session, which was another cornerstone of Psymetrics and for which you paid a fee. When you invested in a closed-door, you invested in yourself.

"How many levels are there?" Dawn asked. Krista told her that wanting a number was magical thinking. Suffice it to say that people above them, people at the highest level, could communicate without speaking. They could cure illnesses that baffled medical science. There were realms of knowledge so profound they lacked names. "You're just at the beginning of the path," Krista told Dawn, which was confusing, because earlier, Krista had told her she was advanced for her age.

During a closed-door, the facilitator asked questions. "How do you feel right now? What are you withholding? What are you hiding and what are you hiding from?" Dawn started with the outside things: "My grandfather's cancer has metastasized. My dad hasn't called us in a year and we can't track him down and my grandpa's going to die and my dad won't know." But Krista always led her to the inside things. "I feel like a freak. There's something wrong with me. When people look at me, I can't walk properly." You could say anything, no matter how secret or seemingly unutterable. "I have dreams about Justin. Sex dreams."

The facilitator never said anything was right or wrong or good or bad, even when you confessed to taking money from your grandmother's wallet to pay for a closed-door, knowing that she was too worried about your grandfather to remember what she had spent between the grocery store and the pharmacy. "No judgment, no fear," Krista said.

After the questions, the facilitator led you through a visualization exercise to dissolve your obstacles. "You are on a road," Krista said, "and that road stretches out endlessly before you, but in front of you, there is a block. A pile of something. Look closely at that pile and tell me what you see."

Dawn, sitting cross-legged on the floor, peered into the darkness of her eyelids. She said, "Darkness."

"Keep looking," Krista said.

Dawn's forehead furrowed as she strained against her own eyelids. "Papers and books," she said finally. She saw her overdue history essay. Her last math test: 23%. Dictionaries, notebooks. Newspaper clippings. A piece of paper with a phone number on it. A tear slipped out of one eye and plopped onto her wrist.

"Good. Good. Now, light a match," Krista said softly.

Dawn tried, but the papers were soggy. They wouldn't burn. She tried again. She tried a lighter, gasoline, a blowtorch.

"The facilitator can only facilitate," Krista said. "Only you can clear the block."

In Dawn's mind, it started to rain.

She opened her eyes. "It's not working."

For a brief moment, Krista looked irritated, but she only said, "No judgment, no fear, Dawn."

"No judgment, no fear," Dawn said. But she judged herself, and she was afraid that if she couldn't get through, she might be blocked for good.

She tried to get Jimmy to come with her to Lighthouse. "It would really help you," she said one evening when they were watching TV. "It's really helped me to see things properly. Like how I always wanted Dad to come back. Or to have a normal family. And that caused me to fall off the path."

"How is wanting Dad to come back falling off the path?"

"Because it's judging, and judging is falling off the path."

Jimmy thought about this. "But if you judge judging as bad, isn't that still judging?"

"Oh, Jimmy," she said, exasperated. "I'm talking about having expectations that arise out of fear and cause more fear."

For some reason, this irritated Jimmy so much that he jumped up and began pacing in front of the TV. "Yeah, well, parents are *expected* to look after their kids. That's their freaking job. It's not like a kid can go, 'Oh, okay, no problem, I'll just be over here in the corner, raising myself.'" He jammed his hands in his pockets and actually glared at her.

"Jeez, settle down. Sometimes people have obstacles, okay? The parent can be blocked." Krista had taken her through an exercise for this. She had visualized her mother, her father, her grandparents, and had painted them over with the white light of acceptance and forgiveness, the clear light of UC.

"Well, it's not my fault they're blocked. They should still raise their goddamn kids."

"See, Jimmy? See how this is all your own judgment and fear?"

"No shit, Sherlock! No shit it's judgment and fear. I was fucking terrified." He was practically yelling.

"You mean the brownies?"

Jimmy's face contorted. "The brownies. Not the brownies. Everything! All the time!"

"That's what I mean. Come to a session with me. I feel completely happy when I'm there."

Jimmy sat back down and turned his eyes to the TV. "I have my own counsellor. Anyways, no offense, Dawn, but it sounds like crap to me."

When Dawn arrived at Lighthouse the next day, everyone was in the back room, talking all at once. Krista repeated the excellent news for Dawn: next week, Andre was leading a ten-day retreat outside of Toronto, for senior practitioners and above, and Krista would be one of the facilitators, and everyone was invited. Although Dawn wasn't nearly far enough along the path to work at that level, she would still benefit from sitting in on the sessions, and Krista would ask Andre to conduct an individual session with Dawn as a special favour.

Dawn said, "Ten days? Next week?" Her final projects were all coming due, and her math teacher had set up a bunch of tutorials so that she wouldn't fail the course. And what would she tell Vera?

"We'll take care of transportation and accommodation, Dawn. All you have to do is pay the retreat fee," Krista said.

Justin winked and raised an imaginary glass. Krista rang the bell for meditation.

There was no way she could ask Vera for a thousand dollars. Vera didn't even know about Lighthouse. Dawn had told her she was attending a study group after school, which was true, because what was a session if not a form of study, but Vera would not understand a retreat, and she would certainly not understand a thousand dollars.

She asked Laura, who looked startled. "Lighthouse?" she said. "That hippy-dippy religious thing downtown?"

"It's not a religion," Dawn said. "It's a philosophy."

Laura said she would have to think about it. Instead, she called Vera, who greeted Dawn after school with "Your mother tells me you've gotten involved in a cult and you asked her for money to go to some camp or other in southern Ontario. Well, you aren't going, and that's final."

Dawn put down her bag, too stunned to say a word.

"Is that where you've been going after school? That's the study group?" She didn't wait for an answer. "I'm at the end of my rope, Dawn. Just when we get your brother turned around, you start. Thank goodness your mother had her eyes open, that's all I can say."

"It's not a cult," Dawn said finally.

"I don't care what it is," Vera said. "You aren't going."

"Fine." Dawn picked up her bag and went upstairs. In her room, she lay on her bed, her mind whirling.

Jimmy knocked on the door. "Dawn?"

"What?"

"They only want money, Dawn," he said through the door. "A real religion doesn't make you pay to join."

"What about the envelope Grandma puts in the basket every Sunday?" Dawn said to the ceiling. "Anyway, it's *not* a religion."

She listened to his footsteps on the stairs. Not going on the retreat meant she would never progress. Worse, she would be left behind. She had a feeling they would all go to the retreat and not come back. Justin wouldn't come back. Her mind strained for a way to go. Then she remembered her university money.

RETREAT

It wasn't actually running away, since she was legally an adult. Dawn thought the age of majority was eighteen, but Krista said it was seventeen. Anyway, legality had nothing to do with it. The law was a technicality. Commitment to the path meant rejecting the technicalities, and even certain relationships, in order to grow more fully. You couldn't drag people along the path with you, but you couldn't allow them to drag you backwards, either.

Dawn left a note beside the phone. She just said *retreat*, not where, and Krista said that non-members wouldn't have access to that information. *Please don't worry about me*, she wrote. *I am with people who are not only my friends but also my mentors.*

They left in the evening and drove through the night. Dawn went with Justin and Krista in Justin's car; Annette and Cassie went in their own car. Perry refused to miss his summer session courses, and Krista said Perry's lack of commitment would have prevented him from gaining anything from the retreat anyway.

Dawn tried to find out what exactly they would do on the retreat, but Krista wagged a finger. "Don't anticipate. Participate."

When it got cold, they gave Dawn a sleeping bag and she watched the lights well up and fade on the car ceiling. She hoped her grandparents were not awake with worry, but then she reminded herself: if they chose to worry, that was their decision. She slept and dreamed that the retreat was in an actual lighthouse, a white wooden structure capped by a red roof, with curtained windows all the way up the sides. When the door opened, everyone was there: her grandparents, her parents, Jimmy, even Geraldine and Amy. "Surprise," they said. "Surprise!"

The car bumped along a rough road and then stopped. "Wake up, sleepyhead," Krista said, but Dawn was already awake. They were parked outside an old farmhouse.

"Where are we?" she asked.

"Where do you think?" Krista said and opened the door. Cold air swarmed in. Justin smiled at her. "Uxbridge," he said.

It wasn't a lighthouse at all, just a crumbling brick farmhouse with narrow windows made of old yellowed glass and a tarpaper addition that had no windows at all. The yard was full of rusted things half-sunk into the wet earth: an old bed frame and part of a plough. Seven or eight other cars were parked around the farmhouse, along with a dirty white van. Dawn followed Justin and Krista, hopping from stone to plank to root to avoid the squelching mud. The grey sky was breaking apart over low rocky hills to show a golden sky. *Be a beacon*, Dawn reminded herself. *No judgment, no fear.* But the wooden huts at the end of the driveway looked like outhouses, and where would everyone sleep?

Inside, the rooms were crammed with boots and sleeping bags and boxes of pamphlets and people standing, sitting, eating bowls of cereal, working an adding machine, reading a novel called *The Fountainhead*. "Krista!" everyone shouted, and there were hugs all around. Everyone flurried and hurried into another room, and Dawn could hear cries of excitement from deep inside the house. Justin had disappeared too. Dawn stayed where she had stopped in the kitchen, repeating *No judgment, no fear* against the other voice in her head that was judging the filth of the floor and the sour smell from the overflowing garbage can, and fearing the next ten days, and wishing she could go home. Finally, Justin came back. "Let's see what there is for breakfast," he said. He looked at her closely. "You okay?"

She nodded. "Just tired."

He hugged her and his hands made circular motions on her back. "I'm glad you're here," he said, and his chest was so warm and solid she wanted to melt into him. He held her arms and pulled away to look at her. "You'll feel better after you eat something." She did feel better, watching Justin set down bowls and spoons and a bag of unsweetened puffed rice.

In the mornings, they attended an open-floor session before getting into a van and driving into Toronto, where they handed out pamphlets on Yonge Street. Krista and Justin stayed behind to facilitate the advanced practitioner sessions with Andre, but after the first day, Justin came into the city with them. On Yonge Street, they were divided into units of three, and no matter where Dawn stood during the count-off, she and Justin always ended up in different groups. At least she managed to sit next to him in the van, and once, he put his head on her shoulder and closed his eyes. She thought she would float up out of the seat with the sheer joy of his curls against her neck.

Toronto, Dawn repeated to herself each morning as they drove into the city. *Toronto!* All those years she'd spent imagining the city Dean had conjured for them, a blaze of lights and billboards, everybody dressed in black, hailing taxis between clubs, and now here she was. She scanned the passersby for Dean, imagining his delight when she fell into step beside him and said casually, "Hi, Dad." It would be the kind of surprise he would orchestrate himself. And she didn't think he would have a problem with Lighthouse. In fact, out of everyone in the family, he was probably farthest along the path to UC. But she didn't see Dean on Yonge Street, and in the evenings, they were too busy at the farmhouse for Dawn to figure out how to find him.

In the evenings, they were divided into either work groups or session groups. Dawn was often in the kitchen with Justin, who was struggling with the fact that Krista said he just wasn't ready to advance. "No judgment, no fear," he said, "but Jesus H. Christ!" He hadn't come all this way to hand out pamphlets. Why had she brought him if he wasn't going to do advanced practice? He knew why. It was because she needed a ride and he had a car. He stopped washing dishes and braced himself against the sink, staring into the water. "I'm sorry, Dawn," he said. "I'm having a hard time with this."

Krista had already confided in Dawn about this very subject. "I'm afraid Justin is slipping off the path," Krista said. "Sometimes people advance too fast and they aren't ready, so in a crisis, they slip back to where they actually belong." She put an arm around Dawn's shoulder. "I want to ask you a favour, Dawn. I want you to keep an eye on Justin and tell me what he says."

"Everything he says?"

Irritation flickered in Krista's face. "No, Dawn. What he says about me." Her face smoothed itself out. "I think you can really be a beacon for him, Dawn. He has a special connection with you."

Dawn's heart missed a beat. A *special connection*. She promised Krista she would try, but now, drying soapy plates with a filthy dishtowel, she wasn't sure how to reach him.

Justin dropped a pot into the sink, splashing them both with greasy water. "I don't know," he said to Dawn. "Sometimes I think I should just go."

Dawn grabbed his sleeve. "Go? Go where?"

"Nowhere. I'm just . . . complaining." Justin patted her shoulder. "I'm not going anywhere."

"Do you promise?" She couldn't think of what else to say, but it worked, because Justin gave her hair a playful little yank and said, "Promise."

She slept on a mattress on the floor in one of the upstairs rooms with three women from Quebec, all of whom ignored her. She lay awake, thinking up ways she and Justin could end up in the same room, and then the same bed, and fell asleep with his imaginary arms around her. On the fifth day of the retreat, she woke up from a dream in which she and Justin were driving down a highway, just the two of them, and he reached over and took her hand and told her, "I love you, Dawn. I have always loved you." When she opened her eyes, she could still feel the dry warmth of his fingers. She got dressed and went to find him. He was chopping wood behind the barn. "I'm off kitchen duty," he said, wiping sweat out of his eyes. "It seems I was lacking kitchen commitment. Actually, this is better for me. Physical exertion. But can you bring me some juice?" She ran and came back with a glass of Tang. They sat on an unchopped log. Justin tilted his head back and drained the juice. She watched his Adam's apple bob. When he put the glass down, he looked at her curiously and said, "What?"

Dawn pressed the palm of her hand to her face to hide her blush. "Oh! Nothing!"

"You had a weird expression."

"I was just thinking—I don't know what I was thinking."

"No judgment, no fear," he said, peering at her. "No? Okay." He stood up.

"I was thinking what if you kissed me," Dawn said. She was breathless now, whirling downstream on a dark, fast current.

Justin sat back down on the log, a slight crease between his eyebrows. "I . . . don't know if that's a good idea," he said, and Dawn's dark current became a whirlpool of shame, but then he leaned over and kissed her. His lips were chapped, and she didn't feel anything at first. Then he licked her bottom lip and her mouth opened. His tongue lapped against hers and heat went through her, softening her arms, which opened on their own accord. She put her hand on the back of his neck, where it was warm and damp, and he put his hand over her breast. She felt her nipples harden against the inside of her T-shirt. He took her other hand and pressed it between his legs. He pushed her off the log into the soft earth and began kissing her throat while his fingers pulled at the zipper of her jeans. She struggled to help him. He pulled up her T-shirt and squeezed one breast while his tongue circled her other nipple. She gasped. "I love you, Justin," she said.

"I love you too," he said automatically. "Lift your legs."

But then he stopped and pushed himself up. "Shh! Listen!"

Krista was calling her. Suddenly, Justin was standing above her. "Get up," he hissed. She scrambled up and did up her jeans, her fingers stiff and trembling with cold. Justin brushed off her back.

"Dawn?" Krista called.

"It's okay," Justin told her. "You're fine. Just go."

"But—" She was desperate for a better ending, anything but "Just go."

"We'll talk about it later," he said, and gave her a gentle push.

Krista was waiting for her on the front porch. "Dawn! Where were you?"

"I was helping Justin chop wood," she said. Her voice sounded odd in her head, like she had a cold. She wiped her mouth with the back of her hand and pulled uselessly at her T-shirt.

"Tonight is your closed-door with Andre! Isn't that wonderful?"

Dawn gulped in air and said it was. Krista told her to go and help carry pamphlets to the van.

Dawn looked back towards the barn. "Should I go get Justin?"

"No," Krista said. "He has work to do here."

"I—I was just talking to him and he's feeling much stronger in his commitment. He—"

"Never mind Justin," Krista said curtly. "Just go."

All day on Yonge Street, she replayed it, from the beginning of the kiss to his declaration. *At last*, she thought. At last, at last: she had a boyfriend. Not some pimply, wheezing debate team co-captain, either, but Justin, who was twenty-two and looked like a movie star and loved her. She remembered every time he had touched her, from the first day. This was the real reason she had found her way to Lighthouse. The only thing that worried her was the way he had said, "We'll talk about it later." She didn't like the "it" part. But he had also said, "I love you too." Would he have said that if he hadn't meant it? If Krista hadn't called her, they would have had sex right there behind the barn.

When they got back to the farmhouse in the evening, Krista was waiting to take her to Andre. "Now?" Dawn said. "But I just got back. I—"

"Now," Krista said firmly, and led her upstairs.

The session was not what she had expected. Neither was Andre. She had had only glimpses of him, usually getting in or out of a turquoise Oldsmobile in the evenings. Up close, he was short and slight, with thin, greying hair and glasses and a spotless white shirt tucked into jeans. Sitting at a wooden desk with a pad of paper, pencils, a calculator, he looked like a high-school principal. Dawn sat in a folding chair across from Andre. Krista angled her chair so that she could see them both.

"Welcome, Dawn," Andre said. "Krista tells me you have remarkable potential."

Dawn dipped her head and tried to arrange her features into an expression of humility.

Andre said he and Krista wanted to talk about her future with Lighthouse, where she saw herself in five years. They wanted to know about her commitment. Did she see herself travelling along the path at higher and higher levels? Dawn said she did.

"Excellent. Now, I understand you haven't yet paid your fee."

Dawn looked at Krista for help. Before they'd left Sault Ste. Marie, she had explained to Krista about her university fund, and Krista had told her not to worry, they would work it out after the retreat. But now, Krista was looking at her the same way Andre was: expectantly. Dawn explained again that she had no way of getting the money because it was in an account her mother had set up for her.

Andre said, "Is the money in your name?" Dawn thought it was. "And you're eighteen?" Dawn said, "Seventeen." Andre asked if she knew the account number, but Dawn only knew the bank name. Andre said they had someone at a branch in Toronto who could look into it. If Dawn had proper ID, something could probably be done. Tomorrow, when they went into the city, Krista would take Dawn to the bank. Dawn could pay all the money she owed at once: the retreat money, plus all the membership and meeting fees Krista had kindly deferred.

That was the end of her session. "Be a beacon," Andre said.

Dawn went to sit on the wooden bench on the porch. It had happened so fast she hadn't had time to protest. No, that wasn't true. She wouldn't have protested even if it had gone slowly, because even after all the weekly meetings and the closed-doors and the open floors, she was still bound by fear. She was afraid that Andre and Krista would be disappointed. Worse than disappointed. But she was also afraid to go to the bank in the city tomorrow. Even if the money was in her name, it hadn't actually been given to her. Even if it had been given to her, it was for university. And if she failed math and didn't graduate, it wasn't right to use it for something else. She didn't want to be arrested for whatever you got arrested for when you took money that was in your name but wasn't technically yours.

But if it was? If it turned out to be hers technically and legally and completely?

She didn't want to give it to them. Her head was full of murk and sludge, but that one thought was clear. She didn't want to give them the money, and she didn't have to, and that's all there was to it. She didn't have to be afraid of Krista's disappointment or Andre's judgment. No judgment, no fear. That was the message of UC, and finally, finally it had sunk in!

She got up and went inside to tell Krista that she had solved her own blockage.

Krista was going over a column of figures at the kitchen table. She didn't even look up when Dawn told her. "I understand," she said.

Dawn said, "I knew you would! After all this time, I finally—"

But Krista went on. "I understand your fear. But you've already committed that money to Andre."

"But it's not my money to commit."

"If it's in your name—"

"But it's still not exactly mine."

Krista said, "Technicalities. You're obscuring the real issue with technicalities."

"The real issue?"

Krista threw down her pencil and folded her arms. Her eyes were cold and narrow. "Your commitment. Is extremely weak."

"But—"

"No. No buts. No excuses, Dawn. Either you're with us or you're gone. You commit fully or you leave."

"Leave?"

"Yes, leave. I'm tired of having to carry people who can't carry themselves."

"You mean—leave the retreat? Or leave Lighthouse?"

"They're the same thing."

Dawn said, "But I have no way of getting home."

"Well, then, stay and honour your commitments," Krista said coldly. Then she sighed. "Look, Dawn, I don't want to lose another of my practitioners."

"Another?"

"Justin left this afternoon."

"What?" Dawn gasped. "Where—where did he go?"

"He couldn't honour his commitments. He was warned. A number of times. He was given the option of staying or going, and he chose to go." Her voice softened. "Oh, Dawn. Don't let yourself be led astray. I know you had a crush on him. But you're worth five Justins." She got up and stroked Dawn's arm. "Listen. You've come too far to fall off the path now. You have more potential than any other practitioner I've ever met. Stay and honour your commitments, Dawn. To us and most importantly, to yourself."

"Okay."

"Okay what?"

"Okay, I'll stay. I'll honour my commitments." Dawn was surprised at how easily it came out. She was surprised Krista believed her. She was surprised she wasn't crying. She didn't feel at all like crying. She was burning with a deep, cold wrath, like she had been on the night she pounded on Laura's door. No judgment, no fear. Just ferocious goddamn fury.

"Good." Krista beamed at her. "I knew you would."

Dawn walked down the driveway to the rough road. She didn't look back to see if anyone was watching her. She didn't care if they were. Anyone could be free. Anyone could choose to fuck you over anytime they wanted, and you were free to let them or stop them. She had had enough. *Fuck you, Krista,* she thought. *Fuck you, Andre.* If they tried to come after her, she would scratch out their eyes. They were liars. The whole thing was a lie. It was *all* judgment and fear.

Under the pines, the shadows were growing dense. The rough road seemed to be running parallel to the highway; she could hear cars somewhere through the trees. She guessed it was around seven o'clock. The light would not last much longer. She would have to walk quickly.

Justin, she thought. *How could you leave me like this?*

He had promised to stay. Then he had left. What was wrong with her that he wouldn't take her with him? She began to run. If she cut through the woods, she could get to the highway before it got too dark.

The earth was soft and springy under her feet. *It's fine, it's fine,* she told herself. *Just walk straight. You'll hit the highway and you'll get a ride.*

The earth began to slant up, and she was breathing heavily. Mosquitoes whined in her ears. She focused on the ground, stepping over logs and roots and rocks. Then the earth fell away into a deep ravine and she had to stop. Below, in the last of the light, she could see withered trees poking up out of a black swamp. There was no way across it.

Out of breath, she slumped down at the base of a tree and pulled her jacket up around her head against the dive-bombing bugs. Maybe Justin was out looking for her. She let that thought grow into a movie in her head. He had come back for her and Krista had told him, "She's gone. She just walked off." Justin was furious. "You let her go? By herself? On foot? You fucking bitch." He stormed over to his car. He had to find her. She couldn't have gone far. He was driving up and down that rough road, and any minute now, he would get out and begin calling. He would have a flashlight. When he heard her voice, he would say, "Don't move, Dawn. Just keep talking. I'll come to you." A beam of light would flicker and disappear, then reappear, growing brighter and brighter, and then Justin would wrap his arms around her and say, "Dawn! I thought I'd lost you."

She opened her eyes. It was completely dark now, except for the car lights across the ravine. Maybe Justin was driving up and down the rough road. Or maybe her father had called home and Vera had said, "Oh, thank god. Dawn's run away," and Dean had said, "I'll find her." Or maybe her mother had called the millionaire with the helicopter and they were flying over the farmhouse right now. She could sit here all night thinking up ways everyone could come back and realize their mistake and fall in love with her and never let her go. But a voice in her head said, *You have no time for that nonsense now*. It sounded a lot like Vera.

And she had to agree. She had to rescue herself.

She stood up.

Turn around and walk back, the voice said.

She had to test each step with her foot, groping at the space in front of her, clutching at prickly striplings to keep from falling.

She stumbled onto the road and skinned one palm on gravel. Even on the road she had to go slowly because it was so dark she could barely see her feet. She walked until the road curved and went over a wooden bridge and ended at tarmac under a streetlight: the highway.

It began to rain, and a car stopped instantly. It contained an elderly couple, the Hendersons, they said, and they were appalled to see a young girl walking along the highway in the dark. Whatever was she thinking? She said she had gone for a walk and lost track of time. "I'm going to call my dad," she said. "He'll come and get me." They let her off at a gas station. Inside, she asked for a phone book and found the number right away, between Turner, C.K., and Turner, Donald. Turner, D.

As easy as that. All this time. He had been in the phone book.

The phone rang. A man answered.

"Dad?"

"Yeah?" But it didn't sound like him, so she hesitated.

The man cleared his throat and said, "Did you say Dad or Dan?"

"Dad."

"Thought so. Wrong number."

"Oh. Sorry."

"That's okay."

Dawn hung up. She would have to call her mother or her grandparents next. Then she dialled D. Turner's number again. Before he could say hello, she asked, "Is your mother's name Grace Turner?"

ONCE REMOVED

Rain ran down the window in rivulets. Inside the gas station, Dawn followed their progress, remembering how she and Jimmy had tried to use telekinesis to move water droplets after seeing a man on TV bend spoons with his mind. Jimmy gave up quickly, but Dawn concentrated until her head hurt. None of the drops had even quivered. She had been so certain she could do it, right up until the moment she was certain of the exact opposite. How was it possible, she wondered, for something to be right and true one minute and impossible and a pipe dream the next? This morning, she had been the most advanced-for-her-age Lighthouse practitioner on the path to freedom and truth, and Justin had loved her. Now she was standing in a gas station, Justin was gone, and the only path she wanted to be on was the one that took her home to her math textbook and bed.

The man behind the counter said, "There are your people." Dawn watched them getting out of the taxi. The bell above the door rang, and they walked straight to her, smiling. Grace was small and bird-like, with bright dark eyes and a wide forehead and short, rusty-coloured hair shot through with grey.

Dawn said, "You—you look like my grandpa."

Grace hugged her and then the man hugged her. "Hello, Dawn," he said. He was tall, with longish dark blond hair. "It's nice to meet a relative at last."

She hadn't told Dan much on the phone, only that she was Frank Turner's granddaughter and she was stranded in Toronto and couldn't find her dad. That seemed to be enough explanation for him. He told her to stay where she was, they were on their way. "This is very nice of you," she said to Grace. "To come and get me."

"Of course we would come and get you," Grace said.

In the taxi, they gave her a can of orange juice. She watched the city grow denser and taller from the window. The taxi pulled up in front of a red brick house on a street of squeezed-together houses. Some had stores downstairs, but Grace's house had a greying front porch and a green lawn. They ushered her in and sat her in an armchair. A purring cat immediately jumped on her lap. "Dawn, you must be hungry," Grace said. "I'll warm you up some soup."

"Ma," Dan said, "I don't think we should inflict that soup on relatives we're just meeting for the first time."

Grace looked surprised. "Why? Theresa made it when she was here yesterday. It's full of vitamins."

"So is pizza," Dan said, picking up the phone. "And it has the added advantage of not tasting like dishwater."

Another cat climbed up and was negotiating for space beside Dawn. She stroked the cats and looked around. The furniture looked old, the wooden floor was bare, and none of the lamps or end tables matched. On the mantel above a white brick fireplace was a rather ugly stone carving of a huge-hipped woman, next to a brass plaque that said, KNOCK AND THE DOOR SHALL BE OPENED. She wondered if Grace was poor or if she just liked things that were old and odd and didn't match. There were also plants everywhere, in pots and trays on the windowsills and tabletops, and a row of photographs on a wooden desk. She got up to look at them: a round-cheeked boy sitting on top of a pile of clothes in a wagon; the boy holding on to a wriggling puppy; the boy being swung by his hands between two women—Grace, obviously, with cropped dark hair, the other with loose curls and freckles; the boy in a baseball uniform; in shorts and a white shirt and a tie; with a cat and a dog; with his arms around the neck of the freckled woman, who was laughing. In each photo, he got closer to the grown-up Dan.

Dan said he was going upstairs to put sheets on the bed in his old room, and Grace brought Dawn another can of juice. "Dan doesn't live here?" Dawn asked. She wasn't sure yet whether Grace was her great-aunt or her grandmother. Most likely her great-aunt, given the fact that Dan called her Ma, but with this family, it was best not to jump to conclusions.

"No," Grace said. "He has his own apartment near the restaurant. He's a chef."

"Really? Do you—do you work at a restaurant too?" It was a ridiculous question, but Grace didn't seem to mind.

"No. I sold my business a couple of years ago. I had a little cleaning company. Now I grow herbs for Dan's restaurant and a few other places."

The doorbell rang. "Pizza's here," Dan called. "I got it." Grace went into the kitchen to get plates.

At the window, Dan pulled a few leaves off a plant. "Fresh basil?" he asked Dawn, who said, "Sure." He tucked three tiny leaves onto a pizza slice and handed her the plate.

Grace shooed the cats off Dawn's lap, then sat on the sofa and accepted a plate of pizza from Dan. "Now, Dawn, how did you come to be stranded in the city?"

"Ma, maybe she doesn't want to talk about that right now."

"It's okay," Dawn said, swallowing. The sharp, sweet taste of basil cut through the hot, oily taste of the pizza. "I don't mind." She didn't feel as bad as she thought she would. She had lost Justin, but she hadn't handed over her university money to Andre. She had lost Lighthouse, but she had found her way in the dark, and then she had found her long-lost relatives. She was actually feeling pretty good. Grace had never heard of Lighthouse or Universal Consciousness, but Dan said, "Universal con artists, more like. They hand out pamphlets on Yonge Street, right?"

They also wanted to know about her dad, where he lived, what he did in Toronto.

"I don't have his new number," Dawn said. "He used to live on Spadina, but that was last year. He was looking for a bigger place. He was working at a club. I don't know the name."

Dan said he could find Dean. He knew people in the business; he would ask around.

It was close to midnight when Dan left. Grace said, "Dawn, I know it's late, but you should call your grandparents and let them know you're here."

Dawn said, "They're going to be so mad."

"They'll probably be more relieved," Grace said. "And surprised. I haven't talked to my brother in years."

Dawn's hand flew to her mouth.

"What's the matter?" Grace asked.

Dawn realized that Grace didn't know about the two ugliest words in the English language.

Dawn talked to Vera first. Vera asked her if she was all right, and was she sure, and when Dawn explained where she was, there was a long pause. Then Vera said, "I'm going to wake your grandfather." Dawn passed the phone to Grace and went upstairs to see the room Dan had prepared for her. It was a boy's room, with a shelf of trophies and a dismantled drum set. Two more cats were asleep on the freshly made bed. She opened the door to the other bedroom, which contained only a bed with a wooden chair beside it and a small dresser. On the dresser, a framed photo of the baby Dan stood next to an old-fashioned hairbrush. There wasn't even a mirror. Except for Dan's old room, it was the barest house she had ever seen, and yet it was perfectly comfortable and clean and warm.

At the end of the hallway, on a little wooden table, a small, polished statue of the Buddha sat between a book called *Zen Koans* and a tumbler of water containing three purple tulips. Under the table, a very old black dog slept on a blue rag rug. He lifted his head when Dawn knelt beside him and looked at her with rheumy eyes. Downstairs, she could hear the murmur of Grace's voice. "This is very sad," she told the dog. It was happy because it was a reunion, but it was also sad because of all the wasted time. "My grandpa's going to die," she said, and her throat ached with unshed tears. "And my dad doesn't even know." The dog put his head in her lap.

The next morning, Grace brought her up a cup of hot chocolate in bed. Her eyes were red, but she smiled at Dawn. "I told Frank we would drive you home. Dan's going to rent a car."

"But we're going to wait until Dan finds my dad, right?"

Grace said, "I'm sure Dan will find him. He knows a lot of people. But Vera thinks—" She stopped and cleared her throat. "Vera thinks we should come right away."

Afraid she would spill her hot chocolate, Dawn put the cup on the bedside table. "At Lighthouse, they said those who couldn't face death didn't understand life. Do you think that's true?"

"Maybe," Grace said, "but it doesn't make it less sad." She studied her hands for a while. "I was just a small girl when my mother died, and I couldn't face it. Frank was older. He was okay. But there's no way around the sadness, whether you face it or not."

One of the cats jumped up on the bed and curled up on Dawn's lap. Dawn scratched between its ears until it began to purr.

Grace said, "If Dan can't reach your father before we leave today, he'll keep trying from Sault Ste. Marie."

Dawn reached for her cup again. "Did you know my dad was adopted?"

Grace nodded. "Oh, yes. Frank wrote me."

"So he's not your son, then?"

"No." Grace looked confused. "Dan is my son."

"But he thinks you're his mother."

"Who does?"

"My dad. He found a picture and a birth certificate," Dawn said. "He thinks he's Daniel Turner and you're his mom. But obviously, if your Dan is that Dan, then you're not my dad's mom."

Grace said, "A birth certificate? But Dan was born before Frank and Vera adopted your father."

Dawn shrugged helplessly. "I don't know. It's all mixed up. I think he only saw the papers once. After that, they hid the box or something. He said Grandma and Grandpa wouldn't tell him anything, but he heard from other people, like neighbours or something, that Grandpa had a sister who had a baby."

Grace said she had left Dan with Frank and Vera to find work in southern Ontario. It took her over a year to be able to set up a home, and when she went back to get the baby, Vera didn't want to give him up, but Frank said they had to let him go.

"They adopted your father after that," Grace said. "But people didn't talk about adoption back then. It was all a big secret. Because it meant the mother had had sex before she got married. That was something shameful in those days."

Dawn nodded. According to Mrs. Ditmars, it was still something shameful. "But did they know who his parents were?"

Grace said, "They got him through the Children's Aid. I don't think they were given much information." She got up. "You know what? I have all the letters."

The letters were in a battered red tin box with flaking gold trim. Dawn sat in bed, with the letters spread out around her. They were written on all kinds of paper, some in pencil, some in spidery blue ink. They were short, one or two paragraphs, but there were dozens, still in their envelopes, which had been neatly slit, and some had photos.

Dear Gracie,

the first one began.

Hope you and the little one have settled in all right down there. Your friend seems like a nice girl, someone to help out, very important if you're going to be on your own. Snow started again after you left. Had to climb through the window to shovel out. Vera in a bad way, missing the little one. I am too. But it is right he is with his mother.

Dear Gracie. Spring very late this year. No sign of thaw. Vera still very low. Sits and stares. Some days doesn't get up. Mrs. *McCabe has been by two or three times. She can arrange for us to adopt. Vera says no, but* Mrs. *McCabe says think about it.*

Dear Gracie. Garden finally planted. Vera somewhat better. Still has low days, but no longer taking the medicine. Made her sleep all the time, anyway. Mrs. McCabe came by with the forms again. Vera still saying she has no heart for it. Mrs. M. says to push her, says everything will change when the baby comes into the house.

Finally got word they have a boy for us. A little older than we expected, just over a year old. Will receive him in two weeks. Weather warming, will plant soon. Love to you and Danny.

The next letter said,

We named him Dean. Mrs. McCabe came by to visit and remarked on how close it was to Dan. Well! It never even crossed our minds. Vera busy but happy. Days very warm, but rain every night. Everything growing very well.

The photo was slightly out of focus: a baby bundled in a white blanket, a white cap on his head.

The next photo showed a child being bathed in the kitchen sink.

Another picture of Dean. Very good baby. Never cries, never fusses to be picked up. But have to wonder the condition of the places he was in before he came to us, three different ones according to Mrs. M. When we got him, he didn't know he had a pair of legs. Walking all over now.

"What does that mean?" Dawn asked. "My dad didn't know he had a pair of legs?"

Grace said, "I think it means he was kept in a crib in the foster homes or wherever he was. So he didn't have a chance to begin crawling."

"But he was a good baby. He never cried."

Grace was quiet for a moment. "Well, you know, Dawn, babies are *supposed* to cry. It's how they call for us."

Dawn said, "When my sister was born, Grandma said that Geraldine—that's my stepmom—was giving the baby the wrong message because every time the baby cried, Geraldine went to see what was wrong."

Grace smiled. "I never did understand how that was the wrong message." She stood up and said she was going to pack for the trip north.

Dawn studied the rest of the pictures, her father in diapers, in shorts, in long pants with a fishing rod. A teenager in a white jacket, his hair falling into his eyes. A wedding picture of Laura and Dean, Laura smiling directly into the camera, Dean talking to someone off to the side. There were pictures of her and Jimmy as babies, as toddlers, opening Christmas presents, standing side by side under the apple tree. *Grandkids with us now*, Frank wrote. *Probably for good. Mother not likely coming back*. She skimmed through the rest of the letters, news of the garden, the neighbourhood, Dawn taking piano, Jimmy starting at a new school after some trouble with windows. The last one, dated eighteen months ago, ended with, *Should get up and fix the leak in the basement sink. Tired lately. Feeling my age, I guess*. The box was empty now, except for two mismatched buttons.

Dawn reread the letter that announced her mother's departure. There it was, the unthinkable written down as if it were the weather report. *Spring colder than usual. Mother not likely coming back*. What made him think that at the time? What had her mother said? How had it all unfolded? Why didn't she know? It was suddenly the craziest thing she had ever heard, not what had happened, but that no one had bothered to explain it to her, aside from her mother's speech about being left holding the bag.

As if she and Jimmy were something to be stuck with. *What a thing to say*, she thought. And her father! "At least you know who your parents are." As if that made it all right. She kicked back the covers, scattering the letters as she got out of bed. As soon as she got back home, she was going to start asking questions, whether people wanted to answer them or not.

Replacing the letters in the little red box, she looked one last time at the first picture of Dean, the hazy white bundle. The thought of a baby crying for someone until he just gave up trying brought tears to her eyes. She wasn't even sure if it was her father she was seeing. *It could be any one of us*, she thought.

Dan arrived in the rental car and handed Dawn a black cotton sweater and a long black skirt. "Left behind by a roommate," he said. "I thought you might want a change of clothes."

Dawn ran upstairs to change. When she came back down, Dan was saying to Grace, "—left a message to call home." He smiled at Dawn. "I found your dad."

"You talked to him?"

"No, someone he works with. We have his number now." Dan smiled. "I'm a pretty good detective, if I do say so myself."

Dawn didn't have the heart to tell him how many ways a phone number did not count as finding Dean.

They got to Sault Ste. Marie at dusk. Dawn had to give directions to Dan, because Grace was no longer sure of the way. They passed the school, the corner store, the cemetery, and then they were on Sylvan Avenue, sitting in the driveway, all of them looking at the three-storey red brick house. Dan said, "Well, it's certainly the most beautiful house on the street." Dawn could see what he meant: the hedges were flowering, roses climbed the trellises, and the apple trees spread their arms over the garden.

Inside, her grandmother would be knitting and her grandfather would be dying, but there was no way around that.

Dawn opened the front door and let Grace go in first. Frank was sitting in the armchair under the lamp, with a blanket in his lap. "Gracie," he said, and Grace burst into tears. Amazingly, she only cried for a second. It was like a sneeze. "Frank," she said. "I'm so glad to see you. Vera, how are you?"

"As good as can be expected, under the circumstances," Vera said.

Then the door opened and Vera's face went slack. Dan strode in, set down the luggage, kissed Vera on the cheek and shook Frank's hand. "Hello, Aunt Vera," he said. "Hello, Uncle Frank."

Jimmy came downstairs, and there were more introductions and handshakes. Vera told Jimmy to bring the luggage upstairs and Dawn to set the table for dinner. She had made fried chicken, and even Frank sat at the table and ate a tablespoon of mashed potatoes. Afterwards, Dan helped clear the plates, and Dawn made tea. Grace watched Frank, Frank watched Vera, and Vera's eyes followed Dan everywhere.

"Did you recognize the neighbourhood?" Frank asked Grace. "It started to fill up after the war. The Cherniaks sold first. After John went overseas. You remember him, Grace?"

Grace held the teacup to her lips, blowing to cool it. "Yes," she finally said, and set her teacup down.

"He came back a different person," Frank said. "Drink? Boy, oh boy. And mean? Scare the fleas off a cat. And his son was the one that got Dean into all that trouble with the law. Left him holding the bag."

Now that, Dawn thought, was the correct usage of the phrase.

"That's a shame," Grace said. A message went between her and Vera that Dawn couldn't read. Then they both drank their tea.

After tea, Dan said he was exhausted from the drive, and Vera and Jimmy took him upstairs. Dan was going to sleep in Jimmy's room, Jimmy in Dawn's room, and Dawn and Grace in the attic room. Downstairs, Dawn listened from the kitchen while Grace told Frank about her business. Her company had cleaned offices at night, Grace said. Her employees had had young children, and they had rotated child care. It hadn't always worked out, though, and sometimes they had lost clients because the head of maintenance didn't care whose kid hadn't come home from school or whose boyfriend had locked her out of the house in her nightgown. He only wanted the wastepaper baskets emptied on time. But the business had managed to survive. It had never made a profit, but everyone had gotten paid.

Dawn had finished drying the dishes, but she lingered in the kitchen, refolding the dishtowels, standing on a chair to wipe down the cupboards and the blue-faced clock.

"It must have been hard, though," Frank said. His voice was raspy, and he had to rest in between sentences. "All by yourself."

Grace said, "Oh, we had a lot of help. Theresa—you remember Theresa—she sent money. Came to stay. Looked after Danny."

"He's a good boy," Frank said.

"He is," Grace agreed. "But it was hard for him. He spent a lot of time at other boys' houses. When he was fourteen, he practically lived at his friend Joey's. They had a nicer house, a car, a backyard full of toys. A father." She sighed. "He always wanted more family than I could give him."

"You did a good job, Gracie." There was pause, and Dawn could hear her grandfather struggle with his breath. "I'm sorry I didn't do more to help you."

"You did the most important thing," Grace said.

"It was hard for her."

Dawn heard a quick little sob.

Grace said, "She'll be all right, Frank."

Over the next few days, Dawn noticed that Vera and Grace didn't like to be in the same room, but Vera and Dan had taken a shine to each other. "Let me do that," he said, taking the broom or the duster out of her hands. He helped with all the cooking and went through Vera's recipe cards, asking questions and copying things down in a little leather notebook. They talked for almost an hour about pastry and the particular advantages of lard. It was funny, Dawn thought, because Dan didn't look like the kind of person Vera would go in for. His hair was too long and his jeans had rips at the knees and he wore a leather wristband. But when he said he would drive Vera to the pharmacy at 3:00, he was ready at 2:45. And when he cooked, he cleaned up as he went along, so that when the meat pies went into the oven, the stovetop was shiny and the counters were clear.

The house was busy. Laura brought a pot of soup, a pan of lasagna. She never stayed for long, but Vera always said thank you for the food. Geraldine brought flowers, and Vera scolded her for wasting money, but she washed out a vase and put them on the dining-room table. Amy sat on a stool beside Frank, who lay on the couch, and showed him photos of her dance competition. Frank could only stay awake for short periods of time. He took in long, slow, noisy breaths, but he said he wasn't in pain. "Do you have to get back?" he asked Grace. She shook her head. "Dan has to go back on Monday, but I'm going to stay."

Dan was planning dinner for everyone for Saturday night, using six kinds of preserves from the basement and all the vegetables in the freezer; Vera was going to make the dessert. A year ago, it would have been almost unwishable: having Laura,

Geraldine, Amy, Vera, Frank, Grace and Dan all at the same table. Even adding Dean to the table, Dawn thought, was not unthinkable. He could probably sit right between Laura and Geraldine; there were so many abnormalities now that one more wouldn't make any difference. But no one mentioned Dean.

Saturday was unusually warm. Dan cooked the roast early in the morning so the kitchen wouldn't get too hot, then made pancakes topped with Vera's raspberry jam and whipped cream, and they all sat on the dark green benches under the apple trees to eat them. In the afternoon, while Grace went to the cemetery and Vera crocheted a doily, Jimmy and Dawn helped Dan in the kitchen, learning the difference between chiffonade and shredding. When the kitchen got too warm, they took Dan down to the creek, where a little breeze skimmed over the green shallows. They walked from one end of the overgrown path to the other, and then squeezed themselves onto the flat rock under the chokecherry tree. "Apparently," Dan said, "my mother used to bring me down here when I was a baby." In the riot of green across the bank, birds carried on a noisy conversation. The sun was strong on their hands and faces.

"Does it look familiar to you?" Dawn asked. It was weird to think that Dan had been a baby here. It was weird to think that they had all been babies here, beside the same creek, under the same roof.

"A little, but maybe magical places look familiar to everyone. Hey—wild leeks!" Dan pulled one out of the ground and nibbled on the green stalk.

Jimmy stripped a handful of chokecherries from overhead and tossed them one by one into the creek. "So, are you like our uncle or cousin or what?"

"Well," Dan said, "your grandfather is my uncle, so that makes us . . . What *does* that make us?"

"And technically, he isn't our grandfather," Dawn said. "You know, by blood."

Dan made a face of mock anguish. "Argh! Now you're just making it complicated."

Jimmy decided they needed something cool to drink and went up to the house for pop. Dawn wondered who Dan's father was, and if he had grown up making birthday candle wishes for his dad to show up. It didn't seem right to raise such a personal topic, but then she thought, *We're family*, so she asked. "Dan, you never met your dad?"

"My mother said he went to war. He wasn't killed over there, but she never saw him again."

"Were they in love?"

Dan shrugged. "I don't think so. She never had much to say about him. She didn't even have a picture."

"That sucks," Dawn said. "Not knowing anything about your father."

"Yeah, it wasn't ideal," Dan said.

Jimmy had come back with three sweating cans of ginger ale. "It's like a hundred degrees," he said, handing out the pop. He sat down beside Dan. "Vera says we're related because everyone in the world is related if you go back far enough."

"Well, that's true," Dan said, draining his ginger ale.

"Did she really say that?" Dawn asked.

"Nah," Jimmy grinned. "First cousins once removed."

"'Once removed'!" Dan snickered at this, then reached over and tested the water with his hand. "Do you guys swim here?"

"In the *creek*?" Dawn was aghast. They had never swum in the creek. Vera would have had a fit. But Dan was pulling off his shoes and socks. He splashed out into the water in his ripped jeans and T-shirt. "Not deep enough to swim," he said, sinking down, "but so nice." The green water came up to his shoulders, and he tipped his head back and doused his hair. "Ahhh," he said.

"What are Grandma and Grandpa doing?" Dawn asked her brother.

"Grandpa's awake. Grandma's making butter tarts," he said. "Laura's there and Geraldine's on her way."

Dan lifted his head out of the water. "Are you guys coming in or what?"

Dawn shook her head, but Jimmy said, "I will." He pulled off his shirt and waded in, sinking down beside Dan. "Come on, Dawn," he said.

She gathered her skirt close and followed him in. The water was silty and soft. They lounged and talked until they heard two car doors slam in the driveway. "Geraldine and Amy," Jimmy announced.

"We should go up," Dawn said, but she was reluctant to leave the cool green water. She arched her back and floated, feeling her hair fan out behind her. Now that they had done it once, it seemed like they had been swimming in the creek all their lives. Jimmy began scooping armfuls of water at her. She splashed him back, and then they both doused Dan. Above them, another car door slammed. Jimmy stopped mid-splash. "Who's that, now?"

"Your father, probably," Dan said, standing up and sloshing towards the rock.

Dawn and Jimmy looked at each other. "Why do you say that?" Dawn asked.

"I talked to him last night," Dan said. "He borrowed a car and was leaving at five this morning."

For a moment, they were afraid to move. "What if it's not him?" Dawn asked.

Through the trees they could hear a medley of voices. "What if they fight?"

"What if Grandma doesn't let him in the house?"

Dan hopped on one leg, yanking socks onto his wet feet. He said, "Of course she'll let him in the house. He's her son. Go!"

Dawn and Jimmy raced up the bank, water streaming off them, yelling, "Dad! Dad!" In the driveway, a car was parked awkwardly between Geraldine's dented Honda and Laura's new Ford. The trunk was wide open, and the engine ticked as it cooled. The screen door was open too, but the front porch was empty. Everyone had already gone inside.

ACKNOWLEDGEMENTS

Thank you to

My parents, Jim and Judy, for allowing me to snip pieces out of their stories and sew them into this novel (or at least for not protesting too much when I got out the scissors)

My agent, Anne McDermid, for her (more than ten years of) patience and invaluable advice

Diane Martin and the team at Knopf Canada, especially Deirdre Molina—for their dedication to this book, and for being such a pleasure to work with

The eagle-eyed Sue Sumeraj

The Canada Council for the Arts

Dan Wilson, for encouragement, playlists, and (especially) the title

Maureen Lennon, for reading, and for reminding me to write

Dr. Peter Steele, for his very generous help when I needed it most

All the mothers who took the time to speak with me about this novel

My brother Jason and my sister Eva, and Pema Dorji, for making me laugh

JAMIE ZEPPA is the author of *Beyond the Sky and the Earth: A Journey into Bhutan*, which won the Banff Mountain Book Festival Award for Adventure Travel Writing. She won the CBC Canadian Literary Award for Memoir and her essays have appeared in *AWOL: Tales for Travel-Inspired Minds*, *My Wedding Dress: True-Life Tales of Lace, Laughter, Tears and Tulle* and *Between Interruptions: 30 Women Tell the Truth about Motherhood*. She has written articles and reviews for *Chatelaine*, the *Globe and Mail*, the *Toronto Star*, the *Literary Review of Canada* and *Ascent*, as well as several UK newspapers. Jamie has a teenage son, and she teaches English at Seneca College in Toronto. This is her first novel.

A NOTE ABOUT THE TYPE

The text of *Every Time We Say Goodbye* has been set in Goudy, (often referred to as Goudy Oldstyle) a face designed in 1915 for the American Type Founders by the prolific typographer Frederic W. Goudy. Used with equal success in both text and display sizes, Goudy remains one of the most popular typefaces ever produced. It is best recognized by the diamond-shaped dots on punctuation; the upturned "ear" of the g; and the elegant base curve of the caps E and L.